LITTLE
Sunshine

© 2024 Layla Frost
All Rights Reserved. No part of this publication may be reproduced, distributed, or transmitted in any form or by any means, including photocopying, recording, or other electronic or mechanical methods, without the prior written permission of the publisher, except in the case of brief quotations embodied in critical reviews and certain other noncommercial uses permitted by copyright law.

This is a work of fiction. Names, characters, businesses, places, events, and incidents are either the products of the author's imagination or used in a fictitious manner. Any resemblance to actual persons, living or dead, or actual events is purely coincidental.

Editing by Editing4Indies
Cover Design by Steamy Designs

FROM THE PERVY MIND OF THE AUTHOR

I'm sitting here, staring at the computer screen, trying to figure out what to write in this spot. Not because I have a shortage of things to say... Trust me, that'll *never* be an issue. But because I have so much to say, and I don't want to ramble.

Those of you who have read the note in Little Dove already know the gist of this story, but I'm going to tell it again anyway.

I wrote Little Dove while I was pregnant with Baby O. To say I was anxious about it—the book and the rainbow baby—would be an understatement. I worried that I was imploding my career by stepping outside of my box with a Daddy book.

But I should've known better because I have the best readers in the world. And they fell just as in love with Daddy Maximo *and* Juliet as I had.

There's always this period of mourning when a book is done. When I'm no longer submerged in a world that I'd been living in. Finishing Little Dove was especially devastating because I'd intended for it to be a standalone. But thanks to all the love, encouragement, messages, and posts, those plans changed.

If you ever feel like your voice as a reader doesn't matter, let this be a lesson that it very much *does*.

FROM THE PERVY MIND OF THE AUTHOR

An extra special thank you to:

Layla Frost's Cupcakes for being the best group on Facebook.

Jenny S/Editing4Indies for your editing magic.

Beth Hale for catching the bonehead mistakes I make while "fixing" my edits.

Maria/Steamy Designs for the gorgeous cover that almost makes me drool.

Ashley/Geeky Girl Author Services for putting up with me being a needy author.

To M, for forever being my muse, my supporter, my coffee supplier, and my lovey.

And to my beautiful readers who demanded the Handsome Goon get a story,
THANK YOU!

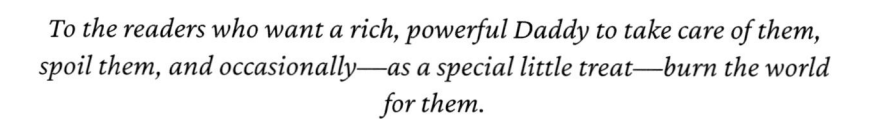

To the readers who want a rich, powerful Daddy to take care of them, spoil them, and occasionally—as a special little treat—burn the world for them.

Because, really, is that too much to ask for? I certainly don't think so.

Anyway, this one is for you...

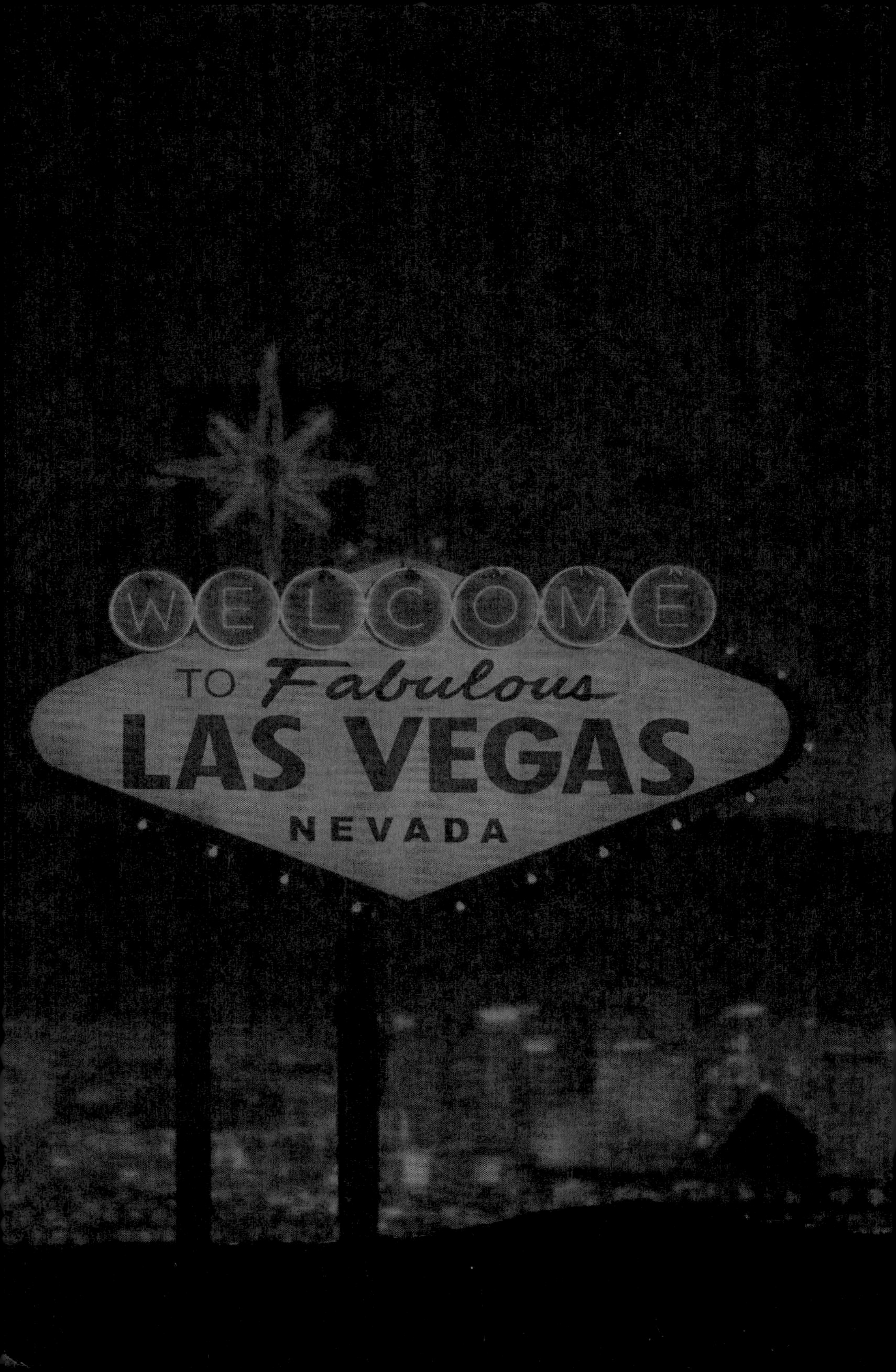
WELCOME
TO Fabulous
LAS VEGAS
NEVADA

PROLOGUE
MILA

"I THINK WE SHOULD BREAK UP."

Wait, what?

Standing in my open doorway, I tilted my head as I looked up at CJ. Tall. Hot in that seventeen-year-old way that was still kinda boyish but almost a man. My boyfriend of almost six months. My first *real* one.

The love of my sixteen-year-old life.

Or so he'd said.

Studying his somber expression, I waited for him to crack a smile and tell me he was kidding. He loved to prank me. He said it was hilarious.

I didn't really agree, but it made him happy, so whatever.

But there was no amusement in his expression. No twinkle in his dark eyes. No look of love or—more commonly—horniness. Not even a hint of a smile.

Instead, his lip was curled in disgust. As if those same lips hadn't just been pressed to mine minutes before. Like we hadn't been making out on my couch while he'd pushed me to let him go further.

Go all the way.

And now he was dumping me.

"Okay," I said. Not because it felt okay. God, it didn't feel okay at all. I should've been used to the feeling, but the rejection stabbed away at my already battered heart.

CJ gritted his teeth at my one word, but his tone was gentle. "It's not you."

But it was.

I didn't fit into his world. Our lives were too different. Maybe he was tired of sneaking over to the wrong side of the tracks. Maybe it was because I wouldn't have sex with him.

Whatever the reason, I knew it was my fault.

For a moment, the invite to my bedroom hovered on the tip of my tongue. It wasn't like I held on to my virginity because it had some imaginary value.

But I wasn't going to sleep with any random guy who showed me interest. Or who I could get something from.

I wasn't my mother.

"Okay," I repeated, at a loss of what else to say. I just wanted him gone.

CJ didn't get the message. He kept talking, making it seem like he was trying to make me feel better when I knew it was the opposite. "I need more freedom. I'm still young. I need to be able to go where I want. Hang out with friends. Just live without someone grilling me and being all…"

Clingy.

He didn't say the word, but he didn't have to.

We both knew it was there.

For someone who'd said it wasn't about me, his reasons were exclusively about me. My faults. My weaknesses.

My *issues*.

"Okay," I said, yet again.

"That's all you have to say?"

I shrugged. "There's nothing else to say."

Irritation tightened his handsome face, and he opened his mouth to cut me down more. It was what he did when I pissed him off.

Although what I'd done to deserve it, I wasn't sure. I wasn't the one dumping him.

I couldn't take it.

Looking around him, I squinted my eyes. "I think someone is near your car."

He was off my busted porch before I could blink. It wasn't a surprise that he quickly abandoned our conversation. He loved that loud thing more than anything. Clearly more than me.

I slammed the door and clicked the lock into place.

Leaving me alone.

As usual.

The small house may have been silent, but my thoughts weren't. CJ's words kept ricocheting in my head.

I hadn't thought I was that bad. Between school and my job as a hotel housekeeper, it wasn't like I had hours to spend hounding him. CJ didn't have a job, so he had plenty of time for friends and whatever else while I worked. But when I was off, I *had* wanted to spend that time with him. I thought that was normal.

Apparently, I thought wrong.

My boyfriend. My own mother.

No one wants me around.

Blinking back bitter tears, I loaded up the slow-as-hell internet on my phone and started searching for apartments. My own place.

Well, I don't need either of them.

Them or anyone else.

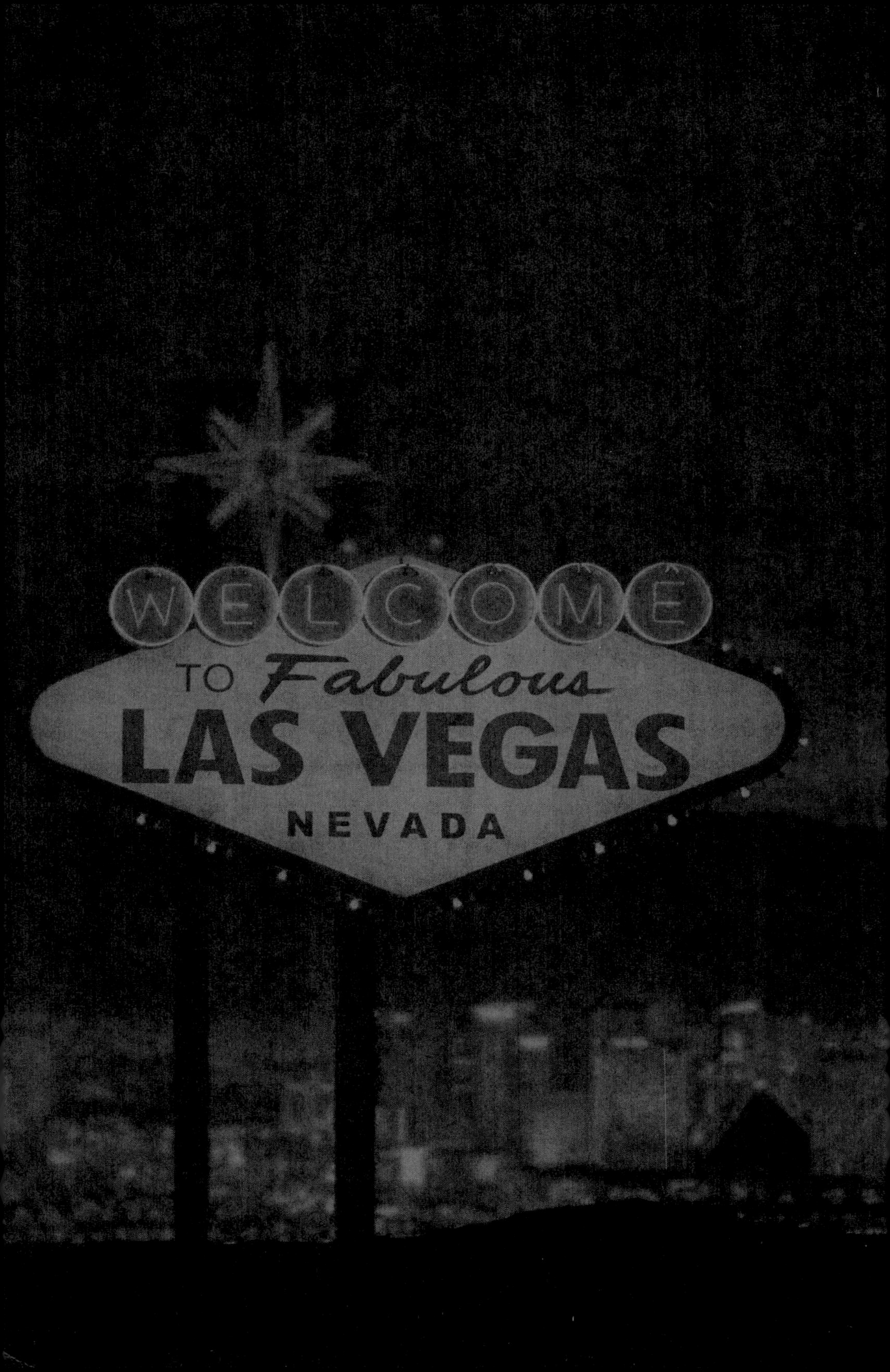
WELCOME
TO Fabulous
LAS VEGAS
NEVADA

CHAPTER 1
LESSONS FROM MILA: DON'T TRUST ANYONE
MILA

"I'M SORRY, MILA, I'M GOING to have to let you go."

And you couldn't have told me before I worked my entire shift?

Standing in the back office of a sleazy hotel, I looked at my even sleazier shift manager—or *former* shift manager. My thoughts raced as I tried to figure out what I'd done.

Nothing.

I'd done absolutely nothing to warrant getting fired.

Like always, I'd gotten to work at four in the morning, had spent the day busting my ass, and I was still there at nearly two even though my shift technically ended at noon.

And I was being fired.

It wasn't layoffs for budgetary reasons—I'd be the last person they'd let go. Not because of my dazzling personality or anything. It was just common sense. I did the work of multiple people, and I did it without a shitty attitude. I never stole from rooms, I kept my head down, and my eyes stayed on my own business. That was more than could be said for anyone else—Todd included.

"Why?" I asked.

But then I saw it. The grimace. The way he looked at me with a mix of pity, disdain, and the usual lust.

The way history loved to repeat itself.

"Veronica."

And there it is.

Veronica Rogers.

Con-woman.

Narcissist.

Professional hot mess.

And my mother—though I was forbidden from calling her that. The fact we didn't share a last name made it all the easier for her to pretend she wasn't old enough to have an adult daughter.

Not until she needed something.

"She came by when you were on break," he continued. "Steve was here, and we had guests in the lobby when she made a scene."

Of course, she did. And of course, she did it while the general manager was here.

I didn't ask why he hadn't said anything when I'd clocked back in earlier. Why he hadn't sent someone to come get me since they all knew where I took my break. Why he hadn't given me the chance to talk to Steve or fix things.

Because there was no fixing it. I'd already received that warning.

"That's not my fault," I tried anyway, but even I heard the resignation in my tone.

Although I had nothing to do with the chaos she caused, my mother was more drama than I was worth.

Story of my damn life.

"My hands are tied," Todd said. "This came from Steve."

It wasn't like cleaning a scuzzy, outdated hotel was my dream job. I could happily live without the smell of mold, dust, and body odor that hung in the air and clung to the walls and furniture.

I couldn't, however, happily live without food. And food cost money.

As did my shitty apartment, electricity, and basically everything else in life.

Dejected, I bit back the load of insults I wanted to spew and focused on the important thing. "Can I get my check, at least?"

"We'll mail your final one in two weeks."

"What about today's?"

But, again, I already knew. Dread filled me, tightening my chest until I thought I was dying.

No lie.

Twenty years old, and I was having a heart attack.

The ache it caused behind my sternum stole my breath.

My fears were confirmed when Todd said, "Steve gave it to your mother."

"That's illegal," I pointed out, not that it mattered.

The Roulette Hotel was lax with health codes, business practices, and labor laws. Handing over a paycheck to an unauthorized person was small fries.

Todd shrugged, confirming it was no big deal to them.

To me, it was my bills and my meager groceries.

Even if I filed a police report, and they somehow tracked down whatever sketchy check cashing place my mom had used, it would take far too long. It would be too little, too late.

"It was that or call the cops on her," he shot back, like they'd done me a favor.

They hadn't.

You should've called them then, you asshole.

Even with everything, a tiny ball of guilt hit my chest at that thought, but I shoved it down.

Standing, Todd came around the desk, and I locked my knees to stop from retreating.

I wouldn't show weakness, even if he totally creeped me out.

"For what it's worth, I tried to get Steve to reconsider." He shifted my long hair over my shoulder, his hand lingering on my back. "You're my best girl."

Barf.

"But this isn't the first time your mom has caused issues," he said as if I needed the reminder.

A couple of years before, the hotel had rented out their lot as parking for one of the big RV conventions. My mother, in all her addled wisdom, had seen the RVs and jumped to the conclusion that the hotel was filled with rich guests—as if anyone with money would stay at The Roulette.

She'd hung around the hotel bar before propositioning the wrong man... in front of his wife. A knock-down, drag-out fight had erupted between Roni and the wife. Property had been damaged. Faces had been damaged. The cops had been called.

On-premise violence was bad enough.

But The Roulette—and likely the guests—had a lot to hide. Police sniffing around, even for ten minutes, was bad for business.

Todd gave a sad shake of his head. "I told you then that it couldn't happen again. You're out of chances."

That was also the story of my life.

I was always out of chances.

Out of options.

Out of a job and money.

Out of time.

I nodded and lied, "I understand. Thanks."

For nothing.

As it often did, his expression changed from friendly boss to something dirty. "Now that you're not my employee—"

"I'm going to clean out my cubby."

Before I barf all over and you make me clean it up even though that's not my job anymore.

Hightailing it out of the office, I didn't stop at my locker since it was empty. I didn't pause to say goodbye—or a well-deserved *fuck you*—to any of my nosy *ex*-coworkers. I jetted from the building before the walls closed in on me, trapping me forever in dodgy stains and mildew.

Even once I was outside, the fresh air did nothing to fill my burning lungs. I moved on autopilot as I went to my bus stop, my mind numb.

It wasn't long before the first bus of my commute pulled up, and I got on. It was a mistake. In the stuffy, enclosed space, my breathing became shallow. My chest squeezed tighter, and spots began to float in my vision.

By the time I reached my stop, a barely restrained panic attack hovered, ready to push in. It mixed with my extreme hunger and left me shaking. If I didn't get it under control, I'd pass out in the street.

Breathe.
Breathe.
Inhale.
Exhale.
I'll figure it out. I always do.

The pressure on my chest lessened, but the hunger pangs and lightheadedness remained. I hadn't eaten since lunch the day before, and that had only been a PB&J on stale bread. The day before that had been the same.

I'd been rationing groceries, counting down until my paycheck.

A paycheck I no longer had.

Rather than going straight to my next bus stop, I went in the opposite direction to an ATM on the off chance I'd miscalculated my balance. Maybe I would luck out with a bank error. It didn't even have to be a million dollars. I'd have settled for twenty bucks.

I wasn't that lucky.

A dollar and some change. That was all I had.

A fucking dollar.

I had no cash on me. I didn't have to check to know my meager food stamp card was wiped and wouldn't be refilled for two weeks.

I had *nothing*.

The pressure was back, but I didn't have time to melt down. I couldn't sink to the ground, surrounded by glamor but filled with despair.

I needed to hurry home before I passed out.

As much as I hated cutting through the ritzy hotels, I didn't have the energy to take the long way to my next stop.

Moving with a fake confidence that hopefully projected I belonged there, I walked into Moonlight—a resort that was the exact opposite of The Roulette Hotel. The place was gorgeous. Every inch was decorated on theme with flowers, shiny moons, and intricate details—right down to the tile under my feet. It was always lively with bright lights, loud noises, and crowds.

I hated it.

For petty and envious reasons, but still. *Hated* it.

I kept to the outside path, dodging people who decided the middle of the walkway was the perfect place to stop for a chat. As I approached a quick service restaurant, the smell of delicious food wafted out. Savory cheese. Spicy pepperoni. Rich red sauce filled with garlic and herbs that weren't from an expired seasoning shaker.

My empty stomach clenched so painfully, tears filled my eyes.

Standing outside the restaurant entrance, a man talked with a woman as they ate. I watched in horror as he tossed half his slice of pizza into the trash. She'd only taken a couple of bites of her giant soft pretzel before adding it to his waste.

I was starving and on the verge of passing out.

Desperate.

And they'd just tossed out food like it was nothing.

That was why I did it.

Passing the man, I deftly slid his wallet from his pocket. It'd been so smooth, there was no way he'd felt it.

I kept my previous pace as I pocketed the prize, my expression blank and calm.

It wasn't like they were the kind of tourists who had scrimped and saved to do a budget Vegas vacation. The kind who stayed at The Roulette because it was better than nothing.

My mark clearly had money. Hell, he had money to literally throw away.

Plus, I wasn't going to take all his cash. Just enough to grab a fast-food burger. No side. No drink. Not even the tiny upcharge for cheese. Just a cheap, plain burger.

Even as I tried to justify my actions, I hated them. I hated my mother for putting me in the position—and not for the first or hundredth time.

I hated myself for being more like her than I ever wanted to be.

But a girl had to eat.

After a few tense seconds with my heart pounding in my throat... nothing happened.

Relief flowed through me.

Phew.

I did it.

But I should've known better than to think fate or luck or the universe would be on my side.

"Return it."

At the rough order spoken from right behind me, a chill shot down my spine. My stomach bottomed out as bile rose to burn my throat.

No.

He's not talking to me.

Just a coincidence.

But, again, I should've known better.

A hand snagged my wrist, halting my steps. I was whipped around until I was face to torso with a mountain of a man.

At barely five-one, I was used to being shorter than pretty much everyone. But between his towering height and muscular build, I felt infinitesimal as the suited man eclipsed me.

I craned my neck to look up at the behemoth with buzzed hair and a full blond beard. His hazel eyes were far too sharp as he stared down at me and repeated, "Return it."

"Return what?" I tried.

He arched a brow, not buying my innocent bullshit. "The wallet."

"I don't know what you're talking about. Now let me go before I scream." I tried to tug out of his viselike grip, but it was impossible.

"Good idea. I'm sure security can help get to the bottom of this."

I swallowed hard. "Security?"

He tilted his head toward where a handsome Black man stood against the wall, an authoritative air about him as he surveyed the expansive room. I didn't need to see the details on the ID badge clipped to his suit jacket to know he was in a position of power.

The bearded man gestured again, that time to where three men were converged, all wearing the typical security guard uniforms.

His focus returned to me. "Go ahead and scream, little girl."

As insulted as I was by the condescending name, I was more terrified at the threat of getting busted. If getting fired had screwed me over, getting arrested would fuck up my entire life.

"I'll return it," I said quietly.

When the man released me, I didn't try to run. He'd have caught me in two of his long-legged steps, alerting security in the process.

My mom was the one who thrived off making a scene, not me.

I slid the wallet from my pocket and backtracked to where the couple still lingered near the restaurant.

Pretending to pick it up, I stood and tapped the mark's shoulder. "Excuse me, is this yours?"

His eyes dropped to the wallet and then narrowed on me.

It didn't matter what trumped-up image I'd tried to project to make it seem like I belonged in the fancy casino. It didn't matter how easily and skillfully I schooled my features into the picture of innocence. To the people who actually belonged in the luxury resort, I still looked like exactly what I was.

Poor trash.

Shit, this is going to be bad.

I braced, my thoughts racing for excuses if he accused me of... well, of the truth.

His gaze went over my head just as I felt someone behind me. "Do you work here? This... *girl*," he spat, making it clear that wasn't the word he wanted to use, "stole my wallet."

"The wallet in your hands?" the behemoth asked.

"Yes, but—"

"The one she just picked up and handed to you?"

"Yes, but—"

"Is anything missing?"

My failed mark opened his wallet to check his cards and count his cash.

An obscene amount of it.

He wouldn't have noticed five bucks missing. He probably wouldn't have even realized if a couple of hundred were missing.

He tucked the bills away. "It's all here."

"Then what's the problem?" the man behind me asked, his voice dripping with impatience.

"No problem," my mark said, even as he eyed me with distaste—like my mere existence was an insult to him. Without another word, he and the woman walked away, not even thanking me for finding the wallet.

I mean, I was also the one who'd taken it, but still. Rude.

Not turning, I quietly muttered, "There, it's returned."

I tried to continue on my way to hell in a flaming handbasket, but a large hand encircled my wrist again. That time, he didn't have to whip me around. I did it myself so I could glare up at him. "I will scream, and it doesn't matter if security hears now."

He didn't seem worried. "Why'd you take it?"

There was no animosity in his tone. No judgment. No ridicule. It was just curiosity, like he was asking what my favorite food was.

Any.

Any was my favorite food.

When I didn't answer, he twisted my arm in his hold, and his gaze darted down.

I'd grown up in Vegas—and not the Moonlight side of it that was all glam and luxury. I knew what he was looking for.

That he'd caught me stealing was embarrassing.

But watching him inspect my inner arm for track marks *killed.*

I'd long ago given up caring about what others thought of me. The assumptions they were quick to make. But for whatever reason, I didn't want this stranger to think I was a junkie.

Turning both my arms so he could see they were unmarred, I kept my voice low as I shared my shame. "I'm just hungry. I was going to take enough to buy a cheap burger and then drop the wallet with an employee. That's it, I swear." Tears blurred my vision as I repeated, "I'm just hungry."

"Then let's feed you," he said simply.

My stomach ate away at itself. The burn of reflux and cramps caused a constant ache that I couldn't escape. Not while I worked. Not while I dealt with a behemoth. Not even in sleep.

But I shook my head, my stupid pride unwilling to accept his charity. "I need to get home."

"I didn't ask. Let's go."

"Really, it's—"

"Now, little girl. Or I'll talk to security. I'm sure a place like this is loaded with cameras that caught your trick."

It was the wrong thing to be cocky about, but I knew it was unlikely any camera had detected my pickpocketing. My movements were trained to be minimal. At most, it would look like I'd brushed by the man.

The behemoth as a witness changed things, though.

I wasn't sure whether he'd actually turn me in, but I wasn't anxious to find out.

"Okay," I relented.

A slow smile spread across his lips, making deep dimples appear under his blond beard. "Good."

I had no idea what was *good* about any of it, especially for him.

I didn't trust his smile or words.

Or him, for that matter.

Despite my agreement seconds before, I dug my heels in. "Why are you doing this?"

"Because you're hungry."

"Okay, and? What's that got to do with you?" I snapped—partially to mask my embarrassment but mostly because I was exhausted and starving.

"Are you always such a ray of sunshine?" he shot back instead of answering. Still holding my wrist, he walked through the milling crowds, not hesitating or dodging out of the way like I did. He didn't have to. Everyone got the hell out of his path, likely for fear of being mowed over.

We followed the signs for the food court, and my eyes landed on an exit.

When we pass, I'll duck out and run my ass off.

I barely finished my thought when he said, "Don't even think about it."

I forced my voice to be light and confused. "Think about what?"

"Running. You wouldn't get more than a handful of steps before I caught you."

"I predicted two steps."

"I was being generous."

"Nice of you," I deadpanned.

He smiled down at me, but he didn't say anything further.

There was no reason for him to be mindful of my ego. Getting caught stealing and then becoming a charity case had already destroyed what little, tattered one I'd started with.

It was officially DOA.

We walked in silence for a couple of minutes before reaching the food court. So many mouthwatering scents hit my nose at once, I worried I'd start to drool.

"What're you in the mood for?" he asked.

Everything.
Anything.
All of it.

My choices were Mexican, chicken, burgers, and a deli sandwich place. I scanned the prices before sticking with my original—and inexpensive—plan. "A burger."

He lifted his chin and guided me over to that register. "Order what you want."

"Can I have a junior burger, please?" I asked the wide-eyed cashier.

Not that I blamed her reaction. Shame-spiral or not, even I knew the man at my back was hot.

Maybe she thought I was a juvenile delinquent out for lunch with my social worker.

Or parole officer.

"Make that a double," the behemoth said.

"Cheese?" the cashier asked.

I shook my head. "No—"

"Yes," the behemoth answered for me.

"Bacon?" the cashier asked.

"No—" I tried, but again, the behemoth contradicted me.

"Yeah. And a large fry, a large drink, and a chocolate milkshake."

Oh duh.

He must be eating, too.

"And a salad," he added, rounding off the meal with something healthy. Like some lettuce would cancel out the thirty million calories in the fries and shake.

He's well over six feet of solid muscle. He probably needs a ton of calories to fuel a body like his.

My cheeks flushed at my thoughts. I had no business thinking about his body.

And I certainly shouldn't have been studying it the way I was.

When I dragged my eyes up to his face, I saw he looked down at me expectantly.

My face burned hotter.

If he'd noticed me checking him out, he didn't say anything. "What dressing?"

"Ranch," I answered without thought before realizing why he asked. I'd assumed the salad was for him. It would be in the end because I had no intention of eating anything other than the burger.

After the behemoth paid a far from cheap total, we moved over to the pickup area to wait.

Between the various smells and the heat emanating from the kitchens, my stomach began to churn. My appetite quickly faded, leaving nausea in its place. Saliva filled my mouth at an alarming rate.

At least I won't embarrass myself by throwing up huge chunks... There's nothing in there but stale black coffee and stomach acid.

Spots floated in my vision before it tunneled suddenly. My hands shot out to grip the counter as I fought to remain standing, but my movements were slow despite my panic. Everything shifted, and the world went sideways.

"Hey, whoa." The behemoth caught me around the waist as I slumped, keeping me upright. He pulled his phone out, likely to call for help.

That was enough to jolt me out of my daze so I could force out, "I just need to eat something."

"I'm calling an ambu—"

"No, no. It's just low blood sugar."

If he called an ambulance, I'd have to explain that I had no insurance and no money to pay the hefty bill for their trip. I'd be in debt for the rest of my life, all so they could tell me what I already knew.

I needed food.

"Please. I swear, I'm fine," I insisted.

He didn't look convinced, but he helped me over to a chair and sat me down before crouching next to me. His worried gaze studied my face. "You're pale."

"I told you, I just need to eat." But the thought of swallowing a single bite made my stomach twist.

With a scowl, he stood and returned to the counter. The cashier handed him the milkshake and an empty cup that he filled at the soft drink dispenser. He set them both on the table in front of me. "Drink."

I only took the soda, sipping the unfamiliar sweet syrup. "Root beer?"

"Yes. It'll help get your blood sugar up without adding caffeine to your system." He nudged the milkshake closer. "This too."

Unlike most of the population, I disliked chocolate. I could tolerate it in candy bars if there were other things—like caramel, cookie, or wafer—but I never chose plain chocolate anything.

"What's wrong?" he asked when I made no move to take it.

"Nothing." Not in a position to be picky about preferences, I took the heavy cup and forced myself to drink. It was cold and sugary, and I didn't care that it tasted like artificial syrup. It was sustenance.

Kinda.

He watched me for a second before surmising, "You don't like chocolate."

"It's fine."

"What flavor do you want?"

"This is—"

"Little girl, I asked you a question."

I glared at him. "Don't call me that."

Apparently, he didn't find a frail five-foot-one woman menacing because he ignored my snapped order. "Answer the question, *little girl*."

"Chocolate is fine."

"Tell me what flavor, or I'll order every single one."

I didn't even have to study him to know he wasn't bluffing. On a sigh, I muttered, "Strawberry, please."

"Don't mumble," he chided like I was a child before walking to the counter.

When he returned a minute later, it was with a new shake and a mountain of food on a tray. He set it all in front of me and sat in the chair opposite mine.

Saliva filled my mouth again, and it wasn't out of anticipation. It was my empty stomach threatening to revolt.

I grabbed the burger that looked bigger than my head. Unwrapping it, I took a small bite. A burst of flavor exploded on my tongue, and I wanted to inhale more, but I knew how that would go. I returned it to the paper and chewed slowly, pacing myself.

His gaze went from me to the barely touched burger. "You don't like it."

"I do."

"If you want something different—"

"It's delicious. But when I'm this hungry, I have to go slow so I don't, uh, get sick."

That made his brow arch. "This happen a lot?"

Shit.

"No," I lied.

And he knew it. He stared at me like he could read my thoughts, and his jaw clenched hard enough to make a muscle twitch. After a long, tense moment, he pushed the fries my way. "Eat."

I grabbed one. "Aren't you going to eat?"

"No."

"Why'd you order all this?"

"For you."

Stopping with the fry halfway to my mouth, I narrowed my eyes. "What's your angle here?"

"What do you mean?" He leaned back, draping a muscular arm over the empty chair next to him. Casual and relaxed and open.

I didn't trust it.

"If you think I have a way to repay you, you're out of luck."

"What?"

I met his surprised gaze. "No one buys a stranger lunch for free—"

"I do." Shaking his head, he muttered, "Try to do something nice, and get accusations. Just a ray of sunshine."

"Sorry, I don't—"

"Just eat," he said, thankfully cutting in since I had no clue how to finish that sentence.

As a kid, I'd taken care of myself. If anything, I'd often filled the role of parent to my mother. At work, I'd always done my job well and without needed supervision or direction.

No one ever told me what to do, but that seemed to be all the behemoth was capable of.

I wasn't a fan.

But I would suck it up since he was feeding me rather than handing me over to security. I could deal with his bossiness for a little while longer.

I took another tentative bite of my burger, giving my stomach time to adjust.

Behemoth opened the veggie laden salad and dumped the ranch on before pushing it over.

"I don't like salad," I told him, too distracted by my nausea to think better of being an ungrateful bitch.

"I don't care. You can't just eat protein, fat, and carbs."

I gestured toward the restaurant counter. "You're the one who ordered this."

"Because you need protein, fat, and carbs. But you also need vegetables."

Gross.

My food pyramid was made up of two zones. Cheap food was at the top. Chicken nuggets. Cardboard-esque budget pizzas. Tater tots. Boxed mac and cheese. White rice. Processed items that could be bought on sale and stretched for multiple meals.

Coffee held the place of honor as the largest section on the bottom. That sludge did a lot of heavy lifting, fueling my body while also giving the illusion of fullness. Some days, it was most of my daily intake courtesy of the unlimited supply at work.

Or, rather, my ex-work.

When there was money in my budget for veggies, it was canned stuff. Not different types of vibrant green lettuce topped with fresh vegetable chunks.

"Eat it," he ordered.

"You're bossy," I snapped before I could stop myself.

Shit, that was rude of me.

Thankfully, he didn't seem insulted. "So I've been told."

I forked up some of the salad, willing to gag down a bite or two if it would help my stomach. But when I grudgingly popped it into my mouth, it wasn't gross.

"Holy shit, this is actually good."

"Language," he scolded, surprising me. He didn't look like someone who would be offended by swearing, but what did I know? Dressed in a gray suit and blindingly white shirt—though no tie—he could be one of the religious folks who rolled through on a misguided mission to save the sinners of Vegas. Although they usually didn't have hands covered in intricate tattoos. "But I'm glad you like it."

My gaze shot to him, expecting a smirk or an *I told you so*, but there was nothing.

"I'm used to wilted iceberg and mealy tomatoes," I said.

He nodded, nudging the salad closer.

I happily ate more because it sat better in my belly than the other food. Once it was halfway gone and my stomach felt more settled, I returned to the burger and fries.

The behemoth didn't ask any probing questions or even talk. I ate while he drank my rejected chocolate shake.

I used the silence to discreetly study him, wondering who he was and why he was there.

He didn't look like he was on vacation or out gambling. My guess was business—either a meeting or one of the countless conventions that took place daily. Or the whole religious, save-a-sinner thing.

I didn't bother to ask because it was none of my business.

When I couldn't possibly eat another bite, I rewrapped the

remainder. He stood and started to pick up the tray, likely to toss it out.

So much wasted food.

Before I could think better of it, my hand shot out and covered his. I snatched it away just as fast. "I'll bring the leftovers home."

I knew the fries would taste like shit reheated and the burger would be a soggy mess, but I didn't care. It was enough for dinner.

Or dinner and tomorrow's lunch if I portioned it right.

His jaw clenched again for some reason—it seemed to be his default reaction to me. But he didn't say anything and just lifted his chin before going to the cashier.

After getting a paper bag for everything, he turned around as someone called, "Hey, Ash!"

The man's gaze shot to me like I'd been the one to shout. He wore an indecipherable expression on his face.

A moment later, it became clear why.

The security guard from earlier approached the behemoth, talking as he moved. It was obvious they knew each other.

Well... I was kind of right.

He is *here for work.*

Because this is *his work.*

With zero hesitation, I was up and running.

I only wished I didn't have to leave my precious food behind.

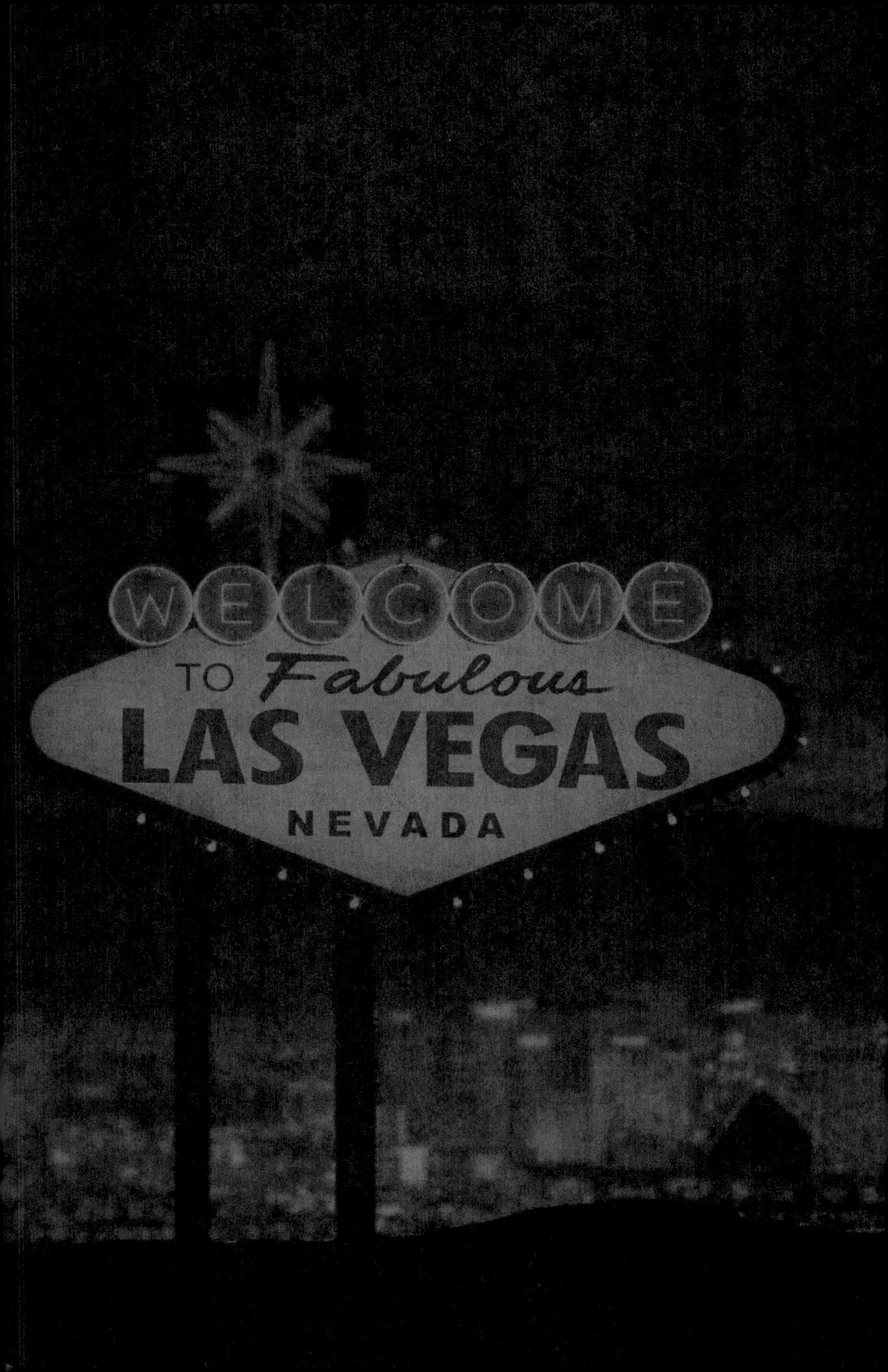
WELCOME
TO Fabulous
LAS VEGAS
NEVADA

CHAPTER 2
DON'T LET THEM SEE YOUR NEXT MOVE
ASH

F*UCK.*
Before I could speak or move, the little thief was out of her chair and gone in a blur of long black hair.

"What's—" Miles started, but I didn't have time to explain.

Blowing past him, I got into the hall just in time to be stopped by a crush of senior citizens heading toward the bus pickup.

Not wanting to ram through and risk breaking old people's hips, I rounded the group and slammed out the exit.

More seniors and tour groups filled the sidewalks. Not seeing her in the crowd, I ducked between two of the buses and scanned the street.

No sign of her.

Damn.

When Miles approached, I knew she'd put two and two together and run. I just hadn't anticipated her being so fast.

For a tiny—and probably malnourished—thing, she could move.

Going back inside, Miles waited in the hall. "Was that the girl?"

"Woman," I corrected—though barely.

She was still young.

Far too young for me.

When Miles and I had spotted her skirting the room, we'd thought she was a minor trying to sneak onto the gaming floor. She hadn't been interested in the slot machines. Instead, I'd caught her nearly imperceptible wallet swipe.

"I looked away for a second, and you were gone," Miles said. "What happened?"

"I brought her to get some food."

He slow blinked. "She stole from a guest, so you rewarded her with lunch?"

"She stole so she could eat. Then she nearly passed out. It was feed her or call an ambulance."

"You sure she wasn't playing you so you wouldn't call the cops?"

People could be human-shaped piles of garbage who lied as easily as they breathed—especially if it meant saving their own asses. I knew when someone was lying straight to my face, but her tears and pain hadn't been bullshit.

My sunshiny thief was starving—and not just from a day or two of not enough food. She was skin and bones with dark circles under her haunting blue eyes. When I'd held her wrist, I'd had to keep my grip loose for fear of grinding the bone to dust.

It was a safe bet she hadn't eaten anything of substance for a long while.

"Positive," I said, without a hint of doubt.

"That changes things."

"What *things*?"

"I was coming to tell you the man with the wallet filed a complaint. He's demanding to see the security footage so he can press charges."

That fucker.

I knew the cameras and angles like the back of my hand. There were two that would capture the area perfectly and one that would be obstructed but still show enough. "Have you watched the footage?"

"Not yet. I came to see if you knew where she was."

I wish like hell I did.

"What'd you tell him?" I asked.

"The truth. I need to speak with the owner first."

"I'll talk to him."

Maximo Black—my boss and closest friend—may have been a hard-ass, but he had a soft spot for the broken. His wife said he collected strays, and she wasn't wrong.

"Make it fast." He started to walk away before turning back. "I'll call you if I see her again."

I nodded, but I already knew he wouldn't. Neither of us would.

She'd dance into hell before she returned to Moonlight.

Not stopping to talk or bullshit with anyone, I quickly made my way through Sunrise. It was one of four—soon-to-be five—Black Resorts properties. Taking the private elevator up, I paused to knock on my boss' door.

Before Maximo met Juliet, I'd have let myself in with barely a knock. But with her in his life, I knew better.

Walking in on my boss and his wife wasn't an experience I was anxious to repeat.

"Come in," Maximo called.

Even if I didn't want to see them making the beast with two backs, I was glad to see his wife on the couch.

Juliet had lived a rough life before Maximo. If any of us could understand the mystery woman's motives, it was her. I doubted I would need the backup, but it was good to have it.

Maximo tore his gaze from her to look at me. "What's going on?"

Starting at the beginning, I told them about the woman, the wallet, her hunger, and how she'd almost passed out. I finished by relaying what Miles had shared. "And now the man wants the footage so he can press charges."

Maximo's face was its usual unreadable throughout it all. "Have Miles—"

"You can't give it over," Juliet interrupted with a sad shake of her head. "That poor, poor girl."

"Dove," Maximo warned, but she didn't heed it.

"She was *starving*." Juliet got up and paced. "I remember what it was like to be hungry, but at least I had some crappy food. I can't imagine how much pain she must be in."

His eyes softened as they tracked his wife, though his jaw was clenched. "Stop—"

"Being hungry with no food is like torture," Juliet shared, lost in her memories. "It's this ache that you can't fill. Not with water or distraction or anything. It seeps into your dreams so there's no break from it."

"Juliet." Maximo's voice was soft but stern. It was enough to make her freeze. "Come here." She did it immediately, and he pulled her onto his lap. "Can I finish a damn sentence now?"

She nodded. "Sorry, Daddy."

He rubbed his thumb across his lip. "You will be once Ash leaves."

Their interaction made my gut clench with envy. I didn't want Juliet. Even if I did, she loved Maximo like he hung the moon exclusively for her each night, and he loved her enough to kill.

I'd have to be a masochist and suicidal to want her.

But I wanted what they had. An atypical relationship that was so smooth, so easy, it made it normal.

Because for them, it was. It was what they both wanted. Needed.

Grabbing his phone, Maximo touched the screen a few times before putting it to his ear. "Send me the footage with the girl." He was silent for a few seconds. "Good."

When the email came through, Maximo played it on one of the monitors that lined the wall across from his desk.

We watched from three different angles as the mystery woman brushed by the man. None of it showed her taking his wallet.

"You sure she even took it?" Maximo slowed the video and leaned forward.

"It was quick."

I wondered again what kind of life she lived where learning to pickpocket with that skill level had been necessary. Her subtle sleight-of-hand work put Vegas magicians to shame.

"God, she's so tiny." Juliet's focus and concern was on the woman, not the wallet. "Did she eat any food before Miles scared her away?"

"Part of a burger, some salad, and a handful of fries."

She scowled. "That's not enough."

It wasn't. Especially since she'd run off without the leftovers.

Focusing on the monitor, I watched myself talk to the woman, struck again by how beautiful she was.

Beautiful and broken and in need of someone to take her in their tattooed hands to keep her safe.

And would you look at that? My hands just happened to be tattooed—under the blood that coated them.

She walked away, and the angle changed again.

"Shit," Maximo bit out before rewinding the footage.

I shifted my attention to watch what happened on the screen, not just the woman.

Taking a few steps, she dipped like she was picking up the wallet. But from that angle, it was easy to see there'd been nothing on the floor before that.

Making it clear the wallet had been in her hand the whole time.

Her theft had been undetectable. If I hadn't made her return the damn thing, no one would've been able to prove she'd taken it.

Maximo echoed my thoughts. "If we share the footage of her walking by, they'll want the footage of her returning."

"I know."

Juliet dragged her eyes from the paused monitor to her husband. "Does that mean you're going to give it to them?"

Maximo shot his wife a look as he picked up his cell and dialed. When whoever answered, he ordered, "Delete the footage. I'll have Cole wipe it from his backups so it can't be retrieved." He was silent for a minute. "Tell him that none of our cameras captured anything illegal, and to protect the privacy of our guests, we will not be sharing the footage. If he has an issue with that, he can take it up with our lawyers." He was silent again. "Right. Yeah. Cole will be in touch."

Juliet threw her arms around his neck the moment he ended the call. "I love you."

"You're not going to love me so much when I make your ass raw for thinking I'd turn that girl over."

"I know." His eyes narrowed, making her give him an innocent smile. "I'll love you more."

"I'll call Cole," I volunteered as I backed toward the door. I got the feeling Maximo wouldn't have time for a while.

"Wait," Juliet said as Maximo clicked off the monitors. "Forward the email to Ash before you delete it."

Maximo's brows lowered. "Why?"

"He likes her." There was an unspoken *duh* in her tone.

Their eyes shot to me for confirmation.

I lifted a shoulder in a half-assed shrug.

I didn't know anything about the mystery woman except she was strong, stubborn, too proud for her own damn good, and beautiful.

So fucking beautiful.

And she sure as shit needed someone to protect her.

Maximo clicked a couple of buttons, and my cell dinged in my pocket. "A little leverage goes a long way."

I doubted I'd ever see the woman again. Even if I searched,

Vegas was a big city with a constant rotation of people. I'd have better odds winning back-to-back jackpots than I would finding a woman who wanted to stay lost.

That didn't mean I wouldn't look.

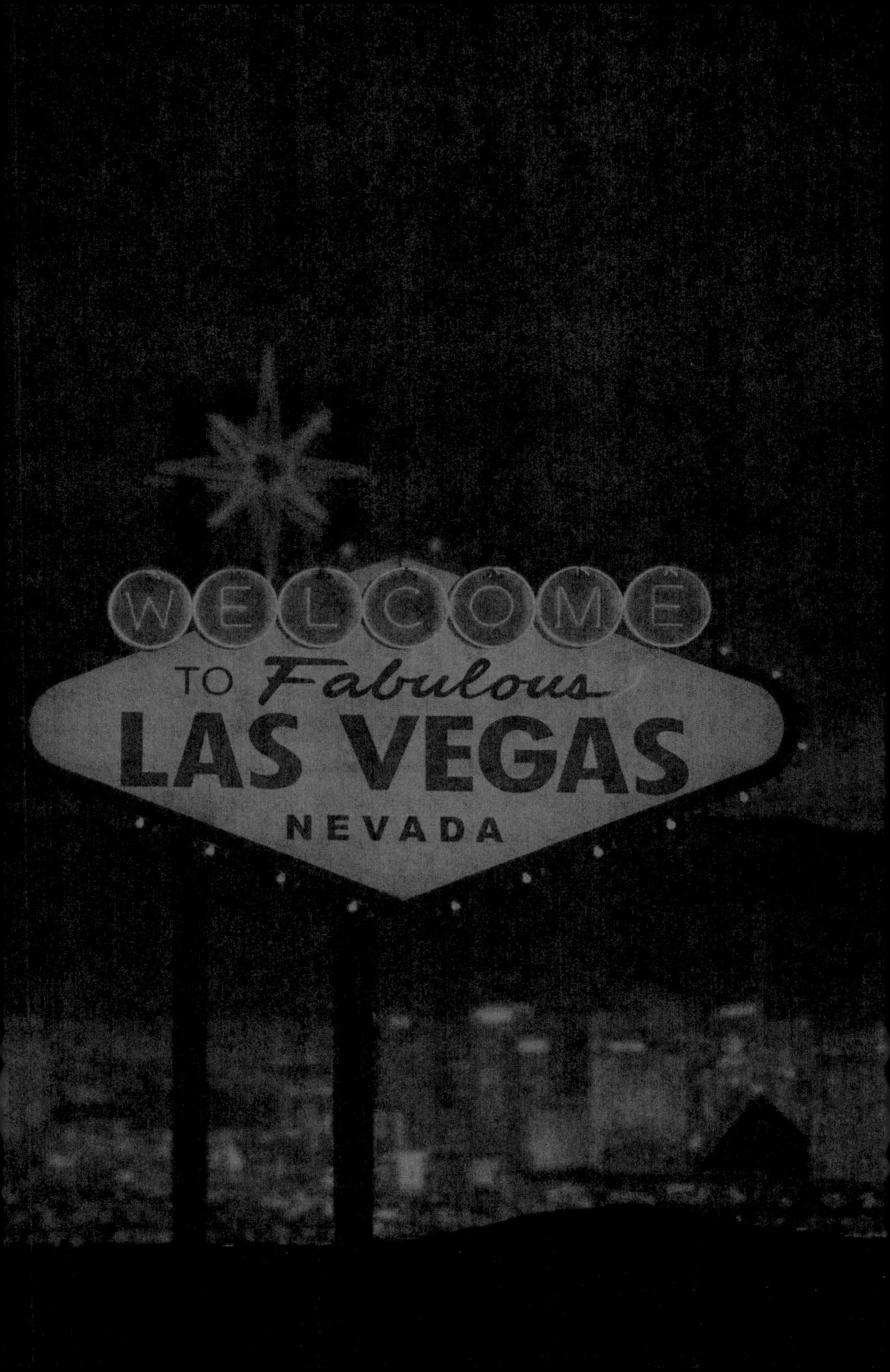
WELCOME
TO Fabulous
LAS VEGAS
NEVADA

CHAPTER 3
BE PREPARED
MILA

TRUDGING UP TO MY APARTMENT, I felt like I was about to die—and not just because walking up four flights of stairs was an intense workout.

I was used to it. My building had an elevator that was perpetually out of order. According to Ron—the building manager who only blew in when rent was due—it would be repaired any day.

Any day was going on nearly two years—the entire time I'd lived there and then some. When new tenants pressed on the matter, they were told the same rotation of excuses.

Just waiting on one part.

Just hit a snag.

Just need a little time to figure it out.

Any day.

It would never happen. The people who could move did so quickly, and the ones who couldn't had to suck it up.

I was in the suck-it-up category since it had the cheapest rent for a place on a bus route.

Usually, I didn't mind the hike up the stairs, but my stomach had already been iffy after I'd eaten the delicious food at Moonlight. When I'd taken off running, that iffy had turned into an outright *no*. I'd barely made it to a side alley before throwing up everything.

I hadn't cared that the few onlookers had loudly taunted me, assuming I was drunk or high. I'd just been happy the behemoth wasn't among them.

The downside was that the hunger I'd finally satisfied was back. And thanks to the retching, it hurt so much worse than before.

Enough nutrients must've hit my blood sugar, though, because I no longer felt like passing out.

Small victories.

Tiny victories.

Infinitesimal ones.

Whatever bright side I tried to look on disappeared as I went to open my door, only to find it already unlocked.

Shit.

A sane person may have seen that and backed away to call the cops.

I didn't bother.

For one, it'd take the cops forever to get over to my side of town. I was too tired to wait.

Mostly, though, it was because I knew the likely culprit.

Positioning my keys between my fingers like a discount, off-brand Wolverine, I rushed inside, not stopping to check that I was truly alone.

Not really caring.

Going right to the kitchenette, my stomach sank to my feet when I saw the cabinets were open. I ignored the pain that radiated as I dropped to my knees and dug around the mess left under my sink.

Please.

Please.

Please, please, please.

But I knew.

Even before I grabbed the innocuous-looking rubber tube of wipes.

Even before I wedged the lid off.

Even before my eyes fully processed what I saw—or, more accurately, didn't see.

Every tiny bit of cash that I'd hoarded away was gone.

Stolen.

When I'd moved out of my mother's house at sixteen, I'd vowed that eviction and homelessness were a thing of the past. No matter how strapped I was, I'd always kept aside enough money for a couple of months' rent. Or, if things really went to hell, it would secure a new, equally shitty apartment on short notice.

At times, I'd wanted to dip into those funds. To splurge on a huge meal. To shop for groceries that weren't on sale.

To go out. Have fun. Join the party that everyone else seemed to perpetually live in.

But I'd never done it. Not when I'd been sad, bored, or desperately hungry. I'd forced myself to be responsible, if only to combat the anxiety and memories.

All that sacrifice, and I had nothing to show for it.

Both dreading what I'd find but needing to know what else had been stolen, I stood on trembling legs. I scanned the place, which was easy to do from one spot because my studio apartment really was that tiny, and I really owned that little.

My small TV was no longer sitting on the rickety stand I'd found by the side of the road.

Drawers were left open.

Clothes were strewn on the floor.

A sleeve of dollar store saltines sat on the counter, left open to get more stale than they'd already been. I didn't care that she'd eaten most of them. In fact, I hoped she'd choked on their dryness. My issue was the jar of peanut butter sitting next to them.

The *empty* jar.

There was a dirty spork on the counter next to it, inviting ants—or worse—to come feast on the sticky mess and the cracker crumbs.

That peanut butter was the only protein I had in my apartment.

And thanks to my mother, it was gone.

Sad as it was, I hadn't realized she knew my address. It wasn't like she'd ever popped in for a visit with her only child. I also had no idea how she'd gotten inside. Even if I had a spare key, which I didn't, I wouldn't have given it to her. She'd never had the patience and intricacies needed to pick locks—that was my skill.

That left one likely option.

Ron.

All she had to do was bat her lashes at him, and the shitty building manager would've let her right into my apartment.

I eyed my bed with distaste.

Hopefully, that was all he did.

Grimacing, I dropped my gaze to the empty jar of peanut butter. The longer I looked, the more enraged I became.

The Roulette Hotel was a cruddy place filled with skeezy people. But I liked my job. Not necessarily where I'd been doing it, but the work itself was good. It was honest. I had solitude. I had independence since neither Todd nor Steve ever had to micromanage me. I had something to be proud of.

Every day was like one of those satisfying viral videos where a house gets organized or a stain gets removed. I liked sitting back and seeing my hard work pay off.

And the money may have been woefully low for all that effort, but it was still money.

Money she'd stolen.

Along with my savings.

My TV.

My job.

And my peanut butter.

For whatever reason, that enraged me the most. The damn peanut butter.

With a frustrated groan, I picked up the jar and threw it

across the room. Thankfully, it was empty and didn't make much noise as it hit with a hollow *thud* and fell to the ground.

The last thing I needed was a neighbor in my business. Or, worse, for them to complain.

I was already going to be frantically scrambling to make rent in time. I didn't need to speed up the eviction process with complaints.

No.

Screw this.

I'm not letting her drown me to keep herself afloat.

My mother or not, it was time to start pushing back.

I just had to find her first.

RILED UP ON peanut butter indignation, I stormed out of my apartment and onto a bus. I took it across the city, waiting for my anger to fade as time passed.

It didn't.

It grew with each seedy bar I'd had to enter searching for my mother. All I'd learned was that she hadn't been to her usual haunts.

Oh, and some of her old drinking pals already had the mother but were happy to try out the daughter, too.

Barf.

Beyond barf.

I should've gone home. My time and effort would've been better spent searching for another job rather than my deadbeat mother.

It wasn't like I was going to accomplish anything by finding her. She wasn't going to pull me into a hug before groveling at my feet for forgiveness. I had a snowball's chance in a Vegas heat wave of getting anything from dear ole Roni.

I knew that, but I was too pissed to think rationally. And the longer I searched, the more that anger festered and grew.

Because it was the principle of the matter.

The stench of stale beer and cigarettes filled the air as I neared a bar Veronica used to love. It'd been her favorite place—unless she got behind on her tab.

I remembered having to come drag her home when she was too wasted to walk the few blocks to our apartment alone.

I'd been six or so.

Instead of doing the smart thing, I did the stubborn one. I steeled my back and tried not to touch more of the sticky door than was necessary as I pushed inside.

It'd been a long time since I'd been there, but nothing had changed. And that wasn't a compliment. The interior looked even worse than the outside—something I hadn't thought possible.

As I approached the corner of the bar, the two bartenders spoke to each other quickly. The man continued filling glasses from the taps while the woman headed my way. Her brows were lowered—not hostile but definitely curious. Before she reached me, a surly, older man moved in front of her. He, on the other hand, looked outright intimidating as he glared at me.

"Get out."

My eyes widened. "What?"

"Ya heard me. We don't need whatever trouble you're about to bring, so just do us both a favor. Go."

"I'm looking for—"

"Don't care if you're looking for a score, a date, or the mystical chupacabra. You ain't finding it here."

I bristled at the insinuations he made, but I focused on what was important. "I'm looking for Veronica Rogers."

That got a reaction.

The male bartender's gaze shot to me as he continued to pour a dark beer until it overflowed. He cursed and shook off his hand before dumping the glass that was mostly foam.

The woman's expression swapped from curiosity to distaste in an instant.

And the older man's glare tightened like he was trying to shoot lasers out of his eyes.

Yup, they definitely know my mother.

Before anyone else could speak, an older woman pushed through a swinging door behind the bar. Her eyes landed on me, and she froze mid-step. "Whatever cookies you're selling, Girl Scout, we don't want 'em."

Ohhhhkay.

So much for a warm welcome and helpful assistance.

The man looked at her. "She's looking for Roni."

Before more insults could be flung my way, a woman flopped onto a stool and nearly fell from it. She turned and nearly fell again. "Roni? What do you want with her?"

Revenge for my damn peanut butter.

"She's my mother," I said instead.

I expected her to be skeptical. After all, if she was my mother, why would I need to search for her in a dive bar?

But the woman must've known her well because she wasn't fazed by the estrangement. "I see it. You've got her eyes."

Our blue eyes were the only trait we shared. That and our poverty-chic frames.

The woman picked up her beer. "But Roni hasn't been around for a while. She's living with her new man."

Unsurprising.

"Do you know where?"

She preened, like having the knowledge made her special. "Of course I know where my best friend lives."

Such is the manipulative power of Veronica Rogers.

I didn't bother to tell her that Veronica didn't have friends. She didn't care about anyone unless she had something to gain from it.

Including her own daughter.

The woman took out her cell and touched the screen a few times before turning it my way.

The fact Veronica had a new man was predictable. But my jaw hit the floor, and my disbelief reached an all-time high when I saw the address where she was supposedly staying.

My first lead, and it's one of Veronica's embellishments.

"You got your answer. Now go," the older man bit out before I could question the woman further. He looked two seconds away from siccing the bouncers on me. The threat on his face was followed by an outright one. "I'm not gonna say it again."

Even though I doubted the address was legit, I gave a small nod and thanked the woman before hightailing it out of there.

I walked down the street toward the bus stop, trying to decide what to do.

It was unlikely the fake address would lead to anything. It was a waste of time *and* money. If I was smart, I'd go home, grab the metaphorical scissors, and cut her out of my life for good.

Yet when the bus stopped in front of me, I climbed on.

What do I have to lose? She's already stolen everything.

You've got to *be kidding me.*

After taking the bus as close as it went, I'd had to walk the rest of the way through a lot of *cute.*

Cute houses with cute little gardens where cute kids played with cute toys.

The longer I hiked, the bigger those cute houses became until I stood outside the address the barfly had shown me.

It wasn't a mansion, but it wasn't far off. It was way nicer than any place I'd expect to find my mother.

Standing on the sidewalk, I was about to approach the door when a racing car squealed into the driveway. Veronica launched herself out from behind the wheel so suddenly, I thought the car would continue rolling until it crashed into the garage.

She snagged herself a man with a nice house and *a garage. Not to mention that expensive car since there's no way that's hers.*

Why the hell did she have to steal my shit?

"What're you doing here?" she hissed at me, her worried eyes darting behind me to the front door.

"Give me my fucking paycheck."

Her voice was low. Wounded. As fake as the rest of her. "Camila, is that any way to talk to your own mama?"

Oh barf.

"I have no *mama*," I hissed back. "No mom. No mother. I have a thief I share some DNA with."

Not that I'm much better up here on my pickpocketing high horse.

"I can explain." Another nervous dart of her eyes. "Later."

History might repeat itself, but she's really got it on a loop.

Most of my childhood memories involved being left alone or with my grandparents. But I'd seen enough pictures of us when I was a baby to know Veronica hadn't minded me back then. I'd been a cute accessory she could use for attention. That'd changed when I'd gotten older. She hadn't wanted people to know she was old enough to have a *kid*. By the time I was five, she'd taught me to call her by her first name.

In her head, we were Roni and Mila, basically sisters.

That'd changed again when I became a teenager. Then I was her secret. Her enemy.

Her *competition*.

Her shifty behavior made it clear nothing had changed. Her new man had no clue she had a daughter.

I was exhausted. Stressed. Sick to my stomach.

It's finally happened. I'm out of patience.

I'm done.

Steeling my spine, I did something I rarely had the desire or energy to do.

I stuck up for myself.

"I'm not leaving without my money."

My mother's eyes narrowed to slits, and I could practically see the vicious insults she had forming on her tongue.

It was our typical routine ever since I was old enough to know she was trash.

That *we* were trash.

Any time I questioned her grand stories, she would lash out and cut me down until she felt superior again.

I didn't give her the chance.

"*Now*," I emphasized, though I honestly didn't expect to get a single cent from her. I just couldn't back down. I couldn't let her continue taking advantage of me.

It needed to end.

Veronica fidgeted with a too tight hoodie that matched the sweatpants that were also too tight and too low on her hips. That was her signature style.

Too.

Too tight.

Too low-cut.

Too short.

Too revealing.

Too much bleached hair, lashes, and perfume.

She clung to the past like she clung to her youth.

Her hands trembled, and fear pinched her features. Her blue eyes brimmed with tears. Whether it was genuine or not, I wasn't sure. She was a brilliant actress. "They would've *hurt* me."

I must've been stupider than I thought because sympathy bloomed in my chest like a daffodil in a cracked sidewalk. If I let it, it would grow and take over, desperate for hints of sunshine. For love.

I didn't let it.

I hardened my heart against it *and* her. "That's not my problem."

There was that edge of hatred in her eyes as she glared at me even while she aimed for pity. "An old... friend found me. He thinks I owe him and threatened to hurt me, Mila. Said he'd tell my new man who I really am and ruin my life. And I *finally* got a good man."

"Then why the hell didn't you have him help you?" I snapped before I thought better of it.

Because I already knew the answer.

Veronica would always come first.

Whatever man she was bleeding dry was next.

And down at the bottom was me.

Her daughter.

Her only child.

The one who'd ruined her life by simply existing.

She opened her mouth, and I could almost hear the excuses. Almost taste the lies.

I lifted my hand, cutting them off before she could start. "You know what, I don't care. About him. You. Any of this. I don't even care about my missing TV and the damn peanut butter. I just want my money."

Her brows lowered. "What TV?"

"The one you stole and pawned for a whole, what, five bucks?"

"I didn't steal your TV," she insisted, indignation filling her tone like she had any high ground to stand on.

Stealing a paycheck is totally fine. Someone's life savings is fair game. A TV, though? Noooo, that's far beneath Veronica.

I shot her an impatient stare. "I'm supposed to believe you broke in and stole my money, but the missing TV has nothing to do with you?"

"I didn't steal anything." Crossing her arms, she truly looked insulted. "I just... borrowed the money. And I didn't break in. Your nice landlord let me in so I could wait for you. To explain and avoid *this*," she said, gesturing around. "But then I had to leave before you got home." It was her turn to give me the stare that said she thought I was a moron. "You think I'm gonna lug that cheap TV down the stairs?" She held out a hand to show off her long acrylics. "It would cost more to fix a broken nail than that piece of shit is worth."

She wasn't wrong.

However, if she didn't take it...

Oh God. Someone was in my apartment.
And I strolled right in.
The fact I wasn't immediately butchered is a miracle.

Taking in the self-righteous way Veronica lifted her chin in that small victory, I forced a sugary-sweet smile. "Oh, I'm so sorry for accusing you of stealing my TV. Now if you'll just return my whole fucking paycheck and the cash that you *did* steal, I'll be on my way."

Her face fell as she grudgingly admitted, "I don't have it."

Even if it's what I'd expected, the confirmation made the ground beneath me bottom out. The thread of hope I'd been desperately clinging to went up in a burst of fire, leaving me to fall.

To hit rock bottom.

Before I could speak—or shout the whole neighborhood down—I took a moment to inhale deeply. To try to get control of my rage and fear and the anxiety that was lodged in my throat, choking me.

I don't make scenes.
I never make scenes.
That's Veronica's thing.
She's already pushing me down to save herself. I refuse to help by lowering myself to her level.

A tiny bit of clarity and calm started to grow in my brain.

Or maybe it was rage suppression that would turn into an aneurysm to kill me.

Either way.

I'd said my piece. More than that, I'd stood up for myself—something I rarely did when it came to Veronica.

It may not have been the return of my money, but it was enough.

"You'll be fine, hun," Veronica said. "You've always been responsible."

She didn't mean it in a good way. In her world, responsibilities were a boring killjoy. But I took it as a compliment anyway.

Wow, this is rare. Ending an interaction with Veronica on a high note.

But that would've been too easy. Too good. Veronica had to go and ruin it. Because of *fucking* course she did.

With a dismissive wave, she rolled her eyes and continued. "There's no reason to get your panties in a twist. It was just one paycheck, Camila, and not a very big one—"

The warmth her—albeit backhanded—compliment had created turned to acidic fire, and I saw red. Rather than anxiety choking me, it was rage that stole my breath as it tightened my chest until I vibrated with it.

"It wasn't one paycheck," I cut her off, my volume growing with each word. "It was my last paycheck because you got me fucking *fired.*"

She winced.

Not with guilt or shame.

It was because my yelling could alert her man to my existence.

"Shut up before someone hears you," she snapped, looking ready to smack me.

It wouldn't be the first time.

My voice was even louder. "Fine by me."

She took a step toward me, violence in her eyes. I didn't dodge to the side. I didn't back away. I didn't cower.

I lifted my chin.

A nonverbal dare.

When she faltered, her eyebrows raising briefly in surprise, I added a verbal one. "Do it, and I'll scream and scream and scream until this whole fancy-ass neighborhood hears. You can explain who I am and why I'm here." I looked pointedly at her front door and yelled, "Explain it to *every*—"

"I'll get you your money," she interrupted, her voice tinged with panic and loaded with anger.

I reared back, more surprised than if she'd followed through with hitting me.

In all the times my mother had stolen from me, she'd never

breathed a word about repayment. In her mind, it was all what I owed her. For ruining her body. For ruining her plans.

For ruining her life.

As soon as the words were out, she tried to backpedal. "I just need some time. A few weeks. Maybe a month."

By that time, I'll be on the street.

It'll be like old times, except we won't have Nan and Pop's couch to crash on like when I was a kid.

That thought led to another. "If you're staying here, what happened to Nan and Pop's place?"

But I knew before her lips pressed into a thin line—her one tell of guilt. It wasn't one I saw often since she typically lacked the soul to feel remorse.

She rallied quickly, raising her chin like she worried her invisible crown would fall.

The Queen of Trash.

"You mean *my* house?" She shrugged. "I sold it."

"When?"

"A few months ago."

The house had been paid off when Nan and Pop were still alive. It wasn't much, but it was nice enough. It would've sold for a decent amount—especially with the way Veronica likely nickeled and dimed the buyer.

She could bleed a leech before it bled her.

How had she gone through all that money in months?

How could she sell the house without giving me the chance to take any of the sentimental items that were stashed away?

And how the hell was I surprised by anything she did?

I didn't bother to ask any of those questions. I focused on the only thing that mattered at that point.

"I'm not waiting a month," I said. "You sold the house, so you should have no trouble giving me my money now."

"I don't have it."

"Then get it."

It took everything in me. Every ounce of resentment, anger, fear, and stress was channeled into my backbone.

Because I knew what would happen when I pushed.

I'd lose her.

She may not have been much, but she was still the one relative I had in the world. The thought of losing that single strand of connection tore at my heart, leaving me feeling isolated.

Just so completely *alone*.

But I pushed anyway.

"Otherwise," I continued, raising my voice once again, "I'm calling the cops. How many warrants do you—"

"Monday," she rushed out, hatred dripping from her words. "Just give me the weekend to get the money together."

"The weekend. That's it."

I could practically hear the vile names she called me in her head.

It was better than hearing them out loud… again.

After hesitating for a moment, I decided to push my advantage. "I need money for a taxi home."

"All that way? That'll cost—" Her protests cut off abruptly when I opened my mouth, the threat of more yelling clear. With a grudging sigh, she stomped to her car before returning a moment later to thrust some crumpled twenties at me. "This is coming out of what I'm giving you."

'What I'm giving you.'

Like it was a gift or loan and not what she'd stolen.

"Good," I said, and I meant it. I had no interest being indebted to my mother.

The interest and strings she'd attach to each penny would be never-ending.

"I'll see you *this* Monday," I added. "Not Tuesday. Not two Mondays from now. Otherwise, I'll be back for another family reunion, *Mother*."

I didn't wait around for her to try to manipulate me, throw insults my way, or maybe follow through with slapping me.

I took my money and walked away.

I had no intention of actually paying for a taxi. A little—or a lot—of walking never hurt anyone. Even once I was at the closest bus stop, I ignored the sleazy catcalls and went about my own wild Friday night.

First, I stopped at the store for a small restock of staple groceries to get me through the weekend. I was extra cautious with what I chose because once I was done, I splurged on a fast-food burger.

It wasn't as good as the one I'd had for lunch.

And eating it alone in my apartment wasn't the same as sitting across from the behemoth.

But at least no one was bossing me around. That was way better.

Right?

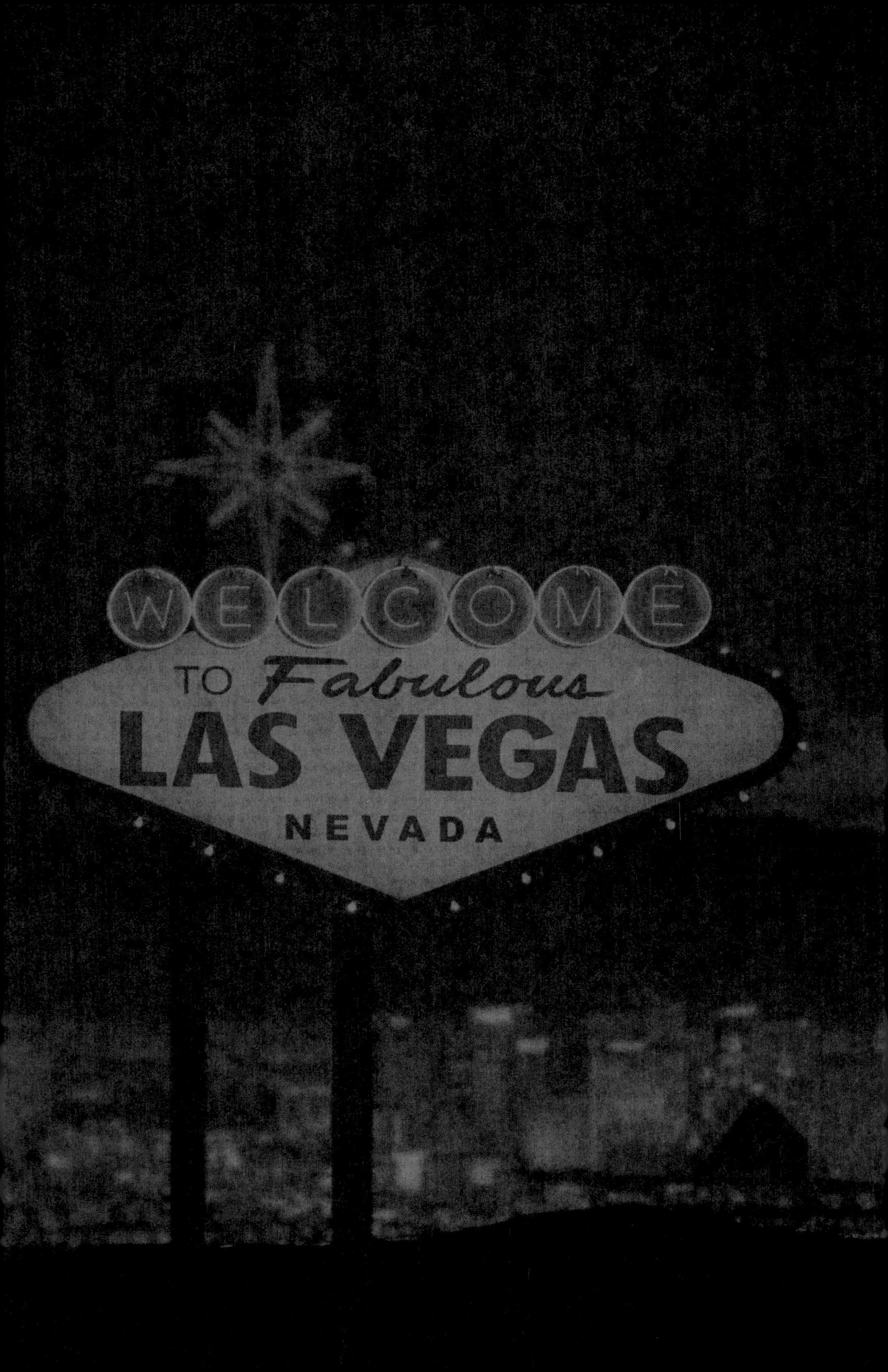
WELCOME
TO Fabulous
LAS VEGAS
NEVADA

CHAPTER 4
WATCH YOUR MOUTH
MILA

I was trapped in a tiny room. I couldn't move. Couldn't breathe. If I did, the whole place would fall apart, taking me with it. I stood there, my lungs beginning to burn when buzzing bees suddenly attacked.

No, that wasn't right.

Another bee attacked.

Opening my eyes, I blinked rapidly to clear the sleep from them. It felt like I'd just dozed off, but when I grabbed my phone—the real source of the buzzing—I saw it was nearly two in the morning. I shook my foggy head as I willed my tired eyes to focus on the waiting text messages.

> Unknown: Meet me here at seven PM.
> Unknown: Pin Drop Location Loading

It took me a minute to figure out who it was.

> Me: Veronica?

My text went unanswered.

I opened the map she'd sent, zooming in to see the meet was nowhere near my apartment. Of freaking course.

> Me: Wow, thank you for making it so convenient for me to get my stolen money.

No answer again.

Letting out a groan, I flopped back in bed.

I wasn't sure why I was surprised she wouldn't just drop it off at my apartment. Veronica had always been self-centered to the point of dysfunctional. She hadn't considered—or maybe it didn't matter—that I would have to take the bus while she had a car. It was just like her to *tell* me what to do and expect me to follow.

And since I needed that money, that's exactly what I would do.

Dammit.

I rolled over, kicking my legs with more force than necessary.

Beneath that anger, though, was a dull hurt that would grow if I let it.

Because she'd *texted*.

All that time, I'd assumed she didn't have my number, but she did.

Had she used it to *ask* for help?

No.

Had she used it just to check in with her only child?

No, of course not.

It was yet another reminder that my relationship with my mother would never be what I wanted because she didn't want it.

She didn't want me.

With that knowledge causing a pit in my stomach that I refused to acknowledge, I was almost back asleep when something hit me.

Once I get off the bus, I'll have to walk by Moonlight.

No way.

I snatched my phone back, cursing my previous snark. After that, it was even more unlikely Veronica would respond. I tried anyway.

> Me: Can we meet somewhere else?

Literally anywhere else.

I wasn't worried about security being sicced on me. If I saw the behemoth—and that was a big *if*—I could likely do a jig in front of him, and he wouldn't recognize me.

It was my ego I was looking out for.

Usually, repression and compartmentalization were skills of mine—especially when it came to all the various embarrassments I'd endured. In that lengthy list, the entire scene at Moonlight was ranked right at the top. Even though I would've loved to block the whole thing out, it'd been hard not to think about the behemoth.

And I did *not* want to think about him.

I didn't want to remember the pity in his hazel eyes.

I didn't want to remember the way he'd fed me like he cared that I was starving.

I didn't want to remember how good looking he was as he sat across from me, cool and sophisticated in his fancy suit. All the while, I'd been fighting against passing out or throwing up.

That was a big ole *no thanks.*

The easiest thing for me and my ego was to forget about the behemoth and avoid Moonlight for the rest of my life. Easy enough. I was too young and too poor to gamble.

I just had to hope Veronica would be accommodating to someone other than herself or her man for once.

But I knew it was highly unlikely.

Well... At least I was right.

That has to count for something.

Veronica hadn't been accommodating.

She hadn't been anything because I hadn't heard a damn peep from her.

There'd been no texts from her. Certainly none that had said she'd reconsidered and would be dropping my money off at my apartment, plus a few grand more for the inconvenience.

I'd tried to call and text a few times throughout the day, but they'd also gone unanswered.

Which was why, though I was far from happy about it, I was in the spot *she'd* picked. At the time *she'd* picked.

Yet Veronica was *not*.

Standing outside boarded-up buildings that'd seen better days, I checked my phone.

Still nothing.

Although it was only September, the strong winds made tiny bumps spread across my skin. Or maybe it was hunger messing with my temperature regulation since it was nearing dinner—my one meal of the day. Whatever the reason, I pulled my hoodie a little tighter as my gaze went to my left.

Again.

For the millionth time.

It was just the edge of a roof, off in the distance.

Moonlight Resort.

It might as well have been an entire world away. Nothing about the run-down block where I stood seemed like it should be in the same state as Moonlight, much less the same area.

When I'd gotten off the bus near The Roulette—another building I would prefer to avoid for the rest of time and then some—I'd had to walk out of my way to steer completely clear of both.

If Veronica would hurry up with my money, I could return to my apartment and never have to see even the edge of Moonlight again.

Which sounds very ominous and dramatic, but whatever.

With an exasperated sigh—both at myself *and* my mother—I

tore my eyes away. I checked my phone, but there was still nothing. No call to explain. Not even a text to acknowledge she was late.

Tired of waiting, I hit call. After only a ring and a half, it cut off and went to her voicemail.

She hit decline.

When it beeped for me to leave a message, I wanted to scream. I wanted to tell her what a shit mom she was. How she was selfish and greedy and ruining my life.

But I didn't.

I kept my frustration and temper in check because if I wounded her giant ego, she wouldn't meet up. I wouldn't get my money. She'd flip the whole narrative around to be the victim. And with an angry voicemail as proof, she could really milk it.

Not wanting to give her any excuses or fuel, I kept my voice as light and non-confrontational as possible. "I'm here, Roni—"

I didn't have the chance to say anything else when two things happened at once.

My phone was plucked from my hand.

And my body was moved against my will—and not gently.

It took a moment for me to realize what happened.

That I'd fucked up.

I'd lived in Vegas and the outskirts my whole life. I knew it was as dangerous as it was glamorous.

As in, the rich areas were glamorous with just a hint of danger to keep it exciting. Outside of that—in the areas I lived and shopped and worked and existed—was the opposite. It was dangerous with just a glimpse of glamor in the distance. Close, yet always out of reach.

Even knowing how dodgy it was, I'd been focused on my phone. My thoughts had been preoccupied by my mother. I hadn't stayed aware of my surroundings.

For anyone, that was a stupid risk.

For a woman, it could be deadly—or worse.

As soon as my brain caught up to my body being shoved against a building, I inhaled deep.

And then I screamed my damn head off.

My mouth was quickly covered, a sweaty palm pushing my cheek harder against the brick. The rough texture scraped and stung as I was dragged farther between the buildings.

Whoever had me spoke, but with my blood roaring in my head and a forearm against my ear, I couldn't make out what he said.

A different, quieter voice responded.

I knew better than to think that voice was some Good Samaritan rushing to help me. If anyone else was in the vicinity—and that was a big *if*—they'd likely lower their head and take off in the opposite direction. A second voice only meant one thing.

There are two of them.

Fuck.

My thoughts raced as I tried to figure out what to do. I needed to scream. Lash out. Kick. Scratch. Bite my way free.

With my heart hammering in my chest and my lungs burning with insufficient breaths, my fight-or-flight instincts screamed at me to do something. Anything.

I didn't.

Couldn't.

His hold was too firm, keeping me faced away. Trying to hit him would only work to hurt me. And with his gross palm covering my mouth and squeezing, I couldn't speak or plead or reason or insult.

I was frozen, both by fear and circumstance.

Right up until someone touched my stomach.

I jolted, trying to shift away as bile rose in my throat when the hand moved to my hip.

It was a light touch. Tentative, even.

But that didn't make it any better.

When whoever touched my ass, I nearly lost the tenuous hold I had on my retching stomach. Rather than feeling me up, whoever only slid my thin wallet free from my back pocket.

My head swam in relief.

It wasn't the first time I'd been held up—that'd happened at the old age of twelve. Replacing my EBT card, bank card, and license would be a pain in the ass, but it was infinitely preferable to what could've happened.

I would even give them my pin numbers so they could hurry along to discover that I was broke. That they'd wasted their time. That I should've been the one robbing them because it was almost certain they had more than I did.

"Nothing," the quiet one whispered.

I could've told you that.

"'Cause you're not looking right," the other bit out, the harshness of his voice sending a chill down my spine even before he pushed in close.

Too close.

Pinning me against the building with his body, he kept his tight hold on my mouth. He ran his other hand along my body. Unlike his friend, he groped at me with a bruising roughness.

Shoving a hand into my hoodie pockets.

My front pockets.

My back pockets.

Lower.

When his hand tried to go between my squeezed thighs from behind, I used what little leverage I had to push off from the wall. The hint of space I achieved was quickly lost when he body checked me back into the brick. His hand on my mouth should've softened the blow, but he jerked my head to ensure it hit hard.

I blinked back tears as he lowered his mouth to my ear. His icy voice was low enough that only I could hear him, yet he might as well have been shouting. "You stupid cunt. You think you're better than me? You should feel lucky I'm touching you."

Either his buddy was getting quieter, or he'd moved farther down the alley before calling, "C'mon, man."

The man holding me rose to his full height. I couldn't stop myself from flinching, and the sick bastard's erection jerked against my back at the sign of fear.

Saliva filled my mouth.

"Let's just go," the nervous one continued.

A leader and a follower.

"You telling me what to do?" the leader asked in such a calm, scary way, I almost felt bad for the other guy.

Almost.

"No, no, of course not."

"Where's your money?"

I thought the asshole was still talking to the jumpy guy, but then he pulled me away from the wall just to shove me harder against it. "I asked you a question, bitch."

"I don't have any," I answered, my words muffled against his palm.

"Fucking greedy bitches, always playing games and thinking their toxic snatches will save them. Being lying sluts must be hereditary for you all." He gripped my cheeks and tilted my head so far, I thought my neck would break. "Tell the truth for the first time in your whore life. In your whore ancestry."

As soon as he removed his hold on my mouth, I insisted, "I am."

If I had enough space, I would have pulled my pockets out of my shorts so dust and moths could fly out like in a cartoon.

"Fuck, Ez," the other guy groaned. "Maybe she's telling the truth."

"First, you try to tell me what to do, and now you wanna let some lying bitch manipulate you?" He wrapped a hand around the back of my neck, and my breaths came in rattled gasps. My face was pushed against the brick as I took the physical brunt of his irritation while the other man got the cold, harsh verbal threats. "You say one more fucking word, I'll keep it all for myself."

Any sympathy I had for nervous guy evaporated in an instant when he remained silent.

The cowardly prick.

"Where were we?" The handsy jerk dropped his head so his mouth was near my ear. He licked the shell, and a shudder went through me. Not of pleasure.

Never of pleasure.

It was fear and disgust that twisted my insides until I was moments from getting sick. The bile rose in my throat, acrid and burning.

But he wasn't done.

Still gripping the back of my neck like I was an animal he needed to keep in place, his other hand shoved between me and the building to palm my breast. My fear grew to panic that seeped into my bones. Not just because he was touching me. It was *how* he did it.

With ease.

Confidence.

He didn't care that his touch was unwanted. It was the opposite.

The way he ground his disgusting erection against me said he *liked* the pain and terror he caused.

I tried to make my voice strong. "Back away."

"Or what?" At my silence, he gave a cruel chuckle. With each word, he squeezed my sensitive flesh harder. "That's what I thought." He slid his palm from the back of my neck to grip the front and tilt my chin up. His eyes were on my lips. "Maybe after I fill your mouth with something other than lies, you'll feel like telling the truth."

It wasn't a scare tactic. It wasn't him using tiny-dick-energy intimidation.

His bland nonchalance filled my veins with ice water.

Even if I knew what money he was talking about.

If I told whatever truth he wanted to hear.

If I gave him all the cash in the world.

I knew, without a doubt, he'd follow through on his vile threats anyway.

Because that was what he really wanted to do.

The mystery money was just an excuse.

My frenzied words spewed without a filter. "I have nothing. Less than nothing. I don't have a job. I don't even have a balance on my food stamp card. I'm broker than you, asshole."

Pain suddenly exploded from the side of my face, the force knocking me against the building so hard, I saw stars.

I scrambled, turning in time to watch his fist fly at my face again. The back of my head hit the brick, and he chose right then to finally move away.

I dropped.

By the time my dazed brain communicated the need to catch myself, it was too late. My sluggish arms were lined with lead, and they couldn't move fast enough to break my fall.

Shooting pain radiated up my spine from my tailbone, knocking the wind out of me. What little breath I had was lost when a hard kick connected with my exposed stomach. I soundlessly cried out as preservation instinct overcame the shock, and I curled into myself.

It didn't do any good.

Gripping my hair, the monster pulled my head back. "What the fuck did you just call me?" He used his stinging grip on my hair to keep me in place so he could punch me again.

God.

I am so stupid.

Being there alone.

Not staying alert.

Mouthing off.

I'd made a lot of mistakes, and with fear and pain clouding my brain, maybe I was continuing to make them. But his anger was better than the alternative, so I let my emotions run the show and my mouth.

Shaking off the mental fog, I glared up at him. It wasn't hard to do since my eye was already swelling. "If you come near me with that dehydrated Vienna sausage you call a dick, I'll bite it off."

He backhanded me so hard, blood sprayed from my mouth. I wasn't sure if it was a busted lip or something more. The sharp, metallic taste coated my tongue, and more droplets dripped down my chin.

His free hand went into his pocket before pulling something free. With a flick of his wrist, a sharp blade clicked free.

Oh fuck.

"Help me get her up," he bit out, pointing that deadly blade at the coward and then me.

Assuming I was subdued enough by the punches, the viselike grip on my hair, and the threat of the knife, the coward must've deemed it safe to approach.

He was wrong.

When he grabbed my foot, I kicked out, catching him right in the jaw.

"Bitch," he bit out, stomping my stomach at the same time the asshole shook me.

Violently.

Like he was trying to snap my head off my neck.

Even if I wanted to keep fighting against their hands, I couldn't. My limbs refused to move. Words wouldn't form, no matter how badly I wanted to shout and insult and plead.

No more screams.

No more kicks.

No tears.

I had to channel every drop of energy into fighting against the black edges that threatened to push in.

Don't pass out.

Don't pass out.

If he did all this while I was awake...

A tremor rocked my body, and I couldn't even finish my thought.

A loud siren suddenly cut through the air and echoed in the alley. It was an ambulance, not the police—I was all too familiar with the difference—but the men must not have known.

The leader's furious gaze locked on me.

He wanted to kill me.

He wanted to do worse.

And he would've had the siren not grown louder. Closer.

He got into my face and said something, the tone of it harsh and poisonous, but I couldn't hear a single thing. Even the siren mixed with whirling in my head, becoming warped until it just stabbed along with the pounding behind my eyes.

The men took off down the other side of the alley, jumping a fence and continuing.

I didn't leave the alley. Not right away. Focusing on my breaths, I scooted to the side until I was hidden away. I took my time, working to stay conscious. Maybe it was only a few minutes. Maybe much longer. My brain seemed to be cutting in and out—like streaming a movie with a sketchy internet connection.

Once I felt steady enough, I used the wall to slowly stand.

I burned.

The brick rash on my face. My hot, swollen cheeks. Even my internal organs felt like they had lava traveling through them. Everything burned like it was on fire.

I wanted to collapse and press my body to the cold ground, but I knew better. It wasn't safe. I needed to get the hell out of there.

Zipping my sweatshirt, I pulled the hood over my head. I kept my face down and moved as quickly as my aching body would allow.

When I reached the end of the alley, I picked up my phone from where it'd been tossed aside. The glass was shattered so badly, it felt jagged against my fingertip. I pressed the power button anyway, but the only thing displayed were the glitchy rainbow lines of a completely totaled screen. I pocketed it and made sure nobody was around before I continued to the street.

I should've gone to my bus stop.

I should've tried to find a taxi to splurge on.

Hell, even walking the long way home would've been a better idea.

I did none of that.

Nor did I go to the police, try to find the ambulance that'd passed, or any of the other million things that would have made sense.

I honestly wasn't sure what I was thinking.

Keeping my slow pace, I walked and walked and walked until I reached the very same building I'd just sworn to avoid. I didn't hesitate before climbing the steps and going inside.

I kept my head down as I cut the line and moved directly to the front desk. "Is the behemoth here?"

"Ma'am?" a man responded.

Why did I say that?

Oh fuck, that's right.

I took a breath, hoping the oxygen would get my brain to function.

It didn't.

I pushed on anyway.

"Ash. Beard. Short hair. Behemoth of a man," I corrected, hoping I hadn't majorly fucked up by taking such a big risk.

Considering how limited my view was—not to mention how out of it I was—there was a good possibility I was in the wrong building.

Even if it was Moonlight, it was also possible that Ash didn't even work there. I'd just assumed so, but maybe I'd met him while he'd been visiting his security friend.

"Ma'am," the man said again, "this lobby is for resort guests. I'm going to have to ask you to leave before I call security."

His voice was filled with equal parts pity and disdain, like I was one of the drunks or druggies who hung around the casinos, hoping to score—either a jackpot or drugs.

Or a wealthy mark to pickpocket.

"Go ahead." My words were clipped with impatience to hide the pain it caused just to speak. "As long as security also brings Ash. *Now*."

I leaned on the counter for a moment, fighting against the wave of nausea that roiled my stomach. From the corner of my eye, I could see the man pick up the phone, but I couldn't hear what he said. The whirring in my head was like a peaceful white noise compared to the hammering that took over the longer I stood. All the bright lobby lighting and reflective glass twinkled around me before bursting like light flares. The black around my vision was no longer hovering, threatening to push in. It was pulsating, thrumming to the beat of my pounding headache.

I need to go home before I get arrested.

No reason to carry on that *family tradition.*

I inhaled and gathered every bit of strength I had before forcing my fingers to release the counter.

"Ma'am, wait," someone said.

Before I made it more than a couple of shuffling steps, the vibe in the lobby was suddenly different. Like the room had shrunk. Like a ripple of awareness moved through it. Like people were in awe or fear.

Or both.

I knew it was him even before he said, "Little girl."

I didn't have the energy to be annoyed at the name I'd told him not to use. I barely had the energy to breathe.

Regretting everything, I kept my head down and ignored him as I continued toward the exit. But suddenly he was there. In front of me. He must've caught some of the damage to my face from the harsh way he bit out, "*Fuck.*"

"It's not—"

"What happened?"

He reached for me, but I flinched away. "I was in a car accident."

The lie tasted bitter on my tongue, but it was far better than the truth.

Actually, silence would've been the best. Which I could've had if I hadn't stupidly searched him out.

This was a mistake.

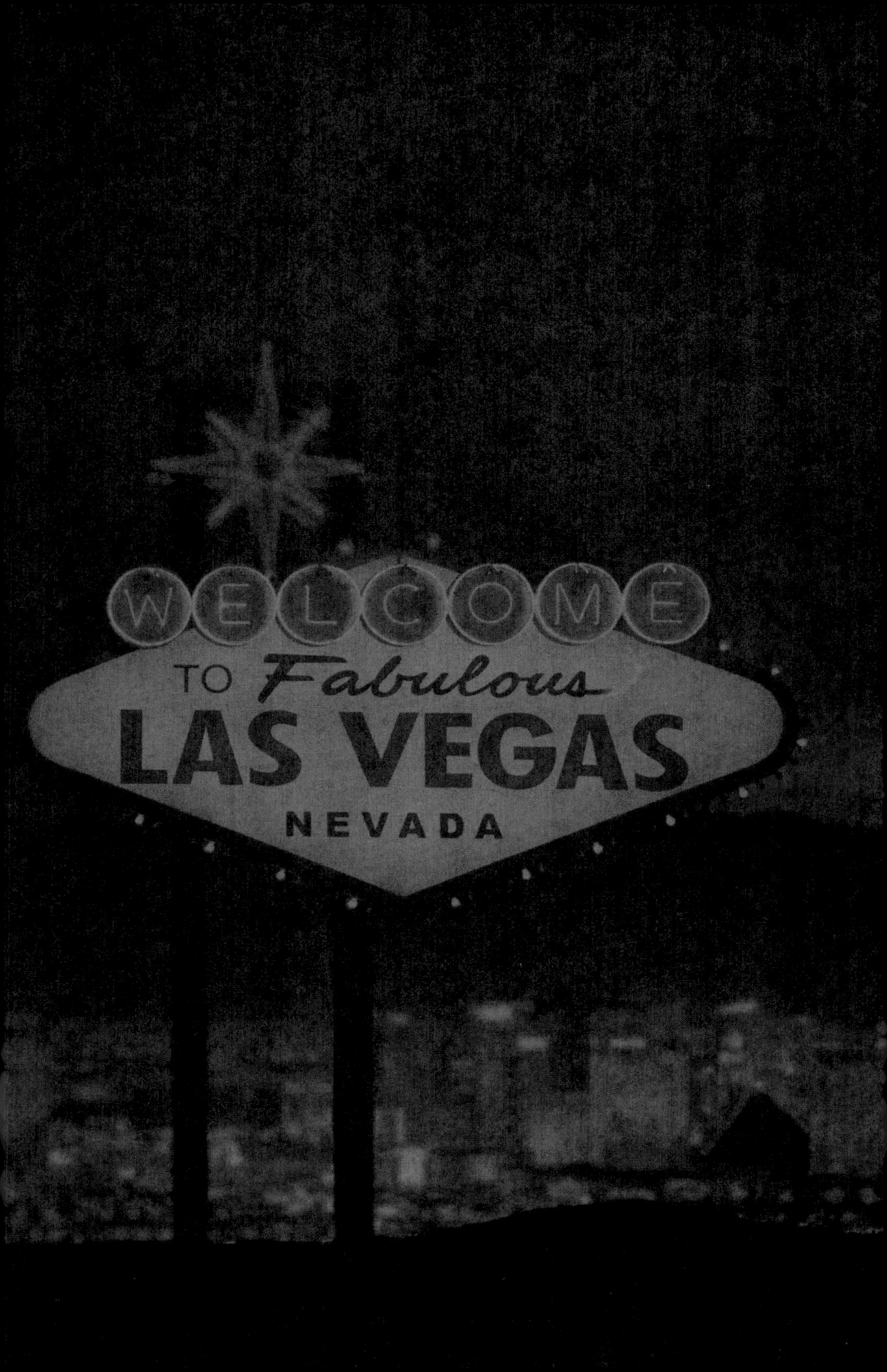
WELCOME
TO Fabulous
LAS VEGAS
NEVADA

CHAPTER 5
STAY AWAY FROM DRUGS
ASH

I*T'S REALLY HER.*
When my gaze had moved from the front desk employee to the woman slowly retreating, I hadn't believed my eyes.

My luck.

When she'd hauled ass away from me like the devil, hellhounds, and costumed card slappers were chasing her, I'd have put all my money on never seeing my little thief again.

At least not in real life. In my head was another story.

But there she was. In the lobby of Moonlight with a hoodie pulled over her head. Even not being able to see her face, I knew it was her.

My *body* had known it was her.

I'd been the sick fuck getting a hard-on from seeing her. All the damn while she was in pain.

I wanted to remove her hood to get a better look at the damage, but I didn't want to spook her. Her shoulders already rose and fell too quickly. Her voice was so small, I could barely make out her words. "This was a mistake."

I didn't get the chance to ask what she meant when she suddenly dropped.

No sway. No wobble.

No attempt to catch herself.

For the second time in a handful of days, I caught her before she hit the floor. But unlike last time, she was out cold.

Lifting her into my arms, I ignored everyone else as I stalked back to the reserved elevator. Calling an ambulance would be fast, but I could drive faster. I just needed my keys from where I'd left them in my office.

When the front desk had called me, I'd been finishing working over a scammer in The Basement—the bottom floor of Moonlight where we brought people who'd fucked up.

The last time I'd had my keys in my pocket during one of those sessions, they'd fallen out and gotten covered in so many bodily fluids, I'd had to disinfect them for a week.

I jostled her just enough to press the button to start our quick rise. Once the doors slid closed behind us, I gently moved her hood aside to see more of her face.

Fuck.

Fucking damn *fuck*.

Her face was a damn mess. Her left eye was swollen. Her cheeks were blotted red. Her lip was split. Scrapes and abrasions covered one cheek, almost like she'd dragged it across sandpaper covered in shards of glass.

Christ, her airbag did a number on her.

Explains why she came here.

She must have a helluva concussion.

The elevator doors slid open, and I stepped into the small waiting room. Cole and Marco were at Nebula with Maximo, so the floor was empty. I used my thumb to get into my office.

Snagging my keys from where I'd tossed them on my desk, I turned back toward the door when she suddenly twisted in my arms. If I hadn't been holding her so tight, she'd have fallen and made her injuries worse.

Her urgent voice pitched sharper. "Put me down. Put me down. Put me down, asshole!"

At her increasingly panicked insistence, I gently set her on the leather couch at the side of the room. She scrambled back, her fear fucking palpable.

Christ.

"Hey, it's okay. It's just me," I said, like that meant a damn thing to her. I kept my distance and lifted my hands placatingly at her. "I'm not trying to hurt you. I'm just taking you to the hospital."

She stopped moving, but her body vibrated with tension. Her eyes widened, giving me a little more of her pretty blues. The swollen one had to hurt like a motherfucker, but she didn't even flinch. "No hospital."

"You said you were in an accident," I told her slowly, wondering how bad her concussion was. "Were you driving?"

Rather than answer, she averted her eyes and whispered, "I have to go."

"Tell me what happened."

She still wouldn't look at me. "Nothing."

"This sure as shit isn't nothing." At her silence—not to mention her refusal to go to the hospital—my mind started going. And I fucking hated the direction it went. Because if she'd been in a car crash and didn't want to get checked out... "You drunk?"

That made her eyes snap to meet mine. "I don't drink."

"High?"

"*Never.*" She was back to scrambling as she hurriedly stood before freezing. Her face contorted from the pain. "I need to go."

"Yeah. To the damn doctor."

She lost what little color she had, but it didn't stop her from taking a step toward the door.

"Christ, sit back down."

"No hospital," she hissed out through gritted teeth.

"Fine. Sit."

She gave a stubborn lift of her chin. "I mean it."

"So do I." I held up three fingers in a scout's sign. "Scout's honor."

Her brow rose before she winced again. "You weren't a Boy Scout."

"Sure, I was." When she just eyed me, I added, "For three whole weeks."

"And then?"

"And then I realized they had too many rules. Now *sit*."

"Talk about too many rules," she muttered even as she sat and practically melted into the couch. Her head rested against the back, and her eyes drifted closed.

"Hey, hey, hey." I'd had more than enough concussions to know she shouldn't be asleep. "You've gotta stay awake, or I'm taking you to the hospital."

"You promised," she said without opening her eyes.

"Tell me what happened." When she didn't answer, I prodded, "Tell me, little girl."

She didn't take the bait. There was none of the attitude she'd tossed my way in the food court. Instead, she remained stubbornly silent.

"Let me see if there's a first-aid kit around here," I said.

She made a small murmur of acknowledgment—or a pained noise—as she lifted her feet onto the couch and wrapped her arms around her bent legs.

Christ. She looked even more frail sitting like that, curled into herself.

Going into the bathroom, I pulled out my phone and scrolled through my contacts until I found the number I needed. The call connected, and I kept my voice low. "May, it's Ash Cooper. I need the doc at Moonlight now."

I gave Dr. Pierce's wife—who also worked as his receptionist for off-the-book cases—more info about my mystery woman's injuries and refusal to go to the hospital before clicking off. After I texted Miles to wait in the front lobby for him, I dug in the storage cabinets for the basic kit and grabbed some damp paper towels.

When I returned to my office, she was still in the same position. Her breathing was even, but her mouth was set to a scowl even as she slept.

She shouldn't be asleep, but I didn't wake her yet. I kept my touch light, barely grazing as I felt around for a wallet or ID.

Nothing.

I used my phone to check my usual sources for reports of a crash or abandoned car.

Nothing there, either.

Maybe that means she wasn't the one driving while fucked up, and she's trying to protect a friend.

Or boyfriend.

If that was the case, that hypothetical motherfucker better hope he was already dead in a ditch somewhere. Because if he'd taken a stupid as fuck risk with her in the car...

Dead in a ditch would be heaven compared to what I would do to him.

Knowing I'd let her sleep too long, I softly murmured, "Hey, let's get you cleaned up a little."

"I'm fine."

"And you'll be better once we get those scrapes clean."

Without opening her eyes, she held out her hand. When I didn't give her anything, she wiggled her fingers. "I can do it myself."

"Not saying you can't."

When I didn't relent, she slowly lifted her head and cracked her lids to watch me warily as I wiped her face. It had to sting like hell, but she stayed stoic.

"I'm sorry," she whispered, her blank expression unchanged as I worked. "I shouldn't have come here."

"You sure as fuck should've."

"I just didn't know where else to go."

If she wasn't two seconds away from passing back out, I'd have allowed myself to like that. Like that she'd come to me. Asked for me.

But right then, my focus was on making sure she was taken care of.

"*Always* to me," I said before I could stop myself—adding being a creepy fuck to being a sick fuck.

It didn't matter anyway. She didn't seem to hear me as she stared ahead.

I reached out to tilt her head to the other side, but as soon as my fingers came in contact with her chin, she flinched away.

And not from the pain since I'd barely grazed her.

"Sorry, just tender," she muttered.

Lied.

What the fuck?

Ignoring the questions I had no right to ask—and had no chance in hell of getting answers to—I focused on the basics. "Tell me your name."

"It doesn't matter."

"It does."

She didn't give me the chance to clean her other cheek before she lowered it back to her knees. Her lids drifted closed. "I just needed someplace to rest. I'll leave in a minute."

The fuck you will.

I didn't say that to her. "If you're going soon, no reason not to tell me your name first."

"No reason to do it, either."

"Is the fact I want to know not a good reason?"

"No," she said with zero hesitation.

My lips tipped at the small sign of attitude.

The silence stretched. I thought she'd fallen asleep when she quietly said, "Mila."

"Mila," I repeated, liking the way it sounded.

Liking that she'd told me.

Wondering if it was the truth.

"Was that so hard, Mila?"

She shifted her head to glare at me before resting again.

I hated to do it, but I ordered, "You need to stay awake."

"But I'm tired." Bone-deep exhaustion seeped into her voice. "So fucking tired."

Contrary to her claim, when the elevator suddenly dinged a moment later, she quickly sat up.

Miles filled the office doorway, and her gaze shot to me.

Betrayal.

Accusation.

Panic.

"It's okay," I tried, but it was too late.

She bolted upright, ready to run.

Or kick me in the balls.

I wasn't sure which.

Likely both.

Miles picked up on her anxiety and raised his hands, flashing her the smile that charmed even the pissy old ladies who stalked the penny slots. "I'm just here with the doctor."

Well-intended as his words may have been, it was the wrong fucking thing to say.

Mila spun on her heel, pointing a finger up at me. "You promised."

"Promised I wouldn't bring you to the doctor. Said nothing about bringing the doctor here."

"That's the same thing." Her head tilted to the side for a moment. "Actually, it's worse."

"How?"

Ignoring me, she stormed toward Miles and the doorway. Her voice was rough—from pain, anger, or both—when she forced out, "Excuse me."

His gaze went over her head to meet mine, and I shook my head. He stayed in place, blocking her exit.

She dropped the niceties. "Move."

"Mila—" I started.

"Move now, or I'll..." She raised her chin. "If you don't, I'll..."

"You'll what, little girl?" I asked from behind her.

"I'll... Oh shit." She darted to the side. Miles shifted to block her, but she wasn't trying to escape. She slammed down onto her knees and grabbed the wastebasket, barely getting it under her before she retched.

"Fuck." I moved behind her, holding her hair away from her face as she threw up what she had in her stomach. From what I could tell, it wasn't much more than water and stomach acid.

"Go away." Another heave mixed with a sob, and she half-assedly swatted at my hand. "*Go.*"

I didn't.

Keeping hold of her hair, I crouched behind her and rubbed her back.

A water bottle appeared in front of her, and she took it from Miles' outstretched hand with her own shaking one. Before she could take a sip, her body leaned to the side, and the bottle dropped. She barely flinched as the cold water spilled onto her bare legs.

Fuck it.

The space I'd been trying to give her was gone as I gathered her into my arms. I sat on the couch with her on my lap but kept my arms loose.

She leaned away from me. "I just need to eat. Or sleep."

"Let the doc look at you." I stroked her hair from her face. "Then you can go."

Even as I said it, I knew it was a lie.

When she didn't argue, I jerked my head for Dr. Pierce to come over. I didn't put Mila down as he poked and prodded. Her eyes stayed closed the entire time, her face blank except for the occasional wince.

After a few minutes, he used a gentle, doctory voice. "We need to reconsider going to the hospital."

"No," Mila shot back immediately.

"Baby," I said without thinking, "if the doctor says—"

"No." The one word was even firmer and backed up by her trying to launch herself off my lap. "I told you, I just need to eat."

"Good. They've got food at the hospital."

"I'm not going." That time when she shoved away from me, she did it so forcefully, I had to release her before she hurt herself. She scrambled to stand, and her body swayed, but she just lifted that stubborn chin. "I appreciate the concern, but I'm good. And I'm leaving."

"Mila."

At my tone, she froze, and tears glimmered in her eyes. Despite all the pain she had to be in, it was the first sign of them. Like she was holding it together by pure spite, only one drop slid down her scraped cheek.

As heart-fucking-breaking as it was, I wasn't going to bend. Not when it came to her health.

I could say that I would feel that strongly about any random person's pain and suffering, but I wouldn't. Years of working in Vegas had shown me most people weren't all bad.

They were worse.

A shitty outer shell that hid an even shittier, rotten inside.

Other than my family and small circle—who were basically family—I didn't give a single, solitary fuck about other people.

For whatever reason, I gave a whole lotta fucks about Mila.

I snagged her wrist and carefully situated her back onto my lap before she passed out.

"If you don't let me go, I'm going to scream." Her threat may have been genuine, but her body contradicted her words. It leaned into me. Her grip on my arm wasn't to shove it away or dig her nails into my flesh.

Instead, she held my arm to her like it was a seat belt she wanted to keep in place.

Or so I thought.

Because with my guard down, Mila struck.

Keeping hold of me with one hand, she used the other to dick punch me. She missed most of the good stuff but caught enough to make me instinctively loosen my hold.

When I did, she bolted to her feet and raised a fist at where Miles filled the doorway. A slight breeze would've knocked her over, but that didn't stop her. "Get out of my way, or you're next."

Christ, that was hot.

Dick punch or not, I had to fight getting as hard almost as much as I had to fight a smile.

Not the time and all that.

Miles' face stayed blank, but I'd worked with him long enough to catch the amusement in his slight brow rise.

I wasn't about to back down, no matter how much rage she packed in her tiny, five-foot-nothing frame. "Mila, if the doc—"

Dr. Pierce didn't have any balls against her steel ones, though, because he cut me off. "I understand. Let me at least give you something for the pain. Are you allergic to anything?"

I opened my mouth to ask what the fuck was going through his thick skull but caught myself.

Getting her some relief is most important right now.

I'll stop her from leaving after that.

Remaining silent, her gaze darted between us—like a skittish doe surrounded by predators—but it kept returning to me.

Like she knew I was the wolf to watch out for.

"Mila, allergies?" he prompted. When she shook her head, Dr. Pierce grabbed a bottle from his kit.

After a long, hesitant minute, she asked, "Just some pain meds, then I can go?"

"Absolutely."

Absolutely fucking not.

Mila shot me a look that bordered on gloating before accepting the pills and a fresh bottle of water. She tossed them back and gave Dr. Pierce—that spineless bastard—a small smile. "Thank you. Sorry for the trouble. And sorry I can't..." Her words trailed off as she scowled before wincing.

"Sit and let those kick in."

A beeping filled the air, and Mila jolted, her hands going to her ears.

It wasn't my cell, but I quickly silenced mine anyway while Pierce looked at his. "I need to take this."

Mila watched him go, shifting forward when Miles stepped aside to let the doc out. When he returned to block the door, she let out a small, frustrated huff. "One minute. Then I've really got to get home before..."

Before someone notices? Someone misses you? Someone gets worried and reports you missing?

"Before *what?*" I prodded when her sentence trailed off. "Is there someone waiting for you?"

If she had a man at home—and he wasn't the one responsible for the accident—it wasn't a dealbreaker. An inconvenience, sure, but nothing I couldn't handle.

It could always just be a roommate she was worried about, and that meant even less.

"Of course, my boyfriend. Sorry, *boyfriends*. Plural." Mila started to rub her forehead before pulling her hand away. "My whole apartment is full of men. Stacked to the rafters."

I knew she was fucking with me, but that didn't stop the surge of murderous jealousy from hitting harder than her fist to my balls.

As soon as you feel better, little girl, you'll pay for that.

She sat as far from me as she could get, and I gave her that—for then. Every so often, she sipped her water, but I wasn't fooled. She wasn't resting. She was covertly checking her surroundings. Waiting for an opening. An opportunity.

If Miles moved even half a foot, she would run.

She wouldn't get far, but that wouldn't stop her from trying.

As I tried to find a way to get her checked out properly that wouldn't terrorize her further, I watched and waited.

For her to throw more attitude my way.

For her to bolt.

For her to nut-check me again.

I'd have bet on at least one of the three. More likely, all three.

And I'd have lost.

Because rather than growing more antsy with each passing minute, Mila seemed to relax. She sank into the couch, her head bobbing.

I didn't buy it.

"Nice try, baby. No one's letting their—" My words cut off when her head dropped back suddenly.

Shit.

I quickly yanked her onto my lap, brushing her hair away so I could see her face. She didn't look as pale as earlier. There was no wince. No scowl.

I thought she was out cold until she whispered, "Sorry."

"You apologize too much," I teased, trying to distract her while my panicked gaze shot to Miles.

He lifted his chin and spun to go get the doc.

"I know. Sorry." Her tone held no matching playfulness.

"That took longer than expected," Dr. Pierce said as he entered the room. I thought he was talking about the call, but his focus was on Mila.

And it wasn't filled with the same panic I felt.

He didn't seem fazed by finding her practically unconscious. Not even a raised eyebrow.

He sat on the table in front of us and put his fingers to her throat, feeling her pulse. Then he opened Mila's lid to flash a penlight in. "Tell me what happened."

"Car accident," I answered for her.

Pierce met my gaze and shook his head before returning his focus to her. "Mila, who did this to you?"

Who.

Acid churned in my gut, the implication of that one word eating at me like poison rot.

"What happened?" he continued when she didn't answer.

Her words and body trembled when she whispered, "He happened. *They* happened."

They.

More than one person did this to her.

Rage twisted in me, mixing with the poison rot until I could hardly see straight.

I could practically smell it. Taste it. Feel the lives I would snuff out.

But none of that mattered. Not right then.

Murder would come later—slow and painful and torturous.

"Who's they?" I asked once I locked it all down tight enough to keep my voice gentle. Mila didn't need me shouting and scaring her worse than she was.

The flinching.

All that fucking flinching.

She lifted her shoulder in a small shrug before burrowing into me. Within seconds, her breathing had evened out.

Pierce stood and started for the door. "Let's get her to the hospital."

I'll be damned.

Literally, once Mila wakes up and turns those tiny fists of fury my way.

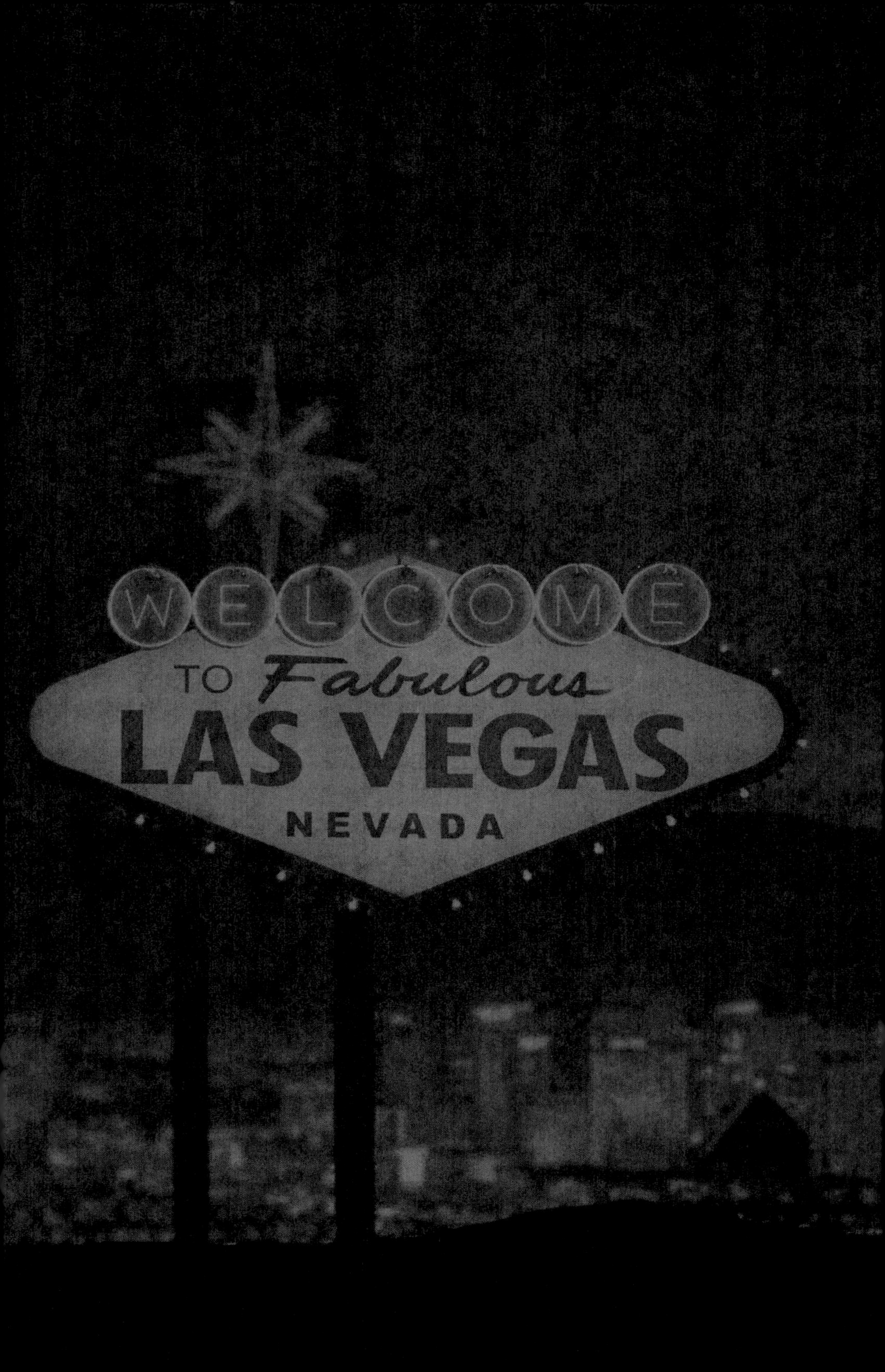
WELCOME
TO Fabulous
LAS VEGAS
NEVADA

CHAPTER 6
KEEP YOUR COOL
ASH

Every time I closed my eyes, I saw Mila swallowed up by the hospital bed—vulnerable and pale with tubes sticking out of her bruised arms.

And every damn time, my murderous rage was stoked.

I paced the private room, waiting for her to return from some scans. My attempt to follow had been shot down by harried nurses who'd bluntly told me I would be in the way.

It made me fucking antsy to have her out of my sight, but the sooner it was done, the better. They'd already run X-rays, blood work, more blood work, and had her hooked to an IV.

She'd slept through it all.

The sedative Dr. Pierce had slipped her under the guise of pain meds wasn't to blame. He'd only given a low dose—enough to relax her and chip away at some of the pain.

My cell buzzed in my pocket, and I pulled it out to see it was one of the few people I wanted to talk to right then. "What'd you find?"

Cole was unfazed by the lack of unnecessary pleasantries. He clacked away at a keyboard, the noise carrying like he was on speakerphone.

The fact he's still at it and unwilling to stop long enough to make this call isn't a good sign.

My suspicion was confirmed when he bit out, "I was able to trace her down the street on the SafeCams, but the farther I got, the fewer cameras there are until I lost her altogether."

Damn.

SafeCams were an extensive system of security cameras that were supposed to prevent crime.

They were also supposed to be confidential.

Cole often and easily hacked into them—occasionally to help us commit a crime.

"Any luck on her background?" I asked.

"Not a lot of luck for me or your girl, it seems."

That raised the hairs on the back of my neck. "What's that mean?"

"She might've been born and raised in Vegas, but she's had shit luck her whole life." Disgust filled his tone when he added, "Starting with the cunt who birthed her."

"That bad?"

"Fucking worse. A few pops for drunk and disorderly, trespassing, assault, typical trash shit."

None of that was earning her a nomination for *Mother of the Year*, but it wasn't the worst we'd heard. Not enough to warrant Cole's anger.

"Handful of CPS cases, too." That made the pieces click together to form a picture that hit close to home for him. "Sending your girl to school in dirty clothes. Not having food in the house." The emotion drained from his words until he sounded cold and robotic. "Leaving her home alone for days at a time."

"And she was able to keep custody?"

"Still digging, but other than losing her for a brief stint after a report of suspected neglect, yeah."

"What'd you find out about Mila's life now?"

"Camila Price. Twenty."

I knew she was young, but hell. A dozen years younger than me?

Unaware of that hit to my underused conscience, Cole continued. "Lives in a studio apartment with more violations than residents. Has worked at The Roulette as a housekeeper since she was sixteen—on paper, at least. Could've been longer. They've been busted for employing minors under the table."

I tried to remember which place that was. "The dump near the old shopping center that got torched?"

"That's the one."

Christ. Just driving by that place could give someone bed bugs and an STI.

I didn't wonder why she worked in a shithole like that. Or why she lived in a slum apartment that was likely worse than the bad I already pictured.

Simple answer.

The universe had a fucked sense of humor.

Pretty girls with haunted blue eyes faced bullshit after bullshit while undeserving assholes like me were born with *gold* spoons in their mouths.

She worked and lived like that because she had to.

Had.

Past tense.

"What else?" I asked, desperately wanting to know more about her. Needing to know it all.

"That's all I've got. She's got no socials. No dating apps. Never seen someone with no digital footprint. Especially someone her age."

"Maybe she uses a fake name."

"If I had her mom, I'd want to go undetected, too."

"You think you can get more info on the CPS cases?"

"Already on it."

Usually, questioning his skills to hack into anything would be an insult, but there was no offense or cockiness in his voice. It was nothing but determination—once again showing how close her history was to his own.

How deep it cut.

"Try not to get busted." My words turned distracted when I

saw Mila's bed being pushed through the double doors at the end of the hall. "I don't have time to bail you out."

"I was trying to be nice, but now you're just being outright rude." He gave a dramatic sigh that was undercut by another burst of rapid typing. "I'll send over what I have so far."

Cole and I—along with Marco—worked for Maximo Black. Not as employees of Black Resorts, but for him personally.

Juliet called us his goons, and she wasn't far off.

Marco put his immense knowledge of causing bodily harm into being his bodyguard.

Cole was a fucking computer nerd—not that I'd ever seriously call him that since he could ruin my life with three clicks of a mouse. He kept all our tech updated and top of the line. Including, of course, Maximo's stalker cameras.

And I was his second. His right-hand. Driver. Bodyguard. Intermediary. Enforcer. Scheduler, fill-in, and, on previous occasions, math tutor to his wife.

We'd earned our places in his small inner circle by being the best at what we did.

Which was how I knew Cole would have the files within days.

If not before.

"Get me the footage from the lobby today, too," I said.

"On it."

I clicked off and opened the door before stepping aside so they could push the bed in. Since they'd been gone a while, I expected Mila to be awake and ready to give me hell. But when transport got the hell out of my way, I saw her eyes were still closed.

I thought she was asleep, but the rapid rise and fall of her shoulders gave her away.

"I know you're awake, baby."

Her voice may have been soft, but it was filled with venom when she gave me the expected hell. She just did it in a way that hurt worse than hurled insults. "You broke your promise."

It'd been for her own good, but fuck, I hated hearing the betrayal in her words.

"Technically, it was the doc." I didn't hesitate to throw him under the bus. Or at least drag him down with me.

"He didn't promise. *You* did." She paused for a moment, a few tears escaping her closed lids. "I knew I shouldn't have trusted you."

With that sucker punch, she rolled over and curled into herself, looking even smaller. Vulnerable.

The murderous rage knocked at my sternum harder, eager to be let out.

Dr. Pierce moved into the doorway and jerked his head.

I brushed Mila's hair from her face. "I'll be right back, baby."

"Take your time," she said sweetly. "A hundred years will be too soon."

"I'll aim for fifty."

It was small and quick, but I caught the curve of her lips before she smothered it.

I would take it.

Once I was in the hall, Dr. Pierce reached around to close the door. "I can't give you specifics about a patient."

I lifted an expectant brow.

"But I can tell you about a hypothetical patient. *Hypothetical.* If you say anything to a real patient"—he tilted his head toward the closed door—"that so much as implies I told you anything, I'll cut off my partnership with Mr. Black. I don't care how mutually beneficial it may be."

Maximo had first seen Dr. Pierce after he'd taken a bullet as a teenager—one meant for his crooked old man. Over the years, we'd kept him busy with an assortment of injuries. In exchange, he was paid a shit-ton.

Not to mention, Black Resorts made generous donations to the different charities and fundraisers the hospital organized.

We weren't the first or only patients Pierce saw off the record. He worked on his own code that wasn't dictated by hospital policy or insurance company bullshit, and the money Maximo donated also went toward that.

"Got it," I agreed.

"The hypothetical patient has a concussion, but the CT didn't show swelling. No broken bones but a lot of bruising." He glanced into the room, his lips thinning out. "I'm going to prescribe something, but she should alternate ice and heat on her face and ribs."

I'll text Marco to drop supplies at my house since I have even less than the understocked kit at Moonlight.

"Her loss of consciousness wasn't from her injuries. They're painful, and even a minor concussion could be dangerous, but they aren't as extensive as I'd feared. The biggest issue is her labs. Her metabolic panel and vitamin levels show she's malnourished."

That wasn't a surprise. It was a safe bet that someone who pickpocketed to buy a burger, didn't blink at almost passing out, and had a system in place so they didn't get sick while eating didn't have unlimited access to healthy food.

"I'm going to start her on some supplements to get her vitamin levels where they should be. I'll get you a list of foods she needs to eat more." Pierce paused for a second before clearing his throat. "I'm assuming you're staying with her, but if not, with a concussion—"

"She's coming home with me."

"Good." His gaze drifted back to her, his expression tightening. "Whoever did this to her caused a lot of pain to a body that was already weakened. I took an oath to do no harm..." He gave me a pointed look.

"But I didn't."

"Good," he repeated. "Now keep yourself together for this next part, or I'll have every security guard in the hospital remove you."

I didn't get the chance to ask what he meant before he opened the door and moved to Mila. I followed him in, staying back and silent even though I wanted to be close. Wanted to make her feel safe.

Wanted to force her to look at me when she wouldn't even glance my way.

Pierce washed his hands before checking Mila over, asking questions as he worked. None of it warranted the warning he'd given me, but Mila still answered like her defenses were a mile high.

When he pulled a stool over and sat close, she eyed him warily but remained silent.

Giving nothing away.

"Do you want Ash to wait in the hallway?" he asked, and I wanted to strangle him with his own stethoscope for even giving her the option.

She can want it, but it ain't happening.

Still not looking at me, she shook her head.

I took the win.

Dr. Pierce gave her the same recap of her test results. She didn't seem surprised by anything other than the lack of broken bones.

"So I'm good to go?" she asked when he finished.

No questions on what to do. No concern for her low nutrient levels. No fear of what anything meant or what could happen to her.

Christ. If she's not going to take care of herself, she needs someone to do it for her.

My chest tightened, but I ignored the sensation. Ignored my thoughts.

Ignored my needs.

"Not yet." Dr. Pierce grabbed a metal tray and pulled it closer. "The most effective way to boost these levels is via a shot." He looked over his shoulder at me before adding, "In the buttock."

That's why he told me to control myself.

He thinks I'll lose my shit over him seeing and touching her ass.

To be fair, I was already possessive of the woman I barely

knew, but not so bad that I'd try to stop the doc from treating her.

He started to explain what he was giving her and any side effects, but Mila didn't seem to care. Didn't question. Still didn't look at me. Stone-faced, she rolled in bed like it was nothing.

Dr. Pierce's body blocked hers as he gave her the shots.

The second he finished, she asked, "Now am I good to go?"

"Almost." He put some space between them but stayed seated at her level. "Mila, we noticed some severe bruising on your breasts during your exam. I need to know if they—"

Bruising.

Breasts.

Fucking fuck.

Pierce hadn't been worried about the shot in her ass. It was how I'd react to these questions. To her answers.

"No," she interrupted.

He kept his voice soft and matter of fact. "If they did, we need to start you on some precautionary medications and run a—"

"They didn't. I've never even..." Her swollen eyes finally went to me, her face flushing.

It took a second to understand why she looked embarrassed. To get what she was saying.

Seeing I had zero reaction to her admission, Mila returned her focus to the doctor. "I swear it. They didn't get that far."

They didn't get that far.

Her words kept cycling in my head, but I heard what wasn't there.

They didn't get that far.

But they would have.

Mila's eyes shot back to me as I shoved my hands in the pockets of my slacks to stop myself from chucking something across the room. It took every fucking ounce of control I had, but I kept my expression blank. Relaxed. I stayed where I was when all I wanted to do was pull her to me and tell her all the ways I'd make those motherfuckers pay.

In graphic detail that still wouldn't come close to what I'd do once I found them.

Standing, Pierce dropped needles in the bin and looked at me. "Because of her concussion, I'll give you a list of things to watch for."

Mila gave a little scoff. "That'll be difficult for him to watch for anything since I don't plan to ever see him again."

Oof, my fucking pride.

Pierce's words were firm. "You have to stay with someone."

"I have a roommate," she said instantly. "He'll wake me up and make sure I'm not dead."

She'd kill in a poker tournament.

I was almost certain she was lying, but there was no tell. No overselling it. No emphasis. No fidgeting. No stuttering.

Pierce called her flawless bluff. "Good. He will need to pick you up so I can give him the discharge instructions before I release you."

Mila's face fell before she quickly caught herself and smoothed it out. "He's at work until the morning."

"You can stay here and rest until then. That'll give the pharmacy time to get your prescriptions ready. Are you allergic to hydrocodone?"

"I don't need anything. I have Motrin." She tilted her head to look at him. "*Actual* Motrin."

I wanted to take her over my knee for being so frustratingly stubborn, but I couldn't.

She was already injured.

She'd already punched me in the dick once that day.

And she wasn't mine.

Rather than threatening her with a punishment I had no right to give, I said, "Don't be a martyr, little girl."

"This is none of your business," she snapped at me.

My lips quirked, but before I could respond to tell her I was making every damn thing about her my business, Pierce sat again. "Mila, you've got some nasty bruising. Over-the-counter pain medication won't cut it."

"It's what I have, so I'll make do."

I had no damn clue why she'd turn down relief when she was clearly in pain. Just like I had no damn clue why her cheeks flamed red under the bright hospital lights.

But Pierce knew. "There's no copay for this visit or any prescriptions."

Her eyes closed as her head dropped back. "I don't have insurance, so not only will there be charges, they're gonna be big."

"Mila, we don't bill people who—"

Mila shot back up, her voice adamant. "I am *not* charity."

"I never said you were. It'd be the same for anyone."

I wasn't sure if that was the hospital's official policy or just the doc's, but it didn't matter.

Her expression didn't look happy, but her body language shifted anyway. Her shoulders dropped. Her muscles loosened.

She relaxed.

All that fight. It wasn't about protecting anyone or a hospital phobia.

She'd been willing to suffer without medical attention because of the bills.

Christ, I'm a fucking idiot.

"While you decide what you want to do," Dr. Pierce said, "I'm going to draw up your discharge paperwork so it's ready when you are."

When the door closed behind him, I took his place on the stool. I wasn't expecting her to acknowledge me, but she quietly asked, "Is he going to call the cops to report this?"

"No."

I'll handle them in a more satisfying way than the law could.

"Actually no, or the same way you weren't going to take me to the hospital?" she pushed.

Ouch.

"Actually no. Why?"

"Trying to mentally prepare."

"Where'd it happen?" Again, I didn't expect her to tell me, but when she rattled off an intersection, I texted it to Cole.

She tucked her hands under her face and fell silent again.

My cell vibrated with a response.

> Cole: Only SafeCams in that area are broken or the lens has been sprayed out. What the fuck was she doing over there?

I had no idea, and it was unlikely she'd tell me.

Not the truth, at least.

> Cole: I'm gonna drive over there, see if there's anything.

I pocketed my phone and returned my focus to the curled-up bundle in the bed.

Neither of us spoke as I tried to pick my words, and Mila did her best to pretend I didn't exist.

I needed to get her to accept a room at one of Maximo's hotels without pissing her off. I just wouldn't share that it would be in my penthouse.

Or that I'd be sleeping on the couch.

When I opened my mouth, my carefully chosen offer wasn't what came out. "Stay at my house."

It wasn't my original plan, but I liked the idea a helluva lot better.

Maximo paid a shit-ton to keep his hotels heavily guarded by security. He'd upped that to a whole fucking shit-ton after a—now dead—bastard from Juliet's past had managed to get his hands on her.

Mila would've been safe in any of the hotels. She would have access to the spa, room service, and all the other bells and whistles that went unused by me.

But they weren't my house.

And that was where I wanted her.

When all she did was blink at me, I went on. "I got a decent-sized place. Food. TV. And a spare bedroom with a lock on it."

Though I wish that lock was on the outside to keep you in. 'Cause I'm betting you'll try to leave the first chance you get.

"I can take care of myself," Mila said.

"Don't doubt it."

"And you're a stranger."

I held a hand out. "Ash Cooper. Nice to meet you."

She didn't take it. "Fine, you're a stranger whose name I *might* know because you could've just made that up." When I reached into my pocket to show her my license, she kept going. "And even if it is your name, I still don't know anything about you."

"This is true."

Her brows rose like she was surprised I agreed. "So why the fuck would I stay with you?"

I let the language and the attitude slide.

Not the time.

Not the place.

Not *mine*.

"Food. TV. Privacy," I recapped before sweetening the deal—literally. "I even have some leftover cake."

"Poisonous cake from a stranger. It'll be like the unhappy ending to a morbid fairy tale."

"Hey, my baking skills are shitty but not deadly."

Her lip quirked—or maybe it was a twitch. "Wow, even more enticing."

"That's why I have a chef buddy who handles all the baking. He makes these unreal cookies. Soft and buttery, they literally melt in your mouth."

Her eyes lit, and I could almost see the need form.

One day, you'll look at me like that.

Not above using my friends to get what I wanted, I laid it on as thick as frosting. I tipped my head and rubbed a hand across my beard. "Actually, I don't think he's ever made anything that didn't make me want to lick the plate clean. He was classically trained in the best French kitchens."

"Cool. *Fancy* poisoned cake."

"Do you always think everyone is out to murder you, sunshine?"

Her expression was the epitome of *duh* as she gestured down to herself—injured in a hospital bed.

I'm a fucking moron.

"Fair point," I said roughly, mentally kicking my own ass. "I won't tell him you accused him of poisonous desserts because then he won't bake for you, and that would be cruel."

She gave a small, one-shoulder shrug as she mentally lifted her walls higher. "Tell him whatever you want. It doesn't matter."

I leaned forward, my eyes meeting hers. "You came to me, Mila."

"I—"

"You were hurt," I interrupted before she could spew lies or excuses of temporary insanity. "And you came to me. You knew you could trust me. *Keep* trusting me."

The silence stretched until I was about to back down and offer her the hotel room.

"Fine," she muttered so quietly, I wasn't sure I'd heard right. "But only for a few days."

"Whatever you say, little girl."

"And stop calling me that."

I hid a smile and started planning.

ARMED WITH A few bottles of pills, a lengthy list of warning signs to watch for, and an exhausted yet somehow still stubborn as fuck woman, I moved through the lobby with Mila. She'd refused to ride in a wheelchair. When I'd offered to carry her, she'd offered to punch my dick again.

Or use a scalpel.

I let her walk.

Other than her hood pulled over her head and her slowed steps, she gave no indication she was in pain. It reminded me of the first time I'd seen her in Moonlight. Her chin was held high as she moved like nothing was wrong.

Like prey hiding her injury from predators.

What have you been through?

Her steps slowed further, and I put my hand on the small of her back and leaned in to mutter, "I will chase you."

She twisted away, but not before I felt a shiver go through her.

Christ, am I going for the dickhead record tonight?

"Mila—" I started to apologize before she cut me off.

"I'm not that dumb. For one, you'd catch me in half a step even with the super juice that doctor injected into me. For another"—she glanced up at me—"there's fancy cake in my future."

"Then why're you slowing?"

She opened her mouth before hesitating. When she spoke, it was with an evasiveness. "Just looking around."

Usually, I hated lies. Doing what I did for a living, I heard them daily. Always stupid ones. Done for self-preservation, greed, or both. It got old. They were predictable and easily spotted.

Mila was different. A challenge.

If it wasn't for the subtle way she favored one leg and the wince of pain that followed, I may have believed her skillful lie.

Moving fast but carefully, I lifted her into my arms.

"Whoa, hey. Put me down!"

"Hush, sunshine."

She looked over her shoulder to see an audience of people looking our way at her outburst. I couldn't find a single fuck to give, but she apparently had a stash of them.

She thumped my shoulder with her fist. I assumed it was meant to hurt.

It didn't.

Kinda tickled.

"I said put me down," she hissed, her cheeks flaming brighter as she hid behind her dark hair.

"No."

"You can't just say no."

"Can and did."

"Remember what I said about the scalpel," she threatened with a huff. Despite all the attitude she threw my way, she folded into herself, shrinking as small as she could.

"You're in pain," I said softly.

"I'm fine."

"Okay, well my legs are longer than yours."

"Thanks, Captain Obvious."

"That means I can get you out of here faster."

Mila paused before her body relaxed in my hold, even as she huffed at the inconvenience of being carried.

Once we got to the garage, I readjusted her in my arms and pulled my keys from my pocket. When I unlocked the SUV and the lights flashed, Mila's gaze went from the Escalade to me.

"Well, at least you don't drive something ostentatious."

My lips tipped. "It's my boss'."

When I opened the passenger door and set her inside, her nose crinkled.

Fuck, she's cute.

Another thought I kept to myself since she'd slam my head in the door if I said it out loud.

When I got in and started the engine, she immediately rolled the window down.

"Not a smart idea to throw yourself from a moving vehicle."

"It'd be worth it for some fresh air." Another nose crinkle. "It stinks in here."

I stopped from shifting into reverse to raise a brow at her. "It's new. Not even three days old."

"*This* is the new car smell everyone raves about?" She shook her head. "What a letdown." She scanned the interior. "Why do you have your boss' yacht of an SUV?"

"I'm his driver," I said, simplifying my job description.

Her own brows rose before she winced. She lowered them but didn't look away.

"What?" I prodded when she continued her silent studying.

I was a man, and her eyes on me... I could only take so much, dammit.

"Nothing." Closing her eyes, she rested her head near the open window.

"You're going to get bugs in your face."

She hesitated for a second, then only moved as much as she had to in order to roll the window up. "It may be preferable."

"I'll pick up air fresheners."

"Don't bother. I'm only staying with you for a couple of days." Her voice was quiet as she added, "Hopefully less."

Ouch, my fucking pride.

Not that I minded a challenge.

Especially when I knew the reward would be worth it.

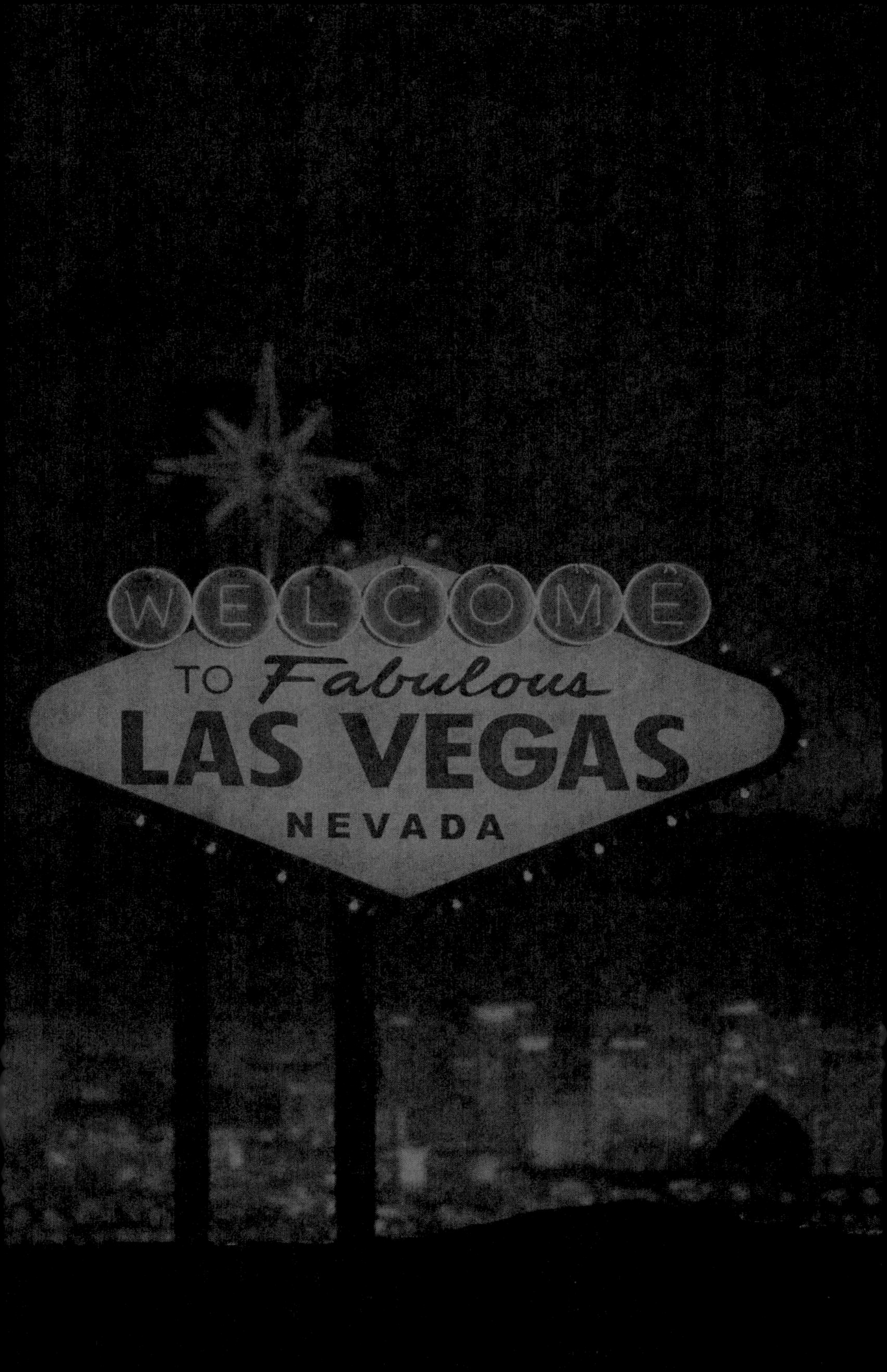
WELCOME
TO Fabulous
LAS VEGAS
NEVADA

CHAPTER 7
DON'T SHARE MORE THAN THE MINIMUM
MILA

"**M**ILA, BABY, WAKE UP." A gentle touch. "Mil—whoa. Easy, killer."

My eyes shot open to meet amused hazel ones.

Standing outside the car, Ash leaned into the passenger side. My wrist was clutched in his large hand, my fingers still curled into a fist.

The man is trying to help me, and I almost punched him.

Meh.

He kind of deserves it.

"Sorry." I only half meant it. "Not used to someone waking me."

"Not even your roommate?" he shot back with an infuriating smirk.

Maybe it's not too late for that punch...

I really thought the doctor would let me go once I'd mentioned a roommate. I hadn't expected him to care enough to confirm his existence. I'd even made my fictitious roommate male so they'd misogynistically think I had someone to protect me.

Glaring up at Ash, I ignored his outstretched hands and carefully stood. Despite my efforts to stay awake, I was pretty sure I'd fallen asleep before we'd even left the garage. I wasn't sure how long we'd driven, but my bones and body ached like I'd been in the same position for centuries, not minutes.

He didn't back away as he studied me closely. "You okay?"

"Not as bad as I expected," I shared honestly. "I really think the doctor snuck me something magical in those shots."

"Yeah. Needed vitamins and nutrients."

Ash hovered close as we walked, and I could barely see anything around his massive frame. From my small glimpse, it was the cleanest garage I'd ever seen. There were labeled storage cabinets, typical yard equipment, and a tarp-covered car that was on cinder blocks.

That explains why he's using his boss' car. His must be broken down.

Having a usable garage put him in fancy house territory, but the busted car was somehow comforting.

Familiar.

I mean, sure, it wasn't parked in the front yard and surrounded by uncut weeds, but still.

Maybe we're not so diff—

My thoughts didn't trail off. They froze.

And so did I.

Because when Ash turned on the light in the kitchen, I saw I was so very wrong.

The one room was triple the size of my entire apartment. Not only was it that expansive, but it was also nicer than any room I'd ever seen in person.

No chips or chunks were missing from the dark cabinets. No scuffs on the gleaming counters. No bong water stains from the previous tenant, faded linoleum flooring, or outdated appliances that looked like fire hazards.

The gorgeous space was something out of a magazine or a display from one of the ritzy home remodeling conventions that came to the city every year.

"Little girl, I asked you a question."

I scowled up at Ash. "I told you not to call me that."

"Tried using your name, but you weren't answering." He didn't look apologetic about the annoying nickname, but he did seem concerned. "What's wrong?"

"Just tired." It wasn't technically a lie. "What did you ask?"

"Are you hungry for some of those vitamins and nutrients in food form?"

I was.

Starving, actually.

But the time on the clock said it was nearing two in the morning. Ash had dealt with my hoopla all night and must've been exhausted. I didn't want to keep him awake any longer.

It wouldn't be the first time I'd gone to bed on an empty stomach.

"No, I'm good. If you want to show me to the guest room or couch—"

"You're eating."

"I'm fine with a floor—"

I didn't get the chance to finish when he carefully lifted me and sat my ass right on the flawless island countertop.

"Why did you bother asking if you were just going to do what you wanted anyway?"

"I was trying to be polite." He gave me his back as he opened the fridge.

"I think you failed," I muttered.

I'm being a cranky bitch.

Before I could apologize, he shot a small smile over his shoulder. "It's a work in progress."

Ash pulled a stack of glass containers from the fridge and set them to the side. He grabbed the smallest one and opened a drawer to get a fork before passing both to me.

"Eat that…" he started, but I was already tearing the lid off.

A salad.

It looked even better than the one I'd had at Moonlight.

I dumped the enclosed cup of ranch on before I dug in.

Ash took another container and opened a drawer, setting it in.

"Uhhh, whatcha doing?" I asked, wondering if he was more sleep-deprived than he let on. Not that he looked it. There were no bags under his eyes, and he wasn't yawning.

Not even a single wrinkle in his pristine clothes.

I didn't know how I looked, and I didn't care.

Much.

So long as I repressed any thought of it.

"Heating up dinner." There were a couple of beeping buttons before the quiet hum filled the silence.

I looked down at what I thought was ordinary cabinetry. "Your microwave is a drawer?"

He lifted his chin like a cabinet microwave was a totally normal thing.

Not wanting to see any more of my surroundings, I stared down at the bowl while I picked at my salad. It was delicious, but my appetite was lost to the discomfort that sat heavily in my stomach. I felt caught between the uncontrollable impulse to scrub my hands so I didn't dirty everything I touched and the need to flee from the house altogether.

I didn't belong in that kitchen. I didn't belong in that house.

I sure as hell didn't belong anywhere near the behemoth in shining armor.

I was there because he felt pity for me.

I was charity.

I have to get out of here.

Only I have nowhere else to go.

Nowhere safe, at least.

"Did you win?"

At Ash's question voiced from close to my ear, I jolted and nearly dropped the heavy glass container. "What?"

"You were having a staring contest with your salad." He took it from me, replacing it with a warm container before stepping away again. "Did you win?"

"I would've, but you interrupted." I glanced down at the new food he'd given me. It smelled delicious, but I wasn't sure I could even politely pick at it.

And not just because of the pit still occupying my belly.

"Meatloaf, mashed potatoes, and green beans," he filled in unnecessarily.

I loathed meatloaf. My nan had made it often. She'd called it cheap comfort food. I assumed the emphasis was on the *cheap* part since hers could've easily been ground cardboard covered in brown water that tasted like it'd once spent time near some beef.

Essence of beef gravy.

Not wanting to be rude—or ruder than I'd already been—I took a small bite. Then a bigger bite. And another.

I may have had the dish countless times as a kid, but it'd never tasted like that. Savory and rich, with a sweet tomato glaze and seasoning. So much seasoning. When I tried the mashed potatoes, it was even better. Buttery and herby, with chunks of actual potato in it.

Nothing like the packets of powdered potatoes I got from the dollar store—and I thought those were pretty good to begin with.

"You like it." It wasn't a question, just another unnecessary statement. If I could've inhaled the whole thing without getting violently ill, I would've.

Still, I nodded.

"Vera was right."

I stopped with my fork halfway to my mouth. "What?"

"She said you needed comfort food."

I didn't know who the all-knowing Vera was, and I wasn't about to ask. It wasn't my business.

Just like I wasn't hers.

I slammed the dish down harder than I meant to. "You told someone what happened to me?"

"Just that you were in an accident." He stepped closer. So close, my knees spread automatically out of his way, though he stopped before that point. "Not any of the details."

Even if he wanted to share, there wasn't much he could. I hadn't told him or the doctor more than the bare minimum.

Less than that, actually.

That didn't mean I wanted the mysterious Vera knowing *anything* about me. I didn't want to picture him and some equally gorgeous woman talking about my misfortune. Looking down at me with pity as they discussed what to feed the poor, starving *little girl*.

"Little girl," Ash said, unknowingly echoing my thoughts. The already annoying nickname cut like a knife.

I easily hid my reaction before letting a yawn free. "Sorry, I'm exhausted." I slid off the counter, expecting him to back away. To give me space.

He didn't.

So close.

Too *close.*

My body nearly touched his, and I could feel the heat radiating from it. If I wanted to meet his eyes, I would've had to crane my neck to do it.

I didn't want to, though. I'd seen enough sympathy for the day.

Or a lifetime.

Looking to the side, I asked, "Can you point me to the bathroom and then the couch?"

"No energy for a slice of fancy poison cake?"

I shook my head as I squeezed out from between him and the island.

He muttered something under his breath that I didn't catch. I assumed it was something about how rude I was, but when I forced myself to look at him, his mouth was curved into a smile.

"What?" I snapped defensively.

"Let's get you to bed." He started for a stairwell on the other side of the room, leaving me to trail him.

Which I did.

When we reached the top, he continued halfway down a

lengthy hall before stopping. Ash pushed a door open and stepped aside for me to enter.

Decent-sized, my ass.

Not following me in, he pointed things out from his spot in the doorway. "Bathroom. There's stuff in there for a quick shower if you promise not to fall asleep and drown. Pajamas on the bed. There's a phone charger and TV remote on the nightstand. Some books in the other room. I forget anything?"

"A chocolate mint on the pillow," I joked, taking it all in.

He chuckled. "My bad."

I turned to face him, trying to muster up adequate words. He may have broken his promise of no hospitals and bossed me into... basically everything, but he could've easily done nothing and left me to fend for myself.

Or called the cops and let them sort out my messy life.

That alone deserved gratitude and not a bitchy attitude, thanks to my own hang-ups.

I didn't get the chance to express any of that before he ordered, "Get some sleep."

And then he closed the door in my face.

Ohhhhkay.

I turned back and stepped farther into the palatial room as I looked around.

Wait.

I don't think this is...

Scowling, I stomped over to open the door and confront Ash, but he was already gone.

"Ash!" I snapped, looking up and down the long hallway.

Nothing.

Shit, I am too tired to deal with this right now.

I closed myself back in the room.

Saying it was nicer than my apartment or even The Roulette's nicest *suite*—and I used that term loosely—was a given.

But when I was a kid, my mom and nan used to watch every show about Vegas—separately, of course.

Travel specials.
News coverage about new hotels or remodels.
Reruns of *Lifestyles of the Rich and Famous*.
If it involved Vegas—but especially the Strip—they watched.
Just not for the same reason.

My nan loathed everything Vegas stood for. It wasn't only because it was packed with all seven of the deadly sins—with many more added for good measure. She hated even the mundane.

The heat.
The traffic.
The various trees and plants.
The street layouts.
The surrounding areas.

When I was a kid, I used to wonder why she didn't move away. When I got a little older, I understood.

She loved to hate it.
To complain.
To clutch her Bible and fake pearls as she bemoaned all the sinners from her position as a self-appointed saint.

Moving would take that from her.

Like most things, my mother was the exact opposite of her own mother. All the reasons Nan had hated Vegas were exactly why Veronica loved it.

She lived for the glitz and glamor. She'd raptly watch each show and special, going on about how it was her future. How she deserved it. She couldn't keep track of picture day or parent-teacher conferences—or even if I'd eaten that day—but she could tell you every last detail about her big plans.

Where she'd stay.
Where she'd eat.
What pool she'd lounge by when that was her life.
Not *our* life.
Hers.

Even at a young age, I'd picked up that exclusion. Yet I'd still eagerly savored that time with her. I would make mental notes of what I'd watched with my nan so I could tell Veronica about it. I would hang on her every word like she'd weaved a fanciful fairy tale and not lies with a hefty side of delusions.

So while my firsthand experience in luxury hotels was nonexistent, I'd seen enough on TV to know that most of those extravagant rooms were a dumpster compared to Ash's *guest* room.

Or so he'd claimed.

Because the more I looked around, the more I was sure it was his bedroom.

The furniture, doors, and molding were the same dark, rich wood. The matching slatted headboard was pushed against a textured black wall, contrasting with the cool blue of the other walls and bedding. The bed itself was massive. I didn't even know they made them that big.

The owner was stupidly tall, so it made sense his bed would be, too.

Across from the bed was a wide, raw brick pillar with a fireplace and mounted TV. I circled the pillar to find a whole other freaking room with two insanely comfortable-looking armchairs and walls lined with stocked bookshelves.

The fireplace was viewable from either side and looked like the best place to spend a rainy day.

As badly as I wanted to flop down on the bed or an armchair or even the lush rug, I needed a shower.

Badly.

I was covered in dirt and grime and *hands*.

A shudder rocked through me as I hurried into the bathroom. Rather than the cool, peaceful blues of the bedroom, that echoingly cavernous space was all moody dark blues and grays.

This is way too fancy for a room with a toilet.

Even the shower was needlessly complicated. I turned and twisted various knobs like I was trying to crack a safe. I was close to settling for a gross scrub down from the sink when the water kicked on.

From the showerhead, *plus* multiple sprayers and a freaking waterfall.

A jet of icy water shot all over me and the floor, and I yelped as I instinctively slammed the etched glass door closed.

Well.

Shit.

Climbing into a cold shower was less than ideal. But so was the idea of letting water spray all over the pristine bathroom while I fiddled with the controls.

Ash probably wouldn't care about the water spots, but I would.

At the thought, an idea formed.

When I'd agreed to go home with Ash at the hospital, it wasn't because I needed someone to take care of me.

I could—and had always—done that myself.

It definitely wasn't because I was desperate to spend time with the bossy behemoth.

It wasn't even the promise of cake—though that'd been a perk.

I'd agreed because those douchebags from the alley had stolen my license. They had my name. They had my *address*.

The new lock I'd installed was better than the old one, but trying to operate Ash's shower would slow someone down more than the flimsy door would.

I wasn't stupid. I wasn't going to be the stubborn, headstrong woman in the action movie. The one who was determined to prove themselves by going alone.

And then promptly being the first to die.

That didn't mean I would hide forever, but a few days would be smart. Long enough to let things cool off. For them to...

Well, I wasn't going to say move on since weak assholes like them moved on by targeting a new woman.

Instead, I hoped that while I took a break in a luxurious house, they moved on by getting hit by a car.

Or maybe eating at a cheap buffet, getting food poisoning, and dying from shitting themselves.

Or having a thousand bees swarm and sting their tiny peckers until they died burning, painful deaths.

Whatever way, I was open so long as the result was them leaving me *and* other women alone.

Although I'd done the smart thing—*hopefully*—by going with Ash, I wouldn't be charity. As I grabbed a towel and crawled around to wipe the water spray, my idea turned into a plan.

While I was there, I would clean. It wouldn't be charity if I was working off my stay.

After I got every drop from the floor, I quickly stripped and dashed into the frozen tundra of a shower. I fiddled with the knobs again, going from icebergs to hell before finally finding a middle ground.

Whoa.

Once I did, my body relaxed for the first time in... forever. Powerful jets worked at my aching, stiff muscles. The pelting heat worsened the burning on my skin, but the way it seeped into my bones was worth the pain.

When I was in danger of falling asleep and drowning like Ash had joked, I wiped the water from my eyes and looked for soap. There was a built-in shelf stocked with men's personal care items. Minimalist black labels marked beard conditioner, sandalwood-and-whiskey body wash, and the like.

On the shelf below, though, was a line of shampoo, conditioner, and body wash from an upscale brand whose name I couldn't pronounce.

I sneered at the items, my brain briefly wondering if they belonged to Vera. But it was just a quick thought because I was too tired and the shower felt too good for me to care.

It was none of my business.

I was just his temporary housekeeper.

Since smelling like his girlfriend would be awkward but smelling like him was awkward *and* intimate, I used as little of the products as I could get away with. Even still, the smell of honey and vanilla filled the enclosed space.

I hated to admit it, but it was incredible.

I turned off the water and climbed out, wrapping my hair and body in plush towels. I used the packaged toothbrush on the counter, but I steered clear of the hairbrush sitting next to it.

Ash's hair was cut close to his head, so it was a safe bet it wasn't his. The idea of sharing *anyone's* brush grossed me out. Using a mystery woman's was totally not happening.

My long hair would knot and tangle to the point it'd take me forever to fix, but I would just deal with that.

Just like I would have to take whatever pajamas Ash had mentioned. It wasn't like I could sleep in my dirty clothes. Or out of them, for that matter.

If using his soap had been too intimate, sleeping with my naked bits all over his bed was definitely off the table.

When I returned to the room and picked up the black set, I immediately dropped the towel, no longer hesitant to wear them.

For one thing, they were insanely soft. Like baby angel wings had been woven together with clouds to make pajamas capable of easing someone to sleep just by wearing them.

For another, tags still hung from the label.

They still may have belonged to someone else, but they hadn't been worn, so whatever.

I could deal with that.

I got dressed before forcing myself back to the bathroom to hang the towels so they didn't make the room musky—a scent that lingered. When I stepped into the bedroom, I froze, tightness settling deep in my chest.

It was far from a cramped room, but it was unfamiliar and dark.

Too dark.

And quiet.

Too quiet.

There was no light pollution. No sounds of traffic. No drunk neighbors loudly fighting. Or drunk neighbors loudly fucking.

I flicked on the bathroom light and left the door ajar so some streamed out. The tightness in my chest instantly loosened, and I inhaled deeply. Not bothering to get under the covers, I flopped onto the bed, and my deep breath rushed out in an exhale that bordered on a moan of pleasure.

This doesn't even feel real.
The cushy bed. The house.
The man.
Maybe I was hit harder than I thought, and I'm actually still unconscious in the alley.
If that's the case...
I'll start throwing hands at whoever wakes me.

I scoffed at my loopiness as I rolled to the side.

It'd been one of the top five worst days in my life, but even I had to admit there were worse ways for it to end.

I was nearly asleep when a hazy thought hit me.

Beyond the strong scent of laundry soap...
I was right.
This bed smells like the behemoth.
And then I was out.

Ash

She's asleep.
I think.
Or she's quiet because she snuck back out through the kitchen and is going to pull a Juliet by getting lost in the desert.

It wasn't possible—no way she could bypass the security system—but the thought set me on edge.

After Maximo had rescued Juliet from her sack-of-shit father and brought her to his house, I'd thought the cameras in her room were overkill. Not only had her door been secured by high-tech locks, but someone had almost always guarded it. I'd figured there was no way she'd get past the lock, one of us goons, and then all the way through the house to the front door.

And I'd thought that right up until she'd done exactly that.

Even once Juliet had decided to stay, the cameras had stayed up. Not because Maximo worried she'd run again, but because he liked to watch her. Something he still did when they were apart.

I didn't judge, but I also hadn't gotten it.

Until right then.

Because with Mila around the corner, I'd give my left fucking nut to see her. In my room.

In *my* bed.

Christ.

My hard cock ached.

I'd tried to explain to it that she was injured.

That she'd been through a shit-ton—and clearly not just that night.

That she wasn't mine.

But my dick and I were sick bastards.

It wasn't just about the possessive need I had no right to feel. I wanted the reassurance she was okay. Sleeping instead of tossing and turning as she relived whatever she'd gone through.

Shit.

I ran my palm down my face.

Once I was sure she was settled, I turned off the muted TV in the loft space and went to one of the guest rooms, heading straight for the en suite. I left the water cold as I climbed in, hoping my dick would get the message.

It didn't.

I made the shower quick and got ready to crash for a few hours before my mental alarm clock would wake me. I was just nodding off when my cell pinged.

I grabbed it to see a text from Cole.

> Cole: One Video

I downloaded the attachment to see the lobby of Moonlight. A few seconds in, Mila walked through the door with her hood up. She kept her head down and face covered as she approached the front desk. The video cut and angle changed as a different camera took over. I could only see the back of her head, but I could hear her clearly.

"Ash. Beard. Short hair. Behemoth of a man."

Hearing her ask for me hit me in the gut.

Hearing her call me a behemoth of a man made me smile.

But hearing and seeing the dismissive disgust from the prick working the counter made me want to take him down to The Basement.

He'd tried to turn her away. With the condition she was in, I doubted she'd have made it far.

Even if it wasn't Mila, that was fucked.

But it was Mila.

My Mila.

Which meant *he* was fucked.

> Me: Are you fucking kidding me?

> Cole: I know. Boss says the desk clerk is fired, and it's your news to deliver.

> Cole: However you want to deliver it.

As tempting as that was, I had more important targets to hunt. My full attention was dedicated to whoever had made it so a walk across the lobby required Mila to clutch onto the counter.

> Me: One of you handle it. I have bigger fish to catch, filet slowly and painfully, and torch.

That wasn't a metaphor.

> Cole: On it.

I watched the clip again before tossing my cell on the bed and leaving the room.

I needed to see that she was okay.

Safe.

That she wasn't trying to hobble her injured ass across the desert.

If I was a better man, I would've stopped outside the closed door. I would've given her privacy. She'd trusted me enough to come home with me, and I was invading the space I'd offered.

I would've at least hesitated.

I didn't.

Opening the door, I moved silently across the room, not needing the light from the bathroom.

Another thing to handle tomorrow.

When I got close to the bed, panic stopped my damn heart in my chest.

Fuck.

Sprawled diagonal in bed on top of the blanket, Mila looked like she'd passed out. I was about to shake her awake when she kicked a leg out and rolled before flipping around to roll again.

Good, she didn't faint, but now I gotta worry she's gonna throw herself out of bed.

Checking on her was one thing. Getting close enough to cover her would push it.

But since I was already watching her sleep—fully owning the fact it was fucking creepy—I did it anyway.

I tugged the blanket from under her and barely dodged the tiny fist of fury she flung my way.

"Don't wanna wake up," she muttered, burying her head beneath a pillow.

"Anyone ever tell you that you're surprisingly violent, sunshine?"

She tilted her head to peek out from under the pillow at me. "Behemoth?"

I'd liked hearing it on the video.

I liked hearing it in person a fuckuva lot more.

"Don't worry," she mumbled. "Still alive."

I let her think that I was there to follow concussion protocol. "Be back in a couple hours with your meds."

Her response was to kick her leg out.

When I returned to my room, there was another text from Cole waiting.

> Cole: She good?

I thought about all that had happened at the hospital. The minimal amount she'd shared. The way she lied like a pro. The smart mouth she let slip through only to lock herself down again.

> Me: No.
>
> Me: But she will be.

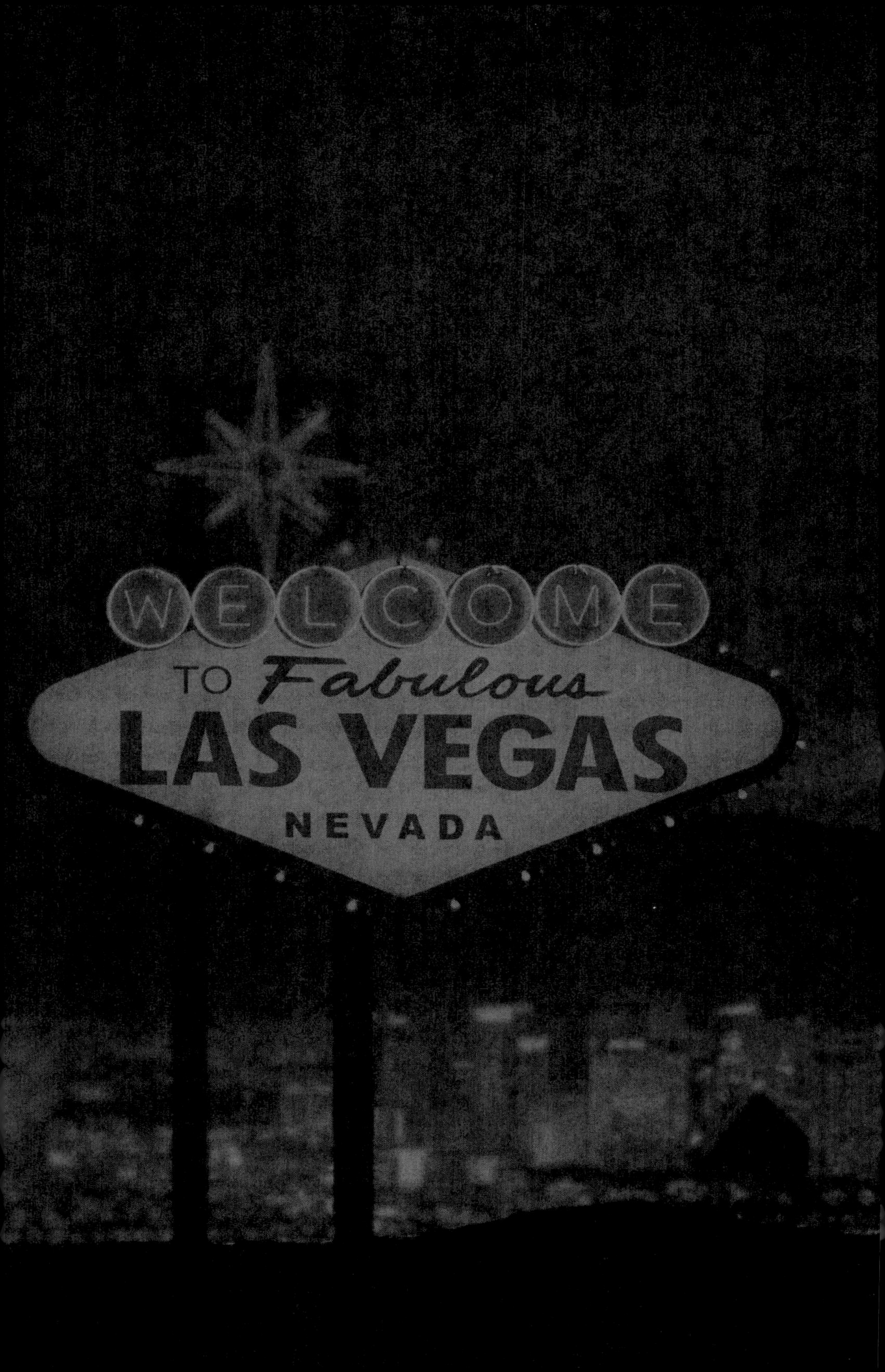
WELCOME
TO Fabulous
LAS VEGAS
NEVADA

CHAPTER 8
Always Have an Exit Plan
MILA

I'M LATE.

I bolted upright in bed.

A bed that wasn't mine.

In a room that also wasn't mine.

It was all very Goldilocks.

So long as Goldilocks had the shit kicked out of her before she'd stumbled into the bears' lair.

Memories of the day before—of the previous few days—slammed into me, and I instantly missed that hazy space I'd been floating in. Not quite awake but also not asleep. I wanted to live there, relaxed and pain-free.

Instead, I'd been catapulted into consciousness by an aching body and panic about a job I no longer had.

I flopped back and hid my head under a pillow, willing my heart rate to slow and my brain to shut up, but it didn't work.

I was awake.

And starving.

Unlike the bed's comfort, the room's luxury, and the bizarre feeling of getting enough sleep, I was used to the hunger pain.

I could ignore it.

So long as I didn't think about cake.

I couldn't, however, ignore the nagging in my head that I was being lazy. I didn't even know what time it was, but I knew I needed to get up and do...

Something.

I stood carefully, but again, it wasn't as bad as I'd anticipated. I was sore. Swollen. I probably looked like hell. But there was no lightheadedness. No nausea. No tunnel vision.

For the first time in a long time, I woke up feeling... rested.

Along with the sore, swollen, and beaten.

I got attacked and somehow feel better than I do on a normal morning.

After using the bathroom and freshening up, I grabbed my clothes from where I'd left them on the bathroom floor. My skin itched at the thought of putting them back on. Like I was about to don a bathing suit made entirely of human hair.

It wasn't because of the awful memories attached to the outfit. If I threw out clothes every time I had a bad day, my limited wardrobe would be gone in a week.

It was just that the clothes were filthy. I still smelled faintly of a sweet pastry from my shower the night before. I didn't want to replace that pleasing scent with brick wall and tiny-dicked douchebag. I also didn't want to leave a dirt trail in Ash's house.

I planned to clean it, not trash it.

Doing my laundry was a smart place to start.

After putting on my shoes—because being in pajamas while barefoot felt too comfortable—I gathered the load and made my way out into the hallway. It took me a second to remember which way we'd come since I'd been basically sleepwalking, but I had it.

Or so I thought.

Because rather than a stairwell that led into the kitchen, I turned the corner at the end of the hall to find a loft that overlooked the entryway and front door. Open and inviting, the sitting room had yet another TV, comfortable chairs, and a dark wooden bar. The far wall was all windows, letting loads of sunlight into the cool space. I continued walking to peek around the corner, seeing yet another hall.

Forget how many TVs there are...

How many rooms are in this place?

Backtracking, I went down the U-shaped stairs, feeling more out of place than a pig in a ballroom.

Not that the house was decorated like a fussy ballroom. There was no chandelier. No ugly artwork. No garish gold details at every turn that tried to jam wealth down my throat.

It was cool and masculine and classy in a natural way without trying too hard.

But like Ash's bedroom, it was comfortable, too. Made to be lived in rather than looked at.

My cleaning plan is going to be harder than I thought.

As curious as I was about the rest of the house, self-preservation took priority.

If things went wrong—and in my experience, they often did—I needed a general idea of my surroundings. What type of gated development he lived in. How close the other houses were. An address.

An exit plan.

Jostling my dirty clothes bundle into one arm, I opened the door and stepped outside.

And then a national emergency was declared.

That was the only logical explanation for the blaring alarm that made me jump out of my skin. It echoed out from the foyer, and it was a miracle all the lovely windows didn't shatter. I expected to see choppers, SWAT teams, and emergency vehicles descend while that one Led Zeppelin song played in the background.

Rushing back inside, I threw the door closed as if that would fix it. When it unsurprisingly didn't, I searched the walls for the alarm control panel. Not that I knew what to do with one, but my brain wasn't thinking that far ahead.

Even over the shrill siren, I could hear a nearby door slam. I whipped around in time to see Ash pull a T-shirt over his head. I caught a brief glimpse of defined muscles and tattoos above his basketball shorts before the black cotton tee covered them.

Before he could start yelling, I stammered my apology. "Sorry. *Really* sorry. I—"

"Hush." He stopped close behind me.

I tilted my head up and did *not* do as he'd ordered. "I was just—"

"Hush, Mila." With one hand lightly on my hip, he reached the other around me to open the discreet panel right in front of my face. I dropped my head to give him privacy, but his hand skimmed my side, continuing up until it reached my jaw. He used the gentle hold to make sure I watched as he walked me through how to disarm the system.

I didn't absorb any of it.

I didn't even breathe.

Once the irritating noise cut off, I stepped away and spun around, needing space. Needing to explain. "I wasn't going to run away."

"Didn't think you'd *try*."

There was just enough emphasis on that word. *Try*. Like even if I wanted to, I wouldn't succeed.

His threat from the night before filled my head.

'I will chase you.'

And like the night before, it moved down my body to settle someplace lower. Someplace it didn't belong.

Someplace that didn't make sense.

"I just wanted to look outside," I said.

It wasn't a lie, even if it wasn't the full truth, either.

"Not a prisoner here. Go outside all you want." He scanned me. "Are you okay? What're you doing out of bed?"

"I can't stay there all day."

"Why not?"

Since that was a loaded question, I returned to his unanswered one. "I'm sore, and my scrapes burn like they're literally on fire, but the sleep helped. What time is it?"

"Almost one."

"Almost... *What?*" I couldn't remember the last time I'd slept so late. I wasn't sure I ever had.

No wonder I feel so rested.

"Why didn't you wake me?"

He looked genuinely confused. "Why would I? You're here to rest. And since you barely cracked a lid when I gave you meds during the night, you clearly need it."

That surprised me—and not just because he had actually gone through the hassle.

As a kid, Veronica—or my nan, for that matter—had never come to tuck me in. No story times, snuggles, or whispered conversations like they showed on TV. They'd certainly never woken up to give me medicine or check on me when I was sick.

Maternal instincts were a lacking hereditary trait.

What wasn't lacking, however, was the amount of creepy *friends* Veronica would entertain. A strong sense of self-preservation had long ago made me a light sleeper. My subconscious knew that if someone was in my room, they did *not* belong there. Yet I'd slept through that.

"Don't worry, sunshine." He softly jabbed his fist into his own chin. "You only tried to punch me twice."

There it is.

Since Ash had dragged his ass out of bed to help with my pain management, I was glad a couple of weak punches were all I'd thrown.

"I'm sorry about that," I said before clarifying. "The punches and sleeping so late. Sorry about both, and I can just set an alarm so you don't—"

"Hush, little girl." Ash stepped closer, and I should've stepped back.

I should've yelled at him for telling me what to do.

Despite the apology that'd just left my mouth, I should've punched him for the stupid nickname.

I stayed frozen. Blank.

His voice was low. Soft yet somehow equally rough. "You apologize too much."

"Sorry," I said before I could catch myself.

I expected... something. Him to laugh or make fun of me or tell me I was annoying.

Instead, he moved away so suddenly, it took my brain a moment to catch up. "You need to get back in bed."

"I actually feel better now that I'm up and stretching."

Ash looked at me for a long moment, like he was weighing whether he believed me. He must've reached the conclusion that I wasn't lying—for once—because he opened the front door and stepped aside. "Make sure you take it easy and rest, but I want you to make yourself comfortable. Explore. Nowhere is off-limits."

"Including *your* bedroom that I'm staying in?"

He looked over his shoulder to shoot me a dimpled, unapologetic grin. "Including that."

For a brief—and wildly irrational—moment, I wanted to push it. To ask if leaving was off-limits.

I wasn't even sure why.

I knew I could. Like Ash had pointed out, I wasn't a prisoner. Not by his design, at least. I was stuck because I had nowhere safe to go since my apartment was temporarily off-limits.

My lack of friends and family and options was depressing.

"Was the room okay? Did you think of anything you need?" he asked.

Yeah. A life.

"A hairbrush?" I asked instead since finger-combing my hair was tedious.

His brows lowered. "There should be one in there." Like he could read my thoughts, he added, "It's brand new."

"Oh. Thanks."

"Want me to help you brush it?"

My heart froze at the mental image that tried to form, but I quickly pushed it away.

"I'm good." I quickly stepped outside in hopes that the fresh air would bring my sanity back.

Wow.

"Wow," I repeated out loud that time. Because thinking it didn't do the beauty justice.

The house wasn't in a development of other identical houses. Positioned on a hill, the sprawling yard of gorgeous desert greenery seemed to go on forever. Other houses were in the distance, but they might as well have been in different zip codes.

Like a god on Mount Olympus, overlooking the mere mortals.

"Go down," Ash ordered, his rumbling voice right in my ear.

My head whipped around so fast, I could practically feel my brain rattle inside. My gaze landed on Ash's chest, and I had to arch my neck to meet his hazel eyes. Whatever words I had on my tongue died there at his closeness.

So close.

The silence stretched for hours—that were actually just seconds—before he jerked his head to the side toward the yard. "Go down to the walkway. The view from there is better."

Oh.

Right.

I barely noticed as my dirty clothes were slipped from my hold, too distracted to even think about protesting. I moved down the steps as he added, "Hold on to the railing."

I did as he ordered and went down before turning around.

And losing my breath.

The house was big, but it wasn't as obscenely huge as I'd imagined. It also wasn't a cookie-cutter show home. It was modern and angular and unique.

But that wasn't the best part.

That honor went to the mountains, which served as a backdrop.

Movement caught my attention, and I looked in time to see Ash's retreating back.

My shoulders loosened even as my belly clenched.

It was a reaction that made sense in its contradiction. Everything about Ash made me feel off-kilter.

Clearly needing the fresh air *and* the distance, I walked farther down the path, moving slowly as I looked around.

Minus the rat infestation in The Roulette, and a smaller appearance of their cousin Mickey at my apartment, I had limited experience with animals. A lizard or cute animal sighting would be fun.

A scorpion—or worse—not so much.

Not that I needed further proof of it, but my guess that he only had his boss' car because his was broken down was *very* far off. In addition to the tarped vehicle and SUV that were inside, a fancy matte-black car and a muddy Jeep without the roof or doors were parked in front of the other *two* garage doors.

Near the driveway, the heavy greenery gave way to a dusty rock section. The plants there looked like they'd seen better days. Curious what'd caused the destruction, I stepped to get a closer look.

Tire marks.
From a wild, ferocious vehicle.
Some animal tracker I am.

I ran my shoes through the dirt, disrupting the imprints.

"Mila."

I looked over to where Ash stood at the top of the stairs.

He held a plate and a can of something, and even though I couldn't see what either was, my stomach growled.

Loudly.

Before I could tell him he didn't need to make me food, his phone rang. He set his load down to quietly answer it. After a moment, he pulled it away from his ear to speak to me. "Nothing is off-limits," he reiterated randomly. Before I could confirm I knew that, he kept going. "Nothing except you leaving. Try that, and I'll chase you over those damn mountains if I have to. You may get farther than Juliet did in the desert, especially if you take a four-wheeler, but I'll still catch you."

Like that wasn't the most insane series of statements, he went inside without another word.

Assuming the food he'd held was lunch for me, I returned to the porch with my stomach twisted in knots. A massive Scooby Doo-esque sandwich, chips, a bottle of water, and a root beer were on the small table between two wooden chairs. There were also a few pain pills and an ice pack. With how sore and raw my face felt, the ice pack was the only thing I was interested in.

The food, view, and everything else had lost their appeal.

After keeping the ice pack against my burning cheek and eye for as long as I could stand, I set it aside. I peeled half the veggies and meat from between the bread so I could actually fit the sandwich into my mouth. It was probably delicious, but it had the taste and texture of the dirt I'd just walked through.

Because as I ate, a few questions rolled around in my head.

One, who was Juliet?

Two, had Ash chased her?

Three, and most importantly... Why did that thought bother me so much?

I COULD STAY *out here all day.*

Never mind. No, I can't.

I totally could've, though. There was so much more to see, and I hadn't even checked out the backyard. But I'd already slept until one. I didn't have time to waste.

Gathering my dishes, I went inside—and got slightly turned around—before eventually finding the kitchen. I loaded my stuff into the dishwasher, but since it was otherwise empty, I didn't run it. Unfortunately for my grand plans, cleaning up my own mess was the only opportunity in there. Otherwise, there wasn't so much as a stray crumb or a sticky beer bottle ring.

Who has a kitchen so clean?

Determined to clean something—*anything*—I moved into the living room next. Starting at the perimeter, I slowly circled around.

Every corner.

Every nook.

Every cranny.

There were no random solo socks under his plush couch or forgotten trash set aside to be dealt with later.

With an exasperated sigh, I decided to branch out to the rest of the house, starting with the upstairs.

Unlike earlier, shades had been lowered over the large windows at the back of the loft to block out the afternoon sun. That room was just as tidy as the others, so I headed down the unexplored hallway I'd seen that morning. I avoided a couple of closed doors, and the others seemed to be guest bedrooms with the same effortlessly cool vibe as the rest of the house. They were set up in a way that made them cohesive to everywhere else, but different enough not to feel like someone copied and pasted the design with zero effort.

And—surprise, surprise—they were all spotless.

I backtracked to the other hall, but the only door led to Ash's giant room.

Going downstairs, I went down the direction Ash had come from earlier. The open door at the end of the hall showed a home gym.

A promising place to start.

I neared the doorway before halting.

It smelled like Ash and sweat and...

Never mind, way too personal.

The next door was ajar, and my foot *accidentally* pushed it all the way open before my eyes widened.

An arcade.

He has a whole freaking arcade in his house.

Okay, maybe it wasn't a whole one, but it was still a lot. I was pretty sure every video game console in existence lined the shelf below yet another big screen TV. In addition, the room had pool, ping pong, and foosball tables, along with a wall of older arcade games.

I chalked it up to Ash being a gamer, but when I walked around the couch, I found something else.

A toy box.

One packed with cars, trains, a few baby dolls, and a huge collection of figures from some popular dog cartoon. None of it was older stuff that would lead me to believe it was childhood toys he'd kept for the future.

Which added another question to the ones already bouncing around my head.

Does Ash have kids?

Since it was none of my business, I forced it from my head as I moved on with my mission.

Unfortunately, in all my wandering, there was nothing to clean. Nothing in need of a wipe down. Not even some freaking dusty blinds.

I tried to devise a new plan to earn my stay because my housekeeping abilities wouldn't cut it in the already immaculate house. I wasn't much of a cook unless it was microwaving a crappy frozen dinner. I definitely wasn't making fancy cake or edible meatloaf. Hell, even the sandwich Ash had made me for lunch was better than anything I'd ever made.

That left me with a whole lotta *nothing*. My daily life was cleaning a shitty hotel, taking a bus home to eat a small dinner, and then falling asleep before the sun had fully set.

Not having friends or family to stay with is bad enough… Realizing my only skill is cleaning up after other people is even worse.

With embarrassment and depression warring for top spot in my head, I returned to my temporary room. I might not have been able to pay, but I could at least stay out of Ash's way.

He'd certainly been doing a good job of it all afternoon. I hadn't seen or heard him once during my exploring. It was a safe bet he was in one of the closed rooms, which wasn't fair to him. He shouldn't have to hide away in his own house just because I'd come to him, turning my problem into his.

I showered again—only slightly soaking the bathroom floor that time—before stepping into the bedroom while wrapped in a towel. The pajama set I'd left on the side table was gone. A new purple set was on the bed.

And right next to it was yet another ice pack for my face.

Shit. Not just did I fail at cleaning for him, I actually added more work.

For all I knew, a housekeeper was ninjaing around the house, always two steps ahead of me. But that wasn't much better. I didn't want to add to someone else's workload since I knew how exhausting that job was.

Stellar work, Mila.

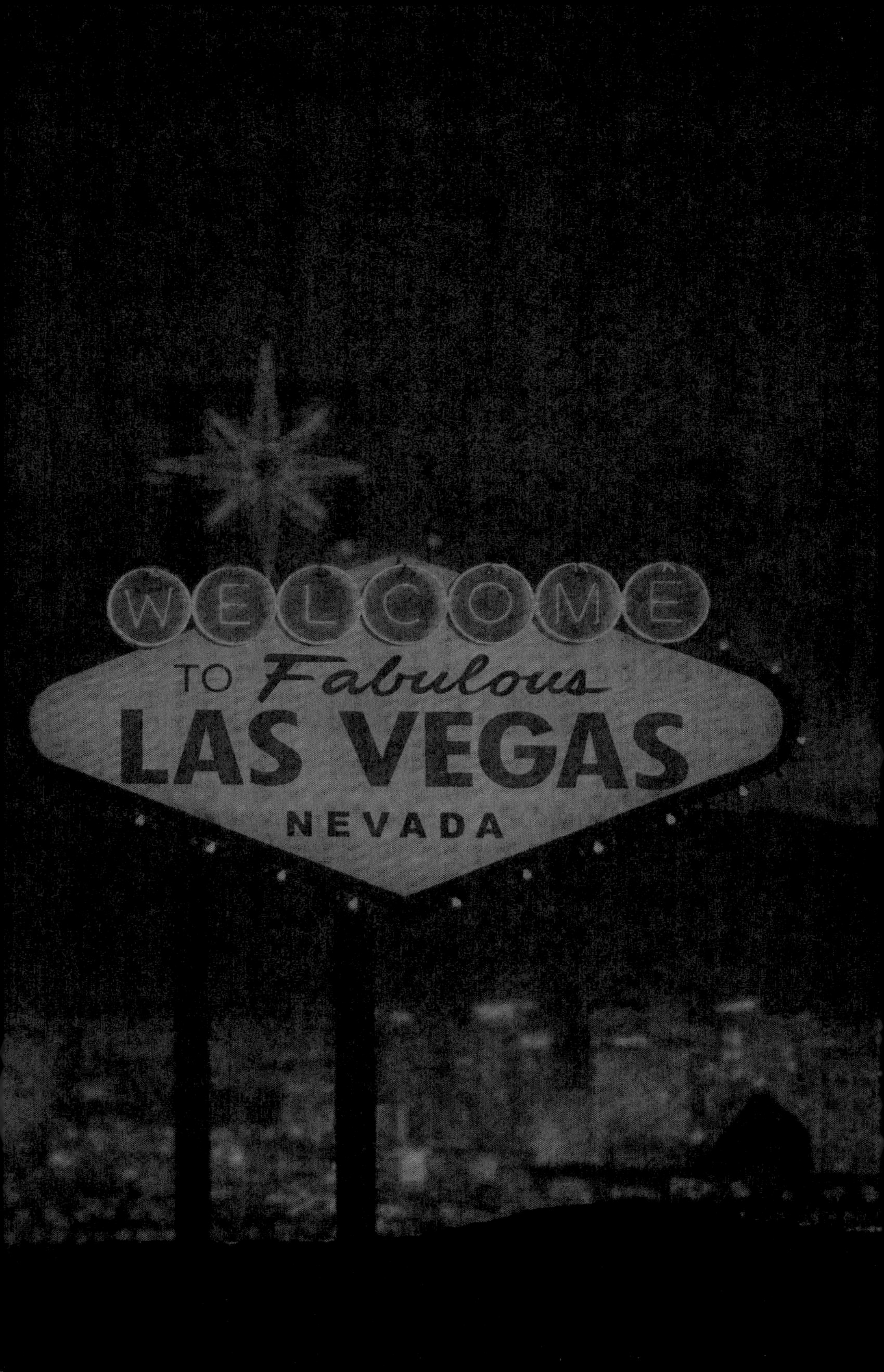
WELCOME
TO Fabulous
LAS VEGAS
NEVADA

CHAPTER 9
HOLD YOURSELF TOGETHER
ASH

Lifting my hand, I tapped my knuckles against the closed bedroom door.

"Come in."

I opened the door to see Mila sitting at the end of my bed with the TV on. The sight of that would've hit me in the dick had it not been for the expression on her face when she aimed her gaze my way.

"Med time?" she asked when I didn't speak.

"Dinner first," I answered. "You need an ice pack in the meantime?"

Earlier, when I'd found her to reapply the ointment, I'd pressed for a real answer on how she felt instead of her dismissive *fine*. She'd admitted what her teary eyes had already said.

Her raw, burning skin was the most painful part.

"No, I'm just tired." A smile tipped her lips. "I don't know how since I slept so late."

'Cause you've been through hell.

I didn't say it out loud. She didn't need the reminder.

She stood and clicked off the TV before approaching.

When she was within reach, I didn't step out of the way. I

caught her chin in my hold and tilted her face up. "You sure you're okay?"

There was a pause. A brief one. Just a millisecond's hesitation. And then it was gone, along with whatever had been weighing on her. Her expression was blank, like her face wasn't covered in scrapes and bruises.

"Like I said, just wiped." She smiled, and nothing about it was forced. But that didn't mean it was as genuine as it appeared. "And hungry."

"Then let's get you fed."

Mila followed me as I went down the rear staircase to the kitchen. She sniffed the air as the scent of garlic grew stronger. "What smells so good?"

"Pasta. Dining room, living room, or out on the porch?"

After a moment, she asked, "Where do you usually eat?"

"Over the sink if I'm inhaling something before bed or on the couch while I watch TV."

"Living room, then."

I'd assumed she'd pick solitude and that convincing her to let me eat with her would require a boardroom-style negotiation. I sure as shit hadn't expected her to choose being with me.

Not giving her time to change her mind, I handed her the plate of pasta and salad I'd already dished out before grabbing my own. She trailed me again, and I set my shit down on the coffee table before handing her the remote. "Got cable and every streaming service you can think of. Put on whatever you want."

"What do you watch?"

"The news." At her grimace, I chuckled and repeated, "Put on whatever you want. I'm not picky."

"Clearly," she muttered as I backtracked into the kitchen for a beer for me and a water for her. When I returned, she blinked up at me. "Can I have a beer?"

"No."

"Why not?"

"For one, you're on pain meds that shouldn't be mixed with

alcohol." There were other spots to sit, but I took one on the same couch. I did give her space by sitting at the opposite end as her, but that was as far as I was going. "For another, you're only twenty."

And the reminder of that makes me feel like a dirty old man because it doesn't stop me from wanting to pull you onto my lap to feed you off my plate.

Mila's eyes widened. "How do you know how old I am?"

Since I couldn't admit to having her cyberstalked, I said, "Lucky guess that you just confirmed." I kept my tone conversational so it didn't come across as an accusation. "I thought you said you didn't drink."

Her cheeks flushed. "I don't. I've never even tried beer."

"Then a dark stout isn't the place to start." I lifted the bottle toward her nose. I couldn't stop the grin when she scowled and shuddered from the small whiff.

"I was messing with you. Are there more *root* beers?"

I raised my chin, and she stood before I could. "In the fridge, brat."

Her steps faltered, and she froze in front of me. Tension infused her body as her wide blue eyes shot to my face.

"Mila?"

Her name seemed to shake her out of it, and her face returned to blank.

Before I could push about wherever she'd just mentally disappeared to, she rushed into the kitchen to physically disappear.

I'll stick to calling her little girl and not brat when I want to get a rise outta her.

She came back a moment later with a root beer for herself and another beer for me. Despite the fact I'd barely taken a drink of the one I held, I accepted the bottle.

Mila flipped through the TV options, her attention on the screen and not the pasta getting cold on the coffee table in front of her.

"Told you already, I don't care what we watch. But if you take much longer, I'm going to put on the news so you'll focus on your dinner."

With a soft *eek*, she bounced the channels back and forth between two shows before settling on a rerun of some police precinct comedy.

"We can watch the other one if you want."

Giving me a smile, she shook her head. "We'll have to watch that one from the beginning to understand." She jerked her head to look straight ahead. "I mean, you'd have to. I've already watched both of these a few times." Her nose scrunched just slightly as she added under her breath, "Or more because I'm a massive loser."

If she wasn't injured.

If she was mine.

I'd take her over my knees.

Because it wasn't playful self-deprecation in her words. They were packed with quiet, cutting venom.

Since I had no right to punish her, I stabbed my fork toward her abandoned plate in a silent prompt. Once she picked it up, I leaned back and reminded, "You're talking to the guy who watches the news."

That got me another small smile. "Good point."

WHAT THE FUCK *am I doing?*

Go to bed, you pathetic fuck.

Walk away now.

I didn't.

After picking at her food, Mila hadn't hauled ass up to her room. She'd tucked her feet under her on the couch and settled in to watch the show I'd barely paid attention to.

That hadn't stopped me from pretending it was my new

favorite sitcom every time she'd looked over to explain a previous storyline or share in a joke.

Since that'd only happened a handful of times, the night was spent with her zoned out on the show and me zoned out on her until her eyes had begun growing heavy.

After she'd gone to bed, I'd taken a spot in the loft to catch up on all the work I should've been doing instead of pretending to watch a show. I was done, and I should've been going to sleep.

I should've been checking the news. The gossip. The rumors that floated through Vegas thicker than the cigarette smoke.

Instead, I stood outside of Mila's door. It wasn't time for her medication. She hadn't made any noise that was alarming. I had no reason to be there.

No reason to go inside.

I did it anyway.

Mila

I'm alone.

I'm always alone.

The house is too scary. Too dangerous. Too dark.

Too empty.

No friends. No family. Nowhere else for me to go. I'm always alone.

Until I'm not.

Hands are touching me. Grabbing me. I try to fight them off, but my arms are weighed down. Slow. Ineffective. I can smell the brick. The monster. He laughs in my ear, and it grows louder.

Higher.

I know that laughter.

Veronica.

Why is my mother here?

"Stupid Mila. Think you're better than me?"

The hands.

"Mila, Mila, Mila."

Too many.

"Mila. Mila. Mila."

All over.

I need help. Just one time. For once, I need someone to help me.

I need...

"Mila!"

"Ash!" I sat up and thrashed, fighting against phantom hands and haunting touches.

"Mila, it's just me."

My movements stopped, though my heart continued to slam against my ribs like it was trying to burst from my chest.

Ash sat on the edge of the bed, stroking my unruly hair from my face. Sweat slicked my skin, and he had to feel it, but he didn't say anything. With the light streaming in from the bathroom, I could clearly see the concern on his face. His voice held the same tender worry when he asked, "What's wrong?"

I shook my head.

It was just a dream.

A nightmare.

I was okay.

Fine.

Completely normal.

I burst into tears.

"Are you in pain? What's wrong? Where does it hurt?"

At the panic in Ash's voice, I started crying harder as I forced out, "It doesn't hurt."

That was a lie.

Such a huge lie.

"Shit," Ash bit out softly, climbing fully onto the bed before pulling me to him. He didn't speak as he palmed the back of my head and held my face to his chest.

Or maybe he did, and I just couldn't hear him over my loud sobs.

Once they turned to hiccuping whimpers, he ordered, "Tell me what happened, sunshine."

"My mother happened."

He paused for a second. "Did she call you?"

I scoffed. "Yeah, right. My phone is broken, but even if it wasn't..." More tears poured down my face. "I think she set me up to get jumped."

"You think your own fucking *mother* did this shit?" His whole body went rigid, but I was too exhausted and emotionally raw to keep my walls up.

They could be down around Ash.

Just for a few minutes.

"It wouldn't be the worst she's done," I said. "She's the one who chose that location. I was only there so she could pay me back when—"

"For what?"

"Huh?"

"Why was she paying you back?"

"She stole my paycheck and my savings. I usually let it go, but I need that money since she also got me fired. I threatened her, and this"—I gestured down to myself—"was her version of payback."

"I don't even know which *what the fuck* to start with, baby."

I'd have laughed had it not been for the fresh wave of tears that started at his soothing tone. It made the echoes of my mother's laughter grow louder in my head.

Taunting me.

A little kindness and attention are enough to make you unravel? Pathetic.

Ash didn't seem to share the same sentiment. He gathered me closer so my front was pressed to his side as tight as it could be at our awkward angle. One hand still palmed the back of my head while his other stroked down my spine. His heartbeat thumped in my ear, chasing away my inner demons and leaving me drained.

I must've dozed off because the next thing I remembered was him shifting me off his chest.

Before I could stop myself, I clutched him tighter.

I blamed being partially asleep, but the truth was, I would've done the same thing if I was wide awake. And not because I didn't want to be alone. That was technically true, but I didn't want just anyone there.

I wanted Ash. Big behemoth Ash who took care of me. Made me feel safe. Who I trusted.

As much as I was capable of trusting anyone, at least.

"Just covering you up, sunshine," Ash murmured, pulling the blanket over us. "You're shivering."

"Sorry." I tried to pull away. "I'm fine now. You can—"

"Hush." The one word was a firm order, softened by his mouth pressing against my forehead. His lips grazed the skin there when he continued. "I've got you."

I've got you.

That time when I fell asleep, it was nothing but peaceful rest.

Because Ash had me.

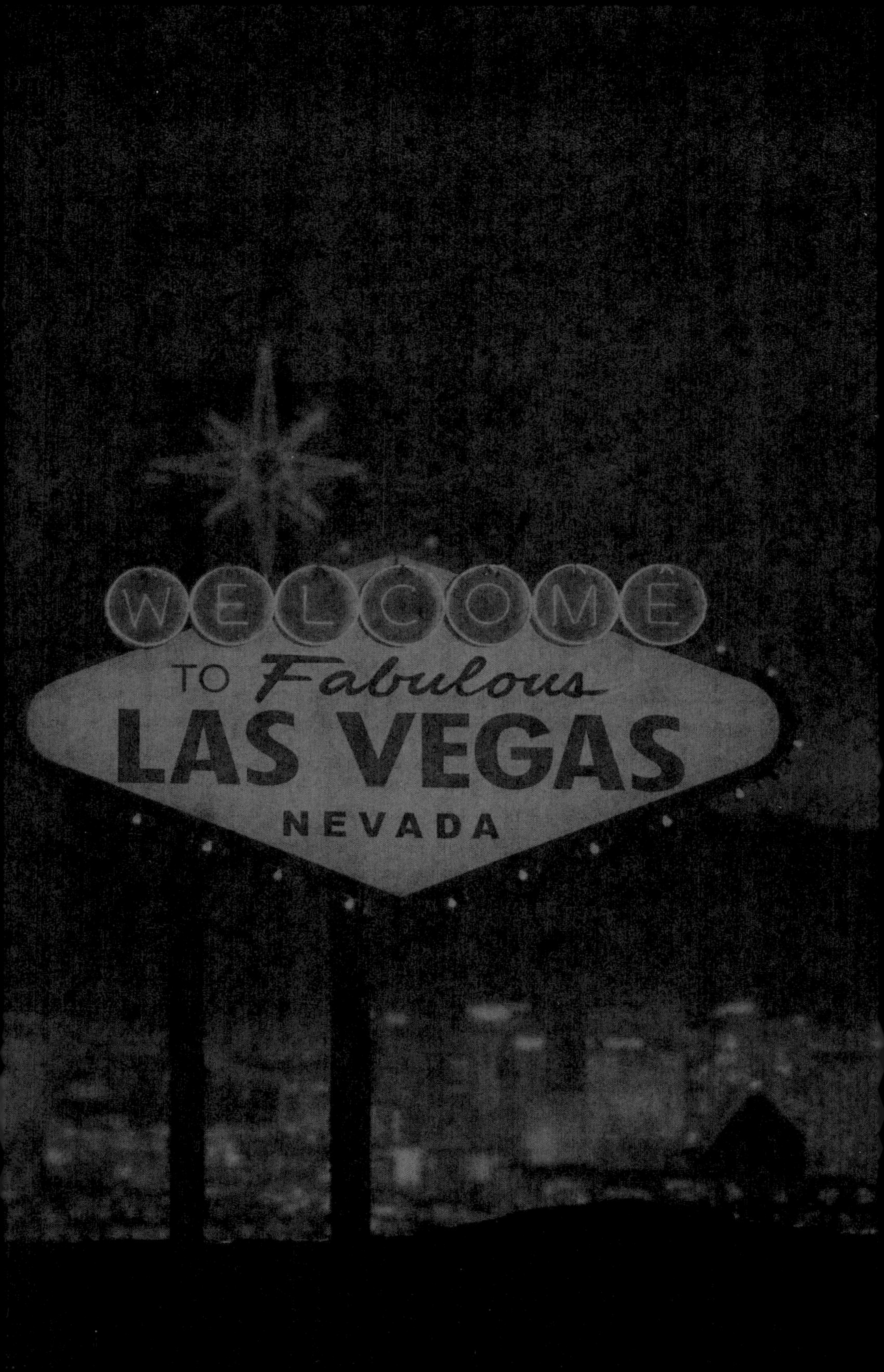
WELCOME
TO Fabulous
LAS VEGAS
NEVADA

CHAPTER 10
KEEP YOUR BIG MOUTH CLOSED
MILA

Waking up the next morning, I didn't open my eyes before trying to bury my head under a pillow. Rather than the soft, supportive comfort I sought, I smacked my forehead against a sharp edge.

"*Ouch*! Shit." I grudgingly opened my eyes and sat up to see my head at the bottom of the bed and my feet aimed up at the diagonal corner. Rubbing my forehead, I pulled my hand away to see a hint of smeared blood on my fingertips. "Shit, shit, shit."

Even though I wanted to stay in bed and ignore the memories for as long as possible, I also didn't want to get blood on the sheets. Those stains were a pain in the ass to get out.

I hurried to the bathroom and cleaned myself up, my mind trying—and failing—to block out the night before.

My nightmare.

Everything I'd shared.

Clutching at Ash and not letting him go.

I can't believe I did that.

Will he ask me to leave? Should I make it easier by offering to?

But I already knew the answer. I had to go.

There was no way around it.

Which meant I had to ask for a ride. It would've been easier to avoid the confrontation and sneak away... right up until I ended up stranded in the mountains.

And then there was his promise to chase me—a threat that made my stomach swirl in a way that was *not* right. Of course, after the night before, that was probably null and void.

I decided to take advantage of one last hot shower before getting dressed in my own clothes. That'd been the plan, but I had no clue where said clothes were. Instead, yet another set of loungewear waited for me.

I'll have to ask Ash, but heavenly soft clothes will have to do.
For now.

I straightened up after myself and made the bed, saying silent goodbyes to the taste of luxury I'd likely never experience again.

When I couldn't stall any longer, I pocketed my broken phone and put on my shoes before going downstairs.

I paused at the bottom when I realized I had no clue where to find Ash. In all my exploring the afternoon before, I hadn't seen or heard him. He'd probably been in one of the closed rooms, but with the size of the house, that didn't narrow it down as much as one would think.

I eyed the front door.

What'd he say about four-wheelers?

Never mind. If I tried to ride one of those, I'd end up lost and *crashed somewhere.*

In the silence, I heard the faint sounds of a rumbling voice coming from the kitchen.

No.

Voices.

I followed them before freezing.

Ash moved around the kitchen, going into the fridge to gather a stack of containers and place them on the counter next to a cutting board and a big bowl. He started slicing strawberries as if he wasn't in a pair of tailored slacks and a deep blue dress shirt. Even untucked, it was clear it was perfectly tailored for him, too.

A blonde woman stood next to him, her voice soft as she spoke while he worked. Her athleisure outfit was more casual than his clothes but no less coordinated. I couldn't see her face until she looked to the side to grab her coffee mug.

Well...

Good for him.

And her.

Good for both of them.

I wondered if the lovely, lithe blonde was Vera, the provider of comfort food. Or maybe the mysterious Juliet. She would certainly be able to run far with those long legs.

Wanting to get away unseen, I took a slow step back. Unfortunately, my stealth skills left a lot to be desired, and two sets of eyes snapped to me.

I braced, expecting Ash to look guilty. Or maybe to treat me being there as no big deal because I was no one. I wasn't sure which would be worse.

It didn't matter, though, because I got neither.

A wide grin split Ash's face, his dimples showing through his beard. It faltered after a moment, and his brows lowered as he set down the knife before approaching. He caught my chin between his crooked index finger and thumb, using his hold to tilt my face up like he'd done the day before.

And, like the day before, it made my brain turn to goo.

He dropped his face closer to me, and I barely held back a sharp inhale at his closeness. "What happened to your face?"

Wow.

Okay.

Fuck you, too.

Sure, my bruises had looked worse in the mirror, but I didn't think it was *that* bad.

I raised my hand to my cheek self-consciously, though I wasn't sure exactly what my plan was. Short of stocking up on Halloween masks, I didn't have a lot of options.

"Your forehead is bleeding," he continued.

"Oh. Yeah." I touched it and pulled away to see another light smear of blood. "Sorry, I thought it was done."

He smirked, but it didn't look right. His hazel eyes held no humor, like it was as forced as his soft tone. "Stop apologizing."

"Sorry."

He used his hold and size to shift me backward to inspect the small cut under a light. I would've let him because my brain was still goo at his nearness, but with the movement, I caught sight of the blonde in my peripheral and was reminded we weren't alone.

I scurried away. Well, as far away as he would let me get, which wasn't far. But at the change in my body language, Ash's gaze dropped from my forehead to my eyes. They darted toward his... whoever she was and then back.

"Oh. Don't mind me." She lifted her mug. "I'm just watching."

If she wants to jump me for being close to her man, she's hiding it well. Or waiting until I heal from my last beating.

For all I knew, they were into that kind of thing. I'd been around a lot of different people in my life. I read books.

Okay, fine. I *thought* about reading books but was too tired to. Either way, I was inexperienced but not naive.

I was also very *not* interested.

The woman talking distracted Ash enough that I was able to dodge to the side and put the needed distance between us. Without his behemoth body blocking the way, I also saw that it was not just the three of us in the kitchen.

There was a fourth attendee at our party. A very tiny fourth attendee.

My stomach churned with guilt. I'd made him sleep in bed with me. I'd taken comfort from his body next to mine. All the while, he had a woman and a baby.

It was totally *not* a girl's girl move.

Not that I shouldered all the blame. It was also on him and made him an absolute douchebag because there was only so much that could be chalked up to his hospitable kindness, but still. Men were stupid. That didn't mean I wanted to be.

Holy shit, I'm turning into Veronica.

The swirling vortex of shame grew into a chasm of it when Ash let me go in order to move toward the woman. With flawless ease born of clear practice, he swooped the tiny human bundle from her arms and rested it against his broad chest.

The same chest I'd slept on.

Fuck it. I don't care if I get lost or end up pinned under a crashed four-wheeler somewhere. I'm so out of here.

I hooked a thumb over my shoulder and inched back. "Well, I'll just get out of your—"

"Not so fast," Ash cut in. "Vi is here to check you over."

That gave me pause. "What?"

The blonde lifted her hand in a little wave. "I'm Violet. An introduction this bonehead should've made the moment you walked in, but my brother has never been great with manners."

Brother.

As she moved to take the spot her freaking brother had just moved from—without the intense body crowding and face touching, of course—I saw it. The same hazel eyes. The light hair. Even the dimples.

I would've felt more relief that I hadn't slept in her man's arms had it not been for Vera and Juliet and whoever else there was. Maybe I'd spent the night in one of their man's arms.

This is a disaster.

Her lips turned down at the inspection of my face, drawing my focus out of Ash's bed and into the present. I shied away from her keen gaze. "Uhhh..."

"Vi is a nurse," Ash filled in.

My eyes went wide, and although the swelling hurt less, the fresh cut on my forehead stung. "I feel better. I'm good."

Ash gave me that damn charming smile. "Never said you weren't, sunshine. But you went through hell. I just want to be sure you're healing okay."

Vi's lips tipped, her dimples coming out to match her brother's. "What he said, *sunshine*."

My hackles rose. Not because of her teasing use of the nickname Ash insisted on using—though they could both shove that where there was no sunshine. My defensiveness was because he must've told her what I'd been through.

Did he include that it was my own mother who set me up?

I took a large step back.

"Sun—" Ash started, setting down the knife.

"Stop calling me that."

He raised a single brow, and that slight movement was loaded with challenge. Or maybe just cockiness. "Whatever you say, *little girl*."

For the sake of the sleeping baby, I fought to smother the frustrated groan that pushed out as a nonsensical noise. "You're infuriating."

"He always has been," Violet said, like nothing was out of the ordinary. "But he's also right."

With a lot of practice, I blanked my expression and my tone. "I appreciate the concern, but I'm fine. I'd know if there was an issue."

"Not necessarily. Car accident injuries can be sneaky buggers."

My gaze shot to Ash to find his own soft one aimed at me. When he added a wink to it, my brain was back to goo.

Vi jerked her head toward the living room. "Let's go—"

Ash deposited the baby back in her arms and lifted me to sit on the counter.

"To the couch..." she finished. "Never mind."

"Lighting is better in here," he said, making her roll her eyes as he took the baby bundle again.

She grabbed a small bag from behind her and opened it, taking out latex gloves, wipes, a bottle of liquid, and the little eye light thingy. Pulling the gloves on, she started with the light, shining it into my eye as she stood close. She moved to my other eye just as the baby began to fuss, and I thought the exam would be cut short.

Saved by the scream.

But Violet didn't even glance away from me as Ash shifted the baby in his hold. He rocked, and the fussing stopped almost instantly.

"You're good at that," I muttered. It didn't seem like a guy Ash's size should be capable of that kind of gentleness. But what did I know? My only experience with babies was hearing them scream from the other apartments in my building.

Violet gave a soft laugh. "He should be. He's a *funcle* times eleven."

"*Funcle?*"

"Fun uncle."

"Oh." The rest of what she said clicked in. "Wait. Eleven?"

Logically, I knew it was unlikely they were all hers, but that didn't stop me from looking at the woman who was seemingly only in her mid-thirties.

She did a double take at my horrified expression before laughing. "No, no. Not me. Charlotte is my one and only right now."

"I have three other older sisters," Ash said. "Emily has three boys, Andrea has two of each, and Maggie has one boy and two girls."

That explains the toy box.

"And Ash has zero," Violet pointed out nonchalantly.

She opened her mouth like she was going to say something else, but Ash cut her off with a warning. "Vi."

The whole conversation felt far too intimate, so I used that pause to change the subject. "So you're a nurse?"

"I'm on maternity leave for another few weeks, but yup."

I tried to scoot back. "Shouldn't you be resting or something?"

She gave me a smirk so similar to her brother's, it could've been copied and pasted. "Trust me. I've rested. I've relaxed. I've binged so much TV, my brain is rotting. I'm happy to get out of the house for a break that involves adult conversation. Even once I get back to work, it'll be mostly cartoons and fart jokes." At my lowered brows, she explained, "I work in a pediatrician's office."

"Does that mean I get a sucker once this is finished?"

I'd meant it as a joke, but Ash moved to open a cabinet near the fridge. He pulled out a large jar packed with lollipops and handed me a pink one. "Why wait until you're done?"

"See?" Violet shook her head. "This is why the kids call him their *funcle*."

I didn't open the package as Violet moved my head around to gingerly clean my face. When she swiped my cheek, I hissed, and tears filled my eyes.

"Hmm," she murmured.

Ash rapid fired questions. "What's wrong? Is it the bone? Should I bring her back to the hospital?"

"No," I snapped.

At the same time, Violet said, "Give me a second."

She reached into her Mary Poppins bag of medical supplies and pulled out something that looked like a headlamp. Once she put it on, a bright light burned my eyes as she inspected my cheek. She ran her gloved finger across it, watching for my wince each time. After a moment, she grabbed something else and warned, "This might hurt."

Ash reached his arm across to offer me his hand, but I didn't take it. I didn't want to accidentally jostle the baby. Plus, after what I'd been through, how much more pain could she really cause?

A lot.

The answer was a lot.

Using the world's largest and sharpest tweezers, Violet stabbed into my face and wiggled. I was pretty sure she'd somehow managed to fit the entire length of the tweezers under my skin.

I clutched my hands in my lap and forced myself to stay still so I wouldn't make it worse. The tears were harder to keep in, but I did my best with that, too.

After an eternity, Violet pulled away. She touched the spot on my cheek, and thanks to her digging, it was raw and tender. But it didn't have the same sting. "Better?"

"Yes."

She held up the tweezers to show a tiny piece of brick squeezed in the tip. "The initial swelling must've hidden it. Do you have ointment?"

"Yes," Ash answered for me since he'd been the one dealing with it.

"Good. Make sure that spot gets some." She removed the light and went back to work looking me over before asking me some basic questions and giving me a few easy commands to follow. "Everything looks good." She offered me a sympathetic smile. "Though I'm sure it doesn't feel good." She shot her brother a quick glare, then returned her gaze to me. "None of this is medical advice or clearance."

"Got it," I muttered.

"I don't have X-ray or MRI vision. I can't say there's no issue brewing below the surface. If your pain gets worse or even if you *feel* like something is off, you need to see Dr. Pierce."

Her knowledge of which doctor I had seen reaffirmed my guess that he was a family friend. Ash clearly had some connection since he was able to make the doctor come to Moonlight and then make my hospital visit so quick.

Well, quick for a hospital.

Ash and Violet spoke for a few minutes while she went over the same list of things to watch out for that the doctor had. Once she was done, she gathered her belongings—including her baby.

Who I probably wasn't supposed to refer to as a belonging, even in my own head, but I did.

"Now if you'll excuse us," Violet said, "my girlie and I are going to grab some Starbucks and spend an hour or five casually strolling through Target."

Before common sense could smack me over the head, my mouth opened, and words spilled out. "Do you want us to watch her so you can have some alone time?"

I had no clue why the hell I offered that. I had no clue what to do with a baby. I didn't know what they ate, when they ate it, or how much. I didn't know how to change a diaper. I didn't even know how to hold a baby.

I'd basically volunteered Ash to baby duty without consulting him. As if he wasn't already generous enough to be on Mila duty.

Relief flowed through me when Violet gave me a dimpled smile while shaking her head. "That's sweet of you, but Charlotte loves Target. She's besties with all the bright lights. Just don't tell the ceiling fan."

I had no clue what that meant, so I just risked a peek at Ash. My relief grew when I saw he wasn't pissed about my blurted mistake. Instead, he looked at me with an unreadable expression. A mix of softness and something more.

Something that made me feel like I had to squeeze my thighs.

When I wiggled in my spot on the counter, the softness left his gaze, leaving only intensity.

He probably thinks I'm trying to hide some pain.

I gave him a smile that I hoped was reassuring just as Violet spoke again. Her voice was light and happy. "Come on, Charlie. Time to get out of your uncle's way."

I was about to again blurt that there was no rush, and I would go, but Ash spoke first. "I'll walk you out."

That was... interesting.

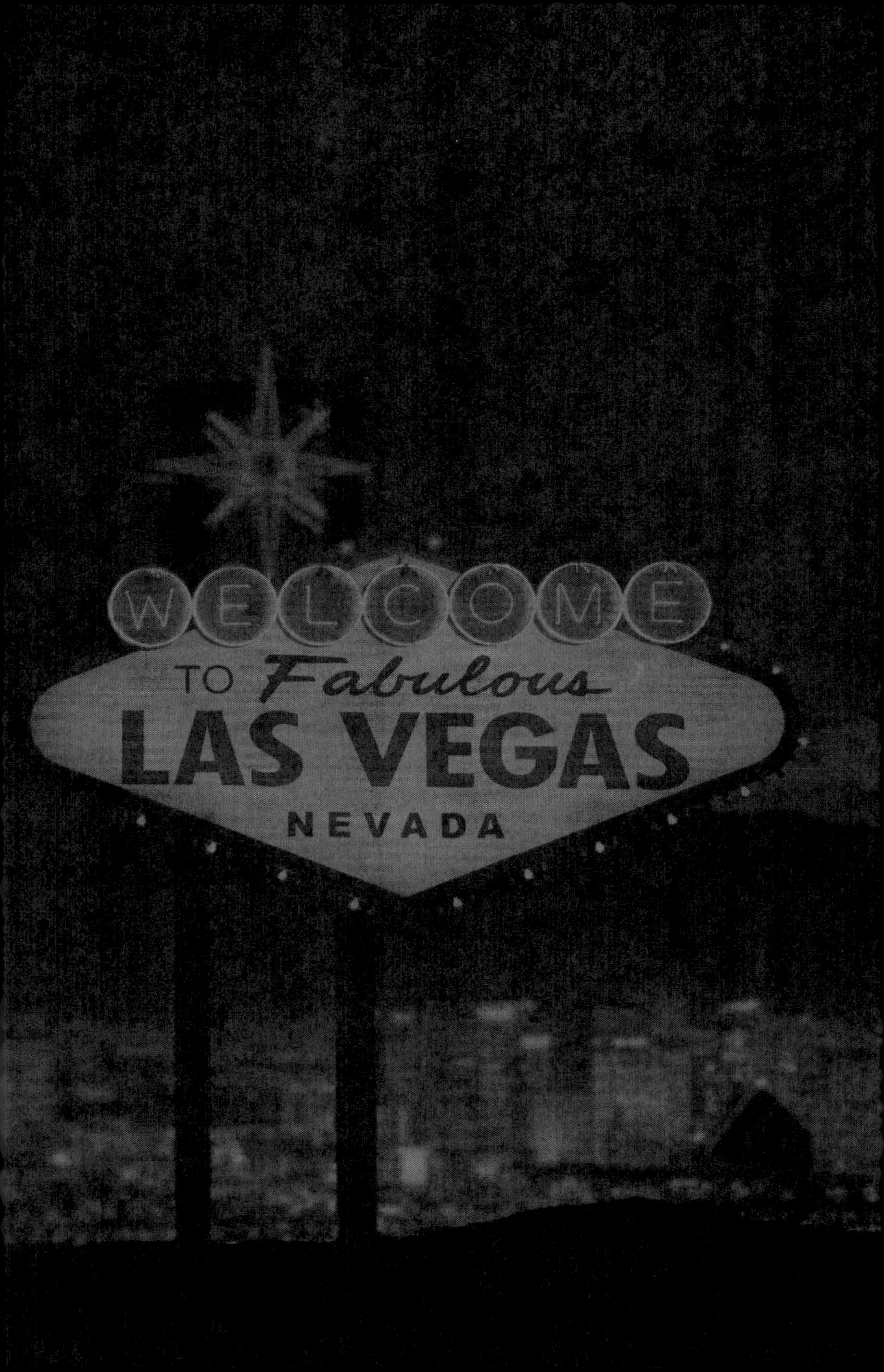
WELCOME
TO Fabulous
LAS VEGAS
NEVADA

CHAPTER 11
BE CAREFUL IN THE DARK
ASH

"**M**ILA SEEMS NICE."

"She is," I said simply, hoping Vi took the hint. She wouldn't.

"Young, too."

I shot my sister a warning glare that she missed as she loaded Charlie into her car seat. My niece's face scrunched with her disgruntlement at the lack of cuddles.

"Do your uncle a favor, Charlie girl, and have a giant diaper blowout right when your mama gets to the good aisle of Target."

"Joke's on you," Vi said, "they're all good aisles. And I have wipes, diapers, and a backup outfit in the bag."

"Have two blowouts. Up the back and everything."

Charlie stretched, her little fists shaking with the effort.

I bumped one of my tattooed fists to hers. "See? It's a deal."

"You're a jackass," Vi told me, but the smile on her face said otherwise. "I'm just saying, tread carefully with Mila. She's young and skittish and has clearly been through it. And you have the tendency to be an overbearing, pigheaded—"

"I get the point."

"Yeah, but I still like making it." At my stare, she held her hands up. "What? It's my sisterly duty to humble you every once in a while."

"Goodbye, *Violence*." I used the nickname I'd given her when we were kids, and she would get the others to hold me down so she could fart on me.

Anyone who said boys were gross never had sisters.

"Keep it up, and I'll tell Mom and Dad you've got a woman living with you. Mom will drive that monster of an RV straight through from Maine so she can start picking wedding themes."

"You wouldn't dare."

Her smirk grew into a grin as she climbed into the car. "Call me if you need anything. Love ya!"

I turned to get back to my young, skittish houseguest when the car stopped, and the window went down.

Vi was smart enough to keep her voice quiet so Mila didn't overhear. "And for God's sake, feed that girl."

I gave her a flick of the wrist salute and went inside to do that.

I assumed Mila would be long gone by the time I returned, but when I reached the kitchen, she remained on the counter. I stopped myself from letting that go to my dick.

But there was no stopping it when she smiled at me.

Fuck, she's pretty.

"I figured it was probably med time," she said.

"You figured right." I grabbed the pills from the bottles and a glass of water before handing them to her.

"I can do this myself."

"Never said you couldn't."

She started to pull her bottom lip between her teeth before stopping. "Then why do you insist on doing it?"

Because I want to take care of you.

Because I want you to depend on me.

Because I want to be your Daddy if you'll let me.

"Because," was all I said.

She shot me a glare before swallowing the pills. Before she

could hop down, I took the cup from her and replaced it with the bowl.

She eyed it. "What's this?"

"Breakfast."

"Wow. Thanks. Super helpful," she deadpanned.

"Strawberry yogurt, berries, bananas, and granola." At her grimace, I reached for the bowl.

She snatched it back, and her arm curled around it protectively.

"I'll make you something else. Eggs and toast?" I offered.

"I want this."

"Then why did you look at it like it kicked your dog?"

"I don't have a dog." When I waited for a real answer, she sighed and admitted, "You keep doing stuff for me."

"And?"

"And I don't like it."

"Get over it."

Mila's brows shot up. "What?"

"You heard me." Before she could unleash any of the insults I could practically see on her sharp tongue, I changed the subject. "Find anything interesting in your explorations yesterday?"

A blush broke out across her cheeks, and as fucking pretty as it was, it wasn't what I wanted.

Right then, at least.

"Told you nothing is off-limits," I reminded so she didn't feel guilty or called out.

But that was clearly what happened. "I didn't go into any closed door. Or into your gym. And I didn't snoop through—"

"You could've gone anywhere you wanted and looked through anything you wanted." Putting my fists to the island on either side of her, I leaned down so my face was in hers. "Nothing is off-limits. Just want to know if you found anything interesting."

More specifically, I wanted to know what she liked or disliked so I knew how to make the space more comfortable for her.

"Your house is really clean."

That wasn't what I'd expected, but she wasn't wrong. "I don't make a lot of messes, and I clean what I do. Vera comes in to do the detail work every two weeks or so."

"Your girlfriend cleans your house?" As soon as the question was out, her blush deepened, and her eyes went saucer big.

Which was fair 'cause I was betting my eyes were just as wide.

"Vera is in her fifties," I said.

She shrugged. "I don't judge."

"Vera is *not* my girlfriend. She's my boss' housekeeper who I poach twice a month because I can clean and do dishes and laundry, but I fucking hate dusting."

She perked up at that. "I can dust."

"No."

She instantly deflated.

What the hell?

I didn't get the chance to question when she asked, "Speaking of boss... Don't you have to go to work?"

"I'm working from home for a few days."

Her eyes moved down my body, and I would've fucking killed to know what she thought. If she liked what she saw. "Why are you dressed for work then?"

"Habit."

"You can be a driver from home?"

Driving Maximo was a small part of my job that any of the others—including Maximo himself—could handle. Keeping his schedule, arranging and rearranging meetings, and tracking his new casino build were all things I could do from anywhere.

My job as his enforcer was a little harder to do remotely, but I was making it work. I just made my threats extra creative over the phone.

"Something like that," I answered.

Her sharp look said she knew there was more, but I wasn't about to get into my full job description.

She already seemed like she was two seconds away from

bolting. Hearing that the man she'd trusted to care for her was cool with some casual torture would seal it.

I distracted her by adding, "Speaking of, one of my coworkers will be swinging by soon."

"Oh." She set the bowl to the side and wiggled forward on the island. "I'll go upstairs."

Without thought, I stepped forward, and her legs spread automatically.

Thank fuck I hadn't tucked my shirt in because there'd be no missing the bulge that'd formed when my dick instantly hardened.

I wanted to close the small amount of distance between us. I wanted to take her mouth and taste sweet berries and something that was sure as fuck sweeter. Something that was all Mila. I wanted to press my hand between her legs and feel if I affected her the way she affected me.

Because I honestly wasn't sure. Sometimes she looked up at me with those damn eyes like she wanted me to do all that and more. Other times, though, she acted like she wanted to be as far as fucking possible from me. Like she was counting down until she could get away from me.

And that was what had me clutching at my control. That and Vi's true words. Mila *was* young and skittish and had been through it. I still wanted her. Fuck, did I want her. But more than that, I wanted to take care of her.

I got the feeling it'd been a long time since anyone had done that.

I didn't want her to feel like that care came with strings attached—and those strings were attached to her body. I also didn't want to do something that'd make her want to leave. Or worse, make her think she *had* to stay and reciprocate.

Once she was healed, and I'd handled the dickheads who'd dared to touch her, things would be different. But for right then, I wanted her to stay in the safety I could provide her. Which meant any of my other wants were on the back burner.

And my hand was gonna continue to get a workout.

Keeping the space between us, I shook my head. "There's no reason to go anywhere. We'll be in my office."

"Okay."

I heard the distant sound of a car door closing, but she didn't move until the front door opened. Her gaze went to the side and then returned to me, and she looked ready to vault herself backward off the island at any sign of trouble.

In my time working for Maximo, I'd dealt with liars, thieves, dealers, loan sharks, and every other aspect of the Vegas underbelly. Some were dumbasses with less common sense than a snail, but others were smart. Sharp. Aware enough of the world they dwelled in to keep their defenses up at all times.

But she had even them beat.

It made me wonder again what the fuck she'd been through that had her fight-or-flight instincts so acute.

I gripped her wrists before she could do anything that'd hurt herself just as Cole came into the entryway.

"Hey, I put the bags..." His words trailed off when he saw Mila on the counter with me standing close, her wrists in my hold. It was barely perceptible, but his mouth twitched in amusement. "I'll be in the office."

"Hold up," I said. "Mila, this is my coworker Cole."

She kept her face partially turned, like she was trying to hide the worst of her injuries from him. She gave him a smile and as good of a wave as she could with her hands still in mine. With my fingers wrapped around her small wrists, I could easily feel her pulse thumping beneath the thin skin.

All of it sent a surge of jealousy through me.

Pushing it down, I asked her, "You got your phone with you?"

"Yeah, but it's busted, remember?"

I grudgingly released my hold on her delicate wrists. "Cole will make it good as new."

With a soft laugh, she shook her head. "It's beyond that. This isn't a little glitch or a needed update." She pulled it from her pocket and showed him the cracked screen.

Cole shrugged. "An easy fix. You cool if I take it with me?"

Mila didn't hesitate before handing it over. "Not like I can do anything with it."

Cole slipped it into the laptop bag he had slung over his shoulder.

Knowing what she'd do if I left it, I moved away from Mila and quickly rinsed the cutting board and knife I'd used before loading them both in the dishwasher. I turned off the sink in time to hear Mila's laugh. I faced them to see her smiling up at Cole as he spoke quietly.

He's fucking lucky I'm not still holding that damn knife.

My homicidal jealousy was forgotten when Mila met my gaze, and her grin grew. "You poured tequila on your own phone?"

"Bourbon," I corrected, grimacing at the hazy memory. "A whole fucking bottle of rare, expensive bourbon."

That detail made her laugh more. "*Why?*"

"I was drunk."

"And?" Cole prompted because the bastard knew that wasn't the whole story.

"And watching a movie."

"*Annnnd?*"

"And I figured if there is gonna be a robot uprising, I wanted my phone on my side. I was being a polite host."

"Oh my God," Mila cried as she threw her head back and laughed.

I didn't give a fuck she was laughing at me. I'd tell her all the embarrassing shit I'd ever done. Hell, I'd recreate the scene with another expensive bottle of bourbon if it made her laugh like that.

Carefree and unrestrained, granting me a glimpse behind her barricaded walls.

Before I did something stupid—like push for more—I handed her back the breakfast bowl. "You see the game room yesterday?"

"You mean your arcade?" she teased.

"Can't be an arcade. Doesn't have tickets or a prize counter.

But yeah. We'll be in the room across from there. Come get me if you need anything."

"Got it."

"It was nice to meet you, Mila," Cole said with a smile. He had a quiet charm that women liked. I shot him a glare so he'd stop fucking aiming it at Mila. He ignored me and grinned wider. "I'll get your phone to you soon."

"No rush," she said, before her own smile faltered. She caught herself and forced it back into place. "And it was nice meeting you, too."

Cole and I headed for my office. Once there was enough distance from the kitchen, he spoke. "Why do I feel like I'm about to be fired from a door duty that I'm not even on?"

His question was a reference to when Maximo had *fired* me after Juliet called me Handsome Goon.

He wasn't wrong.

"I'LL HEAD HOME, see what else I can dig up." Cole stood and gathered his shit as my phone beeped. "That the boss?"

I checked my phone. "Nope."

> Vi: She had two blowouts and a projectile, you bastard.
>
> Vi: If it wouldn't send poor Mila up those mountains, I'd pay to fly Emily's and Maggie's kids here so I could dump all eleven off with you at the same time.
>
> Vi: You bastard.

"What'd you do to piss her off?" Cole asked, reading over my shoulder.

"Baby shit curse."

"Evil."

Cole had come over to drop off some clothes for Mila and get her broken phone. He would transfer her data onto a new one and dig into the texts from her bitch mother to see if there was any merit to her suspicion. Since he was already there, he'd stuck around for a few hours to go over work shit with me.

"Almost forgot." He pulled something from his bag and tossed it to me. I looked down to see a small plug-in light. "She afraid of the dark?"

"Think so." The light she left on in the bathroom could've just been so she could navigate the unknown space in the night, but I got the feeling it was more than that.

"Make sense. She's had a lot of monsters hiding in the dark."

"Now she's got one in the light, too."

He shook his head, but he did it smirking. "You've got it bad already."

I didn't say anything because he wasn't wrong. I tossed the light onto the desk and started walking him out.

He kept his voice low. "Let me know if you decide you want the cameras, and I'll get them together to install when I bring the rest out here."

I lifted my chin, not wanting to say more in case Mila was around.

I didn't see her, but that wasn't a surprise.

I bet she's hiding out in her room.

I'd have lost that bet.

I opened the front door to find Mila sitting on one of the porch chairs. A book sat open in her lap, but it was only on the third page. Either she'd just started, or she found the mystery book as slow as I had.

There was a reason it'd been the first book to come to mind when Maximo had been punishing Juliet with the most boring shit he could pack her reading app with.

"Nice to meet you again, Mila." Cole grinned at her, and I was pretty sure it was more than he'd smiled for the previous month combined. I was also pretty sure he was doing it to fuck with me.

"If Ash is being a dick, just ask him about the lobsters at Parisian Crescent."

"What?" she questioned.

But I bit out, "I'll remember this. Payback is going to be a fucking bitch when your time comes."

Cole just laughed as he jogged down the steps to his car.

Mila turned to blink up at me. "Do I want to know?"

"Probably, but I'm not telling you. I haven't been a dick."

"I'll give it five minutes then," she said solemnly.

"You feeling leftover pasta, a sandwich, or a wrap?"

"For what?"

"Lunch."

"I'm not hungry."

"Don't remember asking. It's lunch time."

"I just ate that big breakfast."

"Hours ago. Not to mention, I saw the container in the fridge when I grabbed water earlier. You ate less than a quarter of it."

"You can't say *not to mention*, and then proceed to mention it."

Fuck, she's cute.

"Lunch, little girl."

Mila gave a soft but dramatic sigh. "I see five minutes was generous."

Biting back a smile at the sass, I headed toward the kitchen. Mila followed a minute later.

"What did you decide?" I asked.

"That you and I have very different appetite levels."

"If you pick something, you can eat in the backyard." Her eyes lit, and I piled on. "It's even nicer than the front."

"I'll reheat some of the pasta," she tried.

"I got it."

"I'll go wash up then."

She returned as the microwave beeped, and I handed her the plate with a potholder under it.

"This isn't mine," she said.

"Pretty sure I'm giving it to you, so yes, it is."

She shook her head. "Ash, this is more than I eat in an entire day."

"And you heard what the doctor said about that."

"I don't need to rectify it in one meal."

"Eat what you want and toss the rest."

Mila's lips curved in a horrified grimace. "I am *not* wasting all this food."

"Then put it in the fridge."

With your yogurt and leftover sandwich.

She opened her mouth to argue before closing it. With a soft inhale, she forced a small smile. "Thanks for making this."

"Mila—"

"Backyard?"

I held her gaze for a few seconds before she broke the contact and looked to the side. She grabbed the book she'd set down and waited expectantly while avoiding my face.

I turned and walked to the back door, sliding it open and stepping out of her way. I was glad I did when I got the profile view of her reaction.

"It's gorgeous," she breathed.

It was the reason I'd bought the house in the first place. After the large deck—complete with grill and built-in pizza oven—the rest of the expansive yard was nothing but nature.

When the real estate agent had suggested tearing it up to put in a pool, I'd nearly fired her. If I wanted to swim, I could do it at Maximo's or one of the resorts. There was no reason to destroy natural beauty—beauty that included a damn creek—for convenience.

I walked to the edge of the deck to point out the chair one of my nephews had dragged out. "There's a creek over there."

Mila didn't need to be told twice. With another murmured thanks, she carried her book and lunch to the chair.

I wanted to stand there and watch her. I wanted to do a fuck of a lot more than that.

I didn't.

Forcing myself into the office, I watched her on the exterior security camera until she came inside.

When the credits of another episode rolled, I clicked off the TV.

With her feet to the couch and her head resting on her bent knees, Mila turned just enough to look at me. I wasn't even sure she could lift her head if she wanted to.

"Bed, sunshine."

"But I'm not tired," she claimed.

A lie.

When I'd finished work, Mila had been in the living room. The book had still sat on her lap, but it'd been forgotten as she'd scrolled the TV.

I hadn't bought it.

The couch and chair had been slightly off. The books on the shelf had been repositioned so they were even.

For a moment, I'd thought she'd been snooping, but when I'd gone into the kitchen, I'd smelled the faint traces of cleaner in my reorganized fridge.

Mila had been trying to clean my damn house.

I'd told her it wasn't necessary, and she'd denied the attempt. Then she'd argued that it was necessary. Then she'd argued that she could cook rather than ordering Chinese delivery.

I'd never had someone fight me so damn hard about so damn little.

She'd finally dropped the fight when I'd told her I didn't want either of us to cook because I wanted to start the other show she liked. The one we needed to watch from the beginning.

Of everything, *that* had been what'd relaxed her.

It was almost one in the morning, and she'd been fighting to stay awake since before ten. Every time I'd said anything about bed, she'd rallied and insisted I put on another episode of the heaven comedy she loved.

"Don't remember asking if you were tired." I stood. "I said bed."

"Okay, good night." She reached to the side for the remote I'd left on the arm of the couch. I grabbed it before she could, and she held out her hand.

"I'll throw you over my shoulder and carry you upstairs."

"You wouldn't. Give me the remote. I promise I won't watch our show." When I didn't give it over, she wiggled her fingers.

I took the invitation she didn't know she made and gripped her hand to pull her standing. Since I didn't move back, the momentum made her body crash into mine.

Her palm went to my chest, and she tipped her head to look at me.

"You gonna tell me why you don't want to go to sleep?"

Just as quick, she dropped her hand and stepped away, nearly tripping over the couch. "I guess it's later than I thought. Bed is probably smart." She yawned, and it wasn't as forced as she'd been going for. "I'm wiped. Good night."

"Good night, sunshine."

"You owe me like ten lobster stories now," she muttered as she headed from the room.

I waited until she was in the entryway before killing the light. I did the same in the entryway, only turning that one off once she was up the stairs. I followed after and waited until the door to the bedroom closed before turning off the hall light.

When I was almost to the loft, the door of the bedroom was thrown open. I backtracked to the end of the hall and nearly crashed into Mila.

"What's wrong?"

"Nothing," she lied, her eyes wide with a surprising amount of panic. "I just forgot my water. And I wanted to grab that book. And I didn't eat my fortune cookie. Plus, I think—"

"Do you want me to sleep in there with you again?"

She started to pull her full bottom lip between her teeth

before wincing at the swollen cut. After a slight hesitation, she nodded.

"Get ready for bed. I'll be right in."

She nodded again and took off toward the room.

I waited until the door closed again before going to the guest room I'd been using. I stripped my shirt off and tossed it into the hamper before undoing my belt and slacks. As soon as I shoved the fabric of my boxer briefs down, my hard cock sprung free from where it'd been stretched down my thigh. It made me a sick bastard because I fucking knew something was bothering her, but my dick didn't get that memo.

Or it did and it just didn't care that it was a bastard.

I fisted it and squeezed until it toed the line of pain. With the image of Mila looking up at me, I knew I would come embarrassingly fast, but I didn't want to risk her changing her mind. Releasing a groan of frustration at the same time I released my hold, I pulled on a new pair of boxers and basketball shorts, tucking my hard-on into the waistband. Since that did jack shit to hide the inches that stuck out past the fabric, I pulled on a loose tee.

I took care of the rest of what I needed as fast as I could before grabbing my phone and returning to Mila. I didn't knock in case she'd crashed, but I did open the door slowly.

Not only was she still awake, but she was sitting on the bed with her eyes aimed at me.

Waiting for me.

My dick jerked.

I tilted my head toward the study side of the room. "Want me to sleep over there?"

Her lip went back between her teeth as she shook her head.

"Want me to take the floor?"

Another shake.

"Like last night?"

She nodded.

Rounding the bed, I closed the bathroom door.

"Wait—" Mila started but her protests cut off when the room

wasn't plunged into darkness. She leaned over to check out the bright light coming from the plug-in. "You didn't have to put that there."

I pulled back the blankets. "Never said I did."

"You can turn it off."

"No need."

"It's really fine."

"Mila."

"Hold on, I'm going to switch it off."

"Mila—"

"I don't need—"

"Little girl."

"Don't call me that."

"Then stop interrupting me before I..." That time I was the one to interrupt myself before I said something that'd have her kicking my ass right back out of bed.

"Before you what?" she challenged. Her voice may have been quiet and raspy with exhaustion, but there was no doubt it was a challenge.

If it hadn't made her visibly upset, I'd have called her a brat again.

"Before I fall asleep and nosedive off the damn bed." I carefully pulled her into my loose hold and covered us. "Go to sleep."

"Eleven lobster stories." She paused before amending. "Actually, twelve for calling me little girl."

I expected it to take a while for her to relax, but within minutes, Mila was out. It took me longer to get comfortable while keeping my hips away from her so she couldn't feel how turned on I was. A task that became damn near impossible when she snuggled into me.

Trusting me in her sleep.

Her monster in the night-light.

Even if she didn't know it yet.

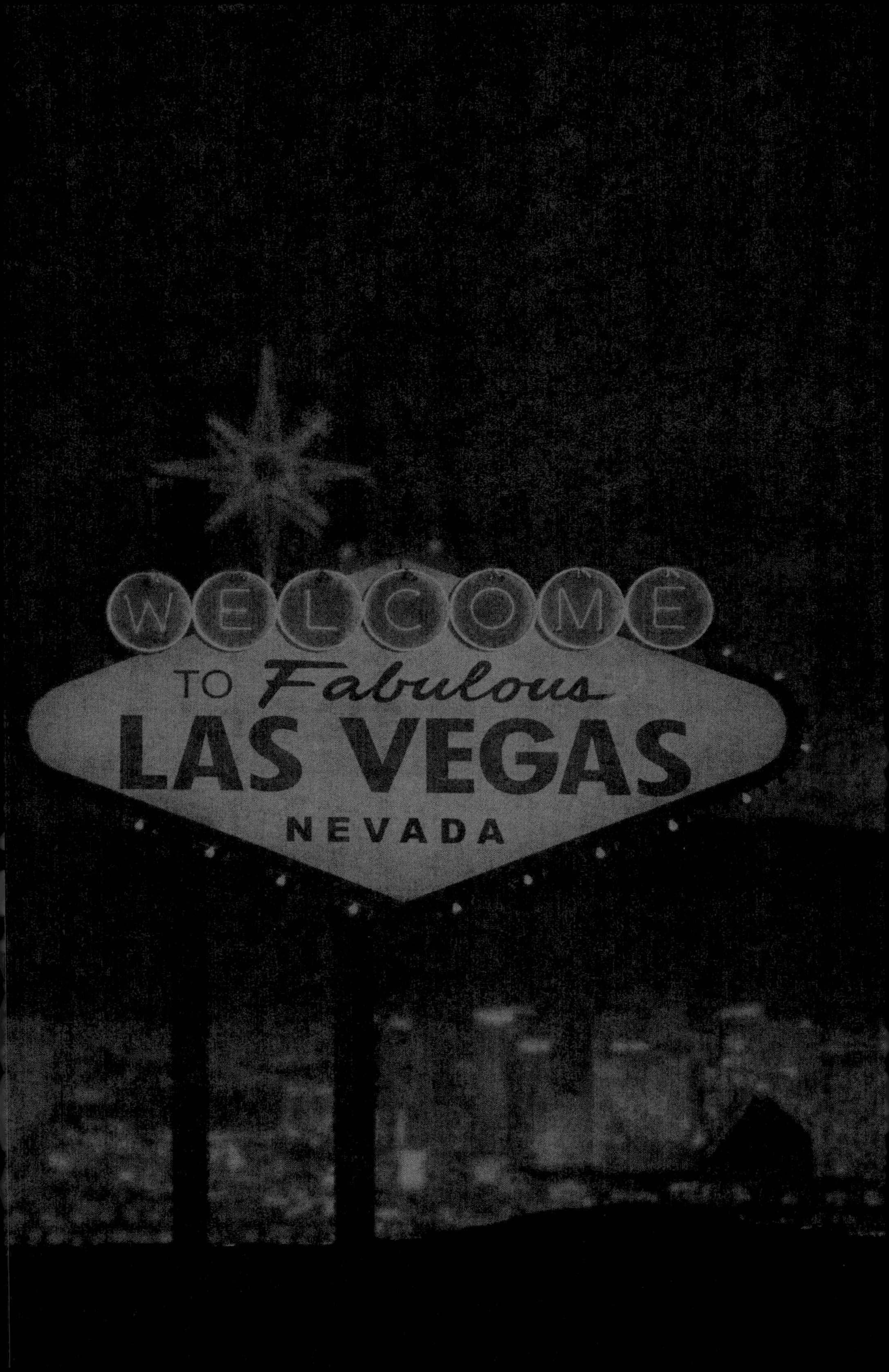
WELCOME
TO Fabulous
LAS VEGAS
NEVADA

CHAPTER 12
KEEP YOUR EYES OPEN
MILA

I CAN'T BELIEVE I ASKED him to sleep with me. Again!
I'm so stupid.
Worse still, he knows it.
A stupid little girl *who is afraid of the dark and has scary dreams. Pathetic.*

Rolling my eyes at myself, I stood from my favorite spot near the creek and went inside to grab some water. My plan went out the window when the intoxicating scent of coffee filled my nostrils.

Like a cartoon, I practically floated over to the fancy coffee maker that wasn't usually on the counter. Opening the cabinets, I searched for a mug. A glass.

I'd drink it out of a measuring cup if that was all that was available.

I'll pour Ash some, too. That'd be helpful.
Except I don't know how he takes it.

Forcing myself away from the delicious scent, I headed through the house toward Ash's office. I peeked into the ajar door, unsurprised to find it was decorated much like the rest of his house. Cool and masculine, with a giant desk topped with three computer monitors.

Ash sat behind it, his phone pressed to his ear as he looked at one of the side monitors. Despite his impatient words, his tone was happy when he muttered, "About time."

Not wanting to interrupt, I backtracked to the kitchen. Finally finding the mugs—on the very top shelf, of course—I hoisted myself onto the counter and carefully stood.

"Camila Price, what the fuck do you think you're doing?"

At the barked question, I startled and lost my balance. My life flashed before my eyes as I seemed to hover mid-air.

And what I saw was depressing.

Rather than cracking my head open on the island and dying without even getting any coffee, strong arms wrapped around to catch me.

I didn't bother to ask how he knew my full name. I was quickly learning there was very little Ash didn't know or couldn't find out. Not to mention, there were much more pressing matters.

Like how I was cradled in his arms.

Or the thunderous expression on his face that contrasted that gentle hold.

"What the fuck do you think you're doing?" Ash repeated, his angry hazel eyes burning as he scanned me.

"Getting coffee."

"And you needed to be a daredevil to do that?"

I bristled at his anger and his concern. Even with as often as I saw the second one from him—and it was far too often, in my opinion—I still wasn't used to it. "It's not my fault you keep the mugs all the way up there. Not all of us are behemoths."

Setting my ass on the counter, he opened the drawer under the coffee maker to show stirrers, powdered creamer, sweeteners, and mugs.

Lots of mugs.

I threw my arms up. "Well, how was I supposed to know those were there?"

"You should've asked me instead of doing something so dangerous."

I rolled my eyes. "This isn't the first time I've had to scale something. I've been this height since I was like twelve."

I wasn't sure if it was the eye roll or my words, but one of them made Ash's jaw clench.

Ah, good to know I still have that effect on him.

His reaction only made me babble more. "I'm a professional at counter climbing. I'd win a gold medal."

"And almost falling?"

"That was *your* fault. Competitor interference. Very unsportsmanlike."

The corner of his lips tipped up and some of the tension left his face. It wasn't a dimpled smile, but it was better than his jaw disintegrating to dust with as hard as he'd been clenching it. "From now on, come get me. Got it?"

"You were on the phone," I said.

Still standing close, Ash lowered his face until it was in front of me. Until he was all I could see. "Don't care if I'm on the phone with the president, the pope, and Elvis from beyond the grave. You can *always* interrupt."

I'd never had someone make me feel like a priority. Even if his words were an empty offer to be polite, I'd never even had someone *pretend* I was a priority.

My stomach swirled like it was made of melty lava, heating me from the inside out. It traveled in my veins, making my heart pound as my nipples tightened painfully.

I'd always considered myself smart. Realistic to the point of cynicism. Even as a kid, I hadn't believed in Santa, the Tooth Fairy, or any other fairy tales. Those few fleeting moments of wistfulness were never worth the crushing disappointment.

Yet as I looked up at his handsome face so close to mine, all my hard-fought common sense fled, and one thought kept running through my brain.

Kiss me.

Kiss me.

Kiss me, kiss me, kiss me.

It was stupid. Insane, actually. Unrealistic and fanciful and...

And I wanted it so badly, I ached.

Literally *ached*.

Ash's gaze dropped to my mouth, and I barely stopped myself from licking my lips. From verbalizing my need.

Or from just kissing him.

Just as quickly, he moved away like nothing had happened.

Because nothing had outside of my wild imagination. For all I knew, I had dried yogurt on my chin that he was too nice to point out.

I discreetly wiped my face while Ash grabbed a couple of travel cups. "We'll have to take the coffee to go, though."

"To go where?"

"Some work came up that I can't do from home. Figured you were probably getting cabin fever."

Yes, in this tiny, dilapidated shack.

"I get to work with you?" I asked.

"You get to hang out while I work."

I had no clue what exactly that entailed. But considering I'd almost thrown myself at a man who was so far outside of my league, we weren't even playing the same sport, I would take it.

I could use the change of scenery.

And to touch grass.

For whatever reason, I'd assumed we'd be going to Moonlight. There'd been a pit of dread and guilt at the thought of returning to the scene of the crime.

My *literal* crime.

Instead, Ash pulled his big SUV onto a private road at a different resort.

"Where are we?" I asked as he swiped something to lift the little bar thingy.

"Sunrise."

I wanted to question that, but something in the distance caught my eye just before Ash pulled into a parking garage. "What was that?"

"What was what?"

"Behind the building. It looked like really tall construction beams or something."

"It's a drop tower."

I didn't respond since I had no clue what that meant other than it sounded not good.

"It's a ride," he explained without me having to ask. "It slowly raises riders to the top and then drops them."

"People *want* that?"

He smiled as he pulled into a spot. "The tickets sell out most days, so yeah. They want it."

"I can't believe people pay for the risk of dying."

"They pay for the wild ride that leaves their heart racing, reminding them they're alive," Ash rumbled before he climbed out and closed the door.

I didn't follow immediately. His innocuous words created a tingle between my legs as I thought about a different way to make my heart pound.

If kissing him earlier would've been a massive mistake...

Scowling at myself, I got out and slammed the door a little harder than necessary.

And then I almost tripped when Ash asked, "Do you want to ride it?"

My brain short-circuited. "What?"

"The drop tower. We can head there now."

Oh. Right. That makes more sense than the gutter my brain traveled down.

What the hell has gotten into me?

Needing to get myself together, I returned to the question I'd wanted to ask before getting distracted by the tower. "So you work here and Moonlight?"

"And Star and Nebula and wherever else my boss needs me."

Sunrise, Moonlight, Star, and Nebula...

It'd been a long time since I'd watched any of the Vegas resort specials because I actively avoided them. But I vaguely remembered Veronica watching one about the remodel of Moonlight, Star, and Sunrise after the current owner had inherited them.

My steps slowed. "Wait, do you work for the owner?"

"Yes." He put his hand to my lower back and nudged me toward the elevator.

"Like directly for him?"

"Yup."

Despite my initial—and very incorrect—assumption that Ash was just a chauffeur, his house made it clear his job was more than that. The small glimpse I'd gotten of him working made it clear it was much, *much* more than that. Still, I'd just guessed he worked for one of the bigwigs.

I hadn't even considered it was the biggest of wigs.

"What do you do?" I asked.

"Whatever needs done." At my growl of frustration, Ash chuckled. "I don't have an exact job title because I don't do one job. I'm Maximo's right-hand. His assistant, driver, security, delegate, and whatever else, all rolled into one good looking package."

The housekeepers at The Roulette never talked about other hotel openings or opportunities, good or bad. If someone knew about a worse hellhole, they didn't give warnings in hopes whoever would leave, and they'd get more hours or better shifts. And if they heard a job was available somewhere good? That was a secret they kept in a vault so they had less competition while they went for it.

Even with that level of selfish subterfuge, it was well known that a job at one of those four resorts was like winning the housekeeper lotto. It was also just as rare. Openings didn't come up often because they had a shockingly low turnover rate for the service industry. From what I'd heard, they didn't even accept applications due to the overwhelming amount of interest.

With so many Roulette-esque dumps in Vegas, a luxury resort that paid its employees well *and* offered great benefits was a dream job.

I hesitated for a second because Ash had already done a lot for me. Too much. But I'd be a fool if I didn't ask for one more thing. "Can you get me an interview with housekeeping? Or just pass along my résumé?"

Right after I create a résumé.

And figure out how to say that I've been cleaning bugs, mold, and bodily fluids since before I was legally able to work.

His brows rose, but I continued before he could tell me what I already knew. "I'm fine to go on a waitlist."

"We'll see," he muttered as we stepped into the elevator, and he pressed his thumb to a button.

I didn't push it further, even if I *really* wanted to.

Other than cutting through Moonlight to my bus stop a few times, I'd never been to the other properties. I wasn't particularly anxious to see all the waste and squandering, but I was still curious to see the design itself. I wanted to know if it was as prettily themed as Moonlight.

I nervously ran my palms down the front of the floral dress that'd been waiting on the bed after my shower. It hit at kind of an odd spot below my knees and was baggy around my torso, but I didn't care. It was gorgeous and made me feel more confident.

Being there with Ash helped, too.

After a second, it became obvious that we weren't exiting in the lobby. The elevator didn't slow to let anyone else on as it kept climbing and climbing.

And climbing.

When the doors finally slid open, it wasn't into a hallway. It was a penthouse. I stepped out and moved through the space toward the floor-to-ceiling windows as Ash spoke.

"Like the house, nothing is off-limits in here. Bathroom to your left. Another is through the main bedroom. The remotes are on the table. I haven't stayed here in a while, so there's no food in the fridge."

Maybe that means there's stuff for me to clean. Not that it'll be much help to him, but it'll help the hotel housekeepers, and they'll appreciate it.

"There's a button on the phone for room service," he continued. "Order whatever you want. I'll be back soon."

I whipped around. "Wait, what?"

The last thing I saw before the elevator doors closed was Ash's dimpled smirk.

Damn him.

I stormed over to the elevator and stabbed the button.

Nothing.

Not just didn't it open, it didn't ding or light up or anything. I tried again.

Nothing.

I looked closer and noticed it wasn't a normal button. It had a fingerprint scanny thing.

Shit, does that mean I'm stuck in here?

I had no plans to leave the space anyway. It wasn't like I had the money or interest to explore the resort. But Ash had me trade one cabin fever for another.

It didn't make sense.

Giving up my escape, I moved through the penthouse. Perfectly pressed suits hung in the massive walk-in closet. A few pairs of basketball shorts and tees were folded in the storage cubes next to them. A pair of shiny shoes sat on a rack next to a pair of sneakers, but that was it. The rest of the space was empty.

And clean.

Not so much as a fleck of dirt on the sneakers.

The whole penthouse was the same. Perfectly clean, if not barren.

And frankly underwhelming.

The suites at The Roulette weren't luxurious by any stretch of the imagination, but they were still painted a light dusty blue that hid grime and fading. The walls in Ash's penthouse were all light beige. The Roulette had generic art on the wall that had likely come from a thrift shop or closeout sale. His penthouse had no art other than a large mirror mounted near the entrance.

With all the raving I'd heard about Sunrise, I was shocked to find it so poorly decorated. Especially since I was sure the price for a single night there would give me an aneurysm.

With nothing else to do, I plopped down on the couch. Rather than reaching for the remote, I grabbed the iPad next to it on the coffee table.

Hopefully there's no password because it's research time.

I pressed the power button, and it loaded right to the main screen. I opened the internet browser and typed in the name Ash had given me.

`Ash Cooper`

A message popped up, telling me it was blocked.

What the hell?

I tried to download a different browser from the app store, but that was restricted, too. Everything was.

Even the already downloaded apps gave me the same message or just didn't load. All except the reading one. That loaded right up to display thousands of books. Everything from highlander romance to true crime to random ancient civilizations.

Bizarre.

As I scrolled through, my fingertip felt something on the back. I flipped it over to see an engraving.

Happy Birthday, little dove.

I had no clue who *little dove* was, but it was a safe bet it wasn't Ash.

For reasons I didn't want to inspect closely, I had the overwhelming urge to throw the iPad across the room. Instead, I settled back and flicked on the TV. I went through the options until I found the show Ash and I had been watching at night. I went to the episode we'd left off on and pressed play.

Watching without him.

The jerk.

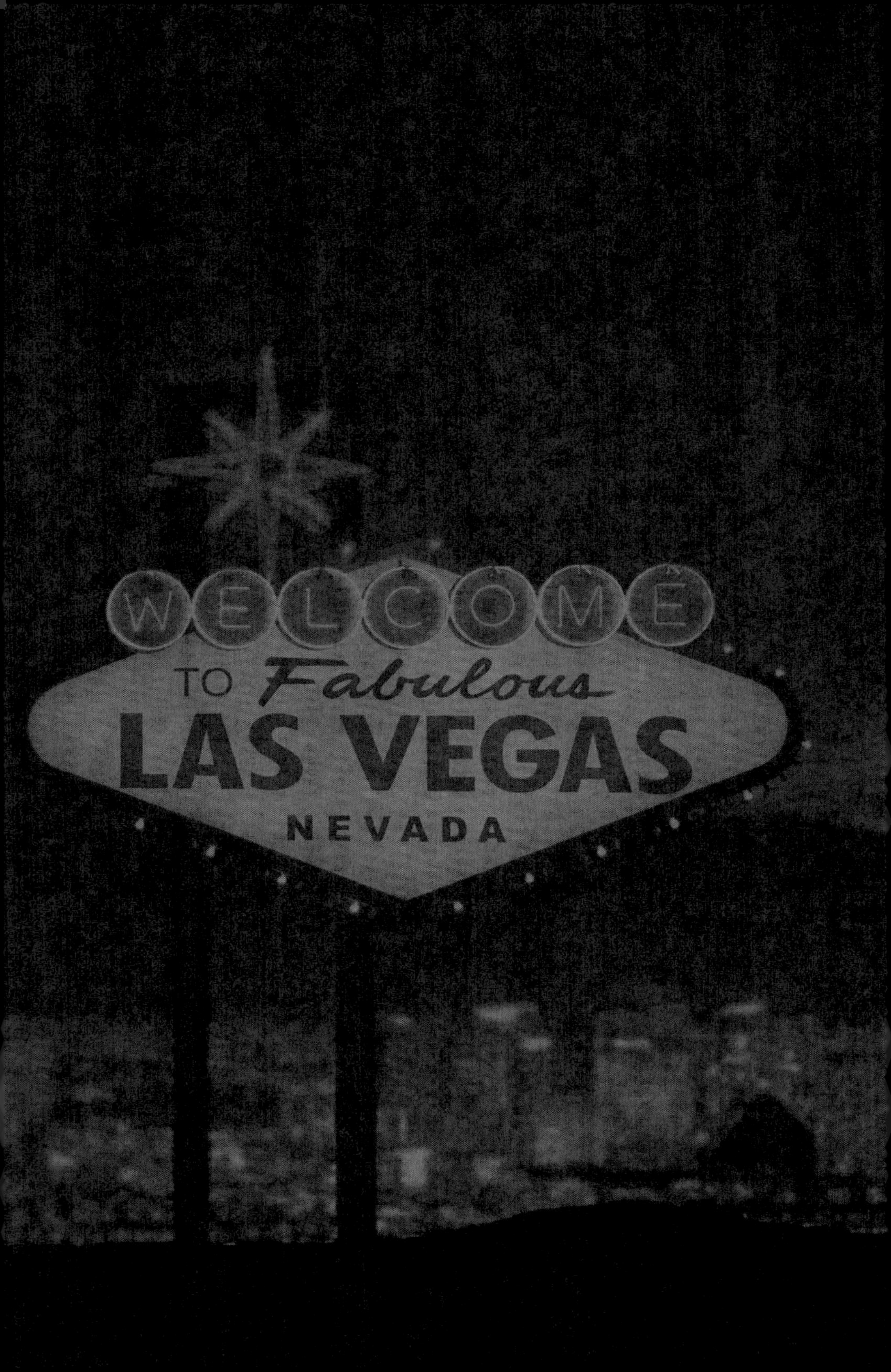
WELCOME
TO Fabulous
LAS VEGAS
NEVADA

CHAPTER 13
HIDE YOUR BELONGINGS
ASH

"WHAT A FUCKING DUMP." COLE scowled, shaking his head. "I can almost feel the sticky everything."

After Mila's nightmare and the confession about her mother, Cole made it his mission to track the bitch down. Her last known address was with a boyfriend in the suburbs, but when he'd gone to recon, he'd discovered her man had recently kicked her out.

According to the chatty neighbor with a yappy dog, it hadn't been an amicable split, either. Veronica Rogers had stood on the lawn, screaming threats and insults until someone had called the cops.

I couldn't picture how someone like that could be related to Mila. The same quiet Mila who tried to clean before she even made a mess. Who apologized for apologizing. Who tried to shrink herself until she blended into the background.

Not that she ever could.

Veronica hadn't left a forwarding address as she'd flipped off her ex and the cops before peeling out, but Cole had gotten her burner number from Mila's cell data. The moment it'd turned on, it'd been an easy trace to the shitty bar we stood outside of.

Cole grabbed the door handle, and his scowl deepened. "Knew it. Fucking sticky."

It reeked of stale beer and fryer oil before we even stepped inside. At barely noon on a weekday, half the stools lining the bar were filled.

The bartender looked up as he wiped down the space in front of him and kept a wary eye on us.

Smart.

Elbowing me, Cole tilted his head to where two women sat with a group of men at the end of the bar. My gaze landed on the brunette first. Her thin face was pinched, with sad brown eyes and thin lips she coated in red lipstick.

Since Mila doesn't act a thing like her mom, maybe she doesn't look like her, either.

But then the bleached blonde looked up, and blue eyes met mine.

Bingo.

A flare of panic went across her face as those blue eyes darted between Cole and me.

Either she's psychic and knows she should be fucking terrified, or she thinks we're someone else.

Whispering to her friend as she stood, she hightailed it down a hallway that I was willing to bet led to an exit.

"I'll take the long way," Cole said while I took off after her.

Veronica Rogers was fast, but she couldn't hop an alley fence like I could. Coming down a small pathway that ran between a porno shop and another trashy bar, she distractedly greeted a small group of smokers while she moved. Her head was turned to watch over her shoulder.

Except I was already in front of her, blocking where the alley met the sidewalk.

"Where you off to, Veronica?" I asked as she was about to knock into me.

She jolted at my voice and froze. "Just headed home... Detective?"

"Not a detective."

She scanned my suit. "Cop?"

"No."

"'Cause you know you have to tell me, right?"

People watch too many movies.

Her voice lowered so the others couldn't hear. "If Sun sent you—"

"Your son didn't send me."

She shook her head. "The other kind of sun."

"Your daughter did," I finished.

Her brows twitched, but she was quick to control it. "You must be mistaken, sugar." Her laugh was dismissive as she glanced over at the group she clearly knew before fluffing her hair. "Do I look old enough to have a daughter?"

Yes.

No. Wait.

Fuck yes.

If she wasn't a fucking bitch, I could see how Veronica Rogers might've been attractive at one point. Smoking, drinking, and the Vegas sun had damaged her skin. The heavy makeup, overly bleached hair, and that whole bitch thing didn't help.

But the thing that aged her most was the calculating look in her eyes. I could practically see the dollar signs in her gaze as she scanned my expensive suit again, all while splitting her focus to watch for a better opportunity.

"I'm here about Mila," I told her.

There was no flash of recognition. No concern. Nothing.

How the fuck did this selfish bitch birth my sunshine?

Someone approached behind us, and I didn't have to look to know it was Cole.

"Like I said, you must be mistaken. I wish someone would send a fine man like you my way." She forced a laugh that was supposed to be sexy as her gaze moved to Cole. "Either of you. Hell, both of you. If that's something I can help you with, then we can talk. Otherwise, I better go."

Before she could take off again—or make my dick crawl

inside me in repulsion from her proposition—I grabbed her upper arm.

Fear blanched her face.

Good. She's not a total fucking idiot.

"Who did you send after Mila?" I asked.

"Wow, you really can't keep your hands off me, huh?" Veronica said loudly with another flirty laugh. She shuffled us farther from the audience before lowering her voice. "What're you talking about? *She* came after *me* just because I borrowed a little money."

"You stole her money *and* got her fired."

She pulled her bottom lip between her teeth like her daughter did. Rather than the cute as fuck shyness Mila had, Veronica's blue eyes darted as she came up with her next move.

Excuse.

Lie.

I cut her off before she could start. "Don't give me whatever bullshit you're putting together right now. It'll just piss me off worse, and that's not something you'll want."

I would never hit a woman. But I had the time, money, skills, and connections to make her life hell. I would still do that for all the shit she'd put Mila through, but the bastards who'd hurt her were my priority.

"I honestly have no idea what you're talking about. But you should know, Mila is a dramatic little liar. You can't believe a thing she says. She's playing you."

Cole made a strangled noise behind me, but otherwise didn't move.

I did.

Crowding in close, my voice was low and lethal. "Mila was waiting for you. In the location you set. You never showed. Instead, two motherfuckers roughed *my* woman up. You saying that's a coincidence?"

"She got roughed up?"

I didn't know if the concern on her face was genuine or a practiced act, but I didn't buy it. "Who'd you send after her?"

"No one. I swear."

"Then why weren't you there?"

Her cheeks flushed, but she lifted her chin stubbornly—just like her daughter did.

The daughter she didn't claim.

The dumb sack of shit.

My grip on her arm tightened briefly, and she finally spoke. "I was getting dumped, okay? And it was all that bitch's fault."

"Mila?" At her nod, I bit out, "How's it her fault? And fair warning, I'd watch your fucking mouth when you talk about her."

"After I borrowed her money—"

"Stole," Cole interjected.

She shot him a glare over my shoulder. "After *that*, Mila hunted me down at my man Harry's place. He saw me talking to her outside, and I said she was a friend's kid. But then he caught me borrowing his money to get her off my back, so I had to admit she's my kid. He didn't want to be hooked to someone with a grown daughter."

I would bet he didn't want to be hooked to a lying cunt who'd ignore her own child, lie about her, and steal, but her relationship bullshit wasn't my concern.

"So instead of calling Mila to tell her you didn't have the money, you sent those assholes to talk to her?"

Veronica gave an exasperated sigh before catching the look on my face. Her attitude disappeared. "I told you, I don't know anything about that. Harry gave me the money if I promised to stop breaking his shit and leave before the cops followed through on their threat to haul both of us in."

I looked over at Cole who shrugged. "Neighbor didn't give specifics about when the breakup took place."

"Harry's neighbors? Those uppity assholes always thought I didn't belong there. Like he's some saint." She looked angrier at that insult than she did at finding out her daughter had been hurt. "By the time I went to the meeting spot, they were gone."

"*They?*"

"Mila..." Her eyes widened as she whispered, "And Abraham."

"Who the *fuck* is Abraham?" I bit out, jealousy hitting my gut.

"*He's* the one who set that location. I told Mila to meet me there first, and then I was meeting him."

"You move on fast," Cole muttered.

"No, you don't understand," she said with a frantic shake of her head. "Abraham is not a friend. He thinks I stole from him, but I didn't. I took what he promised. He found me last week and demanded it back. The money I got from Mila was supposed to be a down payment because he threatened to blow up the good thing I had going with Harry." Her lip pushed out. "Which happened anyway."

Figuring she wasn't dumb enough to run, I released her arm. "How much do you owe Abraham?"

"I don't remember." Unlike her daughter, she was shit at lying.

"How much do you have for the down payment?"

"Nothing," she muttered hesitantly.

"What?" Cole gritted through clenched teeth. It was obvious the conversation was stomping through some areas of his past that were better left buried. I glanced over at him, but he gave me a subtle chin lift as he continued glaring at Veronica. "What happened to the money from Mila?"

"And from Harry?" I added.

"He kicked me out! I'm homeless and sleeping on my girlfriend Jeannette's couch, for fuck's sake. When Mila and Abraham didn't show, I figured I should use the money to get back on my feet."

"Do you have any of it left?"

But I knew the answer even before she said it. "No."

I was far from an expert, but I'd grown up with four older sisters. I knew enough. Her hair was recently done since no roots showed. The clothes she wore were new and quality—unlike the threadbare shit her daughter used to wear.

Used to.

Formerly.

Not any-fucking-more.

She'd treated herself to a spa day and shopping spree rather than pay back her own daughter. Or settle up with a man who'd threatened her.

Running my palm down my face, I mentally went through my options. "You got a number for Abraham?"

She shook her head. I was about to ask for a last name since it'd help Cole find the info quicker, but she said, "I know where he is, though. But I don't have money to give him. And I don't want him to know where I'm staying now. He's dangerous."

Clearly not as dangerous as me if you're continuing to fuck around.

"I don't give a shit," I told her bluntly. "Not if he's behind Mila's attack."

"Well since you seem to be blinded by Mila's uptight, better-than-everyone—"

"What'd I say about watching your damn mouth?"

She forced an acid smile. "Since you seem to *like* Mila, you should give a shit. I never told Abraham about her. If you go confront him, and he doesn't have anything to do with this, you'll be putting her on his radar."

Yeah, I'd already considered that.

"Not if I settle up your debt."

Relief, excitement, and a different, nauseating kind of excitement lit her face. She tried to hide it, but too many gears were turning in her calculating eyes. "It's a lot."

I didn't say anything to that since my money wasn't her business and paying off her debt wasn't about her. None of this was. It was about Mila, and *that* I did share.

"This is a one-time thing. You step in shit again, you clean your own mess. Don't smear it at Mila's feet. You try to *borrow* money from her, you upset her, you even look at her sideways, I will put every resource I have into destroying your life. You got me?"

She didn't try to deny the help. Didn't pause to think it over. Didn't even hesitate for a second before nodding rapidly.

Meanwhile, it's a battle just to get her daughter to let me make her a damn sandwich.

Veronica gave us the address where Abraham might be, and Cole plugged it into his phone.

With another warning, we returned to the car. I watched as she sauntered back to the bar, not even a shred of guilt or worry on her face.

"Need me to drive?" I offered.

"Nah, I got it."

I looked at him as he pulled away from the curb, trying to gauge whether the interaction had fucked him up or just pissed him off. His expression was blank as he navigated through the side streets.

Before I could speak, he did.

"Well, she's a gem."

"You sure this is the place?"

"This is what she said. But it's just as likely that bitch lied." Cole glanced at the navigation on the screen, then back at me. "Maybe more likely."

I'd figured we'd find Abraham in a bar, club, or some similar dump, and that Veronica had raided a register, safe, or drug stock to get on his bad side. I sure as shit hadn't envisioned Eternal Sun.

According to the signage on the wall surrounding the place, the sprawling property was a center for health, wellness, and spiritual clarity.

I had no clue what the fuck any of that had to do with Veronica's debt, but when we turned into the gated entryway, the answer became obvious.

It had jack shit to do with it.

She'd lied.

"Want to turn around and hunt her down again?" Cole asked.

I was about to agree when someone approached from a guard booth. Cole rolled down his window.

"Hello," the man greeted in a voice that was too damn chipper. He scanned the car as he spoke. "Visitors?"

Might as well be sure.

"Is Abraham here?" I asked.

"Do you have an appointment?"

"No."

He gave another smile that seemed as freakishly happy as his voice. "Give me a minute to see if he's available."

"This place is kind of creeping me out," Cole muttered when the guard stepped away and pressed his phone to his ear.

I lifted my chin, still not expecting much.

The guard came back and handed two visitor badges through the open window. "Abraham is waiting for you."

"Really?" I asked before I could stop myself.

"He makes time for all who visit Eternal Sun. Continue up this path to our solarium. Have a blessed day."

Cole rolled his window back up and followed the smooth road. "I take it back. This place doesn't kind of creep me out. It fully does."

He wasn't the only one.

Parts of it looked like a nature center. A full garden spread farther than I could see. There were people gathered near a large fountain doing yoga or some shit. A row of small cabins lined the outside edge of the garden near the wall. Other buildings in the distance looked industrial.

Cole slowed in front of a building marked as the solarium. The front of it was all glass, including the roof, before changing into concrete.

"What the fuck is this place?" Cole muttered.

"Got no idea, but I think we're about to find out."

A man in his early fifties stepped out of the glass doors onto the cobblestone landing. In linen pants and button-down, he looked dressed for vacation, not work. His tan skin added to that. When Cole and I climbed from the car, his lips curved down briefly. There and then gone, replaced by a salesman smile. "Blessed afternoon, and welcome to Eternal Sun. I'm Abraham. I heard you wanted to see me."

Still unconvinced this wasn't an attempt to waste my time, I asked, "Do you know a Veronica Rogers?"

His eyes narrowed, and his body language changed as his shoulders pushed back. Despite the fact no one was around to overhear my quietly spoken words, three other men suddenly came from inside the building, all wearing similar linen outfits. The warning in my gut grew when a gust of wind showed at least one of them was strapped.

Abraham held up a hand behind him to stop their approach. "Yes. Roni used to be a member here."

"And *here* is..." Cole prompted, looking around.

"Exactly what the signs say. Eternal Sun is a health and wellness facility that focuses on clearing the dark negativity of the world from people's bodies and spirits."

Riiiiiight.

Since I didn't give a damn about other people's bodies or spirits, I cut to the chase. "I understand Roni owes you money."

That time when the men approached, he didn't try to stop them. They silently flanked his back as he spoke. "Then you also understand that I've been incredibly patient with Ms. Rogers."

No more Roni. It's Ms. Rogers *now.*

"I could—and should have—gone to the police and let them handle her. Instead, I went to her directly as soon as we tracked her down."

I carefully watched his reaction. "And then sent men after her daughter."

His brows shot up, and he didn't attempt to smother his surprise. "I wasn't aware she had a daughter." His skin lost some of the tan. "H-how..." He cleared his throat. "How old is she?"

"Twenty."

His shoulders didn't just relax, they *sagged*. "Well, as I said, I wasn't aware of her existence. Even if I was, I don't send men after anyone."

"Except Veronica."

"I visited her myself, and it was simply to remind her how much better life can be without the dark burdens of lies and secrets." He smiled as he gestured around us. "It's the philosophy I've built the center around, and our members find more fulfillment with those practices than they do with shopping sprees and cheap vodka."

"And her debt was delinquent membership dues?" Cole asked, still as confused with the details as I was.

"No. Ms. Rogers became unsatisfied with Eternal Sun and our personal relationship. She was under the impression that her role in both would be of much more importance."

That doesn't surprise me.

"When the truth became clear to her," he continued, "she took some of our funds as a parting gift when she left."

That also doesn't surprise me.

Abraham's tone grew more cautious. "If the daughter is anything like the mother, then I'd guess there is no shortage of people who would come after her."

"She's not," I said plainly.

A guy in his late twenties came through the door. Like the others, he wore the same linen uniform. Unlike them, he didn't carry himself with the same confidence. His gaze darted around before he called, "Sir."

Abraham flashed that smarmy smile. "My assistant. Give me a moment."

When he moved into the solarium with his three backups, Cole stepped closer. He kept his voice low. "You buy it?"

I thought it over before lifting my chin. "That he didn't know about Mila, yes. The rest? Don't know and don't care. You?"

"I'm still gonna do some research, but my gut says his surprise was genuine."

Which was fucked for a couple of reasons.

First, we were back to square one with finding the fuckers who'd hurt Mila.

Second, I'd just served her up on a silver platter to a man who I was pretty damn certain led a cult and had a grudge against her mother.

"You're paying the debt," Cole surmised.

It wasn't a question, but I answered anyway. To keep any blowback away from Mila, it was an easy choice. "Yup."

Abraham returned, though the others kept their distance again.

Cutting off the exit I knew he was about to make, I got to the point. "I'm willing to pay off Veronica's debt, if you're willing to go back to not knowing about her daughter."

"I'll happily forget they both exist. But it's a considerable debt. Fifty grand."

That fucking bitch stole fifty thousand dollars and then still *pocketed the money she stole from her man and Mila.*

I didn't blink, though I wanted to drive back to Veronica and throttle her. "Get me the account info, and I'll wire it now."

He gestured his assistant over and whispered to him. As the man took off, Abraham looked at me with new interest. "Would you care for a tour while we wait? Our center offers guided yoga and meditation, massages, two Olympic-sized pools with a top-of-the-line steam—"

"We're good," I interrupted before he brought out a Power-Point presentation and contracts with fine print that'd sign my bank accounts away.

Abraham opened his mouth like he was tempted to push it but decided against it. His assistant was back a second later, handing him a note card before disappearing just as fast.

When he handed it to me, I used the info to wire the money from my untraceable account into what I bet was his own untraceable one. When I was done, I held the card out but didn't release my hold. "This is a one-time thing. Rope Veronica back into this shit, it's between you and her. If her daughter so much as gets a brochure in the mail—"

"She won't. I have no interest in dealing with Veronica Rogers ever again." He pocketed the card and looked over as a small group of women walked down the street, waving at him.

Young women in tight leggings paired with sports bras.

He returned his focus to us briefly. "Now if you'll excuse me, it's time for me to lead meditation."

"Yeah, I'm sure it is," Cole muttered.

Happy to get the hell out of there, we returned to the car. I opened the door when Abraham called out again.

"Gentlemen, if you ever change your mind, all are welcome at Eternal Sun. I'm sure Mr. Black could also find some peace and tranquility away from the toxicity of Sin City. Please extend my invitation to your boss. And have a blessed day." With that, he jogged over to the cluster of women.

Since the car is registered to Black Resorts, it'd be easy enough to run the plates. Still fucking weird.

Cole and I locked eyes but didn't speak until we were in the car.

"Now I know why he looked disappointed when he saw us. He was expecting Maximo." I shook my head. "It's enough to give a guy a complex."

Cole rolled his eyes. "I feel like I need to shower off the creepiness."

"And sweep the car for bugs."

His brows rose. "And that."

I didn't see anyone get close to the car, but that didn't mean shit.

I didn't trust Abraham or that fucking place.

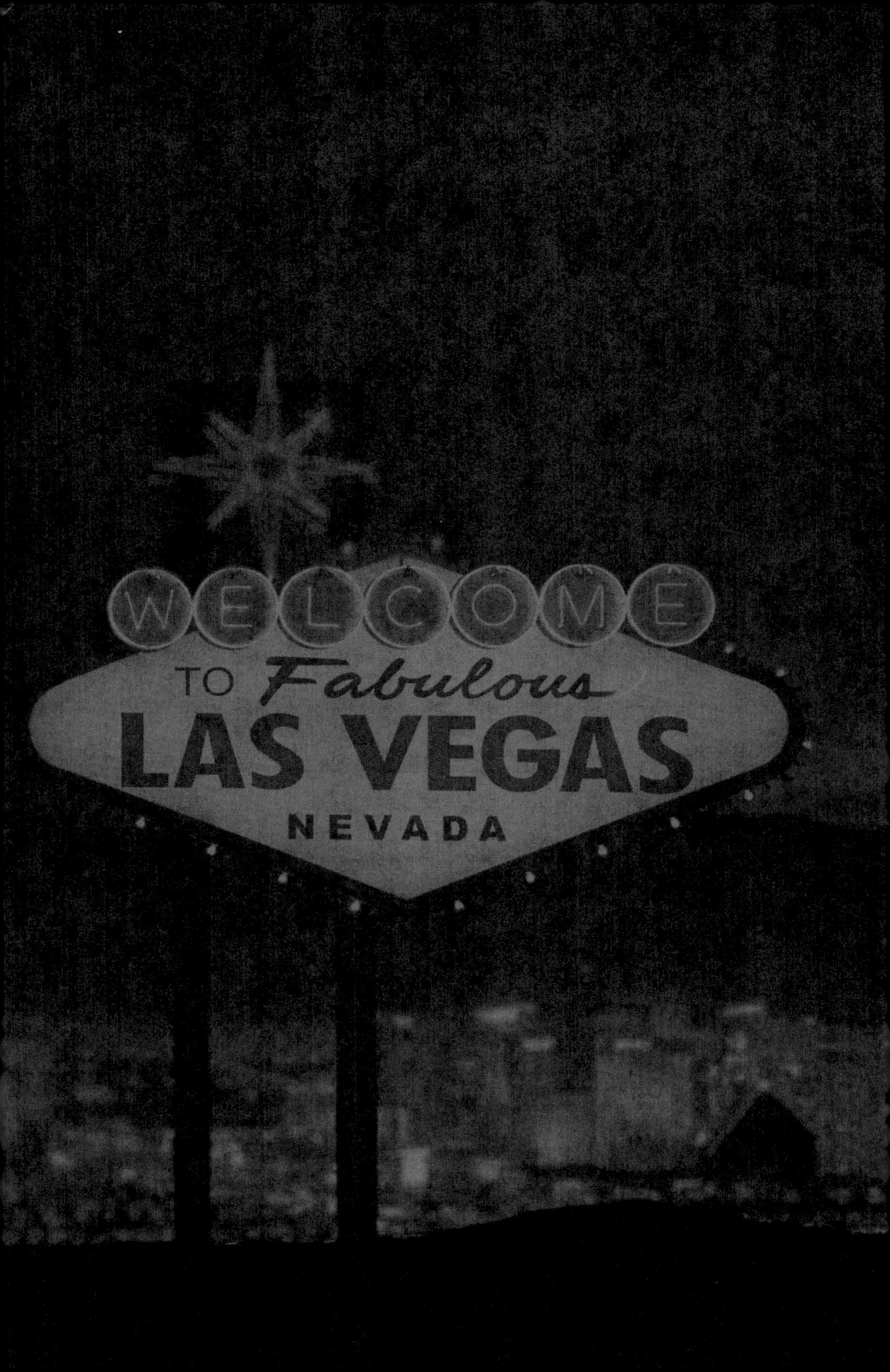
WELCOME
TO Fabulous
LAS VEGAS
NEVADA

CHAPTER 14
HIDE YOUR EMOTIONS
MILA

BY THE TIME THE ELEVATOR dinged, I was in a bad mood.
No.
I was in the *worst* mood.

When Ash had said I was going to work with him, I figured I'd be able to see something. *Do* something.

Instead, he'd locked me in the dull penthouse.

It hadn't made sense. Not at first.

Then it'd hit me.

Given what'd happened at Moonlight, Ash might not trust me. He might not feel comfortable with me around the resort guests at his place of employment. And with all the valuables in his grand house, he might not trust me alone there, either.

A highly secure, barren hotel penthouse was the perfect place to stash me.

As depressing as it was, I couldn't even blame him. Which somehow sucked even worse.

The rest of my bad mood was thanks to the damn iPad I'd returned to out of boredom. After scrolling through the wild number of options, I'd opened a book with a cover of a hot, shirtless man. Unlike the awful mystery I'd tried to read at his house

—which was also weirdly on the iPad—that book had immediately grabbed my attention.

Then overheated me.

Then made me mad.

Because as much as I'd tried to ignore the voice in my head, I hadn't been able to stop thinking about *little dove*. Whether she had the same reaction when she read. Whether she went to Ash to help her.

And whether he kissed her when her thoughts pleaded for it.

By the time the elevator doors slid open, I was already standing. Only it wasn't Ash who stood there. It was his coworker who'd come by the house.

Cole.

"Hey, Mila. Ash is downstairs, so I said I'd come get you."

No alarm bells went off in my head. And based on what I'd seen at the house, he and Ash were friends.

"Okay." I put my shoes on before impulsively grabbing the iPad so I could finish the damn book that I hated to love.

Cole used his thumb to open the elevator doors again, and we stepped inside. Once we were moving, he handed me something. "Your phone."

"Thank..." My words trailed off when I actually looked at it. "This isn't mine."

Not unless his repair skills involve changing out the screen, body, specs, and every other damn thing.

He gave a sheepish smile. "Yeah, sorry, it was too damaged for even my abilities."

I tried to hand it back. "That's fine, I'll figure something out."

"No need. Now you have a new one."

Something about his words made Ash's previous ones float through my head.

Cole will make it good as new.

Realization dawned. "This was his plan all along."

Cole didn't deny it. Nor did his smile look anything but amused. "Take it up with Ash."

"Oh, you better believe I will," I murmured as I looked down at the shiny screen. It was pretty. And a nice gesture.

But nice gestures didn't pay the bills.

My old cell was a piece of shit with spotty service, but it was a piece of shit for a reason. That was what I could afford. If I couldn't add minutes that month, I wasn't locked into a contract that would take the money anyway.

The elevator doors slid open, and I followed Cole into a waiting room that was far nicer than the penthouse. It was a place of business, but I still felt like I should take my shoes off so I didn't track dirt in.

Ash stood in a doorway, his profile to me as he laughed.

I'd never got what people meant when they talked about getting butterflies. It definitely didn't sound like a good thing. Insects flying around someone's stomach sounded like the plot of a bad sci-fi movie.

But as I watched Ash laugh before he rubbed a large, tattooed hand across his beard, I suddenly understood. My belly and heart both seemed to flutter, and it was far from unpleasant.

Unlike the taunting voice that followed. A voice that sounded a lot like my mother.

If he wanted to kiss you, he would've. You were practically begging for it. Instead, he locked you away all day because he knows you don't belong here.

He just pities you, little girl.

With more effort than it ever took, I blanked my mind. It was just in time because Ash glanced over. When he saw me, a dimpled smile spread across his face.

God.

I pushed that down, too, and focused on my irritation. That was easier to deal with. Holding up the cell, I gave it a little shake while I glared.

He just smiled wider.

The ass.

That was an emotion I didn't suppress. "You owe me another five lobster stories, you ass."

He chuckled.

And he wasn't the only one.

Reaching out, he snagged my wrist and pulled me into the expansive office, where two other people stood in front of a wall of security monitors.

With tattoos peeking out from his expensive suit, the man was hot. Not Ash levels of hot, but still. His dark hair was pushed back and slightly disheveled, and his dark eyes were sharp and serious despite the small smile that tipped his lips. I moved my attention from the attractive yet terrifying—or maybe terrifyingly attractive—man to the exceptionally pretty woman in his arms. Her strawberry-blonde hair was pulled into a high ponytail, and she wore a dress that looked a lot like the one I wore.

They both winced as they took in the damage to my face, but she was quicker to hide it. The angry glower he shot at Ash made me inch closer to the behemoth. I wasn't sure if it was an inept attempt to protect Ash or have Ash protect me, but it didn't matter. There was no threat and the man's expression smoothed out.

Ash kept hold of me as he made introductions. "Mila, this is my boss, Maximo Black, and his wife, Juliet."

The one who ran?

She didn't seem like she was there against her will and wanting to escape. With the way she leaned into her husband, I didn't see anything forced about her body language or her smile.

"Uh, hello," I greeted, my cheeks burning red hot. "I, uhh... Sorry."

The woman—Juliet—waved away my apology. "No, no, you're right. They're all asses. A job requirement to work for my husband is they have to be bossy and domineering and heavy-handed—"

"How would you like my heavy hand to make your ass red, dove?" her husband cut in.

My breath caught at the threat, and my alarmed gaze shot to hers. While her eyes were also wide, she didn't look horrified like me.

Not.

At.

All.

With a bat of her lashes, she bit back a smile. "Hey, you hate liars. I can't get in trouble for telling the truth, Daddy."

That time when my breath caught, it wasn't from fear.

It was something much different. Something that settled in my quickened heart, swirling stomach, and areas lower.

Despite his threat, he smiled adoringly down at her, and that made my heart rate go funnier. He said something else that I didn't catch, but it made her cheeks flush.

Not wanting to do or say something stupid, I tore my focus from the couple and looked down. "Oh." I held the iPad out. "I think this is yours."

"Ash said you might like my taste in reading material better than his." She took the tablet and glanced at the screen. "That's one of my favorite books. Major hangover afterward." She offered it back to me. "Do you want to borrow it so you can finish reading?"

And add literary fuel to my already stoked and ready to combust fire?

Hell no.

I shook my head. "Thank you, though."

"Text me the title, and I'll put it on her phone," Ash said.

"No, you won't because I don't have a phone."

Everyone's eyes dropped to the phone I literally held in my hand. When Ash's returned to mine, a smirk pulled at his lips.

I wanted to kiss it off him.

Or maybe shove the cell in his mouth.

I wasn't sure which.

I kept my own mouth shut since I'd already made a mini scene by calling him an ass in front of an audience. I didn't need to make it any worse.

He spoke instead, his smirk changing to a sweet smile. "You ready?"

Between Ash's nearness, my reading material, his boss' interaction with his wife, my hypocritical sadness at his lack of trust, that damn smile, and... Well, everything to do with Ash, I needed to get control of myself before I was stuck in the SUV with him. It didn't matter how big that sucker was, it was still too confined.

"I'm going to pop into the restroom first," I said before facing forward. "It was very nice to meet you Mr. and Mrs. Black—"

"Maximo and Juliet," the man corrected. Although the way he subtly gripped her ass said he liked the reminder they were married.

"Right," I agreed, not that it mattered.

I'd likely never see them again.

Ash

I knew Mila was annoyed.

Her calling me an ass had kinda clued me in.

I'd assumed there'd be worse once we were closed in the elevator, but I got none of the snapped attitude I'd expected.

Wanted.

Craved.

Instead, she'd stood as far off to the side as she could get and stared straight ahead like she wanted to be anywhere but there.

"Mila—" I started.

But the doors chose that moment to slide open, and she hurried out. She slowed after a few steps. A few more, and she stopped altogether. "Where is your car?"

"Getting some work done," I said since that was easier than explaining Cole needed to check it for listening devices.

Her nose crinkled. "Trying to get that awful new car smell out, huh?"

I chuckled before trying again. "Mila—"

That hint of humor was gone just as fast. "Which car?"

I pointed toward a gray Range Rover. "But hold up."

She didn't, hightailing it to the SUV. She tried the door, but it was locked, giving me the chance to box her in with my hands on the roof. She kept her back to me.

"Look at me." When she did, I dropped a hand to her hip to turn her so she faced me.

"I am capable of moving myself. You know that, right? You don't always have to move me how you want me."

That statement and the images it created hardened my dick to the point of pain. I ignored it and focused on her. "Look, I know you're pissed. I get it. But it's a safety thing. And I'll never risk that."

Sadness. Christ, so much fucking sadness filled her blue eyes as she slowly nodded.

Her sass made me hard.

But that expression on her face broke my damn heart.

"You don't have to keep it," I said. "But at least use the phone while you're staying with me."

It wasn't a lie. I just wasn't sharing how long I intended to keep her with me.

Her mouth opened and then closed before opening again. "What?"

Wondering if my assumption was wrong, my eyes narrowed. "Is there something else on your mind?"

"No." She blinked a few times. "I'm just shocked you're compromising."

I wasn't sure which I wanted to do more—swat her smart-ass or find a better way to occupy her smart mouth. Since neither was a possibility yet, I stepped away before I lost that shred of control I had.

I waited until we were in the car before asking, "You got a taste for anything?"

"Not really."

Even if she did, it was unlikely she would tell me.

"Mexican?"

Her expression lit.

"Mexican it is," I said before she tried to lob the decision back to me. I drove in silence for a few minutes. "So... Did you find anything to clean?"

Her brows shot up quickly before she let out a long sigh. "No. For such a fancy hotel, the rooms are really boring."

"Not the rest of them. That's my personal penthouse, so when the last remodel was done, they left it for me to set up how I want. I haven't gotten around to it."

If I thought the mention of Mexican food had excited her, it was nothing compared to her reaction to that. "There are so many possibilities. What do you think you'll do?"

I shrugged. "Haven't thought about it."

"Was it recently remodeled?"

I thought for a second. "Five years ago or so."

Her lips parted, and fuck, I wanted to kiss them.

Fuck, I wanted to do so much more.

I shifted in my seat to hide my growing hard-on. "What was the book you were reading?"

A small squeak escaped her, and her face didn't just flush. It turned bright red, the color spreading to her chest.

I'd asked the innocent question to get my mind off my dick, but her reaction had the opposite effect. Given the books I'd overheard Vera and Juliet talking about, I was no longer just making conversation.

I *needed* to know what Mila had read.

And what part of it she liked so much that it made her blush like that.

She turned away to look out the window. "Nothing really, I mostly flipped through. Juliet has a lot of books. A lot of random ones, too." She took a dramatic pause before glancing my way. "I mostly watched TV."

I slowed to a stop at a red light and gave her my full attention. "What were you watching?"

But I knew. The evil smile that split her face said everything.

"You're a cold-hearted woman."

The evil laugh that followed confirmed it.

"We have to talk."

I'd waited until after Mila had picked at her tacos before starting the conversation that would upset her. Otherwise, she wouldn't have eaten the small amount she had.

She sank back in the secluded booth and crossed her arms as she looked near me. Not *at* me. Her gaze was settled somewhere over my shoulder as she waited.

Elbows to the table, I leaned forward. "I went to see Veronica today." At her lost expression, I clarified, "Your mom."

If Mila's eyebrows could've hit her hairline, they would've. "You know my mother?"

"I do now."

Her lips curved down, and anger radiated from her. "You shouldn't have done that."

"I wasn't trying—"

But her anger wasn't aimed at me or my interference. "Veronica Rogers is a succubus. She digs her claws into everyone in her orbit and bleeds them dry. I don't want her trying to drag you into her problems."

Too late.

I didn't tell her that. If Mila had been that upset about a phone, I didn't know how she'd react to finding out I'd paid her mother's debt.

And I sure as fuck didn't want to find out.

"That won't happen," I stated since that was the truth. "But you gotta know, she didn't have you attacked."

She scoffed. "Let me guess... She batted her fake lashes, pushed her tits out, and claimed she'd *never* do something so vile?"

Pretty much except she claimed she didn't even have a daughter because she's a moronic cunt.

I didn't tell her that, either. "We checked her story. When you were supposed to meet, she was in the middle of getting dumped."

Hope filled Mila's eyes before she worked to tamp it down. "She has my money?"

No, she spent it on herself.

I lifted my chin anyway since I would give her the money—and anything else she wanted.

"I can't believe this." Genuine shock filled her face. "It really wasn't her?"

My folks weren't good parents.

They were the fucking best.

I was tight with them and all four of my sisters. My dad sent hockey scores like I couldn't just check ESPN. My ma still threatened to come cook me chicken soup every time I was sick.

If they weren't spending their retirement RVing across the country, she probably would've.

I couldn't imagine either of them would accidentally hurt me, much less suspecting they'd purposefully set me up to be hurt. But Mila had truly believed it because it was plausible.

Which was its own kind of jacked up.

"She had no clue," I answered. "Showed up later, but you were gone."

The hint of happiness disappeared quickly, and blankness took over. When she caught me watching her, she forced a smile. "So it was just an ordinary, run-of-the-mill mugging? Boring."

I hated to make her relive it, but we had nothing else to go on. And from the haunted look on her face, I got the feeling she was already thinking about those bastards. "Tell me more about what happened."

Grabbing a tortilla chip from the basket, she broke it in pieces over her plate as she gave only slightly more detail than what I knew. "There were two guys. One was tall and lanky. He had this"—she wiggled her fingers under her nose—"awful pube facial hair. He was blond, I think? Or light brown. He only got close to me for a minute. The rest of the time, he just, uh, watched." When she'd turned the first one to dust, she sat forward and grabbed another chip but just held it.

Stared at it.

"Sunshine."

She jolted at my voice.

"We can st—"

"No, it's fine." Sweeping at imaginary crumbs on the table, she peeked up at me shyly. "I was just trying to figure out how to politely phrase that he had tiny-dick energy."

It was a fucked time to laugh, but I couldn't stop myself.

Thankfully, that made Mila relax, and she leaned back again. "The other guy called him Ease. Or Ezz. Something like that. He was shorter than the other guy but still probably around five-ten. Kind of muscular, kind of bulky. Dark hair. Mean." She shivered. "*Really* mean. He's the one who..." She forced a smile as she tossed the chip down. "At least I get the satisfaction of knowing it was a pointless mugging since all they got was my license and debit card with nothing on it."

"What?"

Mila fidgeted with her hands and fake laughed. "Not actually *nothing*—"

"They stole your license?"

"Didn't I tell you?"

"All the details of your *car accident*? No, sunshine, you weren't exactly forthcoming."

"Yeah," she drawled, scrunching her nose. "Sorry."

I didn't bother to tell her she apologized too much since she would just apologize for that, too. Pulling my phone from my pocket, I shot off a text to Cole before pocketing it again.

I watched Mila stack the dishes and tidy up the table and do basically everything to avoid looking at me.

That need deep in my chest pounded closer to the surface. Like an itch I couldn't scratch. Not right then.

Maybe never.

Mila fought me on every-damn-thing. There was a good possibility that she wouldn't ever let me take care of her. That she wouldn't hand over her submission and let me worry about everything else.

That she wouldn't want me to be her Daddy.

I was coming outta my damn skin.

I sat in the loft with my untouched drink. I had no fucking clue what was happening on the muted baseball game or with the files I was supposed to be going over. My mind was on Mila.

My mind was always on Mila.

The same traits that made me good at my job—the way I fixated and obsessed, going over every variable and outcome—had made her the target.

Unfortunately for me and my fucked-up brain, Mila didn't share that driving need to be around me. When we'd gotten home from dinner, she hadn't wanted to watch one of her shows with me. She'd barely muttered good night before locking herself in the bedroom. After the conversation we'd had, I got her need for space. And since my control was close to snapping, I'd wanted to give it to her.

For one night.

I'd made it a few hours.

That was close enough.

Mila wasn't due for any meds, so I didn't have that excuse to fall back on if she woke up, but I didn't care. I needed to make sure she was okay.

That she wasn't having another nightmare that emotionally shook her until she literally shook.

That she hadn't moved around so much, she'd fallen out of bed.

I needed to see her.

Like the first night when I'd checked on her without her knowledge, I felt no hesitancy. No doubt. No guilt. The only reason I paused outside the door was to listen for the TV or movement.

When there was nothing but silence, I turned the knob.

Fuck.

Locked.

If I was a good man, that would've been the end of it.

But I'd never been a quitter.

Jogging downstairs, I hunted around my office and then the junk drawer in the kitchen for the small key that unlocked the bedroom from the outside. Finally finding it, I went upstairs and popped the lock before slowly pushing the door open.

Moving quietly across the room, I stopped next to the bed. In the soft light, I could see everything.

Putting in a night-light was a genius idea.

Mila's body was stretched across the horizontal length of the mattress with one arm under a pillow and the blanket covering her side. Her other leg was kicked out, her sleep shorts barely covering her pussy. Her hard nipples pressed against the thin material of her top.

In my whole damn life, I'd never wanted anyone as badly as I wanted Mila. My control had never been so dangerously close to slipping.

My dick had never been so hard.

Fuck it.

I'm already heading to hell anyway.

Might as well upgrade to a first-class ticket.

Shoving my hand into my shorts, I fisted my cock and squeezed. There wasn't enough room in the confined space, but I ran my hand along the length as best as I could. That was all I'd intended to do. It was already too much. But the longer I looked down at her, the more I stroked until I needed to tug the stretchy waistband down to free myself.

I held the material out of the way with one hand while my other wrapped around the base. I slowly moved up, circling around the head and choking back a moan.

Mila's words from the garage echoed in my head, but I didn't shut them down like I'd done earlier.

I let them run wild.

'You don't always have to move me how you want me.'

I thought of all the ways I'd pick her up and move her. Positioning her exactly where I wanted her. Tying her there. I thought about how she'd let me.

How she'd beg for more.

Beg for *me*.

It took every-damn-thing I had to stop from coming on that pretty pussy, those perfect tits, or her beautiful face.

Once she was mine, I would do it.

But I didn't want the first time I saw my cum splattered across her skin to be when she was asleep. I wanted it to be when she was awake and begging me for it.

Tucking myself away with a soft hiss, I carefully covered her, checking to make sure she was away from the edge. With one last look, I left, going straight to the en suite in the guest room I was using.

After adjusting the temperature of the water to match the fiery flames of hell waiting for me, I barely entered the shower before wrapping my fist around my cock.

It was embarrassingly fucking fast how soon my balls tightened, the pressure building until my cum hit the wall in front of me. My hand shot out, slapping the tile to stop me from face-planting as my vision returned to normal.

Like every other time I'd jacked off that week, the orgasm took the edge off.

But it wasn't enough.

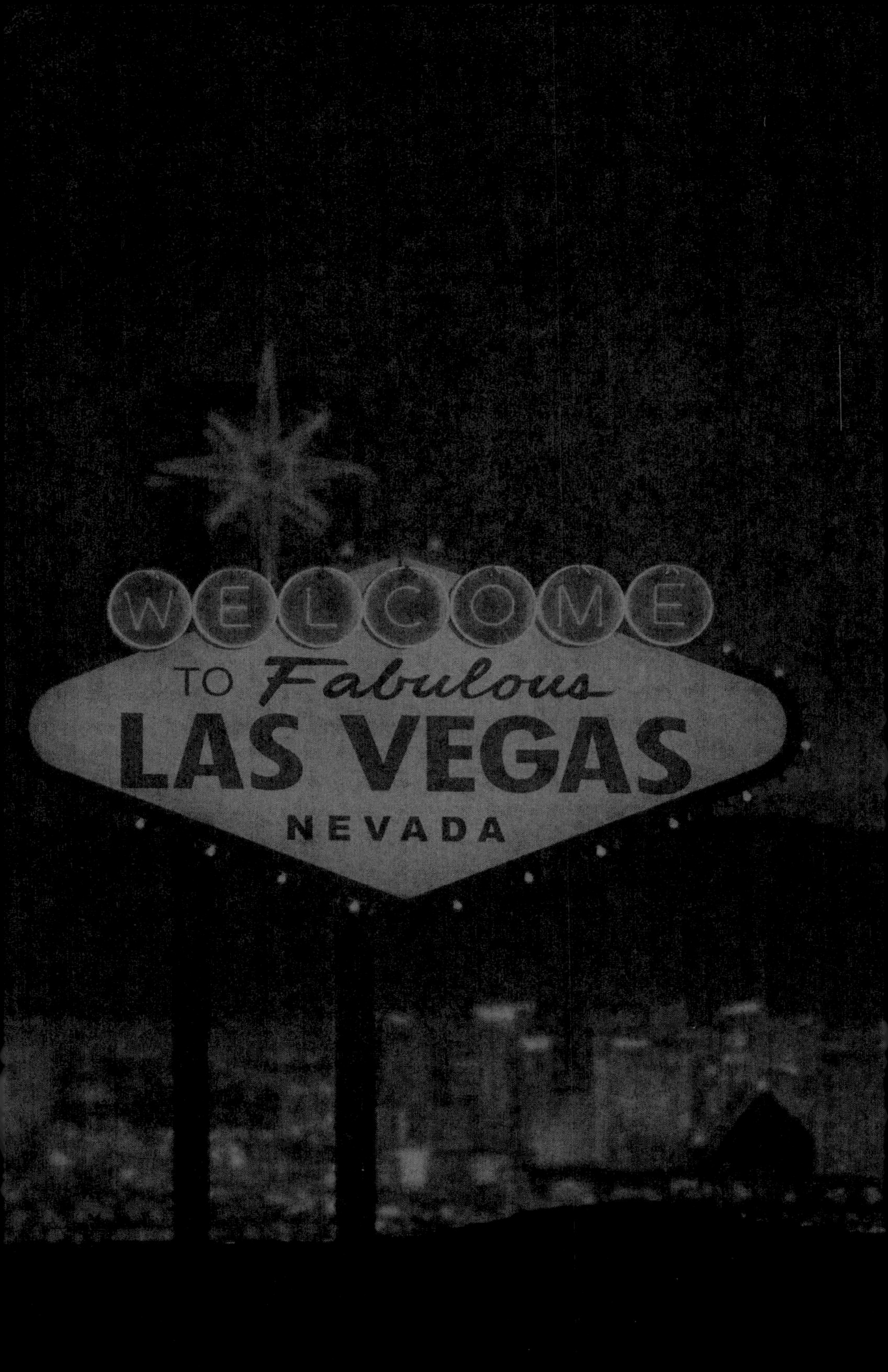
WELCOME
TO Fabulous
LAS VEGAS
NEVADA

CHAPTER 15
EXPECT THE WORST, AND YOU'LL NEVER BE DISAPPOINTED
MILA

"Easy, sunshine, it's just me."

Cracking a lid, I peeked up to see Ash sitting close in one of his pristine suits.

After getting back from the best Mexican food to ever touch my tongue—which wasn't hard when the competition was frozen burritos and value menu Taco Bell, but still—I'd done the smart thing.

I'd locked myself in the bedroom like a coward. *Alone.*

Veronica hadn't been behind the attack and, even more shocking, she'd repaid my money. There was no nefarious plot. It'd been random bad luck—the only kind I ever had.

I would still stay for another couple of days if Ash let me, but pretend time was officially nearing an end. I would be able to return to my apartment. Maybe get a new one if I found a job quick enough.

I could move on.

Which meant I needed to prepare for that. No more binging shows with Ash. No more sleeping in bed with him.

No more building up fantasies in my head that his tender affection meant he wanted to kiss me.

He'd had enough opportunities and hadn't. Not only did I need to get the message, I needed to reread it until it sank in.

I also needed to find out why the door was no longer locked, and I was no longer alone.

I tried to rub the sleep from my eyes, but my wrist was firmly in his grasp.

"You're quick with that right hook." Ash released me when I gave my arm another tug. "You ever think about joining the boxing circuit?"

Since I had the upper body strength of an overcooked spaghetti noodle, I would've laughed at that hilarious joke had it not been for the fact my brain and sense of humor were both still asleep.

"What's going on?" I croaked.

"Hate to wake you, but we've got to get to Moonlight."

"'Kay, have fun." I flopped back, my eyes already closed. I knew it wasn't that early, but after a restless night—filled with sexy yet unsatisfactory dreams—I was still exhausted.

"You're coming with me."

I caught myself before I asked why. It was likely the same reason he'd brought me to Sunrise the day before, and some suspicions were better left unconfirmed.

"Get ready, and I'll make you breakfast for the ride," Ash said.

I waved my hand and listened to his retreating chuckle before I bolted upright to call, "And coffee!"

After a quick shower, I came out to find another sundress on the bed. I scowled down at it.

It wasn't that there was anything wrong with it. It was lovely.

But I would never be able to repay Ash. Adding even more to my tab made my stomach clench like debt collectors were already calling.

I walked by the bed and went to the closet to find my shorts and hoodie from the first day. They weren't exactly chic, but I wasn't going to Moonlight as a guest. Even if I was, there was always a mix of overdressed, underdressed, and barely dressed in Vegas.

And since I'd likely be stuck in a room or penthouse again, what I wore didn't matter.

Except my clothes weren't in there. A few other floral dresses and skirt sets were hung on the mostly empty rack next to Ash's loaded side.

The man had a lot of suits.

Not wanting to be an ungrateful *brat*, I hurried to get dressed before I made Ash late.

"Ready?"

I hadn't even realized we'd parked until Ash had spoken.

Reaching over, he undid my seat belt and turned me to face him. "You feeling okay?"

"Just tired," I said. He likely wouldn't have believed the lie—he rarely did—if it weren't for the actual yawn that accompanied my claim.

He climbed from the SUV and came around to open my door. His hand stayed on my lower back as we entered the lobby.

Walking through Moonlight was a completely different experience that time.

I was still out of place among the gamblers, tourists, and glitz, but it didn't matter. I wasn't trying to fit in. I didn't need to avoid security. Ash was there to work, and I was there because...

Well, because he'd said so.

He steered me toward a private elevator, and as we rode up, my stomach and heart fell. I mentally prepared for another day alone.

I should've taken Juliet up on her offer to borrow the iPad.

I thought about my reaction to the book and the dreams it'd caused.

Never mind.

Sure enough, the elevator stopped at another penthouse. We stepped out, and Ash immediately turned back around. I thought he was going to make a quick escape like at Sunrise, but he tapped some buttons on a control panel as he spoke. "The bedroom is through the door on the right. There's a full bath in there, too. There's a large pool downstairs, but there's also a small infinity pool out on the balcony."

"All the way up here?" I didn't mind heights and would actually be intrigued if I knew how to swim. But I was pretty sure I'd want to see when it was last inspected and check the builder's credentials before I even dipped a toe in.

As if it wasn't an insane feature to have, Ash simply raised his chin. "Room service menu is on the kitchen counter near the phone, but if you want something from one of the restaurants, text me and I'll have it sent up."

"I don't—"

Ash took a cell from his pocket and tossed it onto a little table. "You've got my number, plus Cole's and Marco's. If you can't get through to me, text one of them. Juliet Black's number is also in there. She's here today and driving me fucking nuts wanting to hang out with you."

"What? *Why?*"

"I'm guessing she wants a friend who isn't a goon."

"What's a goon?" I asked.

"Me." He grinned. "And Marco and Cole, but I'm the best one." Grabbing my wrist, he pressed my thumb to the scanner, touched a few buttons, and pressed it again. "If you don't want to hang with Juliet, I'll tell her to drop it. But I think you'd like her. You have a lot in common."

I didn't know what I could have in common with his boss' pretty, glamorous wife other than possibly our ages.

"I'll text her," I said because the idea of staying cooped up all day made me claustrophobic.

My motives were selfish, but the pleased smile Ash shot me would've made me agree to it anyway.

Because I was an idiot.

Needing to break the spell, I turned and studied the kitchen like it was the most interesting one I'd ever seen. It didn't last long, and Ash wrapped a hand around my hip to turn me back.

I'd heard wild, mystical tales that there were some people who were just comfortable with physical touch. Ash was definitely one of them. Usually, I didn't mind it.

Fine, I liked it.

But things were different.

"Did you forget that I said I could move myself?" I snapped.

"Nope, I remember," he said, though his hand stayed right where it was. "Your print is in the system now, so you can come and go. Text me before you leave the room. And if I text you, I expect an answer."

I tried to twist away from him, but he grabbed my chin. Since I was still in the process of moving, his fingers squeezed my cheeks, forcing my lips to part. He bit out something that was rough and quiet, but I couldn't hear what over the blood rushing in my ears.

I'd literally spent the night harshly reminding myself that my crush on Ash was stupid and a disaster waiting to happen. The mean voice in my head had helpfully added that I was pathetic for misconstruing his pity in the first place.

After *everything*, I would've thought some sense of self-preservation would kick in.

It didn't.

I held my breath. Waiting. Hoping.

Needing.

And again, I felt like a silly little fool when all he did was drop his hand and say, "I mean it. I don't care if you're just running down for a coffee and a hand of blackjack. You text me, sunshine."

Since distance wasn't possible with his firm hold still on my hip, I crossed my arms to put some space between us. The fact it also hid my hardened nipples was just a bonus. "Adding a cute nickname doesn't undo your bossiness."

"Get used to it, little girl."

"And that *not* cute nickname definitely isn't helping."

"Get used to it, too." Letting me go, Ash stepped into the elevator.

"Maybe instead of owing me lobster stories, I'll go back to junk punches."

A smirk curved his mouth. There was an edge to it that kind of scared me. But mostly, it thrilled me in a way that *definitely* scared me.

As did his rumbled, "Can't wait."

And then the door slid closed.

I SHOULD TELL *her something came up.*

Or that I'm ill.

I'll say it's my stomach. No one *asks follow-up questions about that.*

After Ash left for work, I'd checked out the penthouse to see it was as barren as the one at Sunrise. There was no real color to the primer beige palette. Not many furnishings. Even less decor.

But it had a freaking balcony pool.

It was a sad waste of potential.

Juliet's iPad had been sitting on the table again, but I hadn't touched it. My hormones didn't need the smutty boost.

When there'd been nothing else to see—and I'd stalled for as long as possible—I'd finally texted Juliet.

I'd wondered if Ash had been exaggerating her interest in hanging out with me. Based on the multitude of texts she'd quickly responded with, though, it seemed like he'd been underselling it.

I'd never had a lot of friends. Even as a little kid, it'd been too hard to explain why their lovingly concerned parent couldn't talk to mine before I came over for a playdate. Or why I could *never* have them over to my house. It'd been easier to keep everyone at arm's length.

The instant I'd agreed to meet her at the pool, regret and my nerves had kicked into overdrive. Juliet wasn't just some random coworker or acquaintance. She was Ash's boss' wife. If I did something wrong—and, let's face it, I was likely to put my foot directly into my mouth—it wouldn't just be an awkward disaster to suppress from my memories. It could have ramifications for Ash.

Hence my mental freak-out as I rode down the elevator.

The door opened, and I stepped out onto the first floor. Juliet had offered to meet me, but I'd assured her I could manage. There was more than enough signage to make her detailed directions unnecessary.

With my focus elsewhere, it took me longer than it should've to realize I was being followed. Acting like I was just taking in the lights and excitement, I glanced quickly over my shoulder to see a uniformed security guard walking a few steps behind.

My chest tightened.

My palms began to sweat.

Anxiety skittered down my spine like a million tiny spiders.

Turning a corner, I looked back again to see he still followed. With my luck, he'd been there to witness my pickpocketing and was about to belatedly bust me.

Run.

Holy shit, run.

It'll make a scene, but getting hauled into the security office would be far worse.

I inhaled deep, slowly releasing the breath as I reminded myself that I was allowed to be there. That I wasn't doing anything wrong.

That I wasn't back in the past.

It's nothing. He's probably coincidentally headed the same way as me. He isn't actually following me.

And if he is, it's probably to make sure I don't sneak onto a slot machine.

I pushed outside, and the warm sun heated my clammy face. I inhaled slow and deep as I took a path past a drink stand and towel racks, hoping the fresh air would help.

It didn't.

Another peek showed security continued to trail me. But his focus was aimed elsewhere as he scanned around.

Oh. Duh. He's probably on patrol or whatever it's called.

It wasn't an overly hot day, but the pool area was packed. Loud laughter and conversation filled the courtyard to create a constant dull rumble. Every cabana seemed to be rented out. Kids splashed around and squealed near a fountain in the middle of the pool. Clusters of people lounged, floated in the pool, chased their kids, drank icy cocktails, and chased their kids *while* drinking icy cocktails. I thought finding Juliet would be impossible, but she stood alone in a far corner.

Weird.

When I hurriedly approached, I saw why the crowd wasn't near her.

Because it couldn't be.

A whole section of the deck was closed off around her. A small cabana was behind her, but a couple of loungers were out in the sun.

I felt like I was lined up to gawk at a celebrity. She was certainly pretty enough to be one. The floral cover-up she wore over her white bikini had slid down one shoulder. It was very classic Hollywood. I was glad that I hadn't been able to find my torn shorts and hoodie after all. I was intimidated enough, making me second—or third or twentieth—guess myself.

But I continued forward since ghosting people was wrong.

For some reason.

I still might've done it if I hadn't known she wanted to see me. Her enthusiastic texts had made that clear even before I watched her scan the crowd. Once her gaze landed on me, she grinned wide and waved me over. As soon as I got close enough, she opened the barrier and greeted me like we were best friends. "Mila! I'm so glad you're here."

"Me, too." And it wasn't even a lie.

Not a full one.

Or maybe just not yet.

"Sit. Sit." Like a natural hostess, Juliet waited until I sat before she did, too. She reached behind her to grab something off the lounger, moving it onto a small wicker cube. I didn't pay too much attention until she asked, "Did you finish it yet?"

"Finish what?"

She gestured to the iPad she'd just moved—obviously one in a collection since another sat in Ash's penthouse. "The book you started yesterday."

I shook my head. "I, uh, haven't had time."

"I hope you can finish it soon. Then we can talk about it after." She smiled again. "Like a book club."

"That'd be fun." I meant it, too. Even if I barely knew her, there was already something likable about Juliet.

A gut feeling that was proven correct the longer we talked. She peppered me with questions without making it an interrogation.

My favorite food.

My favorite color.

What I liked to do for fun.

Superficial things that were far easier to answer than ones about my family, my past, or even my future.

And I got the feeling that was exactly why she was doing it.

Juliet was even more glamorous up close. Her hair was in another high ponytail, and she had a smattering of freckles across her face. She was a couple of inches taller than me, but she wore her confidence in a way that made her seem taller. Older, too.

People likely took one look at her and assumed she was vapid. An attractive face with not much happening behind her eyes. A trophy wife in a white bikini and floral cover-up. That she was…

Dumb.

They probably thought she was dumb as a rock garden and twice as nice to look at.

But they would be wrong. And dumb themselves for underestimating her. A sharpness in her green eyes seemed to take in everything around her.

It made me remember Ash's claim that Juliet and I had a lot in common. I wondered about who she was beyond just cheery and sweet. Since I didn't want to answer any probing questions, I also didn't ask them.

I wanted to, though.

She moved the iPad off the cube and opened it to reveal it was actually a cooler. Grabbing two water bottles, she handed me one and kept the other for herself.

I took a refreshing sip.

"Last time I was out here and didn't hydrate enough, I ended up with a major dehydration headache and a sore, spanked ass."

And then I choked on the refreshing sip.

"Sorry," she said, though she didn't look it in the least. "I figured I'd address the elephant in the room. Or the Daddy."

My body heated in a way that had nothing to do with the Vegas sun and everything to do with thoughts of Ash.

Because, again, I was an idiot.

"I saw your surprise about Maximo and me, and I didn't want it to be a whole *thing*." Juliet's words might have been nonchalant and conversational, but the way she watched me was anything but.

She's definitely more perceptive than she lets on.

I had no issue other than a swirl of jealousy so strong, it might as well have turned my skin green.

Since those were my own problems and not a judgment of her life, it was easy to keep my expression neutral. She didn't volunteer any more information, and I didn't want to push. Well, I wanted to, but I wouldn't. I did allow myself to ask one thing because otherwise, I might've died of curiosity.

I might die from the answer, too.

"Does Ash...? Like, is he...?"

"A Daddy?" At my nod, she shrugged. "No idea."

That doesn't help.

With that in the open, the conversation returned to lighter topics, and we both relaxed.

A while—and two bottles of water—later, Juliet's phone rang. A content smile pulled at her mouth. "It's my husband." She sighed. "I'll be right back."

When she stepped into the cabana, I stood because she wasn't the only one getting a call. In my case, though, it wasn't a gorgeously devoted husband calling.

It was nature.

I left her little corner of solitude and weaved through the crowd. That time, it didn't take me long to realize I was being trailed again. A quick look behind me proved it was the same man.

What the hell?

In case Juliet was off the phone and watching, I didn't acknowledge security. I didn't want to bring him to her attention. I definitely didn't want her to witness a confrontation that might or might not involve accusations of a wallet I might or might not have stolen. I played it cool. I didn't make a scene. I lifted my chin and kept walking.

"Miss Price."

That was harder to ignore. I stumbled and barely caught myself before I flopped into the pool.

Did I imagine that?

Like I'd spoken the question aloud, the man repeated, "Miss Price."

I spun my freaked-out gaze his way.

The older man smiled and gestured toward the row of doors on the far side of the building. "The restrooms are through there."

I could've come up with a million reasons to explain why he followed me. But his knowledge and use of my name narrowed it down to one.

Ash sent him.

I'd already suspected Ash didn't trust me. Hell, on some level I'd been suppressing, I knew he didn't.

But the confirmation nearly took me to my knees.

And that was what finally did it. What killed my crush. What hardened my stupid heart.

What severed the glimmer of hope that there could be something more.

There would *never* be more.

It wasn't just the confirmation that Ash trusted me so little that he had security follow me.

It was because he was *right* to feel that way.

We'd met when I'd tried to steal a wallet. He didn't even know about all the times I'd succeeded.

That I'd gotten attacked and was able to play pretend for a while didn't change anything. Not who I was or what I'd done.

People like me could venture into the opulence. Our buses could pull next to the chauffeured cars. Our penny slots could be right outside the high roller rooms. Our simple burger restaurants could be down the hall from the upscale steakhouses, where the overpriced meals didn't even include sides.

The windows of our budget hotels—The Roulette and others like it—may have faced the same direction as their luxury resorts, but the views were not the same.

We could be in the middle of it. We could enter and spend time there, but it wasn't for us. We didn't belong.

We belonged in the slums and dives and abandoned blocks. Where trash lined the ditches, windows were boarded over, and apartment elevators never worked.

Where stale crackers and peanut butter were a treat.

My skin suddenly felt too tight. The pit in my stomach grew to a bottomless abyss. Mortification froze me in place. I probably looked like a deer caught in the headlights.

It would've been comical had it not been for the fact my pride was no longer wounded.

It was eviscerated into nothingness.

Before I could figure out what to do, the man's gaze went

behind me. I turned to look at the far end near the doors I'd come out of.

Like a torpedo locked on its target, Ash stared me down as he easily made his way through the crush of people who darted out of his path.

With security distracted and Ash headed right for me, I did the only thing I could.

I ran away.

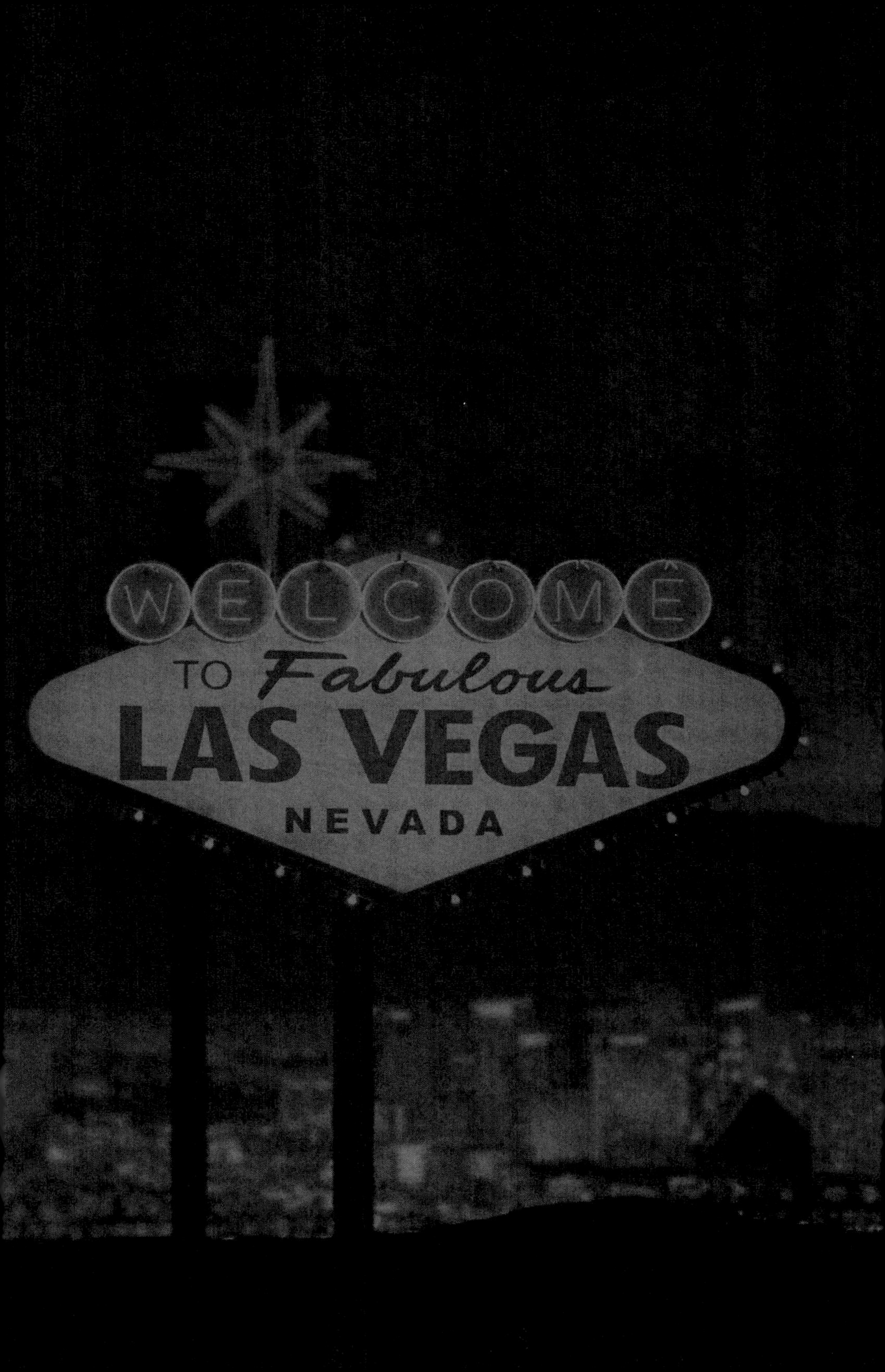
WELCOME
TO Fabulous
LAS VEGAS
NEVADA

CHAPTER 16
NEVER MIND, YOU'LL STILL BE DISAPPOINTED
ASH

After getting Mila set up in my penthouse, I went down to Maximo's office.

Cole was already on the couch with two laptops—one opened on his lap and the other on the coffee table in front of him. He had his screen shared to one of the monitors on Maximo's stalker wall.

"Hope you've got your messages turned off before a sext pops up," I joked.

"Yeah, that won't happen," Cole said with a dismissive laugh. His clenched jaw said he didn't find it all that amusing.

Huh.

Since the screen next to it showed Juliet in their own penthouse, I asked my boss, "Juliet know we're watching? *Us*, not just you."

Because the one time she hadn't known, she'd flashed the camera. None of us had seen much, but that hadn't stopped Maximo from wanting to stab our eyes out.

It wouldn't be the first time he'd done it after someone looked at Juliet.

"Yeah, she knows. She's ordering fabric, so she's unlikely to move in the next four hours or so." He tapped his pen on the desk. "Your woman going to get in contact? Juliet has been talking about it all morning."

I lifted a shoulder. "She said she will, but who knows."

Juliet might have the entire world at her feet now, but she came from almost nothing. It'd been better than Mila had, but not by much. Having someone who got it could be good for Mila. Especially if she lost her mind enough to let me be her Daddy. I would go slow and ease her in, but she would likely still have questions, and it would be helpful to have Juliet.

After Mila told me the pricks had taken her license, I'd texted Cole to see if he could check SafeCams near her apartment in case they had showed up to finish what they'd started.

Despite the fact she lived in an especially shitty area, there'd been none around for him to hack. It'd sat in my gut like a cereal bowl of razor blades and salt water, but I'd thought that was the end. We had nothing else to go on.

My plan had been to give it a few more days while Cole added better security in Mila's building and her apartment. That way, if she told me to fuck off, her place would be safe to return to while I figured out my next steps.

After checking on her during the night, though, I hadn't been sure I could hold off even those few days. That was why I'd been glad to wake up to a text from Cole that he might have something.

I looked at the screen he shared. "What's up?"

"You know me, I don't accept technological defeat easily, so Marco and I took a drive over to her neighborhood last night to see if there was a doorbell camera or something else I could tap into. Which, first off, her building is even worse than the already bad I expected. Don't let her go back to that shithole. But diagonal from it is a liquor store. We gently persuaded them to hand over all their exterior security footage in exchange for us staying quiet about what they really sell."

"What do they really sell?"

He shrugged. "No idea. But even in Vegas, no legit store

needs that many 4K res cameras." He clicked his mouse, and the image on the monitor changed. "This is the only one with a good angle of the front of her building. I wasn't sure whether you'd rather bring her down here to go through the footage or do it privately."

I pictured her reaction at dinner. How pale she'd become when she'd gotten lost in her memories.

If just thinking about them had shaken her, I didn't want to force her to see them. Not unless there was no other option.

I also didn't want to get her hopes up if nothing came from it.

Since she'd described them to me, I said, "Let's roll through it first."

"This is set about twenty minutes before she came into Moonlight. Unless the assholes can teleport, this should cover it." He tapped a button to roll the footage at an increased speed, slowing it when someone neared her building. It was mostly residents, a few lost tourists, more than a few prostitutes or dealers, and other people walking past.

The later it got, the less frequently he had to slow it. The timestamp showed it was after two o'clock when someone came into view, and I sat forward.

"Go back a few seconds."

Cole rewound the video until right before he came into frame. I watched as the man looked over his shoulder and then kept his head down as he walked into the building. A couple of minutes later, he exited again.

My gaze kept landing on the timestamp.

If she would've gone home... Thank Christ she agreed to stay with me.

"That was an efficient drug deal, lightning-speed sex, or—"

My gut, the hairs on the back of my neck, and Mila's vague description all said the same thing I said out loud. "It's him."

It was obvious that Mila had been born with shit luck. But that was before me.

Because the angle when he'd entered hadn't given much to work with, but when he left was a different matter.

Rather than heading back the same way he'd come, he went in the opposite direction.

Right by the cameras.

Cole took a screengrab and cropped it. He grabbed his other computer, his fingers typing rapidly. "Come on. Come on." It didn't take long before he whooped. "Got ya, fucker." He switched back to the laptop with the shared screen just as a text popped into the corner.

> Freddy: I'm at Moonlight, where are you?

There was nothing unusual about it, which didn't explain the frantic way Cole clicked it closed.

Other than a quick look between us, neither Maximo nor I said shit as we pretended we hadn't seen it.

What everyone did was their own business.

Cole cleared his throat. "Allow me to introduce Edward Zale." A mug shot popped up of a loser trying to be a tough guy.

"You want to bring this up to Mila to confirm?" Maximo asked.

I shook my head. "That's him. Edward Zale. Ez. The rest matches her description, too, right down to the tiny-dick energy. Now we just need the partner."

"I might have him, too." Cole brought up another mug shot. "His roommate and known associate, Ronald Jacobs."

"Just as she described him, including the pube mustache."

"You know, your woman has a real way with words."

I grinned. "Almost poetic."

"It's scary how quick you find this shit," Maximo said to Cole as he looked between the computers and monitor.

"Where Big Brother has eyes, so do I. And since Big Brother has eyes everywhere..."

"Glad you're on my side."

"As you should be." My phone dinged before Cole told me, "Address is sent."

Maximo stood. "Then let's go."

LITTLE SUNSHINE

"Your girl finally texted mine. Don't think I've ever seen Juliet use so many exclamation points in a single message."

I glanced at Maximo before returning my focus to the run-down door in the run-down motel that rented rooms by the hour or the week, and nothing between. "Good."

"Juliet's already at the pool, and Mila is headed there now."

I checked my phone. I already knew I hadn't missed a text, but I wanted to give her the benefit of the doubt.

It was the least I could do since, if all went right, her cute ass would be paying the price for ignoring my order.

"You got Miles keeping an eye on her?" Maximo asked.

I shook my head as I shot off a text. "He was at Moonlight for the wallet incident, so she'd be uncomfortable. But Marco and Miles both suggested Elliot, so he's on his way to meet her."

"Marco is headed out, too." He gestured around. "Between this and Juliet's love of mischief, I figured an extra set of eyes would be good."

Especially since we had no clue how long we'd be sitting there, waiting for Zale and Jacobs to show.

The fact that Maximo was staked out at the Bed Bug Motel with me said a lot about the kind of man he was. None of it was his problem. I was the employee there. Assisting him was my job, not the other way around. He didn't have to be there. Hell, with all the money he had, he didn't have to work at all. He could move to an island and sit on the beach all day.

Technically, so could I, but the point was the same.

Maybe I was becoming a sentimental asshole in my old age because I looked over at him and said, "You know... Out of all the bosses in the world, you're probably not the worst one."

"Wow," he deadpanned. "I wish I had that in writing to frame in my office."

"You're welcome."

"We'll see if you still feel the same when I've gotta take a piss in your empty coffee cup."

I threw my arms up as best as I could in the small space. "Way to ruin a beautiful moment."

Before Maximo could apologize—or, more likely, *try* to fire me—my phone beeped.

> Marco: Your girl is outside, and she doesn't look good.

My gut clenched.

> Me: Not good how?

> Marco: Off. Shaken. Want me to talk to her or should you?

I was pretty sure I knew what was up, but I wouldn't risk it. I was about to call her when another text came through.

> Marco: Never mind, she seems okay. Nervous.

That was exactly what I'd figured.

> Me: Let me know if it changes.

A while later, as a whole lot of nothing was happening on our side, Marco was having better luck.

> Marco: Juliet is playing wingwoman and grilling Mila about shit she likes. I'm taking notes for you.

Christ, between everything the three of them are doing, a man could almost cry.

Too bad I gotta look like a scary motherfucker, and that's hard to do with bloodshot eyes and dripping snot.

"I owe your wife," I said.

"This about Juliet playing investigator? She told me she was going to try."

"I'll give her a Get-Out-Of-A-Snitch-Free card."

"What the fuck?" He lifted his hands. "What happened to your gratitude toward me?"

"Yeah, well, then you threatened to piss in my coffee cup."

Another message came through, and I expected Marco's demands for the insider info, but it was Cole.

> Cole: Tracked down an active number for Ronald Jacobs. Don't ask how, and if the FBI comes around, I was with you.
>
> Cole: Location Loading

When the map loaded, I turned my phone toward Maximo. "The only way this could've gotten easier is if they were at a Black Resorts property."

He might've smiled, but there was nothing cheerful about it.

Nothing but luck.

Maximo made some calls while I drove us back to Moonlight. I was already headed through the gaming floor on my way to see Mila when Marco called.

I hit answer. "What's—"

"Your girl is talking to her tail, and she doesn't look happy. Want me to intervene?"

"I'm twenty seconds away."

"Might want to book it. She's about to run."

I clicked off and grinned.

Like I said…

Nothing but luck.

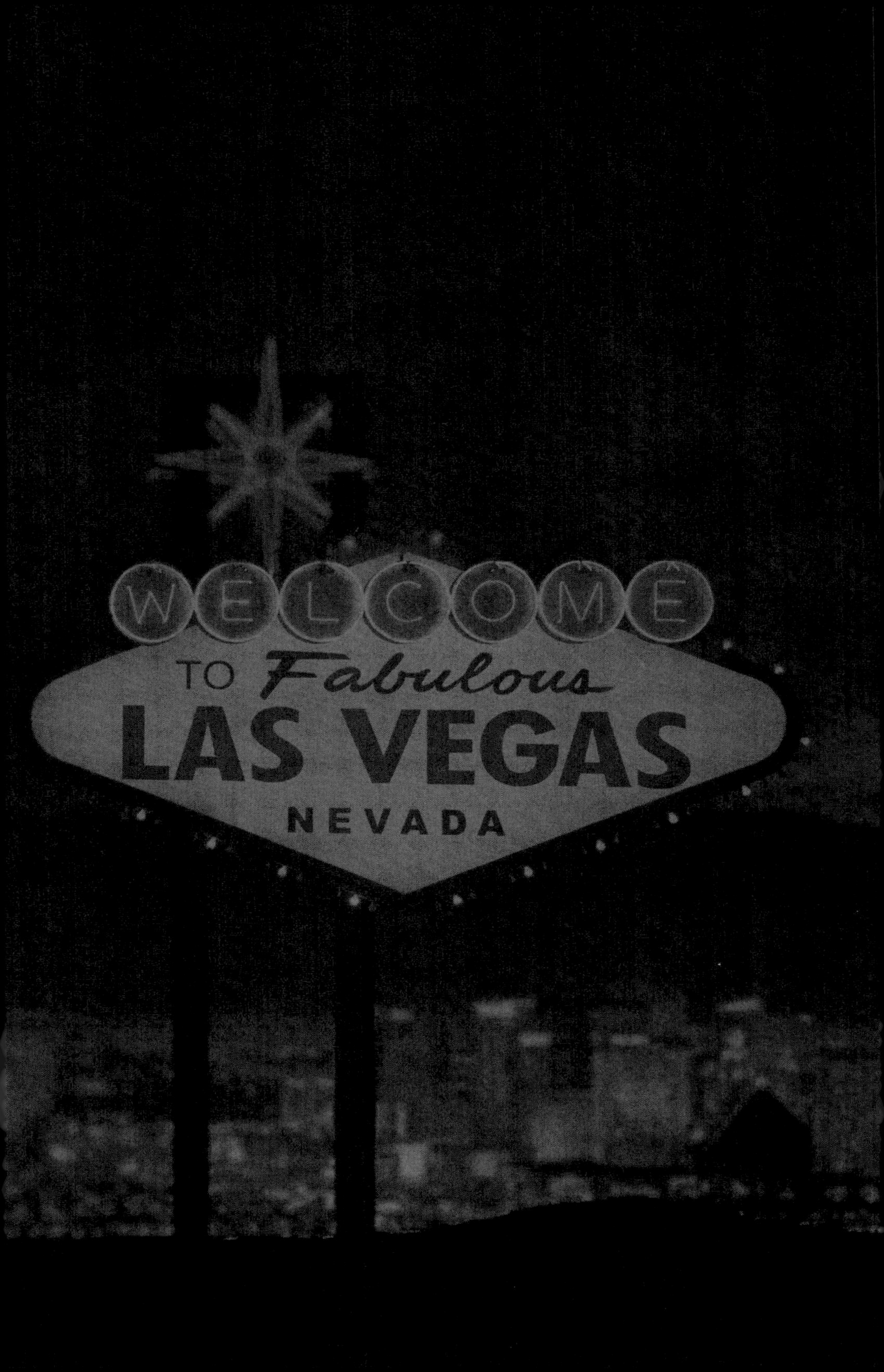
WELCOME
TO Fabulous
LAS VEGAS
NEVADA

CHAPTER 17
IF YOU EVER GET INTO TROUBLE... RUN
MILA

I HAD NO CLUE WHAT got into me.
Some primal flight instinct was triggered, and I just took off. My breath came in heavy pants. Adrenaline made my legs shake and my pulse pound at the base of my throat. All I knew was I needed to go.

And not just from the resort.

With the distance and crowd between us, I thought I'd get farther.

I thought Ash wouldn't chase me at his work.

I thought he wouldn't chase me because he didn't care enough to.

A stolen glance over my shoulder proved I thought *wrong*.

Seeing how close he already was, there was no way I'd reach the doors security had pointed out. There was definitely no way I could make it over the tall fencing surrounding the space. Even knowing I couldn't swim, I was tempted to try to cut through the pool.

With no choice—but hopefully some overdue luck—I dodged to the side like I was starring in an action movie. I didn't risk looking behind me. I kept my eyes on an opening between the fencing and the building.

It looked large enough for me to slip through but small enough to keep a behemoth caged.

Almost.

Almost there.

I just need to get away from him.

I barely slowed as I neared the gap.

And then I stopped so suddenly, I almost fell.

It wasn't a gap. It was a tiny alcove that held some utility panel.

A dead end.

Arms banded around me, and I should've admitted defeat.

I didn't. I thrashed and kicked and fought.

It made no difference. Ash tossed me over his shoulder like I was nothing.

"Put me down," I ordered.

He ignored me.

"Put me down right now, or I'll scream."

His rough chuckle was edged with barbed wire. "I hope you do."

In a last-ditch effort, I played possum. I forced my body to go slack as I waited for an opening. When he stepped inside, I suddenly pushed off.

And got exactly nowhere.

"Will you please put me down?" I tried nicely.

No response.

I growled my frustration. "This isn't cool."

Nothing.

"I'm allowed to leave."

More nothing.

The reality of the scene I'd made, that his boss' wife had witnessed it, and that I was literally being carried through a crowded public place sank in. Knowing I was exactly who I vowed to never become made my head swim worse than the upside-down angle. "I want to leave."

The loudest nothing I'd ever heard.

That time when I went limp, it wasn't an act. It was with resignation while I waited to see what would happen.

After a minute, Ash paused and then took a few steps. I pushed my hair from my face to see we were in the elevator, but I was too disoriented to know which direction it was headed.

Up to the penthouse or down to the garage.

Regret tangled my insides. For what I'd done. For who I was.

For what could've been.

There was a soft whoosh as the doors slid open. Ash barely stepped out before my world flipped right side up. I didn't have the chance to acclimate before my back was pressed to the wall, and Ash was *on* me.

His mouth.

His hands.

His body as it pinned me in place.

Ash is kissing me. He's kissing me.

Holy shit.

Why is Ash kissing me?

Despite my hurt and confusion, I couldn't resist him. It was too much. Too tempting. Too demanding. I was about to give in, but apparently, I took too long.

Like earlier, Ash's tattooed hand gripped my chin and his fingertips dug into my cheeks, forcing my lips to part. He took the access he'd given himself. His tongue plunged in to taste and dominate.

Own.

The mental whiplash was almost as disorienting as the physical.

Moments before, I'd been sure he didn't want me. I'd been sure I didn't want him anymore. But the way he touched me—like he couldn't get close enough—was unbelievable.

Literally.

Life wasn't one of the romance books from Juliet Black's iPad. I'd learned long ago to keep my defenses high. To never hope or dream for anything.

No matter how foolishly I might want something.

I tried to turn my head, but his hold stayed firm. I pushed against his shoulders, but he simply used his torso to force my legs apart. Traitor that my body was, they wrapped around him instantly, lifting my dress in the process. With the fabric hiked up, I was hyperaware that only a thin layer of cotton covered me.

Hunching to keep our mouths connected, he lowered me down his body and stopped only once his hard-on was pressed to my sex. I gasped at the contact.

The hardness.

The *size*.

He took advantage of my reaction by deepening the kiss.

And I took advantage by biting his tongue.

Rather than shoving away like I'd expected, Ash's husky grunt filled my mouth. He ground against me so I could feel him grow somehow even harder. When he finally pulled away, it was just far enough to rest his forehead on mine. "Fuck. Fucking hell. *Fuck*, Mila."

They were angry words, but the way he said them was anything but.

"Sorry," I said anyway since it was pretty much my default.

"Not yet." His fingers on my face tightened. That time when my mouth opened, his hazel eyes dropped to watch as he smeared his thumb across my lips before sliding between them. "But you will be."

I wasn't sure what it said about me, but the goosebumps that spread across my skin weren't from fear.

Ash lowered me to stand. He kept hold of my waist until he was sure I was steady before moving into the penthouse.

I stayed right where I was as my shoulders slumped in relief that he'd let me go.

And disappointment that he'd let me go.

More the latter, but whatever. I was ignoring that.

"Tell me what happened that made you wanna try out for the track team," Ash ordered as he shook off his black suit jacket and tossed it over the couch.

"Nothing."

"Something sure as shit did. What was it?"

"I was just leaving because—"

"Christ, sunshine," he cut in, which was good because I had no clue how I would finish that sentence. He rolled the sleeves of his dark blue shirt. "Usually, I don't mind your secrets. I'm a patient man. I've got all the time in the world to wait you out. But not with this."

Since evasiveness wasn't working, I switched to deflection. "You need to go back to work."

"You're more important," he said with no hesitation.

And God, just that sentence alone made me waver.

I gathered up my backbone and tried again. "Okay, you need to go because I said so."

He put his hands in his pockets and stood there.

"Fine. Then I'm going."

A smile—if it could even be called that—twisted his mouth. "Try it."

Calling his bluff, I pressed my thumb to the elevator button.

Nothing.

It didn't even flash green to show it was activated.

I turned back around.

Usually when Ash spoke to me, it was gentle. Charming. Cautious.

Not right then.

Like a predator stalking his prey, he slowly approached as he spoke. "Told myself I had to go slow. Give you time to get used to me. Be gentle with you."

I retreated until my back hit cold metal, but he didn't stop his advance.

Not until his body was almost touching mine. His hands went to the elevator door on either side of my head, caging me in. "I can see now what a mistake I made by letting you get wrapped up in your own head. That's my bad, sunshine. It won't happen again. We're fixing this *now*."

"Wh—" I started, but my voice was barely a whisper. "What does that mean?"

"First, we're gonna have the talk we should've had from the start. Then I'm going to spank your ass for all the lies you've said straight to my face. After, if you earn it, I'm gonna make you come because just the thought of it has been driving me outta my head."

There was a lot to take in. Important things that I really needed to focus on.

But when I opened my mouth, it was to bizarrely ask, "You want to make me come?"

"More than I want"—he closed the last inch of distance so I could feel his impossibly hard cock against my stomach—"my next breath."

I didn't have the chance to say anything more before my feet were off the ground and he was kissing me. I tried to break away, but his massive hand cupped the back of my head and kept me in place as he carried me through the penthouse. Even when I bit his lip, I was met with another grunt of pleasure.

Ash sat with me straddling him before he pulled away, and I saw we were in an oversized chair in the bedroom. "Tell me what happened."

"I already told you, it was nothing."

His brow lifted as he waited expectantly. When I didn't say anything, he gave a single nod. "Fine, we'll start with spanking."

"No way," I scoffed as I attempted to scramble off his lap, but his hands might as well have been padlocks.

"I warned you."

"Yeah, but... but... You can't actually do that."

"I don't do empty threats."

"And I didn't lie," I totally lied.

His hold loosened, but it wasn't to release me. It was to flip the world upside down.

Or just my world.

Draped over his bent legs, my head hung down with my hair

in my face. I tried to right myself, but before I could find leverage, Ash slid my panties down so they were bunched under my ass. And then his palm slapped down on my bare skin.

At least I assumed it was his palm. Based on the size and sting it caused, it might have been a solid wood cutting board.

His touch was gentle as he caressed the spot. "Wasn't gonna do this until after we talked. Until you agreed to be mine. But you've been mine since the second you came to me for help. And it seems like you need it as bad as I do."

His?

"No the fuck I'm not," I snapped. "And no the fuck I don't."

"Guess I'm adding extra for two more lies." Ash's palm landed in a different spot. Neither had actually been that hard. Just enough to startle me. "Say stop, and it stops instantly. I mean it, Camila."

Say it.

Say it.

Just fucking say it.

I didn't. I had no clue why I didn't.

I was an adult. I'd been slapped, pinched, shaken, hit with a wooden spoon, and an assortment of other punishments as a kid.

Contrary to his assertion, I didn't need more.

But try as I might, I couldn't force the word from my mouth.

Not even when his hand came down again harder. And again. And again. Tears streamed from my eyes. I wiggled. I kicked. I hissed and cried out and begged.

All without ever saying stop.

The burn spread and took over, making each blow blend together until I wasn't sure how many there'd been.

How many there would be.

It was like I was stuck in an unending loop of pain and shock and something else.

It started slow. A trickle of warmth. A hint of calm.

It grew and grew, leaving me raw and off-kilter until an overwhelmed sob broke free. Once it did, there was no stopping it. It wracked my body, hurting far worse than his spanks.

With one last slap, Ash gathered me upright and adjusted my panties into place. My head swam. My ass stung. My tears didn't slow.

He held me through the worst of it before leaning me back so he could see my face. "Talk to me."

I hadn't been able to force myself to tell him to stop. But at his firm order, the truth came flying out in a jumbled mess of run-ons and residual tears. "You don't trust me. And I get it. That's my own fault. But that doesn't mean knowing you won't leave me alone at your house doesn't suck. And then it sucked like a million times worse that you had security follow me. Which, again, it's my fault. Blah, blah, blah. That doesn't make it any better." I swiped at the dumb droplets still trailing down my cheeks. Like a dam had been broken on them and my mouth, all the suppressed insecurities and thoughts spilled free. "And you put me in a stupid dress again because my clothes aren't good enough. And I'm not good enough. And I don't belong here, so if you'd just release me, I'll go."

Ash remained silent through my rambling, his face blank and giving me *nothing*.

Something was definitely karmic in that, considering how often I used my own masking abilities to keep people from reading me.

He slowly nodded, and my heart sank all the way to the underground garage.

I needed to get away so I could curse the cruelty of the universe in solitude. But when I tried to wiggle off his legs, Ash's hold remained unbreakable.

No, it *tightened*.

I'd be surprised if he didn't leave finger-shaped bruises.

Mementos of what could've been.

"I mean this in the nicest way possible," he said, making me brace, "but what in the *actual* fuck are you talking about?"

Oh my God.

It was probably never that serious to him, and I just unloaded an entire warehouse of crazy.

I should've just kept my mouth shut.

I tried again to push off him, more frantic than when I'd been facing an impending spanking.

"Camila," he bit out in warning, and I stopped fighting. "Let's start at the beginning. Why don't I trust you?"

"Because of the whole thing here," I muttered, the cheeks on my face flaring hotter than my other ones.

His brows lowered. "What thing?"

"When I tried to steal that wallet. Now you think I'll steal again so you made me go to Sunrise and here, and then you had that security guard follow me to make sure I wouldn't do something. Which, like I said, I know why—"

"I had you come with me because I like you close. I feel like I'm coming outta my skin when I'm too far from you."

"You do?"

I wasn't acting coy or trying to be cute. I also wasn't faking being obtuse.

There was nothing fake about it.

"Mila, if I had my way, I'd tie you to me."

Even though I knew it was an exaggeration, my mouth went dry.

Areas farther south on my body had the opposite problem.

"As far as security, it's not because I don't trust you." He lifted a hand to cup my face and swept his thumb over where my cheek had been scraped and bruised the worst. "It's other people I don't trust."

"But that was just random, not a planned setup. There's no threat."

"There's always a threat."

It hadn't occurred to me that the guard was for my benefit since I'd been taught that security was always bad. When I was young, they would follow Veronica and me through stores. They'd been right to because once she caused the distraction, I stole whatever she'd told me to.

No one ever suspected the cute kid.

When I was older, they would follow me around because I had poor-person stench on me. Since I carried a lot of guilt from my earlier crimes, the reminder was never a pleasant experience.

I also wouldn't have ever guessed that Ash's motives for bringing me with were positive. I'd been left alone for days at a time—or longer—for as long as I could remember. My mom hadn't wanted to be around me. Nan and Pop had liked a day or two, but they'd been older. They hadn't been equipped to raise another kid.

Friends. Crushes. My first boyfriend.

They'd all left after deciding they couldn't deal.

But not Ash.

Word by word, he dismantled the fortress of justifications I'd built in my mind until it started to resemble a flimsy house of cards.

"If that guy wasn't you secretly keeping tabs on me, then why didn't you just tell me about him?"

"First off, if I wanted to secretly keep tabs on you, I wouldn't send a uniformed guard to do it. This place is wired with enough cameras and undercover security, I could track you from the time you exited the elevator till you left the property. About not telling you, you're right. That's my bad. My mind was on something else, and I'm used to guard duty being commonplace with Juliet."

"Wait, Juliet has a guard?"

"A rotation of them."

"Why?"

"I want security on you as a precaution because I know how dangerous Vegas can be. Juliet *needs* security on her because she's married to Maximo. Any target on his back is also on hers. And as a business owner, he's collected his fair share of enemies. Now that shit is more settled, it's typically just hotel security with her, but if one of us goons isn't busy, we volunteer. Usually, it's Marco since his main job is bodyguard anyway. Didn't you see him?"

I thought about my time by the pool. My attention had been on Juliet and the guy I was aware of. I hadn't even noticed anyone else.

I shook my head.

Ash squeezed my waist. "I might've mentioned it had you texted like I told you to."

My petulant decision not to tell him in retaliation for his bossiness seemed even stupider.

"Now what the hell was all that shit about the dress?"

Oh. Right. He had excuses for two things, but there's still more.

Too afraid to believe him—of being burned for the countless time—I fought to reinforce the remaining cards. "You bought me dresses."

"And?"

That's a fair rebuttal 'cause when I say it like that, it's not exactly the crime of the century.

"And I don't want you to buy me anything," I said.

"I told you this when you said you didn't want me doing things for you, but I'll say it again. Get over it."

"You can't just tell me to get over it or get used to it."

"Yeah, I can." He lifted the hem. "You don't like them?"

"That's not the point. You've already done enough for me. Too much. You shouldn't be buying me anything just because my clothes don't meet your standard or whatever."

"I'll buy you whatever I want, but it has jack shit to do with my opinion on your clothes. I don't care what you wear." His expression softened, and I hated it even before he gently said, "Baby, your hoodie had blood stains. Tried to get them out, but it didn't work. I asked Juliet for something you could wear to Sunrise since I didn't think you wanted to go in pajamas. I saw how much you liked that dress and had her send more over."

"I'm wearing Juliet's clothes?"

The majority of my clothes were preowned. I very rarely bought new. I'd had a lifetime of hand-me-downs. I was used to it. But something about wearing one of her dresses in front of the beautiful and glamorous Juliet was mortifying.

Well, I can never see her again.
That sucks.

"You're wearing clothes she made that I bought from her," he said slowly, like it was something I should know.

"Wait, what?"

"Juliet designs and makes clothes. She didn't tell you?"

No, because I'm a shitty fledgling friend who didn't ask much since I was too scared to answer questions.

That explains why our dresses looked similar yesterday and why the fabric on her cover-up was familiar.

There was a skirt in the closet with the same one.

That it wasn't a pity donation made me feel a lot better. But something else regarding Juliet had been lurking in my head that I hadn't asked. I hadn't wanted to know. But I couldn't keep it in any longer. "You chased her?"

Ash didn't need an explanation or even blink. "Not in the way you mean. Not in the way I just chased you, desperate to have you and fuck you. Maximo chased her. The three of us helped *for him*."

That was enough to blow down the last of my laughable house of cards.

My heart wanted to soar, but a lifetime of... well, my life kept it weighed firmly down. The cringy memory of me silently pleading for him to kiss me was front and center in my mind as I eyed him skeptically. My voice was barely above a whisper, like even it was too afraid the bubble would burst. "I don't get how you want me all of a sudden. What changed?"

As soon as the words left my mouth, I wanted to rewind time and swallow them back down. If that wasn't an option, I'd settle for the earth opening up to swallow me.

I hated sounding insecure and needy. Even worse, I hated that I *was* insecure and needy. I wanted to be effortlessly confident. As aloof and uncaring as my defenses usually allowed me to be.

Before I could tell him to forget I asked or smother myself—

or maybe him—out of embarrassment, Ash tilted his head. "That's a good segue into our next discussion."

Uh-oh.

Something about the way he said that filled me with trepidation. "Ash—"

My words cut off when he gripped my chin in that way that made my breath freeze until my lungs burned. He ducked down so his face was all I could see. "From now on, it's Daddy."

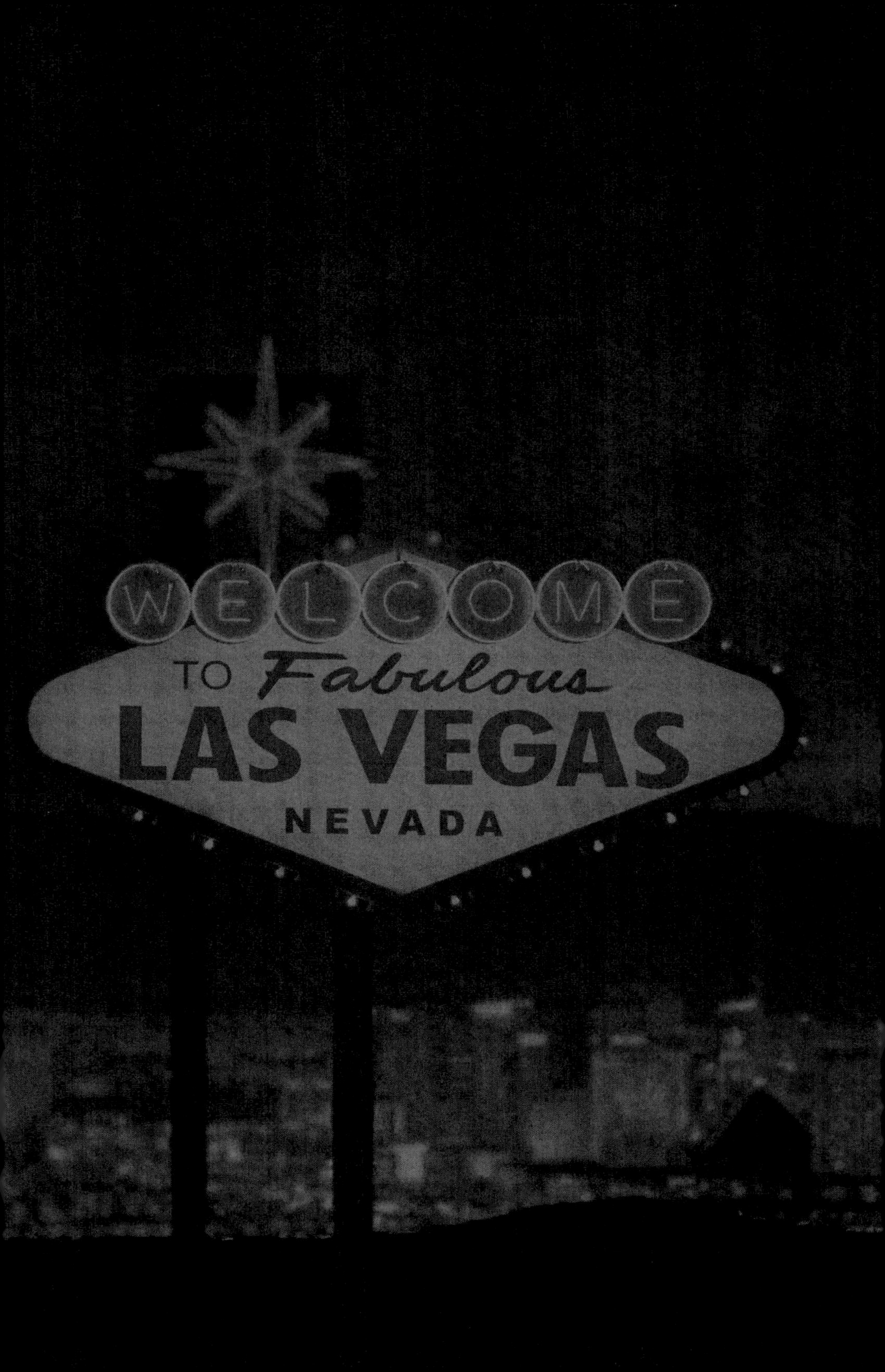
WELCOME
TO Fabulous
LAS VEGAS
NEVADA

CHAPTER 18
YOU CAN'T GET REJECTED IF YOU NEVER EVEN TRY
MILA

"Daddy?" I breathed, not trusting that I'd heard him correctly.

His lids closed, and he inhaled sharply. Still holding my chin and hip, he tugged me closer so my ass slid from his knees to his lap. His hardness pressed between my spread legs. "Say it again."

"Daddy?" It came out airier and even more unsure than before, but that didn't seem to matter to him.

His cock jerked in response. He held me there for a moment before repositioning me on his knees. "Is that something you're into?"

"Yes."

At my immediate answer, Ash gave another of those pleased smiles that made me feel like I'd done something amazing rather than just mutter a single word.

I hated to ruin it, but once my brain caught up with my hormones, I amended, "Maybe? I mean, I don't know."

I really wish I would've grilled Juliet about her relationship to know what it actually entails so I'm not giving a wishy-washy answer.

Ash, of course, didn't take it like that. "It's okay, it's a lot. That's why I was trying to take it slow."

"Would it be like Juliet and her husband?"

"No."

At his blunt denial, disappointment I didn't even understand, much less have the right to feel, hit my chest.

But Ash wasn't done.

Spearing his fingers into my hair, he tilted my head back. "Maximo is obsessed with Juliet." His hand fisted, pulling the strands. "But I could be consumed by you."

In my long life of always being left wanting, I didn't think I'd ever wanted anything more.

"To answer your question," he said, and it took my stunned brain a moment to remember what it even was, "it's not all of a sudden. I've wanted you since the first time I saw you nick that douchebag's wallet." He dropped his hands to my thighs, and his thumbs stroked soothingly. "And what's changed is we found the motherfuckers who hurt you."

In everything I thought he'd say, that wasn't anywhere on the list. It was so far off the list, I wasn't even sure I understood.

"The guys who attacked me in the alley?" I asked.

"You have someone else who's hurt you?"

Yes. A long list. Grab a protein bar and a notepad.

"No, I'm just lost. How did you even find them?"

"We're good with this shit."

I was rocked. I couldn't believe he'd found them. I couldn't believe he'd worked so hard to do it. Because I had no doubt a ton of effort had gone into it. There was no shortage of lowlifes. Sifting through to find them—especially with no real info to go off—would be like finding two specific needles in an even bigger stack of needles.

Violence happened in Vegas all the time.

No.

Violence happened *everywhere* all the time. In the big, scary cities and the wholesome tiny towns.

Getting hurt was awful, but I'd still been more fortunate than others. I'd survived the random attack. I'd moved on.

But Ash hadn't.

"What do they have to do with you wanting me?" I asked.

"You trusted me to take care of you, and I don't take that shit lightly, Mila. I didn't want to do something that would make you feel like you weren't safe with me. Or worse, like you owed me. Before I did anything, I needed to make it so you could tell me to fuck off and then safely leave." His lip twitched. "Temporarily."

"And I can leave?"

Any trace of humor was gone, and his jaw clenched as he repeated, "*Temporarily*."

God, that's hot.

Why is that hot?

"But not this minute," he tacked on. "We found them, but I still need to deal with them."

Maybe it made me a bad person, but I didn't ask how he was going to deal with it because I didn't care. Both those men deserved whatever threat or legal trouble they faced.

Ash stood suddenly, bringing me with. He took a few steps to the mattress before setting me down. He didn't join me. "I'll be back soon."

"Wait, you're going?" I cried. "Earlier, you said you were going to make me..."

An amused smile tipped his mouth, and he played dumb. "Make you what?"

I may have wanted to throw something at him, but I wanted to ease the tightness in my lower belly more. Gritting my teeth, I forced out, "Make me come."

"It'll have to wait." He leaned down to brush his mouth across mine. "I'm guessing you don't want to go back to hanging out with Juliet?"

I would rather dive in the deep end wearing a bikini made of plugged in toasters.

"I would not," I said instead.

He gave me a knowing look but didn't push—though I got the impression he wanted to.

I knew I'd have to talk to her eventually if I wanted to salvage our fledgling friendship. But I had enough other stuff to deal with right then. I didn't want to add trying to explain to her what was raw in my head.

"I want you to stay in this room until I get back," Ash ordered. "I'll bring dinner with me, and we'll talk. Until then, relax."

"You know how I said you couldn't say *not to mention* just to mention it? You also can't say we need to talk and then tell me to relax. Those two are mutually exclusive. Totally incompatible."

"Noted," he said as he walked from the room.

My reeling brain was cycling through our lengthy conversation when he came back a moment later with my phone and the iPad from the table. He set both on the nightstand before pulling a bottle of water from his pocket.

"I thought you were just happy to see me," I joked.

Ash chuckled, but it was husky as he snagged my wrist. He pushed my flattened palm against his abs and moved it slowly down before stopping above his belt. "When you're ready, I'll show you exactly how happy I am to see you. And it'll be a fuckuva lot more impressive than that water bottle."

If he were any other man, I'd chalk the brag up to male ego and exaggeration.

But it was Ash. And I'd felt that hardness between my legs.

He was understating it.

"I want that water gone by the time I get back," he ordered. "Keep an eye on your phone. I'll text about dinner."

"And the iPad?"

"When Maximo and Juliet got together, she had a lot of questions she researched. Figured you'd have the same."

"I can't look that stuff up on her iPad."

His brows lowered. "It's not Juliet's. Though she was the one who suggested I get it for you."

"It's mine?"

"Cole loaded it with the same books she has. She said something about a book club?" Plucking it from my hold, he flipped it over and handed it back. "Water. Texts."

"Right."

He was almost to the door when he turned back. "And Camila?"

Since I'd been staring at his retreating back—and ass—he already had my attention. But that wasn't enough for him, and he remained silent until I responded. "Yes?"

"No touching that pretty pussy. Understood?"

I hadn't been planning to, mostly because it took too long when I did, and he'd likely be back before I finished. But it was still an unexpected order.

Shocked, all I could do was nod. But again, that wasn't enough, and he arched a brow as he waited expectantly.

"Okay," I said.

"Good girl." Without another word, he left.

My eyes stayed aimed at the doorway long after he was gone before I dropped them to look at the iPad.

And the engraving on the back.

My sunshine

Short. Simple. Sweet.

And so very possessive even before we'd talked.

"What the hell do I do now?" I whispered to myself.

I did the smart thing.

I drank my water and started researching.

Ash

Daddy.

Fuck. Just the memory of Mila's nervous voice was enough to have me adjusting my dick in the elevator. I wasn't sure I'd survive the lack of blood to my brain if she said yes.

I wasn't sure I'd survive—*period*—if she said no.

I'd always been a Daddy, even before I knew there was a label to put on it. My buddies in high school and college used to joke that I would put myself in the permanent friendzone with the thoughtful way I took care of girls.

Like friendship was akin to a blown apart, sinking ship.

Like I was owed something.

Like treating women like shit was the way to get them.

Inevitably, they'd see whatever bullshit dating advice they'd read was wrong, and that what I did worked. They'd try to copy me, but it never lasted.

Not everyone was a Daddy. Not everyone got off on that carefully calibrated level of control, nurturing, dominance, and power exchange.

But I did.

If someone had asked me that morning whether I could be with Mila without her calling me Daddy, I'd have said yes. But after hearing her say it twice? I wasn't so certain.

Not without the memory of it haunting me.

I knew without a doubt, though, that I could never turn off my actions that backed up my words. I was obsessive. Arrogant. Over-the-top protective.

I couldn't soften that with anyone, but especially not Mila. She sparked every instinct I had, stronger than I'd ever felt it.

Running my palm down my face, I knew I was getting ahead of myself.

The elevator opened, and I stepped into the waiting room outside of Maximo's office. "It's me," I called, moving slowly. "I'm nearing the plant. Now the chairs. I can almost see into the room."

I smiled at Juliet's laughter.

Maximo was less amused. "Get your ass in here before I shoot you."

"And have to hire five people to replace me? Go for it." I moved into the open doorway and held my hands up. "And I just wanted to give you ample time to hide your shame."

"Ain't no shame in what I've got." He winked at Juliet. "Any of what I've got. Not to mention, you just texted a minute ago."

"A lot can happen in a minute."

And I've walked in on it.

"If that's true for you"—he gave a slow, sad shake of the head—"no wonder your woman ran."

I shot him the middle finger. My gut hurt at the memory of her trying to run from me while my dick wanted to harden at the memory of chasing her. I kept it in check as I glared at Juliet. "Snitch."

She sat on the side of his desk and crossed her arms smugly. "Payback."

"And I was gonna give you a Get-Out-Of-A-Snitch pass. Never mind now."

"Dammit. Is it too late to lie and say Marco told?" Her flippant attitude dropped, and she looked concerned. "Is she okay?"

I wouldn't share Mila's business, so I went for the vague truth. "She will be."

"Good. Please tell her about my run through the desert so she knows she's not alone. At least her escape attempt didn't require a snake murder. And feel free to embellish my heroism."

I lifted my chin since that story would probably help.

I could've waited to ask Maximo until we were in the elevator, but I wanted Juliet's opinion, too. "At the beginning, did you worry Juliet would reject you as her Daddy?"

"No," he said.

Helpful.

"I knew there was a possibility she would, but I wasn't worried about it." At Juliet's gasp of outrage, he shot her a warning look that was mostly bullshit bluster. "Because it wasn't an option. Not one I'd accept anyway."

That time, it wasn't a gasp from Juliet, but an exaggerated eye roll she would undoubtedly pay for later. "Don't listen to him. I think the wedding ring on his finger is somehow cutting off blood flow to the part of his brain that houses his memories."

"My dove." That warning wasn't bullshit bluster.

Juliet continued despite it. Or maybe because of it. "Either that, or he's getting forgetful in his old age."

"Juliet Black," he bit out.

I was already backing away. "I'm going."

"Wait."

At Juliet's tone, I stopped and looked back to see her standing.

"Since you asked specifically about him being my Daddy, I'm guessing the same applies to you."

"Correct."

She smiled but did it shaking her head. "I knew you all were disproportionately bossy." Her smile fell and her words were earnest. "Maximo might've felt like that, but he gave me a choice. Options. When I handed him my... *everything*, it was my decision. It wasn't pried away from me. It wasn't because I felt stuck. I willingly gave it, and that's the only way this worked." She glanced at him and then put her hands behind her back—a position that covered her ass. "That and he was beyond bluntly honest about what this was, what he expected, and how things would be."

That was what I needed to do. Lay it out. Good intentions or not, my attempt at taking it slow and careful had backfired. She'd managed to get shit twisted until she was sure I didn't want her.

"You need to give some thought to what those honest answers are for you. The entire time I was with Mila today, she didn't ask for a single thing. She didn't complain about a single thing. She is go-with-the-flow to the point it could drown her. She's also *very* guarded. And that's coming from me. I get the feeling she doesn't let people in, but every time she mentioned you, she smiled. If she thinks the only way to be with you is as your submissive or in whatever capacity of kink you follow, she'll probably do it, even if it doesn't work for her. If you can be with her without it, I think that's what she needs to hear so she has a choice." Her eyes narrowed and she lifted a finger. "But only if that's true. Otherwise, you'll be the miserable one."

"I'll tell her," I said as soon as she stopped talking. I didn't have to think about it.

"Good because I want this to happen." I started to smile, assuming she wanted the handsome goon to be happy, but she continued. "I already really liked her, but then watching as she made you chase her? Not to be dramatic, but she's literally my favorite person. So you better make sure she sticks around, or I'll kick your ass."

"What was that, little dove?" Maximo asked, his tone too calm.

"I said favorite person, not favorite Daddy."

"Still not okay. I'm your favorite Daddy, person, human, everything."

"Oh God," she muttered, clearly holding back an eye roll.

"Yeah, that too."

There's my cue to leave.

I started for the door, and Maximo said, "Hold on."

"You don't have to come. You've got enough to worry about with the fight coming up."

"That's what I pay Serrano for."

It may have been true, but that didn't mean Maximo wasn't involved in every aspect of his resorts and the events held there—along with the underground ones at the warehouses. He'd already given up his morning to stake out The *E. Coli* Corral Motel.

"Seriously, we've got it."

He shot me a glare. "I saw the lobby footage. I saw her. I know what these dickheads did to your woman. I'm happy to be here." His lips tipped before he added, "Behemoth."

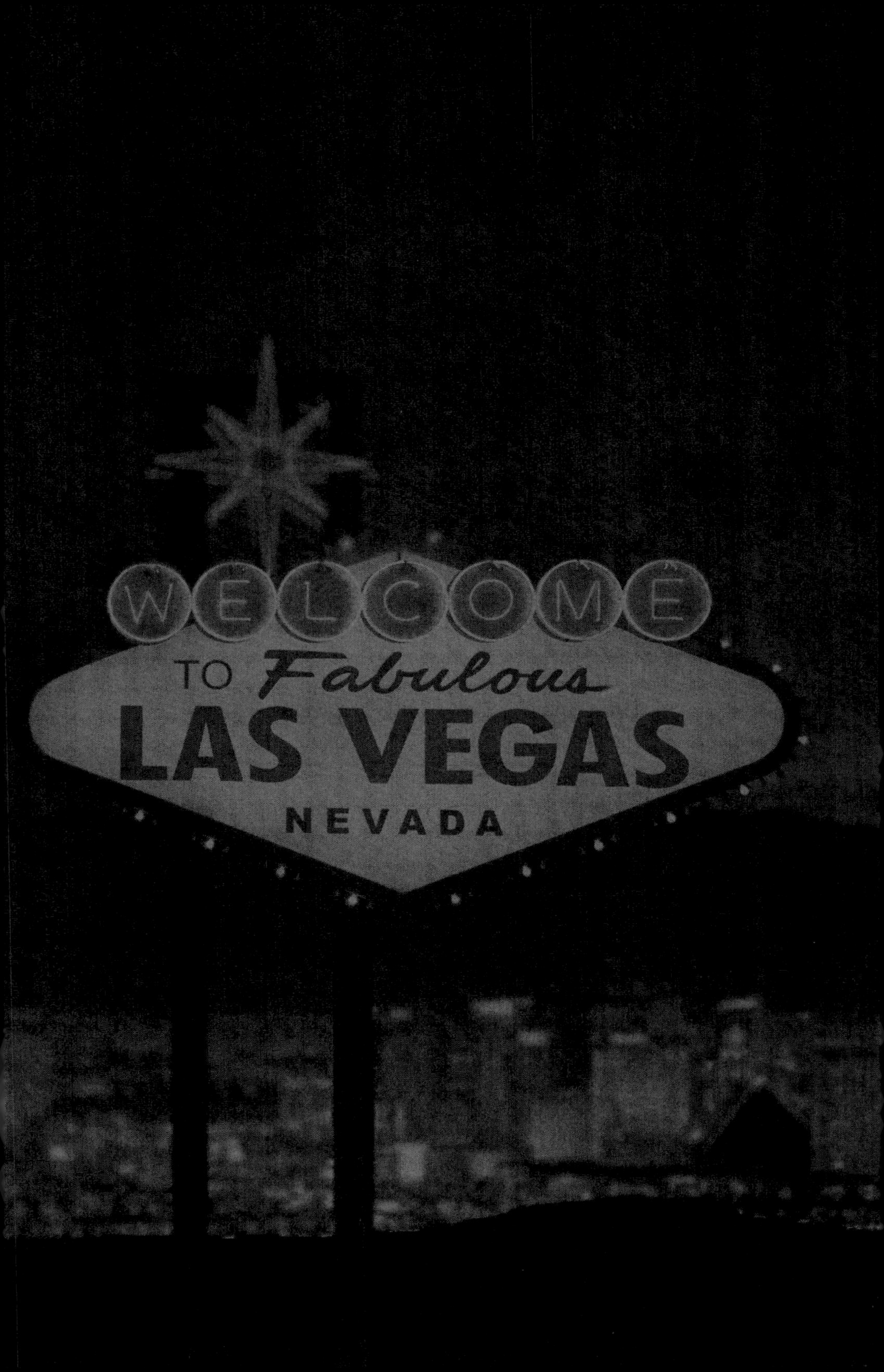
WELCOME
TO Fabulous
LAS VEGAS
NEVADA

CHAPTER 19
DON'T LET YOUR WORDS COME BACK TO BURN YOU
ASH

Between the trust fund from my grandparents, what I'd already made, and my investments, I didn't have to work. I especially didn't need a job that had long, irregular hours, frequent bullshit, and aspects that often put me on the wrong side of legal.

I did it because I liked Maximo, Marco, and Cole. I liked what we did. I liked the variety and the organization and the satisfaction.

I liked the excitement and the chaos and the violence.

Even with that, I'd never been happier to work there than I was right then. Cole had located the assholes at a strip club owned by one of Maximo's connections.

Maximo had sent a few guys from his promotional team over to lure them in with an offer of food vouchers and a poker chip giveaway. That'd been all that was needed, and the dumb bastards had strolled into Moonlight on their own accord.

They just hadn't remained free once they arrived.

I could and would make them pay for what they'd done to Mila. And when I was done, I'd go up and celebrate by making her come with the same hands that'd taken two lives for her.

And that was why there was a motherfucking pep in my goddamn step.

"You got a plan?" Maximo asked as we rode down to The Basement. Usually, that kind of job would be done off property. But since Mila and Juliet were both at Moonlight, we'd decided to stick close.

Like the pathetic bastards we were.

"I always have a plan."

I'd been plotting how I'd handle them since the moment I'd found out Mila's injuries weren't from a car accident. Her last-minute divulgence the night before had forced me to tweak it a little, but that was fine. I always calculated for possible variations.

We turned the corner to see Cole in the hallway with his phone in hand, rapidly typing at the screen.

"Anything else I should know?" I asked.

"Knights signed a new goalie." Cole glanced up and gestured to the door. "They're exactly what we thought. Losers for hire. Nobodies with nothing that no one will miss. Got disposal spots lined up."

"Think we'll only need one," I said.

"Okay," he drawled, but no one questioned me as I opened the door.

Two sets of eyes shot to me.

One filled with stark terror.

Smart.

The second filled with rage, attempting to mask his terror.

Moron.

This is going to be fun.

Dragging a chair from the wall, I moved it between the two men. I plopped down and kicked my legs up on the table, looking back and forth at them. I wasn't on guard since they were both cuffed to the latches on the underside of the table.

I'd have preferred rope, but no one else had my knot skills.

"Who the fuck are you?" the cocky one—Edward Zale—bit out when I didn't speak. "We were promised free poker, but when we got in here, some pricks jumped us. They came after us, so why are *we* the ones in cuffs?"

"Oh, don't like that, huh? Don't like getting randomly attacked?"

"What—"

I kicked the table away. With their arms cuffed to it, the momentum pulled them forward and both smashed their faces into the hard steel.

Blood was instant, but neither nose looked broken.

Yet.

Both men—and I used that term loosely—cried out their confusion, but the mean fucker was the only one dumb enough to follow it with insults.

"You pussy-ass bitch. Uncuff me and try that shit again. I fucking dare you."

With a shrug, I held my hand up. Maximo tossed me a key ring that I used to unlock the guy's wrists.

Rather than come at me—and I'd really been looking forward to that—Zale backed away and rounded the table toward the door.

"I thought you dared me." I tilted my head in exaggerated confusion before holding my arms out. "I assumed the rest of your plan wasn't to tuck your tiny dick between your legs and run."

He spun back like he was going to dive at me. And, again, I looked forward to it. I wanted it. His quiet, crying partner wasn't going to be any fun.

I wanted to play with my prey.

Instead, he muttered some nonsense and continued to the door where Maximo and Cole stood. Both held guns at their sides but were otherwise relaxed. Like they didn't see the man as a threat.

It added insult to the injuries I would inflict.

"I'm going to own you," Zale blustered. "All three of you. I'm going straight to the owner."

"Why wait?" Maximo held out his hand. "Maximo Black, owner of Black Resorts."

He blanched but quickly rallied. "This is even better. I'll own you *and* your damn casinos. I'm going to the media and getting a lawyer when I get out of here."

"*If,*" I corrected, but he was too stupid to get it.

Zale looked over his shoulder at me. "There's no *if*. When I sue you, I'll get all of this and everything else you three have to your name. Plus those fuckers who jumped us. Casinos are loaded with cameras and—"

"Not where you were brought in." Maximo gave a dark laugh. "And certainly not down here."

He wilted a little before puffing his chest out. "I'll let my lawyer handle it. Out of my way."

"No."

"You can't keep me here."

Like it was nothing, Maximo lazily raised his gun to press it under Zale's chin. "Can and will."

By the time Zale realized what was happening and a delayed sense of self-preservation kicked in, I'd already stood and rounded the table. He scrambled back just to crash into me. I didn't give him the chance to turn before shoving him against the concrete wall. Palm to the side of his head, I pushed hard as I dragged him against the rough texture.

Tearing at his cheek.

Making it *burn*.

Just the beginning.

Keeping a firm hand pressed against his head, I reached into my pocket and pulled out my phone. I whistled as I swiped through until I found what I wanted.

Who I needed.

It was a screengrab from one of the security cameras at the back of my house. Even if the quality wasn't the best, Mila looked so damn pretty sitting near the creek. He didn't deserve to see her, but I needed answers.

And he needed to know why this was happening to him.

I put the phone in his face. "Recognize her?"

"No. Should I recognize some random bitch?"

I slammed the edge of my cell into his already swollen nose. "Look again."

He growled before inhaling sharply.

"You recognize her."

It wasn't a question, but he shrugged. "Maybe. What's some honey-ass tweaker got to do with this?"

Another drag along the rough wall before I turned him. "Some *what*?"

"That scrawny bitch was hanging out on a fucking street corner where all the other whores in the world work." His eyes darted to Maximo before returning to me. I thought he'd put the pieces together, but the two-piece puzzle was clearly beyond his shit-for-brain capabilities. His throat bobbed as he swallowed nervously. "Look, if she's one of your girls, my bad. But she didn't have any money on her. So if that bitch said I took it—"

Using my hold on his shirt, I pulled him away and slammed his head against the wall. His eyes went unfocused before he rapidly blinked.

"She"—I slammed him against the wall again, though lighter that time since I didn't want him losing consciousness—"isn't a *honey-ass tweaker*. She"—another slam—"isn't a whore. She"—one last one before I released him to collapse in a heap—"is *my* fucking woman."

"I didn't know, I swear. I thought it was an easy score of her bankroll."

"Did that require touching her?" My voice was calm. Even. "Are you such a weak little bitch that robbing a small woman required you to beat on her first? Or were you compensating for your tiny dick when you grabbed her tits so hard, they *bruised*?"

"I didn't know, man. I didn't know," he rushed out.

Not that he was sorry. Not that he regretted touching her. Just that he didn't know she was mine.

The world is about to be a better place.

Tears and snot mixed on his face as the gravity of his situation finally penetrated his thick skull. Or maybe it was the concussion. It didn't matter anyway.

I stepped back and met Cole's gaze. He started typing out a message without me having to say anything.

Sick minds think alike.

Knowing it was handled, I turned toward the table and swung my gaze to the other man—Ronald Jacobs—who still sat in the chair. A sharp, metallic tang in the air grew stronger, and I glanced down to see his wrists were dripping blood as he worked to dislodge himself.

"Going somewhere?" I asked.

His beady eyes darted between me and the slumped man on the floor. He hesitated for a few seconds, like he wanted to protect his friend. That kind of stupid loyalty would've been commendable had he placed it with someone who deserved it.

And had they not come after my woman.

His sense of preservation kicked in, and he flipped. "I didn't do nothing."

"The double negatives," Cole muttered.

Jacobs didn't correct his grammar as he repeated, "I didn't do nothing. It was all Ez. He said that girl was an easy hit and then we could party big that night. He was the one who touched her. Not me. I just kept watch, but I didn't touch her, I swear."

"You pathetic *nobody*," Zale started, standing up and moving forward like he was going to attack. When Maximo blocked the way, the dumbass was smart enough to launch himself back against the wall. He kept spewing his insults, though. "You're nothing, and you'd be less than nothing if it weren't for me. Dead in some gutter, and no one would notice."

I reached into my coat pocket and pulled out my black kit.

I came from a family of overachievers. We'd all inherited trust funds from my paternal grandparents that we could live on but didn't. My dad had been a judge and my mom had been a professor before they'd retired—though Ma still did guest lectures when bribed or flattered enough. My four sisters were competitive among themselves. Violet was a nurse. Maggie owned a restaurant in New York. Emily was a CFO of a media company in California. And Andrea was a chemist.

One who headed a facility with a lot of funding and very little oversight.

I pulled an already loaded single dose shot from the kit and tapped it against the table. "The fact of the matter is, my woman ended up bruised. Cut. Hurt. So one of you will pay." I set it on the table and stepped back. "You two can decide yourselves."

Zale didn't have the same battle with loyalty that Jacobs had. There was no hesitation. No delay. Without the cuffs that kept Jacobs in place, he did exactly what I wanted.

He stormed forward, snatched up the needle, and jabbed it in his *friend's* arm.

I'd honestly expected him to at least think about stabbing me with it. Or try to use it as a threat against us to free himself. It just confirmed that he was a narcissistic moron.

Jacobs let out a cry. His pale face stayed scrunched as he hyperventilated, his heavy breathing echoing in the silent room. After a minute, he pried his eye open to look at me. He took in my smirk and opened his other eye. He whispered some prayers as tears flowed down his cheeks. "You were just trying to scare us. Holy fuck. That's all this was. A scare. It worked." More tears. "It fucking worked."

"I, uhh, knew that," Zale tried. "I was just calling their bluff, but I knew nothing would happen—"

"Fuck offfff." Jacobs' voice warbled, his lips turning down. "You're full of..." Arching in his chair, he winced.

I talked quickly before the pain stole his ability to listen. To comprehend the magnitude of his fuckup. "Not a scare tactic. A very real poison is flowing through your veins. It's going to feel like your skin is slowly being peeled from your body. It'll *burn* like your blood is being boiled from the insides." I held up the kit. "I have a compound that can neutralize it within seconds. All that pain, your impending death,"—I snapped my fingers—"gone like that."

He scrambled for it. The table screeched as he dragged it along the floor, trying in vain to get relief from the slow building agony.

My laugh was cruel even to my own ears as I tucked the case away. "You don't get that. Like you said, you just watched. So now we'll just watch."

He tried again to squeeze his hand through the cuff. When that didn't work, he slammed it against the table—likely in an attempt to break the bones into being more pliable. A sheen of sweat broke out over his face as he continued thrashing like a trapped bear.

Actually, bear gave him too much credit.

A trapped weasel.

When he couldn't break his own hand, he switched his focus to the table. He knocked it onto its side and futilely tried to break it. Then he tried to drag it with him as he lunged for me in desperation.

A stiff breeze could've knocked him over, so I plopped into a chair and kicked the already toppled table. It pulled him back, and he clutched his side, curling into himself. Another cramp tore through him, and he turned his desperate eyes to me. "Please."

"Nope."

No hesitation.

No sympathy.

Nothing but watching.

He looked at Maximo. "Just shoot me."

"Nah," Maximo said with the same heartlessness.

"Fuck, fuck, fuck," Zale chanted over and over. But not with guilt at the torturous death of his friend that was his fault—in the actions that'd landed them there and literally since he'd injected the dose of hell. He was only worried about himself as he scanned the room repeatedly, trying to save his own ass.

Far sooner than he deserved, the last weak breath left Jacobs.

It was quick, but it wasn't a pain-free death. Those last minutes of his life had likely felt like an eternity of suffering.

While we just watched.

Like he deserved.

Something thumped loudly, and Zale jolted, letting out a high-pitched screech.

"Are you four?" Cole asked with a mocking snicker as he opened the door.

Marco stepped in with his hands full, and I righted the table so he could set the load down.

Meeting my eyes, he tipped his lips in a barely-there smirk and quietly chuckled. "You're a sick bastard."

I put my hand to my heart. "Thank you."

His expression returned to stone as he tossed me a pair of gloves. "Freddy says if you ruin those, you owe him a new pair."

"Noted."

I stood and rounded the table, going the long way as I set the gloves down next to the rest of it.

"W-what is that?" Zale haltingly asked. He sniffed, trying to get more of the mouthwatering scent.

I didn't blame him. The heavy scent of blood, sweat, terror, and death that'd clung to the small space was replaced by something sweet.

"Dessert." I stopped in front of him and jerked my head toward the door. "You can go."

"W-what?"

"Yeah, I want to enjoy dessert, so get out." I walked back toward the table, discreetly removing a new pen from my kit as I went.

I could hear him scramble to stand, stumble, then scramble some more like a cartoon character running in place. When he reached the door, Cole and Marco moved out of the way. A relieved sob escaped him as he yanked the door.

It clattered loudly but didn't open. It wouldn't without the correct thumbprint. That didn't stop him from trying again. And again. That time, an anguished sob tore through him.

I almost felt pity for the poor bastard.

Moving behind him, I jabbed his neck with another needle. He spun around, his hand lifting toward the stinging wound.

You ain't seen nothing yet.

Before he could touch his skin, his arm dropped uselessly. I grabbed a chair and slid it behind him. Just before he fell back, Marco shifted it out of the way so Zale crashed to the floor, knocking his head against the edge of the metal seat.

My laughter cut off. "Hey, wait, this means I have to lift this fucker into the chair now."

Marco kicked at Zale's torso and shoulder until he was positioned near the drain. "More convenient now."

"Smart." I crouched next to the frozen man. He could hear. See. And most importantly, feel. I told him as much. "This is going to hurt. *Burn*. You'll feel every excruciating moment."

Soft whimpers were all he was capable of. Those and the tears that steadily streamed down his face.

I pulled on the heat proof kitchen gloves before placing a metal funnel in Zale's malleable mouth. I'd originally planned to use fryer oil, but when he'd called Mila a *honey-ass tweaker*, I realized how short sighted that was.

Boring.

Overdone.

The scalding honey and sugar mixture was much better.

It wouldn't burn away at the layers of his esophagus. It would cling to his insides *while* it burned away the layers of his esophagus. And then, if that didn't kill him, it would harden to suffocate him from the inside out.

Far more poetic.

Careful not to injure myself in the process, I slowly streamed the sweet mixture into his mouth. It pooled there until instinct kicked in, and he reflexively swallowed. His eyes screamed what his body was incapable of.

Stop.

Please.

Kill me now.

I'm a fucking waste of space dickhead who should've been swallowed or wiped away on a cum rag.

The last one might've been what I thought, not him, but it was still true.

Blood and who knew what else flowed out of the side of his mouth. His ears. His nose. And then his eyes. I cut off the syrupy stream as the light went out behind them, his chest no longer a rapid rise and fall.

"That is fucked." Maximo chuckled. "But fitting."

"It's no dove carved into a back," I pointed out, referencing his own payback.

"And see?" Marco gestured to the leakage going down the drain. "Easy cleanup."

"You know your shit." I set the pot down and removed the gloves before kicking the dead man at my feet. I looked at Maximo. "He'll have to get disposed of, but I'll dump Jacobs at their place. If anyone bothers to do an autopsy, all it'll show is an OD. They'll assume Zale took off. No blowback."

Maximo lifted his chin in approval. "This is why I keep you around."

"I thought it was my color-coded organization."

"Aren't they the same?"

He wasn't wrong. The same thing that made me good at keeping chaos organized was the same thing that helped me think ten steps ahead. It was a fucked skill to have, but it was a skill nonetheless.

"You can take off," I told my boss. "It'll be a while before I can dump pube 'stache at the motel. I'm going to go back to Mila, and then come back around midnight."

Marco and Cole looked at each other, communicating silently before Cole spoke. "We've got this. You can both go."

"No, that's—" I started before he cut in.

"You can make it up to me when I've got someone else to spend my nights with besides this grumpy bastard."

It was my mess, and any other time, I'd stay to clean it up. But not then.

Not with Mila waiting.

After going over the plan, I retreated to the elevator and pulled out my phone. Since I didn't have bodies to dump, there was no reason to stick around.

> Me: Change of plans, sunshine. We're going home.

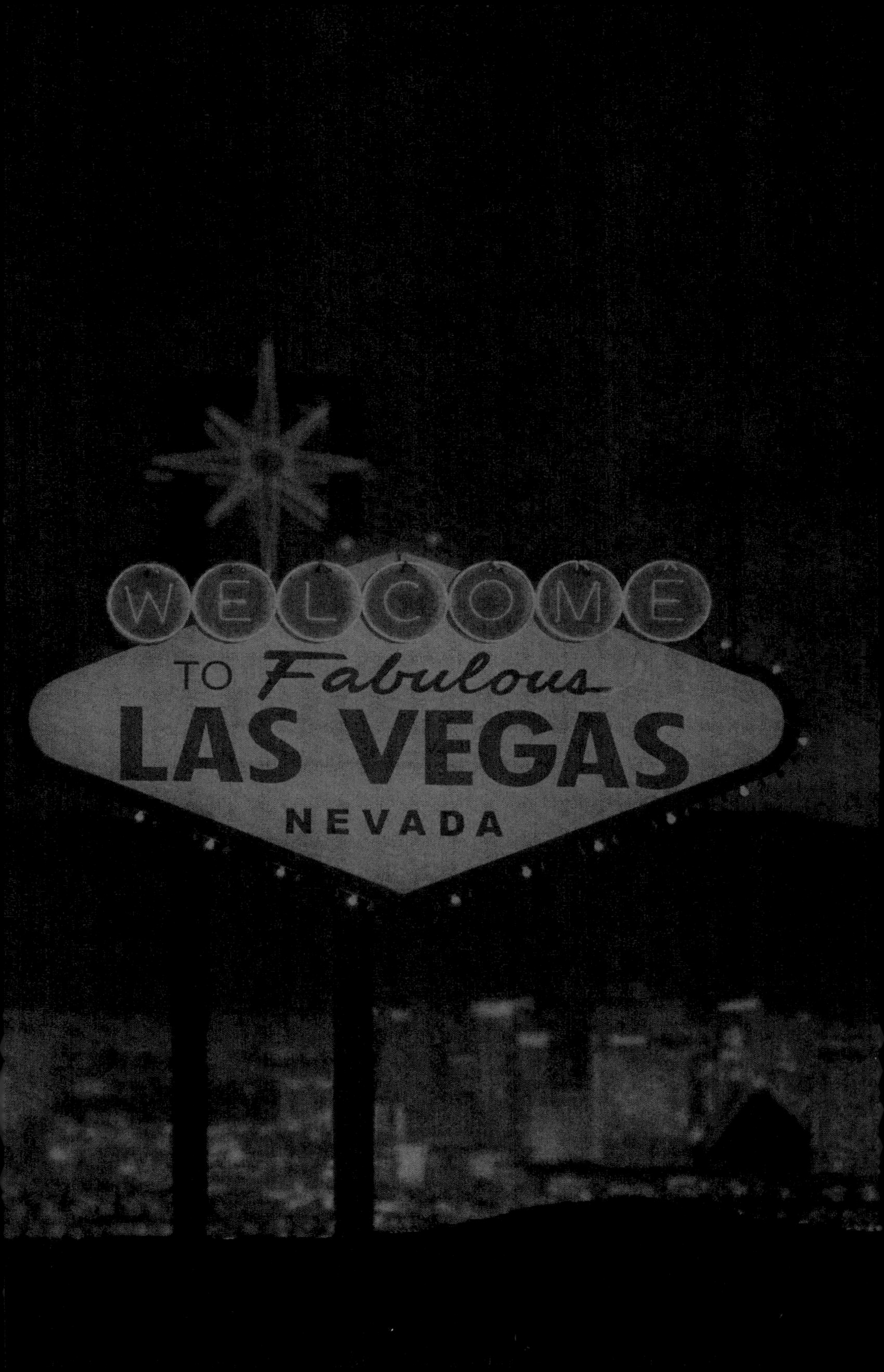
WELCOME
TO Fabulous
LAS VEGAS
NEVADA

CHAPTER 20
DON'T PUSH PEOPLE'S BUTTONS FOR FUN
MILA

"What do you know about Daddies?"

Oh thank God.

After leaving Moonlight, I'd wanted to talk. No, I'd wanted *Ash* to talk. But like it was a normal day and nothing had changed, he'd only asked about what I wanted for dinner.

As if I could eat at a time like that.

And though my stomach had been in knots, that's exactly what he'd made me do. Eat while we watched TV and pretended everything was normal.

That I wasn't hyperaware of how good he looked sitting at the other end of the couch, still wearing his slacks and button-down, but with the sleeves rolled to show more of his muscular, tattooed forearms.

That my mind wasn't replaying the memory of his mouth on me in a constant loop.

That I wasn't obsessing about our impending conversation.

A conversation it was finally time for.

"I looked some stuff up," I shared, "but there was a lot. And most of it was contradictory. So, uh, not much."

Ash's expression was soft when I met his hazel eyes. "That's a good thing. It means there's less bullshit for me to undo while I show you what a *good* relationship is." I watched as a blazing fire replaced the warmth in his gaze. "While I show you a fuckuva lot more than that."

Even without knowing the specifics, his words had me fighting the need to squeeze my thighs to relieve the building ache.

My voice came out airy. "Like what?"

"What I like. What *you* like. How good it can be." Ash's deep voice was gravel and fire. "I'll give you anything. *Everything.* But I'll demand everything from you in return."

"You're in the market for a shitty apartment? Or some packages of almost expired instant rice?" I rolled my eyes and gave a self-deprecating laugh. "Otherwise, I've got nothing."

He didn't share my amusement. At all. Like a flip was switched, the desire was gone in a flash and somberness took over. It was impossible—and not just because he was already massive—but he seemed to get bigger. More menacing. Daunting.

Hotter.

"Live and fucking die to give you every-damn-thing, and it still won't come close to what you can give if you choose to, Camila."

"How can that be true? I have literally nothing." I flung a hand out toward the grandeur of his home. "What could I give you that you don't already have?"

"Your honesty. Your laughter and sweet smiles. Your stubborn as shit attitude. Your time. Your desire. Your body. Your trust. Your submission."

I might not have seen the value in any of that, but they were at least easy to offer him.

Right up until the last two.

In a short time, I already trusted him more than I'd ever trusted anyone, but that wasn't saying much. And with the other thing...

"I don't think I can give you my submission," I admitted, hoping that didn't automatically spell the end before anything really began. "I can't give it to anyone because I don't think I have it. Like you said, I'm stubborn."

"Which is what will make it that much sweeter every time you submit or listen or follow a rule. Because I know it's not easy. That you're doing it for me. Because you trust me."

"There are rules?"

I'd barely had any actual rules when I was a kid, outside of shut up, stay out of the way, and don't talk to cops, teachers, or bill collectors. And never, *ever* call her Mom in front of a man.

Any chores I had were by choice because I hadn't wanted to live in Veronica's filth.

I worked to suppress a tremble of apprehension as my imagination ran wild with the possibilities.

And none of them were good since my points of reference were male-centric porn and online horror stories of abuse passed off as BDSM.

"Yeah, sunshine, there will be rules." He leaned back and stretched his arm across the back of the couch, like we were talking about the weather or a movie. "Let's start with the one that'll be hardest for you."

"Okay," I drawled.

"If something bothers you, tell me *immediately*. No lies. No downplaying. And sure as hell no letting shit fester until you run from me. If you would've asked me why I wanted you with me at Sunrise, it would've saved you pain." He dropped his eyes to my ass before raising a brow. "A lot of it."

"You're right, that will be hard," I admitted. "I'm not good with stuff like that."

"That's okay, I'm patient." I already didn't like his smirk even before he added, "I'll happily punish you however many times it takes."

That should've been a terrifying threat. But down to my soul, I knew it came from a place of caring.

Not that I was anxious to sign up for another spanking—caring or not—but I couldn't ignore the warmth that spread through me.

Ash twisted a finger in my hair and tugged to get my attention. "I don't know what the fuck you've been through that you've convinced yourself you're an imposition. I'm not gonna make it a rule you have to tell me—*yet*—but I hope you will when you're ready. In the meantime, I'm gonna work to undo those knots." His lip quirked. "Or replace them with my own. And that requires you to be honest when something is wrong."

"So you can tell me to get over it or deal with it?" I shot back.

"Yeah, sometimes," he said, completely unrepentant. "I'm used to giving orders and having them followed." My insecurities didn't even have the chance to flare up before he clarified. "At work. It doesn't occur to me to stop and explain myself. I'll try to be mindful of that while you're still getting used to me. Not saying I'll bend to what you want. Actually, I pretty much guarantee I won't. But I can share my reasoning, even if it's as simple as I *want* to buy you shit."

"But I don't need anything."

I prepared for another *get used to it* that never came.

"You agree to this"—he gestured back and forth between us—"there're gonna be a lot of changes in your life. One is that it's no longer about the bare minimum. You won't have to settle for only what you *need*."

That was such a bizarre concept. I couldn't even picture what that would be like beyond what he'd already shown me.

And he wasn't done.

"I *want* to do it. It makes me hard to see you wear the clothes I bought or eat the food I made. It makes me happy to take care of you. Fuck knows you need it."

The way he said it didn't sound like an insult, but that was exactly how my pride took it. As if I was incapable of caring for myself.

"I don't need to be treated like some helpless kid. I've lived alone since I was sixteen, but I've been on my own a lot longer than that. I might not have a closet full of suits in my big house or boring-ass penthouses, but that doesn't matter." Aware that it made me look like the child I'd just insisted I wasn't—and a petulant one at that—I crossed my arms. "I've been doing just fine."

Ash's jaw clenched, but his voice was gentle when he pushed. "And how tired are you from everything falling on your shoulders? How burned out does it make you feel?" He reached over and cupped my jaw, forcing me to look at him. "How lonely?"

With each rapid-fire question, the mental exhaustion I barely held at bay pushed in. It pulsed around the edges, threatening to take over. To drag me down once and for all.

Surprise tears burned in my eyes, and I took a shuddering breath as I fought to keep them back.

Ash knew he had me there and went for the kill. "Wouldn't it be nice to hand all that weight over and let someone else carry it for once?"

It should've been irresistible. A literal dream offer from a literal dream man.

I was just the wrong... everything.

"I would *never* date someone because of what they could do for me," I insisted, nauseous at the concept. "I'm not a user. Or some gold digger. I'm not..."

Veronica.

"Christ, I know that," Ash bit out. "That's not what this is."

"Are you sure? Because it sounds pretty accurate." I grabbed the fabric I wore and shook it. "In exchange for pretty dresses, I do fucked-up shit like crawl on the floor to you, let you spank my ass, and call you Daddy sometimes—"

"All the time."

His interruption made my brain stutter for a moment. "What?"

"You call me Daddy all the time. I don't care where we are or who's around." He tilted his head and rubbed his beard. "If you really feel uncomfortable, I'll occasionally settle for Behemoth."

"I thought this was a, uh, bedroom thing for most people."

The heat in his eyes flared like a warning that I was on thin ice. I wasn't sure if he wanted to kiss me or spank me again.

I wasn't sure which I would prefer.

"I'm not most people," he rumbled. "And about the crawling, that isn't something I like, but if that's what you're into, I can accommodate."

"No, that's not... I'm just saying..." I bit back a growl of frustration, though I wasn't sure which of us it was aimed at.

His hand returned to my jaw, and his thumb covered my lips. "And none of this is fucked up. The insinuation that you're a whore is what's fucked. The insinuation that you're a whore, *and* I'm the kind of asshole who has to pay for pussy is why you're lucky you're not back over my knee. This isn't a transactional arrangement, and it isn't only sex."

My question came out muffled. "It's not?"

"Fuck no." His hand dropped to slowly push under my skirt. Up my thigh. Higher. Achingly slow, he teased me over my panties. "Don't get me wrong, it'll be that, too. Christ, I don't think my hand or dick have gotten a break since I saw you, so when I finally..." He took a sharp breath. "But it's not only sex. I want you. *All* of you. If you give me you, that's it, Camila. There's no half-assing this. No running every time you tangle yourself up in your head. You let me handle that. Let me handle everything. In exchange, I'll be greedy with your time. I'll expect you to listen to me, and I'll reward or punish you accordingly. Most importantly"—his strong finger zeroed in on my clit—"everything you get will be from me. Because *I* take care of you."

Almost.

Almost there.

I just need to get closer to him.

It wasn't lost on me that my thoughts mirrored the ones from when I'd been running away.

How quickly desperation changed.

My lids fluttered closed. My breath grew shallow and shaky. My pussy clenched around nothing, needy and wanting.

Just as the edge neared, and I prepared to dive over it, Ash didn't just ease off.

He *stopped*.

The monster.

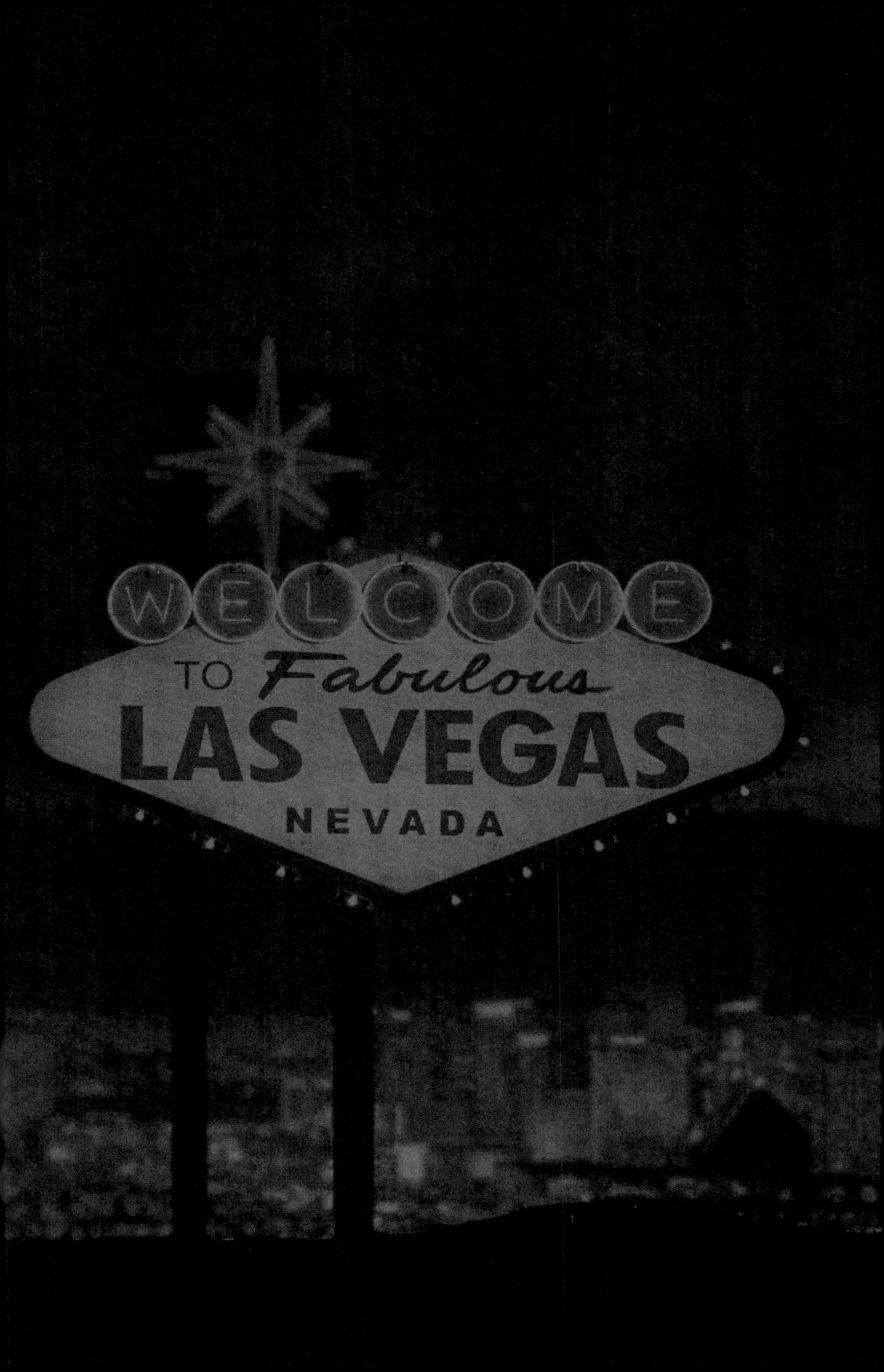
WELCOME
TO Fabulous
LAS VEGAS
NEVADA

CHAPTER 21
MAYBE TRUST SOMEONE
ASH

I LEANED AWAY, GIVING US both space before the thin hold I had on myself was gone. "Tell me what you're thinking."

"I'm thinking that there aren't enough lobster stories in the world," Mila said with a little huff that shot straight to my dick.

"About this."

Surprisingly, she didn't ignore my order or claim it was nothing. "I read some stuff."

I kept my response just as vague since that could mean anything from her horoscope to restraining orders. "Okay."

"And I, uh, have questions." She barely looked at me as she toyed with the hem of her dress. I doubted she even realized how badly she tormented me with each flash of her thigh. "You said you want me to call you Daddy all the time."

It wasn't a question, but I confirmed. "That's right."

"And do what you say all the time."

Again, it wasn't a question, but I answered, "In a way."

She shot me an exasperated glare.

"I'm not going to micromanage your whole day. You'd have

your rules. The occasional extra order. But unless I have plans for you, how you spend your time is up to you."

"Okay, so how would that work once I move out?"

"Easy. You won't be."

"I have to. I need to get back to my life. My apartment." Her face scrunched, and I could see and hear the stress spiking. "I haven't even started looking for a new job."

"You don't need one."

Mila reared back, looking more shocked and outraged by that than anything else we'd talked about. "I can't just *not* work. I've been doing it since I was thirteen and getting paid under the table."

"Then it sounds like you need a break," I said when what I really wanted to do was time travel back and shake the shit out of the adults in her life.

"I don't *want* a break."

"Did you love what you did at The Roulette? Was it your dream job? The best way you could imagine spending the day?"

"Well, no, but that doesn't matter. Most people hate their jobs, but they still have to—"

I twirled my finger in her hair and gave a gentle tug. "You're not most people."

Not anymore.

Not if you say yes.

Her pouty lips bowed into a frown that I wanted to kiss away.

Or fuck away.

"I can't just take time off. It'll make it impossible to find something new once we're..." Her words trailed off, but I knew what she was thinking.

I wasn't sure if I was more pissed that she was already planning the end or amused that she thought she had a choice once she agreed to be mine.

"This would be a different conversation if you had your dream career, but we both know that's not the case. And my woman isn't going to be on her hands and knees, cleaning jizz stains out of a hotel carpet." She opened her mouth, but I cut in.

"And if you're thinking that's not something that happens at the nice resorts, you're wrong. Nebula is one of the best places in all of Vegas, it costs a shit-ton a night, and we've got a diplomat who was banned for leaving a room covered in piss. It was on the damn ceiling." Mila already looked green at that, but I still tacked on, "And that's not the worst story I have."

"It was... *why*? Was he drunk, or was the bathroom broken?"

"It's a kink."

She grimaced at the visual and moved on. "If I'm not working, what would I do?"

"You want to pick up a hobby, great. You want to take some classes, also great—so long as your schedule is flexible around mine." She opened her mouth to argue further, but I reminded, "I already told you I'd be selfish with your time."

She remained silent while she thought that over for a minute. "When we... When things are done, will you pass along my résumé to the housekeeping department at one of the hotels?" She didn't give me the chance to respond before she amended, "Not necessarily at Black Resorts since that'd be awkward. I'm fine with any you have connections with."

A few things struck me.

For one, she could've asked me to guarantee her a job. Instead, she just wanted me to hand off her résumé.

For another, she could've asked me to guarantee her a job working reception, in the offices, or, hell, as a fucking showgirl. Instead, she hadn't tried to take advantage.

But I focused on the most important part.

No longer amused, my fingers that'd been playing in her long dark hair fisted. She turned her wide eyes to me as I tugged harder. "Gotta say, sunshine, I'm not big on your use of the word *when*." At her lowered brows, I explained, "That's twice in this conversation alone that you've talked about when this is over. Kinda hurts my ego that you're ending shit in your head before you've even agreed to anything."

"Sorry."

"Mila."

"Sor..." She smiled shyly. "I'm a planner."

I went back to gently playing with her hair. "That's fine. Plan something else. Not that."

"Right," she whispered.

"What other questions do you have?"

I watched as she started to shift before catching herself. "Would you tell me what to do in the bedroom?"

In the bedroom. The office. The kitchen counter.

This couch, if the conversation goes well.

I didn't say any of that out loud and turned it on her. "Would you like me to?"

Her small but immediate nod sent a surge of blood to my dick. "I, uh, don't really have much experience, so I think it'd be reassuring to know I'm doing the right thing. I've always been a quick learner, so—"

"Camila."

Her words cut off as she looked at me.

And that made me harder.

"If you want to finish this conversation, you gotta stop torturing me."

"I'm not."

"You are."

That time, her smile wasn't shy. It was a real, full smile that held a hint of satisfaction.

It boded well for the relationship but not for my sanity.

"What else?" I asked.

"Do you have any fetishes or kinks I should know about?"

Yes.

You saying fetishes or kinks.

Actually, just you. Full stop.

Again, I didn't say it out loud. I should've let it fly so she knew exactly what she was getting into. But when it came to my growing obsession with her, I still held back.

At least until she agreed.

Moving my hand from her hair, I cupped the back of her head

and pulled her closer. Even then, it wasn't close enough, and I lifted her to straddle me with her ass on my knees. "New rule."

She pulled her lip between her teeth and braced.

"If we're sitting, you're on my lap."

"Okay."

Okay.

Easy as that.

It took me a moment to remember her question—and that she hadn't agreed to anything, so putting her on the coffee table and dropping to my knees to eat her pussy until she screamed wasn't happening.

For then.

"The diplomat and I don't share a piss kink, if that's what you're worried about."

"I wasn't, but it's still reassuring to know."

"I'm guessing you read about BDSM today."

"I did."

"I like the first two parts. BDS. Bondage and discipline. Dominance and submission. The other SM isn't my thing." I watched for a reaction that never came. "Most classify being a Daddy as a kink, but I don't. It's not something I role play. It's not some added fun. It's unconventional, sure, but it's just who I am."

She studied me, her words carefully nonchalant. "I read about how people do this to cope with a trauma."

"I'm sure that's true for some, but not in my case. There's no reason for it. Nothing happened that triggered some big change. I've always been like this." I thought about Juliet's advice earlier. "That said, this isn't an either-or situation."

"What do you mean?"

"It's not that either you get on board with what I like, or this doesn't happen. You don't just have a say in it, you hold the power. You decide whether you want to hand it over to me or not. I want this. I think it'll fit and be good for both of us. But even if you don't want me to be your Daddy, I still want you."

Mila leaned back so far, she would've toppled off my lap had it not been for my hands on her waist. "You'd go vanilla for me?"

I lifted my chin. "Not saying it'll be a one-eighty. I'm a bossy prick. I'll want to spoil you. I'll have suggested guidelines regarding your safety and well-being because I know how dangerous Vegas can be. But they won't involve being bent over my lap if you don't follow them."

Of all the ways I'd have to change, that was the only part that didn't sit well with me—and not just because I'd loved reddening Mila's cute ass.

Her gaze went over my shoulder. "Wouldn't you miss it or be unsatisfied?"

"Fuck no. I can't deny that I liked hearing you say Daddy, and that I like control. I get off on it. But it's not about making you do shit for me. It's about knowing that you depended on and needed me."

Mila took a shuddering inhale, but otherwise, her face was blank. "And you'd like that kind of neediness?"

"Can do without a lot of the other shit if it means having you, but that part is mandatory." I tested my own control by tugging her closer so she could feel my hard cock stretching down my thigh. "I need you to need me."

I wanted Mila to tell me she did so badly, I was close to begging.

I'd never begged before, but I'd also never volunteered to tone down the Daddy in me.

"What happens if I don't like something you do?" she asked instead.

"Like buying you stuff?"

She shook her head.

"Spanking you?"

She shook her head again. "That wasn't as bad as I thought. I don't even know why I was crying so bad. It barely hurt."

I knew why. It was a release of all the emotions and frustrations she kept bottled up. A tiny fraction of that weight on her shoulders being melted away.

One side of my mouth curved up. "I can fix that."

"No, no. I'm good." She tilted her head. "Just, like, other stuff. What happens if I don't like something?"

Rather than answer, I asked a question that we needed to discuss anyway. "Is there something you don't think you'd like?"

She averted her eyes and looked at the buttons on my shirt like they were the most interesting thing in the world.

I wanted them back, but it was obvious she was gathering her nerve to say something more important.

Her hands trembled as she quietly spoke. "I can't stand yelling or name-calling. I read that some people like being called degrading names, and that's great for them, but I... I..."

Seeing *and* feeling how overwrought she was becoming, I gently grabbed her chin. "Name-calling beyond *brat* or *little girl* isn't my thing. I already know you don't like the first one, so that's out."

"I'm not exactly wild about the second one, either," she muttered, though her wobbly smile said otherwise. "But it's fine."

"As far as yelling, I can't guarantee you won't hear me if I'm working from home, but I promise to always do it in a different room."

She visibly deflated. "You don't have to do that. Just don't aim it at me. Though I'd rather get screamed at than get the silent treatment."

"I'd never do either one."

"I'm okay with you not talking, but if I say something, and you ignore me..."

"I would never ignore you. I could never ignore you. It's not something you have to worry about." When she didn't add more, I prompted, "What else?"

"I'm not comfortable with being, um, *shared*."

I reflexively tightened my hold and didn't bother trying to loosen it. "That's okay because I sure as fuck don't share. Ever." Hoping it was the correct bet, I showed a glimpse of my possessive cards. "When I say I'm going to be greedy with your time, I mean to the point where you won't have a second to even think about anyone else." I didn't hesitate before adding, "And that already goes both ways. Anything else?"

"The spanking was fine, but anything like actual hitt—"

"Won't happen."

"But what if I make you *really* mad?"

"No level of mad would make me hit you. Or any other woman, for that matter. If you do something to earn a punishment, and emotions are running too high, it waits. We step away. Take a deep breath. We talk about it until you feel comfortable. *If* you feel comfortable. But even in the heat of the moment, I have control of myself. They'll feel never-ending, but my spank count is accurate. They'll never be hard enough to do damage. And they end the second they're over. Whatever you did to earn them is done and forgiven, and we move on."

Her lips tipped. "I had briefly wondered if they'd last forever."

"Now imagine when I'm not taking it easy on you because, fair warning, I was. If there's a next time, it'll hurt worse. Depending on the infraction, you might get more of them, or they might be mixed with other punishments that you also won't like."

"Such as?"

"Ropes. Edging. Complete orgasm denial."

"That's not that bad," she said more to herself than me.

Famous last words, little girl.

"But whatever it is, we'll talk it through first. Handing out punishments is part of being a Daddy—"

"Why, though?"

Since she'd done more than a two-second browse online, she likely knew the answer to that. I got the feeling she wanted my specific answer and not a generalized one.

"None of the rules are arbitrary. They serve a purpose, and usually it's to protect someone's safety or well-being."

"And sitting on your lap is..."

"For my emotional well-being."

Mila rolled her eyes, but it didn't bother me. Even if she said yes, it wouldn't be a rule that she couldn't do it. It wasn't hurting anyone.

And I liked the show of comfort in her defiance. It was better than her forcing herself to shrink because she didn't want to be a bother.

"If you agree, these rules are to keep you or our relationship safe. I wouldn't be a good Daddy by letting them go broken like they don't matter because then it means protecting you and the relationship doesn't, either. Like the praise I'll give, it's another way to show I care about you and what we have, that I value the trust you've given to me, and that I'm doing my job to protect all three." I ran my hands along Mila's thighs and squeezed. "Even if it's from yourself."

I barely finished my sentence before Mila moved suddenly. Not to push away or punch me in the dick for that last bit.

No.

Leaning up, Mila kissed me.

And sealed her fate.

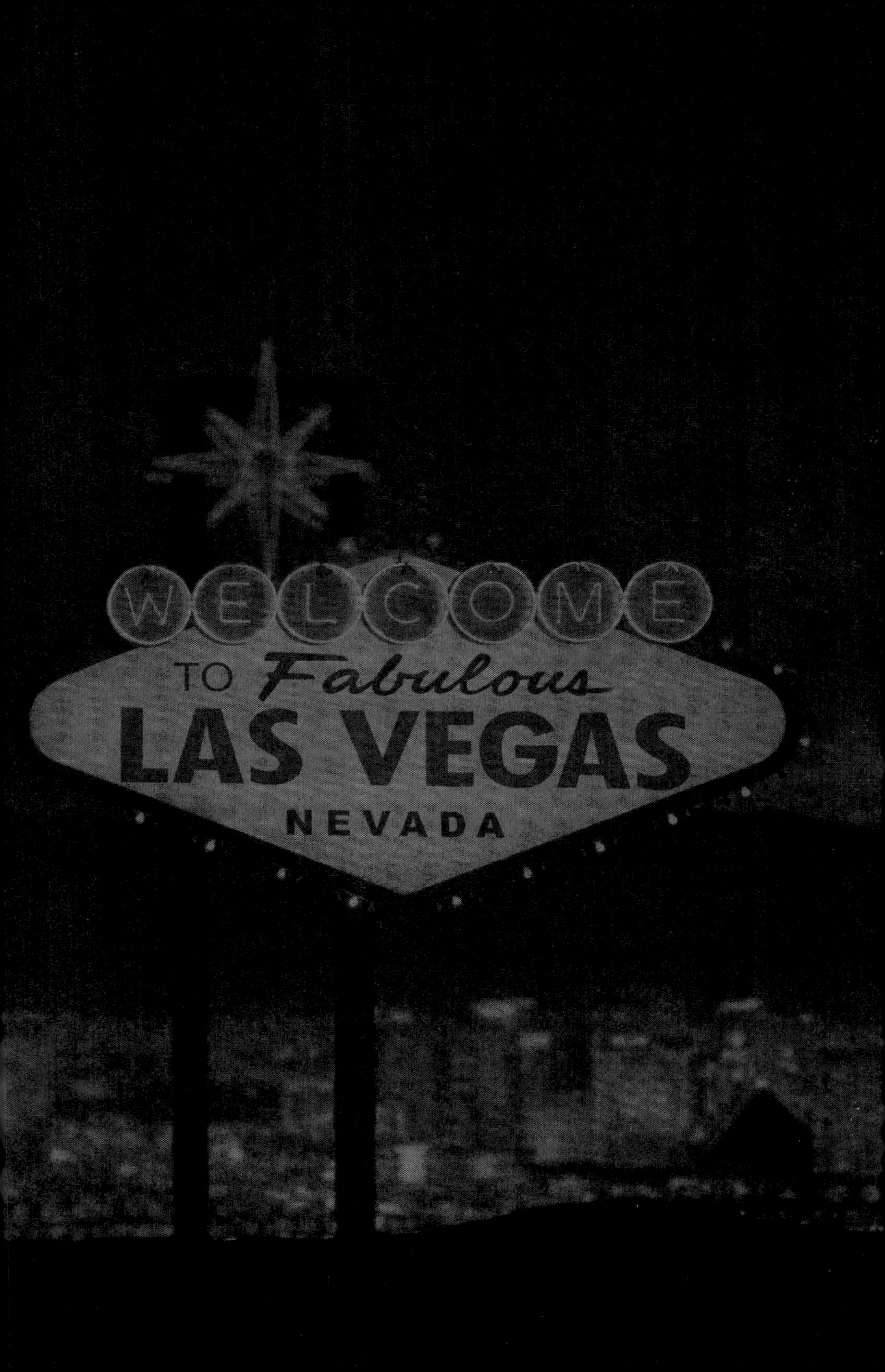
WELCOME
TO Fabulous
LAS VEGAS
NEVADA

CHAPTER 22
And Occasionally Stand Up for Yourself
MILA

In the short time I'd known Ash, he'd said a lot of sweet things. Stuff that made me feel warm. Stuff that made me feel hot. Stuff that I filed away and hoped I'd never forget because no one had ever talked to me with such nonchalant affection.

But even with all that goodness, none of it came close to what he'd just said.

At the insinuation that I was someone worth caring about...

That I was valued...

That I was worth his protection...

I'd tried to swallow past the razor blades of tenderness that eviscerated my insides and my defenses, but it'd been impossible.

So I gave in.

I kissed him.

And not just a peck. Not even a forceful but closed-mouth one.

My neediness that he saw as a positive and not a personality flaw I needed to fix. My happiness. My excitement. My appreciation. Even my fear and doubts. I put it all into the kiss, hoping it said what my scarred heart was too hesitant to.

That I wanted him.

That I wanted what he offered.

I shook with nerves and the anticipation of what was to come, but when he touched me, it wasn't to return my kiss.

It was to shift me away from him as he ordered, "Stand up."

Panic set in, and I worried I'd done the wrong thing. Words tumbled from my mouth. "Sorry. I'm so sorry. I shouldn't have… Am I supposed to ask—"

Ash leaned forward and brushed his mouth across mine in a small show of reassurance before it was gone. "What did Daddy tell you to do?"

Holy shit.

Holy shit, shit, shit.

I swallowed hard. "To stand."

"I don't like to repeat myself."

Confused and aroused—and confused by how aroused I was—I scrambled off his lap. He stood at the same time, his face staying even with mine initially until I was upright, and he kept going, forcing me to crane my neck to keep the eye contact.

Two people standing at the same time shouldn't have been sexy. Nothing about it was inherently erotic.

But that didn't change the fact that it very much *was*.

"Panties off."

Reaching under my dress, I did as he said.

"Sit on the coffee table."

Since I'd have agreed to investing in a timeshare on Mars if he was the one asking, I sat.

Ash gave a shake of his head. "Lift the back of your skirt and then sit."

That gave me my first hint of pause. "But you use this table, and I'm…"

His eyes closed, but not in anger or irritation. Even I knew that. When he opened them again, he pushed. "You're *what*?" My answer didn't come quick enough for him because he kept going.

"Are you wet for me? Dripping with it?" He reached down and snagged my wrist, pushing it against the massive hard-on that tested the fortitude of his slacks. "Do you need me so bad it hurts?"

My nod was immediate.

"Then sit so Daddy can take care of you. Because if I have to say it again, I'm going to bend you over the table and spank your ass instead."

I bunched my skirt up and sat, not caring anymore.

I was so soaked, the fabric wouldn't have offered any barrier anyway.

A pleased smile curved his mouth. "Good girl."

I wasn't sure if it was possible to orgasm from two words, but my sex rippled like it was close to it.

Ash reached for my chin, tipping it so I looked up at him. "Unless I say otherwise, you never have to ask to kiss or touch me. I want you to do it. Often. Constantly. Kissing me was the right thing to do. I know how difficult it can be for you to put yourself out there like that, and I appreciate it." He squeezed in that way that sent another ripple through me. "Which is why Daddy is going to reward you." He paused. "Remember, say stop and it stops. Always. Got it?"

Since forming a word without working lungs was impossible, I nodded.

The breath that was frozen in my lungs was forced out when I watched Ash drop to his knees in front of me. His hands started at my own knees, spreading them wide and positioning himself between them. He slowly ran his palms up, careful not to drag my dress up in the process. Reaching the top, his thumbs teased my slit before pausing there.

Touching me, but not.

"Lift your dress for me, sunshine. Show me what you're giving me. Show me what's mine."

Ash may have been the one on his knees, but there was no doubt he was still the one in command. If he had just pushed the fabric out of the way, it would've been simple. There'd have been no choice. And that was the point. He wasn't letting me take the easy way out.

He wanted me to make the decision to offer myself. To expose more than just my body. It was terrifying.

It was exhilarating.

I bundled the soft material in my clenched fists and lifted.

There was no pleased smile as a reward. I got something so much better.

An expression of sheer hunger. Not like he was starved and desperate for anything set in front of him. It was different. It was the look of a satisfied man who wanted to eat anyway.

Devour.

And that was exactly what he did.

Using his thumbs, he spread me and bent forward to bury his face between my thighs. The first swipe of his tongue made my ass lift off the table. His groan was muffled as he moved an arm to wrap around me, pulling me tighter to him.

It was good. *Amazing.*

But it still wasn't enough. Not for either of us.

His other hand gripped my thigh and tugged me to the edge. I nearly fell back, barely getting an arm behind me to prop myself up. His tongue lapped at my pussy, dipping in to taste and tease before going back to broad strokes. Moving up to my clit, he circled and flicked until I couldn't stop my hips from rocking.

My legs trembled. My thoughts were a clipped jumble of half-thoughts and base needs. My heavy breaths and whimpers mixed with his groans and the messy, obscene sound of his mouth on me.

When his lips latched on to my clit and he sucked, my free hand shot out to hold him there. I started to drop it away when he shifted back just enough to order, "No. Keep it there."

I dragged my nails through his short blond hair before holding the back of his head like he wanted.

"Christ, such a good girl with such a perfect little pussy." He grunted, and once again, rewarded my obedience. Sucking my clit into his mouth, he held it between his teeth and rapidly flicked his tongue.

I had no clue how he did it. How it felt so good. How it was somehow too much and not enough, all at once.

My thighs shook, fighting to close, but his shoulders held them spread as he greedily took the access he gave himself.

His pace was steady and demanding, and the pressure in my lower belly coiled tighter. It built higher and faster than I'd ever been capable of doing with my fingers. There was no chasing. No rearranging and repositioning in frustration. No slow acceleration to a disappointing finale.

I didn't have to work for it. I didn't have to do anything at all. I took what Ash gave and had no choice in the matter. And when I came apart from his skillful mouth, it was nothing short of euphoric. Blinding pleasure chased by lava and popping candy mixing in my veins wiped all coherent thought from my mind.

Everything except one word.

Ash.

Only I didn't just think it.

I knew I'd said it out loud when his husky voice asked, "Who am I?"

I didn't answer. Not because I didn't want to. I'd already made my decision that I wanted him and everything that came with it. That I liked it.

But getting my sated brain and my mouth to cooperate enough to say it was another matter altogether.

Ash sat up. Even with me on the table, he was taller. "Camila."

I'd always hated my name. But the gruff way he said it, like it was a prayer and a warning, burrowed into me. It twisted and tightened in my lower belly, making me feel hot.

Bold.

Sure.

"Who am I?" He pinched my clit between his fingers and another aftershock slashed through me.

"Daddy," I hissed out, my eyes closing.

I forced my lids open in time to see a look of peaceful contentment filling his expression as he inhaled deeply. He leaned forward, cupping the back of my head to tug me to him.

I turned my head at the last second.

"You got two seconds to tell me why you just turned away from my kiss," Ash rumbled.

"You just... I... It's..."

Even though I hadn't finished three separate sentences, he got what I was trying to say. "Kiss me, or I spit your taste into your mouth."

I blinked, caught off guard by his threat and my body's response to it.

He dropped his hold like he was going to squeeze my cheeks to open my mouth, but I moved before he could and kissed him. He took it further, plunging his tongue in to force me to taste it. The sweet tang of my arousal mixed with something that was all Ash.

It wasn't bad or gross.

I may be on the verge of sensory overload and death by orgasm, but I'm willing to risk it if he keeps doing stuff like that.

Ash pulled away to stand while my arm slowly slid out from behind me until I was flat on my back on a—thankfully sturdy—coffee table.

He just has to give me five minutes.

I got approximately twenty seconds before Ash picked me up. "Let's get you upstairs."

I assumed he meant that in a euphemistic kinda way, but after carrying me to the bedroom, he set me down near the bathroom. "Get ready for bed while I lock up the house."

Wait, what?

I didn't have the chance to ask before he left the room. I stood and looked at the empty doorway before snapping out of it. It may not have been what I thought we were doing, but a good idea was a good idea.

And after everything that'd happened on the coffee table, I desperately needed a change of clothes.

I grabbed a pair of pajamas and went to the bathroom to get ready. By the time I finished, the light was off, and Ash was already in bed. Shirtless. As in, no shirt. Splashes of colorful tattoos swirled with black and gray ones, but I couldn't make out any of the details in the dim light from the plug-in. He was typing something on his phone, but as soon as he saw me, he put it down and tossed something my way.

I caught it and unraveled the plain gray tee that was as soft as butter.

"From now on, you sleep in my shirt."

Since that was fine by me, I went back into the bathroom to switch clothes, and then put my refolded pajamas away before returning to the bed.

I climbed in, feeling more awkward than I had the other couple of times we'd shared a bed. Likely because there was the possibility that our sleeping together could change to *sleeping together*. I was tense, waiting to see what he'd do.

I didn't have to wait long. Before I could even pull the covers over me, Ash sat and lifted the tee I wore. One second, my panties were there. The next, they were being tugged down my legs and flung across the room. "In my shirt and *only* my shirt."

Surprisingly, that was fine by me, too. "Okay."

"Okay," he repeated, positioning me so I was on my side with my head on his bare chest. He pressed his lips to my forehead. "Go to sleep."

I was sated and exhausted, but even in the stretching silence, I couldn't obey him. It wasn't my mind keeping me awake—though it did keep replaying the *Greatest Hits* from my day—it was my body.

It was restless.

And curious.

My only serious boyfriend had claimed that men had to orgasm every time they got hard, or their balls could explode. I hadn't believed it as a sixteen-year-old, and I sure as hell didn't believe it as a twenty-year-old.

But I was still surprised that Ash was going to sleep without any relief. I'd seen and felt how turned on he'd been. Thick and hard and just as massive as the rest of him.

Thinking of it sent another tremor through me that was part apprehension but mostly arousal.

Ash misread it as a shiver and pulled the blanket higher.

Pulling my lips between my teeth, I barely breathed as I slowly set my hand on his chest near my face.

Then I lowered it to his abs. His many, many, *many* abs.

It took a few minutes to build the confidence to move again, and even then I didn't just lower my hand. Nope. As smooth as freaking sandpaper, I feigned an itchy nose and lifted my hand to scratch it. When I set it back down, it landed much lower on his abdomen.

Just a little farther and...

I yelped when Ash's long fingers wrapped around my wrist, thwarting my progress. His voice was thick and rough. "What exactly are you doing?"

"I, uhh, was just trying to get comfortable," I lied.

"You wanna touch my dick for comfort, you do it any time. Starting tomorrow."

"But you made me... and you didn't..."

Maybe I should finish a sentence.

I didn't get the chance before Ash spoke, his tone firm and clipped like I'd upset him. "There are gonna be plenty of times when I get you off 'cause I want your scent or taste or just because I can. It's not quid pro quo."

"You mean quid pro *O*," I muttered.

He chuckled at my bad joke, and his voice was lighter. "Point is, this isn't transactional. You don't owe me. You *never* owe me."

"I know," I said even though I didn't. Not really. In my experience, everyone was out for themselves. I wasn't used to Ash's selflessness. But it didn't matter since that wasn't the only reason I'd been trying to touch him. A fact I shyly shared. "It wasn't that I thought I had to. I wanted to."

"Today was a lot, sunshine. I want you to think it over. Do more research if you need to."

LITTLE SUNSHINE

"All I ever do is think and overthink," I told him honestly. "And I don't need to research stuff when I don't know what applies to you or not. Anything else I need to know, you can teach me because I want to be with you. With all of it. Everything."

Ash shifted to reach off the bed, and the small light flared brighter. He propped himself up to look down at me. "Be sure you know what you're agreeing to. Because once you give me you, it'll take a restraining order to get me away." Smirking down at me, he shrugged. "And even then..."

I wanted to laugh at his joke, but I couldn't.

A tiny voice of doubt warned me that the unknown was too dark and scary, like the infinite void of space. And that if I wasn't careful, I was going to end up alone and lost in it—or in that timeshare on Mars.

That doubt wasn't new.

The feeling of rightness that overpowered it was. I wasn't sure I'd ever felt more confident in a decision.

And that certainty came through when I said, "I want you to be my Daddy."

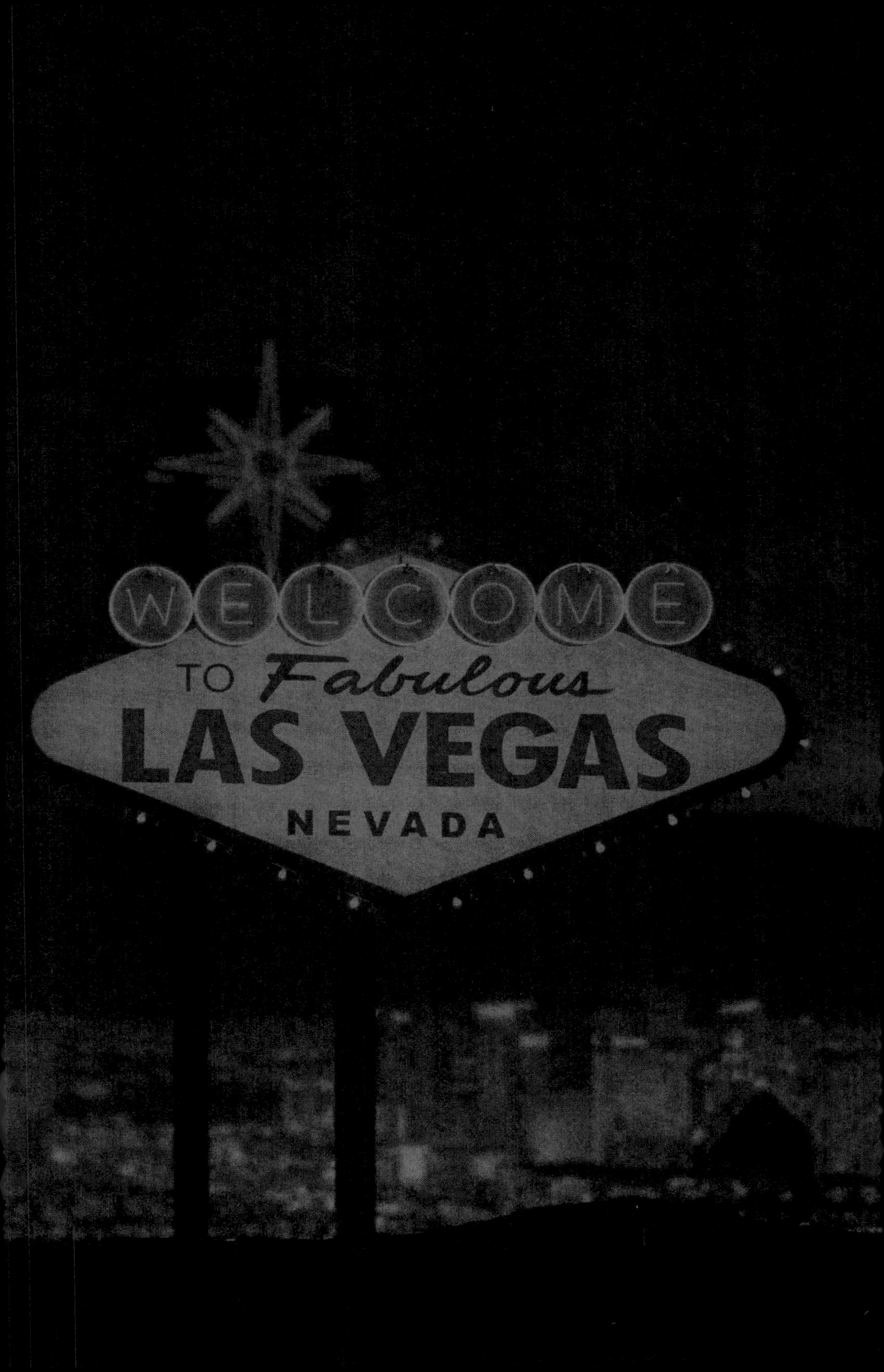
WELCOME
TO Fabulous
LAS VEGAS
NEVADA

CHAPTER 23
LET SOMEONE ELSE DO IT FOR ONCE
MILA

There was no more talking.
No more questioning.
No more anything but Ash's mouth on mine.

With a frantic desperation that built my ego even as it was mirrored in my own kiss, he rolled me to my back and covered my body with his. My tee was up and off, our mouths barely separating to let it past. He cupped my breasts in his large hands. I had a fleeting thought that he might be disappointed in their small size, but the way he eagerly dropped his mouth to tease my nipples said he liked them just fine.

As good as it felt—especially when he held a hardened peak between his teeth and flicked his tongue like he'd done to my clit—I could only take so much. I was empty. I ached. I needed more.

I pushed his shoulders, but he just bit harder and made me gasp.

"Please," I begged.

"What do you need?" he asked, trailing his tongue between my breasts to lick and kiss my neck. His beard teased the sensitive skin there.

"You."

"Fuck yeah, you do." Ash went onto his knees. "Take my cock out."

Like downstairs, if I wanted it, Ash made me prove it.

My hands shook as I pushed his shorts down. His hard-on sprang free, and the apprehension I'd felt at the idea of his size grew to fear at the reality of it.

Logically, I knew the human body was made to do miraculous things. Stretch and all that. But there had to be limits to its capabilities.

And Ash's massive cock would definitely push those limits.

Terrifyingly intimidating or not... I couldn't wait.

I reached out to touch it, but fingers wrapped around my wrist and held it away. My confused gaze shot to Ash. "You said I could touch you."

"Not right now," he gritted out through clenched teeth. "I'm already gonna come embarrassingly fast. If you touch me, there's a good chance it'll be your hand covered in my cum before I even get inside you." He took a ragged breath. "That's still a possibility."

His cum on my skin didn't sound so bad. For a different time. Not right then.

Right then, I wanted him in me.

Which was why I let out a distressed noise when he started moving down the bed.

"Hush, baby. It's going to hurt, and I'm sorry I can't take that away. But I can get you wet to help."

"I'm already wet," I said.

"*Wetter.*"

Ash's skilled tongue speared into me, fucking my pussy while his thumb stroked my clit. My hips rocked, pressing myself against his hand. Against his face. It didn't take long for the pleasure to build.

Close.

Almost.

Nooo.

Just as I was about to shatter, Ash stopped. Switched. Using his lips and teeth and tongue, he played with my clit. His thick finger inched into me. Hardly anything, but it twinged already.

I don't think I can do this.

Ash bit down hard before sucking. That burst of pain and pleasure melded with the added pain of his finger filling me completely. He crooked it, hitting a spot that made my eyes close.

Or maybe my vision flickered out.

I have to do this.

He removed his finger, only to plunge two back in.

"Oh God," I moaned.

"No, not God," he said against me, the vibration of his words adding to the sensory onslaught. "Daddy."

I was right back on the edge. Teetering. My heart slammed as if I leaned over a cliff and stared down into the nothingness that awaited me.

My body was ready to leap.

But Ash stopped.

That time my protest wasn't a distressed noise. It was a growled threat. "If you don't let me finish, I'm going to die."

His chuckle rumbled against me as he lapped at my pussy while his thumb lightly teased my clit. Both were light. Too light.

"Or kill you. Probably both," I said.

"Told you, I have to get you ready."

"I'm ready. I don't think I could get more ready. I've been ready since I turned around and saw you for the first time at Moonlight."

Ash's big body froze. After a long moment, he moved to cover me again. My legs spread to accommodate him, and his cock pressed against me. He thrust, coating himself in my slick arousal before shifting back to fist his cock.

My mouth went dry.

Another thing for a different time.

Positioning the head at my entrance, he didn't stop to talk.

Or ask if I was sure. There was no reason for it, and I was relieved he didn't prolong my torture.

He switched to a different kind.

With more control than I had, he went achingly slow as he pressed in. Barely any of his length. Just the tip.

I already felt full.

Holding his weight off me with one hand, he used the other to pin my pelvis in place as he rocked into me. Easing in inch by way too many inches.

My breaths hissed between my clenched teeth, though they did no good. I felt like I was breathing too much yet somehow not enough. My vision blurred, and I closed my eyes as I fought to hold the tears back with sheer will.

One fell anyway.

"Look at me."

I forced my lids open.

Ash's hazel eyes seared into me as he thrust deeper. Dipping down, he didn't wipe my tear away. He trailed his tongue over it before taking my mouth in a bruising kiss. When I couldn't do more than pant through the burn of being torn in two, he moved his hand from my hip to hold my jaw open so he could continue taking.

My mouth.

My body.

My virginity.

My everything.

His fingers squeezed my cheeks to the point of pain. It distracted my focus from the fiery stretch as he gave one last forceful thrust.

He muffled my choked whimper with his kiss, and more tears spilled down my cheeks.

Ash didn't keep thrusting, even gently. Planted fully inside me, he froze with his forehead pressed to mine and his eyes closed. Our heavy breaths were the only sound in the otherwise silent room.

After a minute, something started to change. The ache was

still there. The burn of being stretched so completely. But something else began to mix with it. A lining of pleasure to soften the jagged edges of pain.

Tentatively, I lifted my pelvis.

Ash's grip tightened. "Gimme a second, baby. I'm barely holding on, and I don't want to hurt you."

The lining of pleasure grew a little thicker as a restless energy tingled through my body like I had energy drink flowing through my veins. "If you don't start moving, it's going to hurt worse." That time when I undulated, it wasn't tentative. "For you."

Placing both palms to the mattress on either side of my head, Ash lifted to stare down at me as he slid out so only the tip remained. My pussy spasmed around him, though I didn't know whether it was trying to push him out or pull him deeper in.

I wrapped my legs around his and tried to get him back. I *needed* him back. I knew I'd regret it later. That the discomfort would be bad.

But I didn't care.

I didn't want to go slow enough for my self-doubt to push in. For me to overthink my inexperience and panic at whether I was messing up. I finally had Ash, and I wanted him to fuck me with the same desperation I felt.

He read my mind—or maybe just my body—and plunged in.

Fast.

Hard enough to shift me up the bed.

I cried out, but that only spurred him on.

Setting a brutal pace, Ash fucked me. I didn't have to wonder if I was doing the right thing because there was nothing I could do besides take what he gave. How he gave it.

And the way he watched me, his eyes blazing, said that was the exact right thing to do.

The orgasm he'd given me on the table had been the best in my life. The pleasure he'd stoked with his hands and mouth to prepare me might've been even better if he'd allowed them to happen.

But none of it compared to what was building right then. His cock and the sheer desire in his eyes worked together to drive my need higher.

Higher.

So high, I didn't think I'd survive the fall.

But Ash wasn't done.

Going up on his knees, the angle he hit changed, and my lids drifted close. My head dropped back as my neck arched.

I won't survive this.

"You're doing so good, baby," Ash praised roughly. Fisting my hair, he forced me to lift my head to look down at our connection. To watch as his thick cock stretched me. As he pulled inch after inch out, just to slam back in and fill me again. "Look how well you take me."

I won't survive without this.

I didn't just fall.

I plummeted.

Each nerve ending in my body seemed to have developed their own nerve endings, and all of them were lit up in the bliss that tore through me.

"Fuck," Ash grunted, his already brutal pace increasing until he lost any semblance of a rhythm. It was just raw power and base instinct as he fucked me through my orgasm and his own.

It was enough to send me over another cliff I hadn't even seen coming.

He gave me his weight as he kissed me with everything he had. It stole the breath I barely had. When he ripped himself away, it wasn't to go far. His hands stroked my sweaty hair back, his sharp gaze scanning me.

At whatever he saw, a dimpled smile split his face.

I smiled, too.

Right until he slid out of me.

The pleasurable pain swapped to a pained pleasure, and I inhaled through my teeth. My eyes went wide as his cum—so much of it—dripped out of me.

Before I could voice my panic, my gaze shot to Ash to find his eyes already aimed there. Only it wasn't panic that filled his expression.

It was raw lust and primal satisfaction.

I pulled my lip between my teeth and held my words in as I fought to close my legs.

He didn't allow it. Hands to my thighs, he spread them wider until more leaked out to slide down to my ass.

I had no clue how it was possible, but his cock jerked, and my pain was forgotten.

For a second.

"Don't move," Ash said as he stood and walked from the room.

Despite the order, I was uncomfortably aware that I needed to go get cleaned up. After pulling on the tee that'd been tossed to the side, I climbed out of bed, but when the ache turned into a sharp stab, I had to pause to steady myself.

"Camila Price, what the fuck did I say?" Ash bit out.

I spun as he stormed across the room. "You don't have to use my full name."

"I do when you're not listening to me." He set a glass of water on the nightstand and moved into my space until I had to crane my neck to meet his eyes. "What did I say?"

"Not to move, but I have to, uh, clean up."

"That's Daddy's job." He lifted me and set me back on the bed.

"You don't have to use my full name *or* move me," I amended. "I can do it myself."

He shot me a look somewhere between a warning and amusement. "That is something you will have to get used to because I like moving you where I want you." Heat infused his expression to mix with the other two as he swiped a warm, damp cloth between my thighs. "A lot."

Truth be told, I also liked it, so I didn't say anything else. Not about that, at least. I tried to close my legs. "I can clean myself."

That look was all warning, and I let my legs fall open. "You're lucky I don't spank your ass. You could've hurt yourself."

I wanted to roll my eyes at his dramatics, but since he was right, I kept my mouth shut.

"Do it again, though, and I won't go easy on you. I have no problem tying you to that bed."

Eek?

Yay?

I wasn't sure what to say to that, so I moved on to something else that needed to be said. "I'm on birth control."

He lifted his gaze but left the warm cloth draped over my tender skin. It felt *heavenly*.

When he didn't say anything, I touched my upper arm. "I can show you the note in my online medical chart from when the clinic placed the implant. And I've obviously never done anything before today, but the clinic runs those tests regardless, so I can show you those, too."

Ash pulled his phone from his pocket and tapped the screen before turning it toward me. Fancier labeling of a private doctor's office aside, the tests and the results listed were the same as mine. "That was from a while ago, but I haven't been with anyone since."

I glanced at the date, expecting a while to be weeks, not *months*.

"Even before then, I've never been with anyone without a condom."

I glanced to the cloth then back at him. "You didn't use one with me."

"Because you're you." That must've been enough of an explanation for him because he moved on by handing me the glass of water and pain pills.

It must've been enough of an explanation for me, too, because I moved on by taking them.

Ash dimmed the plug-in light to the usual brightness before climbing into bed. That time when he rolled me, it wasn't to position me with my head on his chest. Instead, I was mostly on my stomach with one leg bent. Ash covered my back with half of his body. After pulling the blankets up, he reached between us and nestled his semi-hard cock between my ass cheeks so it stretched down to my pussy.

My breath caught as I waited to see what else he did. But that was it. He didn't try anything more as he pressed his lips to my head.

"We can't sleep like this," I said, though I wasn't sure which part I had an issue with.

"Why?"

I went with the easier option that would fix both things. "Because you're a giant. You'll squash me."

"You survived the other nights."

I tried to roll to face him, but I was pinned. "What?"

"Don't know if you know this, sunshine, but you move around a lot. Once I put us like this, you settled, and I wasn't dodging that right hook of yours all night."

"Yeah, but we were wearing clothes."

"You're wearing clothes."

"A shirt."

"Which is a piece of clothing." He gave my waist a squeeze. "Go to sleep."

I let out a little huff, knowing there was no way I could sleep.

I was out within minutes.

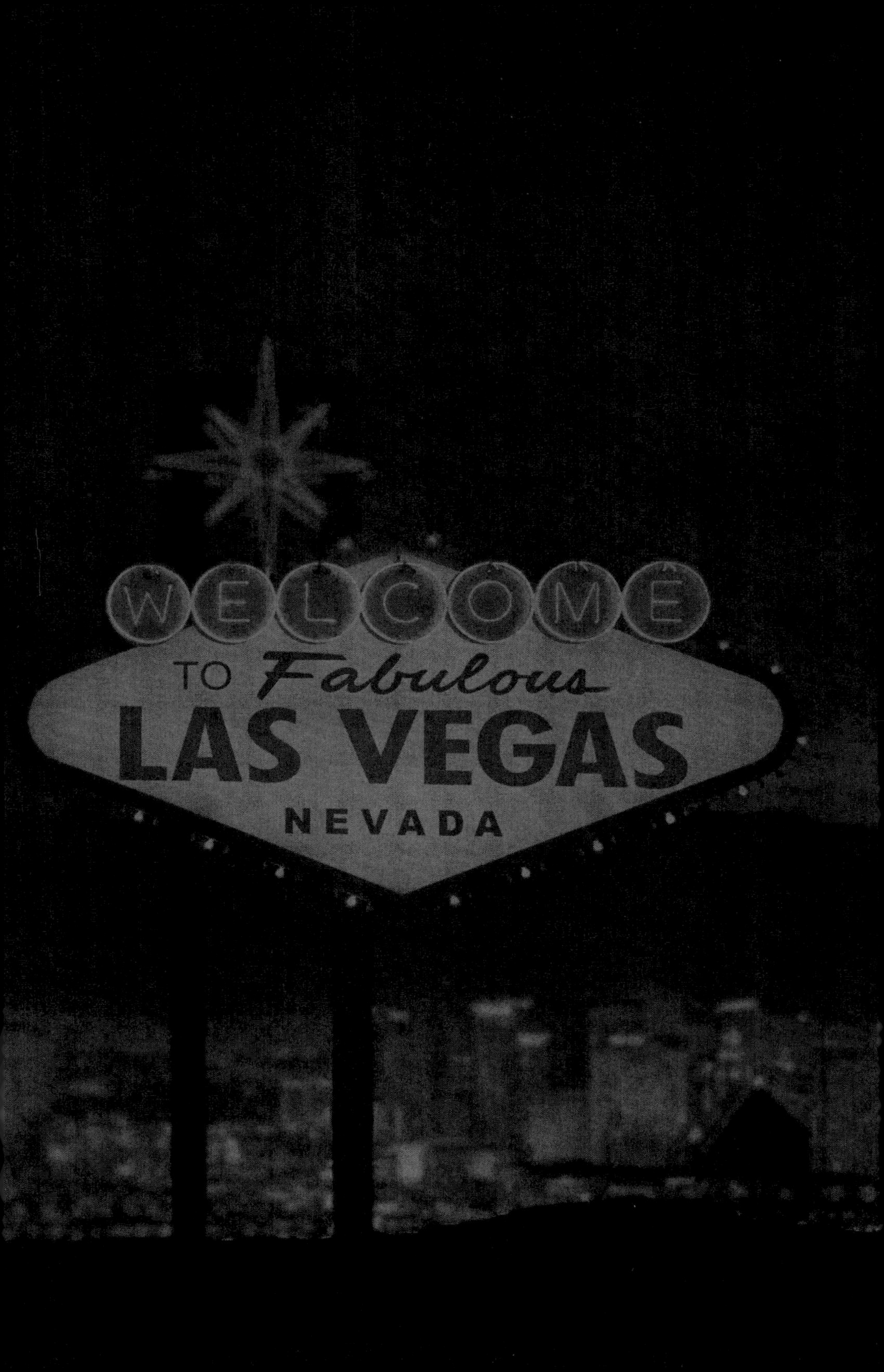
WELCOME
TO Fabulous
LAS VEGAS
NEVADA

CHAPTER 24
DON'T GET YOURSELF TIED UP IN KNOTS
MILA

I WAS SURFING.

Which was weird because I'd never been surfing.

I didn't even know how to swim.

But I was wet. And the wave I rode was growing. Growing. Growing.

Waves couldn't do that.

They couldn't just build. They had to crash eventually. And when they did, I would drown.

This is a dream.

My body tingled.

This is the best dream.

"Glad you think so," an amused voice said, dragging me into reality just in time for the wave to build even higher. But it wasn't a wave. It was the pleasure that Ash was fueling with his mouth.

Knowing I was close, I tried to reach to hold his head to me, but I couldn't. I pried an eye open before rapidly blinking.

That behemoth actually tied me to his bed.

I pulled again, expecting the loose rope to unknot and fall away, but it didn't.

It *tightened*.

"Ash—"

"Who am I?" he bit out before he resumed licking and sucking. Biting and flicking.

"Daddy." I tugged the rope again. "You actually... You... I'm..." My words trailed off and my eyes went unfocused. "Daddy!" I cried out, but that time it wasn't to get his attention.

With what he did and the addition of the rope, there was no more surfing the wave. It crashed over me, leaving me gasping for air like I'd actually nearly drowned.

Once it ebbed away and my brain worked, I wiggled my arm. "You did it. You actually tied me to the bed."

"Yup."

That was it. No apology. No remorse. Nothing.

"*Why?*" I asked when it became obvious he wasn't going to offer an explanation.

Ash stood and rounded the bed to stand at the side near my bound wrist. "'Cause yesterday you ran from me."

"But I'm here now," I pointed out.

"And I ensured you *stayed*. Problem solved." He made no move to free it as he leaned over to kiss me.

Despite the warning the day before, I turned my head.

He didn't give me the chance to explain before he squeezed my mouth open and did exactly as he'd threatened.

It should've been disgusting. It should've made my stomach churn. It should've made me barf or yell or maybe even cry.

It didn't.

It made me needy all over again.

I am sick.

Ash followed it by kissing me, hard and deep. "I don't give a shit if you don't like the taste—"

"It wasn't that," I interrupted. "I have morning breath."

"Don't give a shit about that, either." He did something I couldn't see, and my hand slid free of the rope. He grabbed my arm before I could move, massaging the skin that tingled slightly.

Since he'd made his point—with the rope and the kiss—I let it go.

It was unlikely I'd have to worry about either one again.

When I was wrong, I had no problem saying so. And at that moment, I freely admitted I'd been wrong about the rope.

Or maybe not so freely in that case.

Because as I sat on Ash's bed, I did it with a raw, red ass and my elbows tied behind my back.

The timing of us... well, becoming an *us* couldn't have been more perfect. Ash had two days off. Actually off, and not just working from home.

The first day had been spent mostly in bed.

And once on the kitchen counter—which had apparently been a fantasy of Ash's ever since my first day there.

The second day, he'd taken me to his favorite Vietnamese restaurant for a sandwich that was more loaded than the ones he made before I'd tagged along on errands. And by tagged along, I meant he'd told me I was coming.

Each night, after he'd settled us with his body mostly on mine and his cock pressed between my legs, he'd included the addition of a rope around my wrist to tie me to the slatted headboard.

Like our position, I hadn't thought I could sleep like that.

But again, I'd been wrong because they'd been the two most restful nights I'd ever had.

That was why I'd been up nice and early that morning. And, after figuring out how to undo the adjustable knot, I'd gone to make coffee for Ash.

Fine, and also for me.

Since that'd been a violation of his rules, I'd ended up with a much more secure restraint. He'd called it a simple elbow tie, but there was nothing simple about it.

Or the addicting helplessness I'd felt when he'd spanked me.

He was supposed to be getting the coffee I'd been trying to start before I'd ended up over his shoulder, but when I heard him return, he was talking.

There was the soft sound of another voice, too.

My heart beat a rapid drumroll against my ribs. Unlike the way Ash usually made my pulse race, nothing about the panic that surged through me was pleasant.

I still wore his tee, but nothing was underneath it. And nothing hid the way I was restrained with black rope encircling my arms.

He's not bringing someone else...

He wouldn't.

Right?

When he filled the doorway, it was just his phone in his hand.

Oh thank God.

That relief evaporated in an instant when he sat next to me, and I saw it wasn't a phone call. It was a video one.

I barely choked down a panicked squeak.

His camera was positioned where only he filled the small window, but that didn't make me feel much better. Especially when I took in the older woman who filled the larger one. I could already guess who she was before she said, "And you know your father. He thinks he can fix anything."

"Yeah, but the roof of an RV?" Ash chuckled. "Remember the time he tried to fix the loose blinds and ended up super gluing the curtains to himself?"

"Or the shoe rack incident," the woman added with raised brows.

"We don't talk about that," a man called from somewhere off-screen.

"Anyway, we found a place that can do the repair, but it'll

take some time. Thankfully, we're staying in this cute cabin." She spun around, but not much could be seen at that angle.

That didn't stop Ash from grinning. "Looks like a great time, Ma. You guys are okay, though?"

"The bedding set is garbage now, but that's an easy thing to replace. I'm just disappointed we can't start back your way. Especially since Violet said you have a woman in your life."

My alarmed gaze shot to Ash, and I was tempted to throw myself out of the room to avoid hearing the rest of the conversation—bindings or not.

He must've known it, too, because his hand covered my bare thigh to keep me in place.

His father's voice was filled with the same kind of warning Ash usually aimed my way. "Lynn."

"What? I'm just excited. When's the last time he had a girlfriend? All he does is work, work, work. I know he loves what he does, but he can't give me grandbabies with his work."

No amount of effort could've stopped the unintelligible noise that escaped me.

Thankfully, it was drowned out by his father. "The eleven we have aren't enough?"

Ash didn't seem fazed by any of it.

"There's no such thing as too many grandkids, Joseph Cooper." She looked back to the screen. "Vi said the poor dear was in a car accident, though." His mother was on the phone. She was a stranger. Yet her genuine concern for me was clear as day. "Is she doing okay?"

"Yeah, Ma, she's good now."

"That's good. The drivers in that city act like they need to race everywhere. Are they worried the casinos are going to close if they aren't fast enough?" She shook her head. "Well, let her know we say hi and we're glad to hear she's okay."

No wonder Ash is how he is.

Who would I have been if I had a mother who worried about strangers instead of a mother who never even worried about her own daughter?

Envy wasn't a new emotion for me. If I allowed myself to feel it every time someone had more than me, I wouldn't ever be able to feel anything else. I wouldn't be able to do anything else.

Yet after witnessing the easy conversation between Ash and his parents, the bitter taste of it coated my tongue. For the first time, though, I didn't curse the universe and fate. I didn't spiral.

If it weren't for my bad luck, I wouldn't be in Ash's bed right then. I'd take that silver lining.

Ash squeezed my thigh tighter, offering support I didn't need. "I'll let her know, Ma. I'm sure she'd love to say hi to you guys, but she's tied up right now."

Never mind throwing myself out of here.

I'm throwing him out.

Just as soon as he unties me.

After a sweet goodbye, Ash tossed his phone to the side.

"I can't believe you took a FaceTime call with your parents in front of me."

"I didn't. I took it downstairs."

"You did that and forgot the coffee. You're lucky I don't kick you," I seethed.

"Go ahead."

I lifted my foot.

He stroked a finger from my shoulder down across the rope. "I know plenty of ties that involve the legs."

I dropped my foot.

"Smart girl." Turning me carefully, he quickly undid the rope. "While I was on the call with Ma, Maximo messaged that he needs me early today."

"Is everything okay?"

"Usual bullshit." Since that wasn't reassuring and I likely didn't look appeased, he pressed his thumb against my frown. "There is a boxing event this Friday. The bigger the event, the more VIPs roll in. The more VIPs, the more bullshit."

"Is this a big event?"

"The biggest Moonlight has hosted. When a VIP starts making

a fuss because they think their money makes them better than everyone else and we should do everything but shake the piss from their tiny dicks for them, Maximo sends me to talk them down."

"Why you?" I pointedly looked around the room. "I mean, you have money, but you're not pompous about it. And you definitely don't have a tiny anything."

And the fact I can barely move without wincing is proof.

He didn't gloat about my comment. He let his arrogant smile do it for him while he answered my question. "Marco would tell them to suck it up or kick them out. Cole doesn't deal with guests. And Maximo is the boss, so he doesn't have to. That leaves me because un-fucking-fortunately, I'm charming and persuasive."

Since I'd just spent the morning tied up, there was no arguing that fact.

Ash gave me his full attention, watching me carefully. It would be disconcerting if it weren't so comforting. Maybe that part should've been disconcerting.

I didn't think too hard on it.

"You can stay here today."

After the previous few days, even my dysfunctional brain couldn't twist that into something bad, like that he didn't want me there.

Trust.

He wants me to know he trusts me.

I appreciated it, but now that I knew why he'd had me come with him, I liked it. It sank into some long-neglected part of my soul and made me happy.

That was why I asked, "Do I have to?"

His brows lowered. "What?"

"Can I come with you to Moonlight?"

"Fuck yes, you can. I'd love knowing you're in the same building, even if I can't see you. But I'm gonna be running all over today."

"That's okay." Asking him if I could go with him was already a big step. I decided to make it a massive one. "Do you think Juliet would want to see me again?"

His expression and voice both softened to velvet. "Yeah, sunshine, I know she would."

"Good." I wasn't sure what I'd say or how I'd explain everything, but I wanted to try. "Are you okay with me telling her about us? Just, you know, if it comes up. And I wouldn't go into detail—"

"Share as much as you want about whatever you want. It'd be good for you to have someone to talk to. But fair warning, if you're out of the penthouse, Elliot will be with you."

"Who?"

"The security guard. You don't have to talk to him or any other detail you might have. They aren't there for you to entertain. Do what you want. Go where you want so long as it's on the property. Ignore your shadow. But you *will* have one."

Once again, now that I knew *why* he wanted me to have security, I liked it. I felt bad for whoever had to babysit me, of course, but that didn't change that it was nice to be protected.

When I didn't argue, Ash stood and gave me that small smile that made me want to bend over backward to earn it more often. He pulled me to stand. "Shirt off."

Assuming he wanted to see me naked, I hesitated for all of two seconds before pulling it over my head. His gaze ran over me as he bit out a low curse that seemed to skitter along my skin to tighten my nipples. When he stepped away, he took my tee with him.

"What're you doing?" I asked.

"Wearing this under my suit. Now go get ready."

As if that wasn't an unhinged thing to do, he left.

And as if that wasn't an unhinged thing to like, I grinned as I went to get ready.

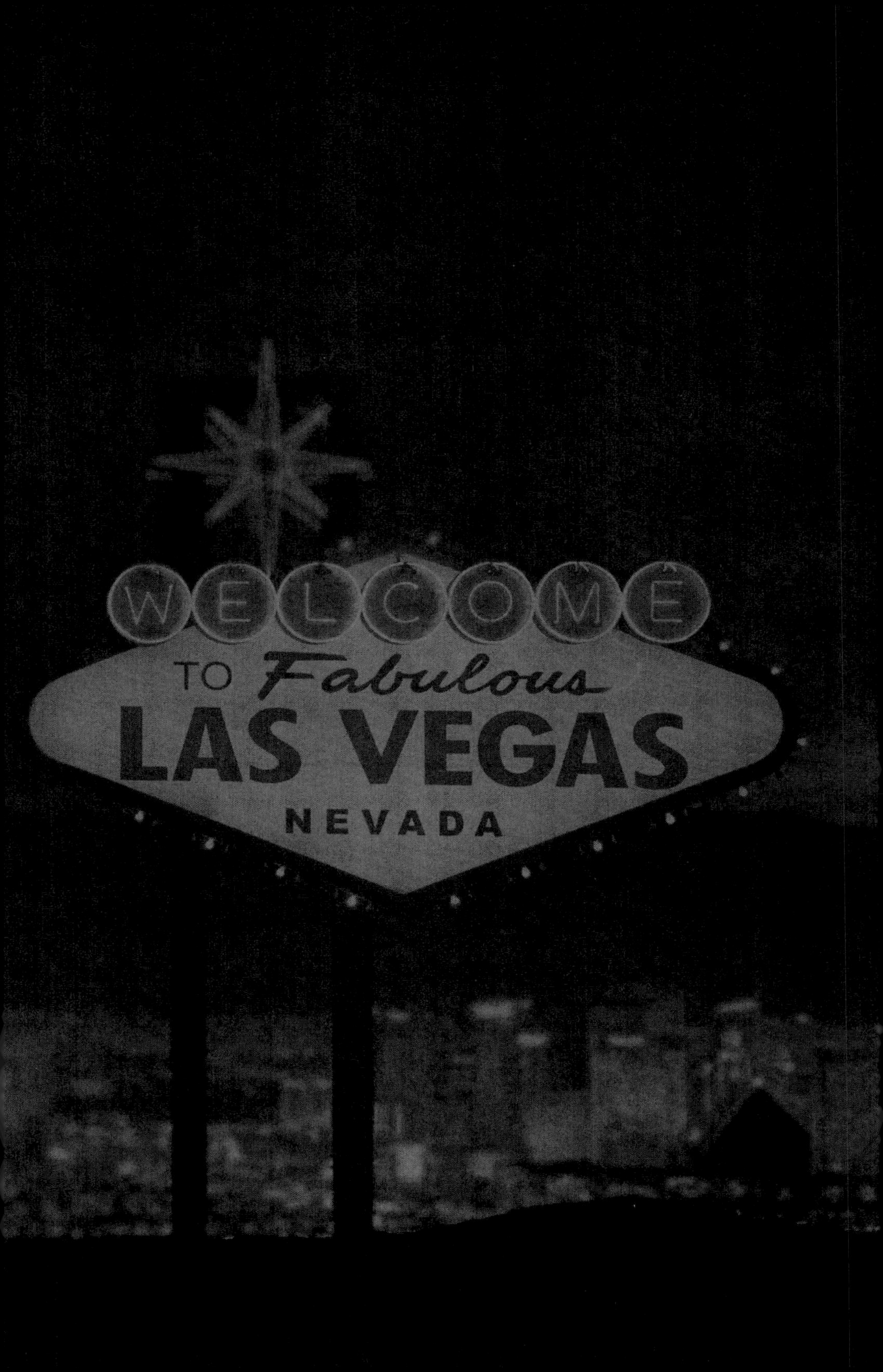
WELCOME
TO Fabulous
LAS VEGAS
NEVADA

CHAPTER 25
DO SOMETHING CALMING
MILA

"**M**ILA!" I wasn't sure I would ever get used to people being happy to see me. Not because I was there to do my work and theirs. Not because they needed a favor. Not because they were a creepy shift manager who wanted to fuck me.

Just plain happy to see me.

But as I approached Juliet's little corner of outdoor paradise, that was exactly how she greeted me.

"Hi," I said, just as happy to see her. Kind of. I would be once I addressed the elephant in the room.

Or the Daddy *and* the security lurking.

"Hi, Elliot," she greeted him like it was no big deal. And from what Ash had said, it wasn't.

He stayed at a distance as she ushered me into her area and played the hostess perfectly again. "Sit. Can I get you anything? Tacos? Cheese plate? Double rum and Coke?"

"Juliet," a suited man rumbled.

A big, *scary* suited man without a single laugh line on his stoic face. I hadn't even noticed him, which was surprising because he was not a slight man. He was beyond muscular, like he went to the gym as a warm-up before going to a secret strongman gym with workouts a normal person couldn't even fathom.

This must be Marco.

Juliet just rolled her eyes at his warning. "Don't mind Marco. He has the sense of humor of a cactus."

"Right," I said.

"But seriously, do you want anything?" She cut off the big guy's interruption with her own. "Other than the cocktail. I have water and Diet Coke, but we can get anything sent over."

"I'd kill for a Diet Coke," I said.

She grabbed us each one from the wicker cooler before picking up a paper bag. "Okay, so this is probably really awkward, and feel free to tell me to shove it."

"Okay," I drawled, trying not to jump to the worst-case scenario.

Trying but failing.

"So when Ash told me that you liked the first dress and he wanted to buy more, I just grabbed stuff from my finished pile for Hilda's."

Am I—

I didn't have the chance to freak out that I'd gotten clothes meant for someone else when she pointed toward the door. "Hilda's is a dress boutique inside where I consign some of my stuff. It's cute. Well, most of it. Some"—she grimaced—"is not my personal style." She took another big breath. "Anyway, hearing that you liked it was great, but seeing you wear those two dresses..." She put her hand to her chest. "It meant so much to me. Because even if it's awesome when I find out someone bought one of my designs, I never get to *see* them wearing them, and that's the fun part. You know what I mean?"

When it came to my own meh clothing, I didn't get it. Not at all. But I could see how it would be different when the clothes were so lovely.

Still, I nodded.

"Anyway, I've been working on a really fun dress. Super sexy. Ash might thank me or vow to forever snitch on me. I'm not sure yet, but I've been dreading handing it over to Hilda's because then I'd never see it again. But it would look so amazing with your dark hair and blue eyes. I took it in and adjusted the length, but if it's not right, I can fix it. And I know the sizing on the other stuff is off because, like I said, I just sent it over. So I can alter that, too."

I already liked Juliet a lot. But at the kind gesture and the nervous way she spoke, I didn't just like her.

I felt a connection to her.

"Oh, it'd help if I gave it to you, huh?"

She passed me the bag, and I carefully pulled out a long black dress. The fabric was soft and made it look almost casual. There was no stiffness or sheen like a formal gown might have. The high neckline of the halter secured with a thick band, and two slits went all the way up each leg. That should've been the sexiest part of it, but it wasn't.

Not for Ash.

Because it wasn't a true backless halter dress. Instead, strips of the fabric had been made to look like rope. Juliet had knotted and woven them together in an intricate design that connected the neckband to the low-cut back of the dress—while still showing *a lot* of skin between.

At a distance, it would look like I was tied with one of Ash's ropes.

"You know," I surmised.

She lifted her drink. "My husband may have let something slip once."

I wasn't sure I'd ever seen something so sexy and subtly naughty before. It would feel like an inside secret between Ash and me. And just thinking about how he'd look at me...

I needed a drink. Or maybe to risk a dip in the pool because my whole body felt overheated.

I carefully folded it exactly as she had it before returning it to the bag and offering it back to Juliet. "I'm sorry, I can't accept this."

Her face fell, but she collected herself quickly and forced a smile. "I totally get it. Like I said, it was just—"

"I stole from you," I blurted. "That's why I can't accept it. I already felt awful and like the worst piece of trash, and then you've just been the absolute nicest. And that was before you offered me this dress that looks like it should be on a runway, not on me. I get it if I ruined our fledgling friendship, and I really am *so* sorry."

Juliet's brows pinched together. "What could you have stolen from me?"

"Well, not you specifically, but from the resort." I bobbled my head back and forth. "Well, not the resort specifically, but a guy who was here."

"Are you talking about the wallet?"

My shocked gaze swung to her. "You know about that?"

She flushed bright red. "No."

Oh my God.

"Does everyone know?"

"No," she tried.

At the same time, Marco said, "I know."

"Not helping," she snapped.

"I don't lie."

I was tempted to run again, but only to hide in the penthouse.

Juliet looked at me with kindness, which was expected, but also understanding. "There was footage, but it's gone now. Completely. And I'm not mad. No one is."

That made me want to run more, but I didn't. I faced the awkwardness. It was my punishment.

"That's—"

My words were cut off when Juliet leaned forward. "Before Maximo, my life was the opposite of"—she flung an arm out—"this. My father and I lived in a tiny house. I was a dropout. We basically only had each other, which really sucked for me because he was *not* a good man. We had food, but there were times when we didn't have enough. I've experienced..." She paused to find the right word. "Inconvenient hunger, and it was awful. You had true hunger. I can't even imagine what that was like."

I swallowed hard and could almost feel that connection strengthening like it was a sentient thing.

That was before she added, "And we don't have a fledgling friendship. We're just friends. Period." She paused for a second. "Though while we're making confessions, you should know that I helped Ash order you more clothes so you wouldn't have a closet of only my designs. I may have gone overboard, and then Ash added even more."

Unease prickled inside my churning stomach.

Juliet studied me for a moment. "Is letting him buy you stuff *a rule*?" She raised her eyebrows with meaning.

"Yes."

"That was a hard one for me to get used to."

"How did you?"

"Because it makes him happy. And with everything he did for me, I wanted to make him happy however I could. And if that meant being selfless enough to accept jewelry and clothes and..." She gave a small laugh and shrugged. "It sounds stupid, but it helped."

We were both quiet for a moment before I tried to hand the bag back to her. "I still don't have anywhere worthy to wear a dress this beautiful."

"Wear it on Friday."

"Friday?"

"Didn't Ash tell you about the boxing event? I figured with as much work as he's been doing for it, he'd have mentioned it."

"He did, but I'm not going. He'll be working."

"They all will. That doesn't mean they can't watch."

"I still don't think—"

Marco cut in. "Ash said he was going to talk to you later, and you're going."

"Oh. Okay." I knew nothing about boxing. I'd never watched it on TV or anything. But I was still excited—especially since it gave me an excuse to wear the dress.

We moved to lighter topics. That was usually the place I loved conversation to stay, but I wanted to talk more.

Speaking quietly, I asked, "That's really how you grew up?"

"Yup."

Rather than discussing more of the Daddy stuff like I thought we would, Juliet and I talked about our lives. First, about her physically abusive and neglectful father and how Maximo had saved her—though she didn't share the specifics. Then, about my emotionally abusive and neglectful mother, my life as a child bandit, and why I'd gone on that poolside sprint.

And even though the topic was different, Ash was still right. It was nice to have someone to talk to who understood.

After a couple of hours Juliet asked, "Are you hungry?"

"Yes," I said instead of doing what I'd usually do—pretend I wasn't so I wouldn't put anyone out.

"Me too, but I have no idea what I want. You?"

I thought for a second. "What were you saying about a cheese plate?"

Juliet smiled.

And she wasn't the only one.

In the first sign of emotion since I'd gotten out there, Marco smiled, too.

Or maybe it was an involuntary twitch. I wasn't totally sure.

Ash

It'd been a motherfucking day.

Between the billionaire who wanted to go through each line of his already itemized bill and the aging movie star who didn't understand why he couldn't do blow at the high roller poker table, I'd put out a hundred other fires. Everyone was finally as happy as I could possibly make them short of tucking them in, reading them a bedtime story, and kissing their foreheads.

I was done.

It was time to go get my sunshine.

Avoiding anyone who'd want to talk, I hurried to Moonlight's French restaurant, Parisian Crescent.

It didn't take me long to find Mila. I just followed the sound of her sweet laughter.

Sitting in a corner booth, she had a huge slice of cake in front of her.

Freddy likes her.

Juliet sat on the other with her own piece of cake. I didn't need to be close to know it was funfetti. Freddy leaned on the table, telling them something they clearly found hilarious.

Marco stood near the table, and Elliot was a little farther away, giving the women space like I'd instructed. I walked over to check in with him and let him know he could take off for the day. Even though he'd been the one to volunteer for Mila duty that day, I asked, "You good?"

"Fine, why?"

"Just making sure you get that this isn't a punishment or mandatory. I asked because Miles and Marco both said they trusted you."

I wasn't sure if the poor bastard had never received a compliment before, but he looked like he might cry.

"I'm happy to do it anytime, and I take it as an honor. I know it's an important job you're entrusting me with."

That was an understatement since, to me, keeping Mila safe was the most important job.

He smiled. "Plus, it beats chasing away minors and dealing with drunken assholes."

I clapped his shoulder as I continued walking.

The closer I got to the table, the more I focused on Freddy's words and not just Mila's reaction to them. "So you've got to picture it, chéri. Ash is in front of a room of VIPs. I'm talking politicians, diplomats, billionaire benefactors, athletes, movie stars, and the like. And the test tube shot he'd confiscated for that little snot-nose punk was in his front pocket. Somehow, the lid comes loose. Not enough to leak at once. It was a slow, steady stream—"

"Okay, story time is over," I cut in.

"Noooo." Mila's grin grew even wider when she saw me. But then she transferred that smile up to Freddy. "What happened next?"

And she likes him.

The damn pretty boy with that damn accent.

I was pretty sure he was laying the French-Creole on extra heavy when he said, "A different time. Otherwise, your man will ruin a good story with facts and accuracy."

A new server I didn't recognize came right over like she'd been hovering close to the important table. "Hi. Can I get you anything, or would you like a menu?"

"I'm good." My gaze landed on Mila. "We're leaving."

Mila stabbed her fork toward her plate. "But I've finally got fancy cake."

Like I wore a mask of normalcy, I let it slip so she could see the need that'd been haunting me all day. "Take it to go, sunshine."

"I'll take it to go."

The server swiftly grabbed the plate and rushed away to box it up.

Marco put his hands in his pockets. "What'd she say her name is?"

Freddy's cheek twitched. "She didn't."

"Callie," Juliet filled in.

Marco nodded and waited a few beats before asking, "What's her story?"

If he was going for casual, his dart wasn't anywhere near the target. It seemed to be stabbed right in Freddy's back if his scowl was any indication.

"No story. Leave my staff alone." He softened his face and forced a smile at Mila and Juliet. "I need to get back into that kitchen before they butcher my recipes with truffle oil on everything. It was nice to finally meet you, Mila."

"You, too. And thank you for the cake. It's even better than Ash raved."

Since Freddy knew I could—and had—knock off an entire one of his cakes myself, that was a glowing review. It was also the right thing to say to get on his good side because his ego was wrapped up in his culinary skills.

Mila and Juliet's goodbye lasted longer than I would've preferred since I was anxious to get her alone, but I sucked it up. However good I'd hoped the day would go, it was obvious it'd gone better. When Mila finally stood, she grabbed a bag and clutched it to her.

Once we were out of the restaurant, I asked, "What's in the bag?"

"A new dress from Juliet."

"Can't wait to see it."

She smiled up at me, but there was an edge to it. Something wicked.

Once we were in the elevator, I pulled her to me and kissed her. Hard and deep and thorough until the bunched muscles between my shoulders loosened. When I was done, I watched her dazedly blink as her tongue swept out to lick across her bottom lip.

I'd have slammed the button to stop the elevator so I could fuck her right then and there if it weren't for the fact Marco, Cole, Maximo, and Juliet might need to use it. I'd have done it anyway, but I didn't want to leave it smelling like sex. That scent was only for me.

As the elevator slowed, I got a text.

> Moonlight: Someone is in the lobby asking for you.

The doors opened to the lobby, and I didn't have to scan to see who it was.

"Veronica?" Mila whispered.

Fuck.

"Mila, wait here," I ordered when we stepped out, but she didn't listen.

She hauled ass across the lobby.

I'm gonna spank your ass for that. Unless your bitch mother opens her mouth and ruins everything.

Fucking fuck.

Reaching Veronica, she quietly hissed, "What're you doing here?"

"I came to see my daughter," Veronica claimed as she gestured to me. "He told me you were attacked. I wanted to see if you were okay. I've been worried."

Bullshit.

I hadn't said a single thing about where I worked to Veronica, but I wasn't exactly surprised she'd found out. Greed was a powerful motivator.

"I'm fine," Mila said, her fretful eyes darting around the busy room. "You can go."

"Camila Price, I didn't raise you to be so disrespectful."

Unlike when I used her full name, Mila frowned at her mother's usage. It turned into a sneer at the rest of the sentence.

"You're right, you didn't raise me. Period. You were too busy—"

Standing at her back, I wrapped an arm around her waist. Not to stop her. It was a show of support. A reminder she wasn't alone.

Not anymore.

At the contact, her words cut off. She leaned into me and took a deep, shaky breath. "Look, I appreciate that you paid me back. And if you're really here to check on me, I appreciate that, too. But I think you should leave."

Veronica's conniving gaze rose to me before returning to her daughter. She opened her mouth, but Mila didn't give her the chance to speak.

Turning in my hold, she said, "I just remembered I forgot my cake."

I looked to the side and crooked my fingers. One of the lobby guards came right over, and I released Mila. "Please escort Mila to Parisian Crescent." I dropped my focus, making my next order to her. "There and right back."

She pulled her bottom lip between her teeth, and her head jerked to the side slightly. A silent plea. At my chin lift, her shoulders relaxed. "Thanks, *Behemoth*."

That might've been what she said, but I heard the Daddy she meant.

Not giving a damn where we were or that her mother was there, I swatted her ass as she walked past.

A taste of what was to come.

When I returned my attention to Veronica, something ugly twisted on her pinched face as she watched the interaction. I didn't give a shit about her opinion, and it showed that she had at least a few brain cells since she wasn't idiotic enough to voice it.

"What're you actually doing here?" I asked once Mila was out of earshot.

"I came to check on Mila."

"Bullshit."

"It's true. We haven't always gotten along, but she's still my daughter." She blinked up at me earnestly. "And hearing she was attacked scared me. I could've lost her. I want to fix things."

I didn't buy it. Not a second of it. And I didn't hide that. "*If* that's true, text her. Let her decide if she wants to talk to you. Don't just show up again, or I'll have you banned from here and half the places in Vegas."

She opened her mouth, but I wasn't done.

"But in the more likely scenario that you've seen she's clawed far enough away from you to land in a good place, and you want some of that for yourself, you can fuck right the hell off. I won't let you weasel your way back into Mila's life just to use her. You've done that enough."

I waited for her to lash out and blow up her act, but she didn't. "Please tell her I'll text her." She began to walk toward the exit before turning around. "Oh, and FYI, I won't tell her that you lied to her about me paying her."

Not *thank you for covering for me because I'm a shit mother.*

Nope. Veronica made it seem like I owed her while also reminding me she had something on me.

It would've been impressive if it didn't piss me off so much.

And part of the reason it pissed me off was because she was right. Mila would flip if she found out. I had enough half-truths and secrets on my conscience. Stuff I couldn't share yet. I'd have to tell her about her mom's debt.

Later.

Since I wanted Veronica gone before Mila got back, I didn't respond.

Mila returned a couple of minutes later. She scanned the lobby, and even from a distance, I could see her relax. A hint of tension returned when her eyes landed on me, and she saw the look on my face.

Quickly closing the distance between us, she smiled and fluttered her lashes, the pretty picture of innocence. When that didn't work, she lifted the container. "I have my cake. And I got a slice for you, too."

"I'm still spanking your ass for not listening to me when I told you to wait near the elevator."

She sighed. "I figured as much. But I had such a good day today, and then there Veronica was. Waiting to ruin it like she ruins everything." That time when she smiled at me, it wasn't fake. Putting her hands around my neck, she went up onto her toes while she tugged me down to kiss me. She didn't let me go as she whispered, "Thank you for handling her so I didn't have to, Daddy."

Christ, she kills me.

I pressed my lips against her forehead. "Any-fucking-time."

"Can you do me another favor?" she asked as we continued to the car.

I braced. "What?"

"When we get home, can you use the rope again? It makes me feel oddly calm." She shot me a nasty look. "Until you take a FaceTime call, that is."

I may have braced, but I hadn't done it enough. For one, Mila asking to be tied was a helluva lot different from just letting me do it. For another, she'd called it home. Not *your place* or *your house*.

Home.

Which was why I repeated, "Any-fucking-time."

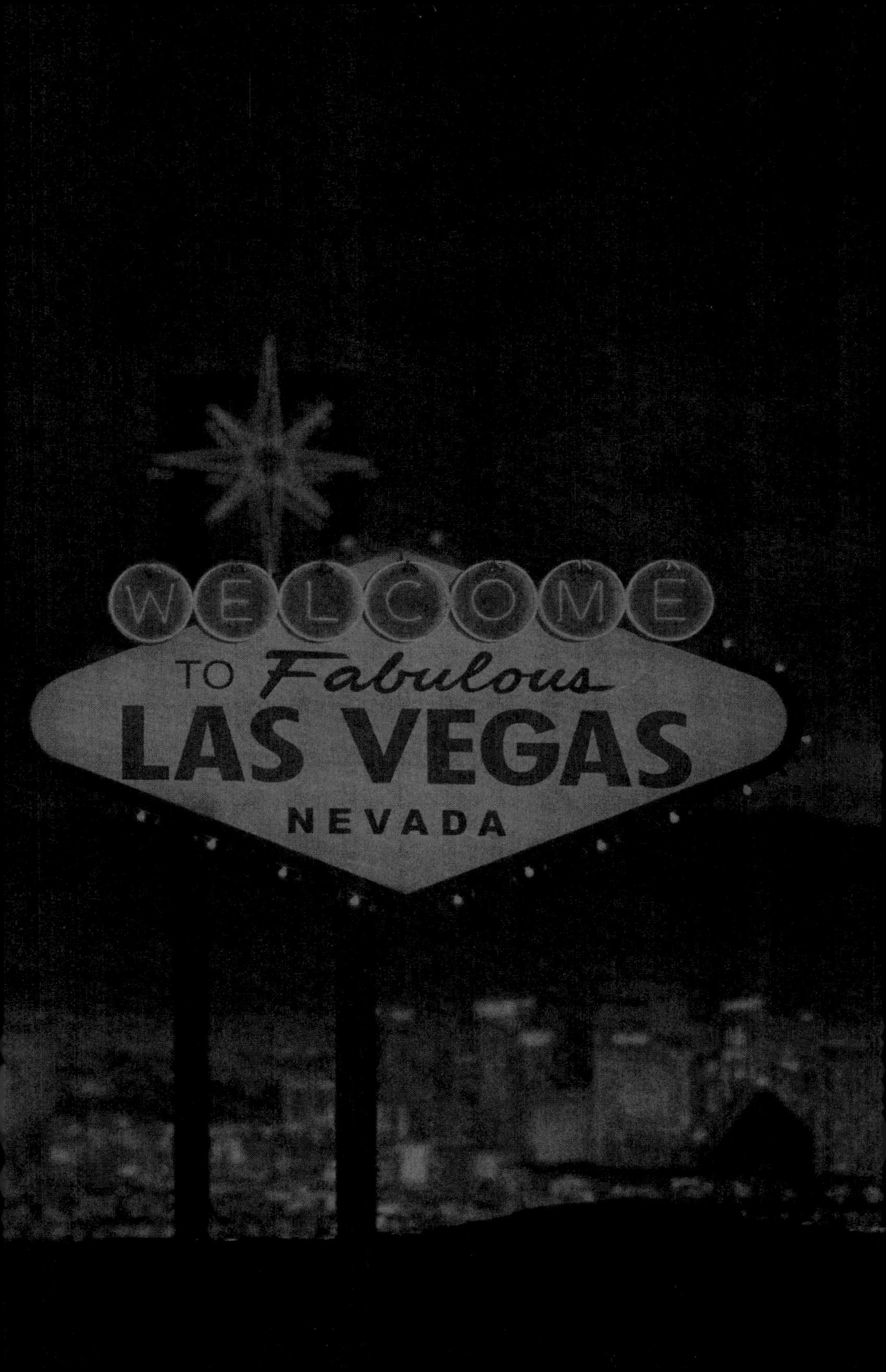
WELCOME
TO Fabulous
LAS VEGAS
NEVADA

CHAPTER 26
CHASE WHAT YOU WANT
MILA

Time was funny.

When I'd worked at The Roulette, each day had seemed to drag miserably. A week had felt like an endless eternity.

With Ash, our first week of being us had flown by in a blink. Yet at the same time, it felt like we'd been together for much longer than we had.

Ash as my Daddy was intense—in the very best way.

Whatever patience he'd used to take things slow before we got together was long gone. He didn't hold back, and he didn't allow me to, either. True to his word, he was greedy with my time. If he wasn't working, we were together. Even if he was working—minus when he'd been out at meetings for a whole day—I went with him.

And every night, I went to sleep with his body on mine, his cock nestled against me, and my arm tied to his bed.

And every morning, he took whatever tee I'd slept in and wore it under his suit.

It was crazy.

It was hot.

It was so crazy hot.

The only sour note in the week had been Veronica's continued presence. Not physically—she hadn't shown up after our interaction at Moonlight—but she'd texted.

A lot.

Asking how I was. If I was okay. When those went without a response, she'd begun to tell me about mundane things she'd seen or heard. Like she was just a normal mom checking in.

I didn't trust it. But at the same time, I hadn't told her to stop. I hadn't blocked her. It was pathetic, but I still wasn't sure I could cut her out of my life.

A voice in my head warned me that if I did that, then once Ash was gone, I'd have no one. I'd be completely alone. I didn't pay attention to it—*much*—but that didn't mean it wasn't there.

Other than that, though, life was good. Not good enough. Not as good as it was going to get.

Just plain good.

And as I finished tying a rope into place, a tremor ran down my side because I knew it was about to get even better.

Stepping back, I inspected my work in the full-length mirror in Ash's penthouse. It wasn't perfect. And it definitely wasn't as easy as Ash made it look. But it was secure.

Hopefully.

I walked around the living room to test it before quickly realizing my error.

I'd wanted to tease Ash.

Yet as my skin rubbed against the soft rope, it was me who quickly grew aroused.

Let's hope he has a similar reaction so it can at least be mutual torture.

After sending him a text that I was headed out, I rode the elevator lobby down to the first floor. Rather than Elliot or one of the other couple of security guards who'd had to babysit me, a different one waited for me. The other man who'd seen me pickpocket.

Miles.

I wasn't hit with the same shame spiral as before, but that didn't mean it wasn't awkward.

Whoa boy, was it awkward.

But I was too excited about the night to let my embarrassment ruin it.

A freak-out would be a waste of this dress.

I pasted on a smile. "You pulled the babysitting short straw, huh?"

"Technically, I'm only walking you to Supermoon, so it's escort duty, and I volunteered."

Considering Ash had mentioned that Miles was the head of security for the whole resort, I didn't believe he'd volunteered for the demotion. But I appreciated his willingness to lie so I felt better.

My brows lowered. "Supermoon?"

"The arena."

Usually when I walked through the resort, it was with Ash when he was in a hurry—either to get to work or get me home. I never asked too much about the place, and he never offered it. Not because he was gatekeeping. I just got the feeling that since he saw it all the time, it didn't occur to him that it was something so spectacular.

Miles was different. Like a tour guide rather than security, he pointed out interesting tidbits. The most popular slot machines. The biggest jackpots won. Which table the poker regulars fought over and which they refused. What celebrities they'd hosted. Which ones they'd banned. Tiny detailing in the decor.

I could've listened to him talk all day, but before I knew it, we turned into an alcove with a single door. He swiped his card to unlock it before leading me down a long corridor. We turned at the end into another hall.

And there, all alone at the end, was Ash on the phone.

I couldn't have planned this better if I tried.

Ducking back around the corner, I glanced at Miles to see that he'd gone alert. I kept my voice as quiet as possible. "Can you turn around?" Then I thought about how Ash would likely react. "And you, uh, might want to stay behind me after this."

Amusement tipped his lips, and he didn't say anything as he turned around.

Moving quickly before Ash left that spot and I lost my opportunity, I undid the hidden hook-and-eye clasps that held the top part of the slits closed.

When I'd asked Ash to tie me earlier in the week, he'd done a knot that'd held my legs spread. Once I'd been capable of thought, an idea had formed, and I'd asked Juliet to add closures to the sexy dress she'd made.

I wanted to tease Ash, not send him through the roof.

When the clasps were closed, the slits started high on my thigh but nothing could be seen. With them open, though, the slits started even higher. And a lot could be seen.

Which was the view I gave Ash.

After peeking around the corner to be sure he was still alone, Miles and I started walking. With each step I took, the black dress draped and the slit opened until the thin black rope I had wrapped around the top of my thighs showed.

No one could ever describe my legs as long. But between the slits and the small wedge heels I'd borrowed from Juliet, they looked long-ish.

Ash turned at my approach, looking devilishly handsome in a black suit with a black shirt. As soon as he saw me, a smile began to form. It froze as his gaze moved down my body. After a stunned few seconds, he snapped out of it and moved.

And he didn't stop until I was in his arms.

Carrying me into a room, he slammed the door behind us and then slammed me into said door. His kiss was wild as his hand roamed up my bare thigh. Hitting the rope, he tugged and groaned.

And I moaned as it pulled taut between my legs.

"I'm going to spank your ass raw for walking through the building like this." His threat lost some of its menace when he tenderly dragged his lips along my jaw, his rough beard teasing.

"And then I'm going to have to spend the night reviewing security footage and hunting down the bastards who dared to look at what's mine. Starting with Miles. Last time I ask him to walk with you."

I knew it.

"That sounds like a long night," I said. "You should probably let me go so you can get started."

"Not until I fuck you so I know it's Daddy's cum dripping out of you all night." He reached between us to free himself, but I stopped him.

"That'll have to wait."

He reared back. "Why?"

"You have work to do."

"You're more important."

It wasn't the first time he'd said that. It certainly wasn't the first time he'd shown it. I nearly gave in, but I held strong.

Barely.

Since evasiveness hadn't worked, I went with the truth. "Then it'll have to wait because I want to torture you."

Though we both knew there were a million ways he could get me to change my mind, Ash went along with it. "Will you at least let me look? And before you answer, know I'm prepared to beg."

Since my plan to tease him was dependent on him seeing me in the dress, I nodded and waited for him to put me down.

He didn't.

Gripping my hips, he slid me up the door before adjusting his hold so my spread legs were draped over his arms. "Move the dress. Show Daddy what my good girl did."

I did as he ordered, tempting my control and his.

The thin rope looped around my hips and each thigh, almost perfectly outlining my black panties. The look would've been more effective without them, but there was only so much I could push myself at once. I knew it didn't matter when Ash spoke.

"Christ. I could die right now, and I wouldn't have to be sent to the afterlife. I've already experienced heaven."

"The knots are trickier than they look," I whispered, not sure what else to say to something like that.

"You did them perfectly."

It was a lie, but one I happily accepted.

Lowering me, he kissed me again before setting me on my feet. "As much as I love how you look right now, Camila, there is no way in hell I'm letting you go out there wearing that. Ropes against your pretty skin are only for Daddy to see."

I reached down and redid the clasps before standing upright.

Ash stepped back so he could take me in again. His palm ran over his beard, his thumb dragging over his lip as he slowly—meticulously—ran his gaze down my body.

The way he looks at me.

The way he looks.

Who needs boxing or plans or anything other than this feeling?

"Ready?" I prompted before I gave in.

Ash held the eye contact as he reached down and adjusted his length. Even then, he had to fasten his suit jacket.

Definitely mutual torture.

Once Ash was set, he raised his chin, and I turned and opened the door. I didn't get into the hall before a hand wrapped around my hip, and my steps were halted. He ran his rough fingertips along the lines and knots of the dress. "I owe Juliet a lifetime supply of Get-Out-Of-A-Snitch cards."

Releasing my hip to take my hand, Ash started down the hall. The closer we got to the doors at the end, the louder the noise became. People were already taking their seats. And like the resort all week, it was packed.

We continued until we reached the first row, where Juliet and Cole already sat. Ash nudged me into a cushiony seat next to them. "I have to do my bullshit and make sure everything is good. I'll try to make this quick, but the opening match will probably start before I'm back. Do not get out of this chair. Understood?"

I nodded.

He stared at me expectantly.

I hesitated, but only for half a second. "Yes, Daddy."

I could've called him Behemoth, and he'd have accepted that, but it wasn't like Juliet would be shocked by the name.

And even if someone else around was, I didn't care. The proud smile he wore was all that mattered to me.

He pressed his smiling mouth to mine and left to do his bullshit. Whatever that meant.

Juliet leaned closer. "Soooo... I take it he liked the dress."

"What makes you say that? I mean, you're right, but what gave it away?"

She hooked a thumb over her shoulder. "Miles told Maximo that Ash barely looked at you before carrying you into a random office."

My brows shot up. "That wasn't his office?"

"Nope."

That made it even better.

She waggled her brows. "Not to mention, Ash's suit jacket is closed. It's never closed."

That made it even better, too.

A charismatic man spoke into a mic as he paced the fighting stage thingy. I knew nothing about boxing, but even I was beginning to get excited with all his hyping. More people streamed in, and every once in a while, Juliet pointed at one while she whispered gossip.

Maximo was back before Ash, and I was about to shift down the row to make room. But he just plucked Juliet from the seat, sat, and then positioned her on his lap.

"It's a rule," she said with an eye roll, like she wasn't grinning about it.

"Ash has the same one."

I wasn't sure if it would apply to a crowded public place that was also his work, and I was surprised to realize I hoped it did—even if it would draw attention.

The lights dimmed, and someone else took over hosting duties as loud music thumped through the speakers. Two boxers were introduced and came jogging down the aisle right next to us. Juliet occasionally leaned in to tell me something, but what little I heard above the cacophony of chaos, I didn't understand.

A bell rang, and the fighting started.

It wasn't bad. Not at first. It mostly seemed like they were dancing around each other. What few punches were swung looked light. But after a few rounds, things changed. The guy in the yellow shorts punched a certain way that left his face unblocked. Juliet again told me what was happening, but I didn't absorb any of it. Not when I was watching a murder.

The guy in the blue shorts found his opening and took it. He got the upper hand and was advancing, forcing Yellow to retreat. Yellow was still trying. He was throwing punches.

But he was mostly taking a beating.

I can't watch this. I have to go.

I darted up and moved before I even realized what I was doing. Before Maximo or Juliet, either, because by the time he reached for me, I was already in the aisle and out of reach.

Turning from the violence and bloodshed, I ran up the aisle.

Ash.

I need Ash.

I was vaguely aware of someone yelling behind me, but then something happened with the fight, and the place erupted into applause and shouts.

The last part just made everything worse.

I ran for the doorway we'd entered through and slammed into it, only to discover it was locked. An arm reached around me to swipe a card, and I looked over my shoulder.

Ash.

Thank God.

Keeping my back to his front, Ash wrapped his arms around my waist and propelled me forward. He stalked down the hallway before entering an office and slamming the door behind us. That time, it was my front pressed to it.

"What'd I tell you about running from me?" I tried to turn to explain, but his large hand between my shoulder blades held me in place. His other hand lifted my long skirt. "I warned you, Camila."

The sound of fabric tearing cut through the air, and I thought it was the dress. I was wrong.

It was my panties.

Ash's finger plunged into me from behind. He added a second, and his thumb circled my clit until I was panting. Before I could come, he took his hand away and gripped the rope at either of my hips to lift me. I gasped at the pressure between my thighs. His body pushed in closer until I was pinned between him and the door.

And then his cock slammed into me. Filled me so completely, it stole my breath. With the tight angle, each inch seemed to meld with me permanently. Like I'd feel him there for the rest of my life. I wanted that.

Needed it.

He fucked me with that same desperation. Like he couldn't get close enough. Like he needed to fuse his body to mine. Connect us until we couldn't be separated.

His palm slapped on the door in front of my face to keep himself upright. He used his other hand on my hip to move me up and down his length as he surged into me.

Over.

And over.

And over.

Like the boxing outside, it was brutal. *Violent.*

Unlike the match, it was also beautiful. It made me feel protected. Wanted.

Safe.

I was right on the verge of coming apart when I heard laughter out in the hall. The speed in Ash's thrusts slowed, but not the power. He pulled out to the tip before quickly plunging in. His tattooed hand covered my mouth.

"Don't let them hear you," he whispered in my ear, his rough voice making goosebumps spread across my skin. He pulled out to the tip and plunged in again. I whimpered, and his hold on my mouth tightened. "If they hear those sweet noises, I'll be forced to kill them. Those are for Daddy." Another hard thrust that made my pussy tighten around him. "All of you is only ever for Daddy."

Choking down the screams that wanted to push free, I didn't just come apart.

I exploded.

My brain was barely functioning when Ash slid his hand from my mouth to my jaw, lifting it so I met his eyes. "I told you if you run from me, I'll chase you." His thumb slid between my lips and pressed to my tongue, forcing my mouth open. His already rough thrusts grew vicious as he pumped into me, filling me with cock and cum until it was being forced right back out to drip down to undoubtedly coat the ropes I was bound with. "I'll always chase you, Camila."

I'll always chase you, Camila.

"I wasn't running from you. I was running to find you because I knew you'd make me feel safe. Happy one week, Daddy," I whispered.

And then I burst into tears.

"Oh, sunshine," he murmured, turning me in his hold to carry me to a chair. He sat and positioned me on his lap. One of his palms stroked up and down my back, but his other stayed wrapped in the rope at my hip. "I didn't realize."

I tried to laugh, but it mixed with my tears to sound like nonsense. "I know that's not a real thing. But it's been the best week of my entire life, and I wanted to show you that I appreciate it by surprising you with the ropes. But then I ruined it by making a scene. *Again.*"

"You didn't ruin anything."

"Maximo and Juliet are going to think I'm insane."

"No, they're going to be worried about you." He dipped into my line of vision. "Just like I was."

I inhaled deeply, not sure what to say. How to explain.

So I didn't. "You have to go back to work." He opened his mouth to argue, but I placed my thumb over it like he did to me.

And he bit me.

"If you don't go back to work, I'm going to feel even worse. I'll never be able to face Juliet again." When he still didn't look like he'd agree, I added, "And that means she'll never be able to make me sexy dresses."

He stared at me for a few stretching seconds. "I'll get you settled upstairs first."

"Can I just stay here? I, uh, don't think I can go back out to the arena, but I don't want to be that far from you."

I got a brief glimpse of his tender expression before he kissed me.

When he pulled away, he asked, "Do you have your phone?"

I shook my head. "You and Juliet are the only people I talk to, and you're both here."

Wow.

That's pitiful.

Ash didn't look like he felt the same way. His smile was all arrogance and wickedness. He stood and sat me on the chair before taking his cell from his pocket and putting it on the desk next to us. Like his openness was nothing, he stated, "Passcode is 9407. If you need anything, text Marco. Don't leave this office until I come get you."

I nodded.

His hands went to the arms of the chair on either side of me as he dipped his face into mine. "You're already going to be punished for getting out of the chair instead of asking Juliet or Maximo to message me. You don't want to add to it. Got it?"

"Yes, Daddy."

"I'll be back soon."

I watched him leave before scanning the office. There wasn't much to it. If it really wasn't Ash's office, I hoped whoever used it didn't return.

At least not until the smell of sex cleared out.

I guess a freak-out wasn't a waste of this dress...

Ash

"You ready to tell me what happened?" I asked once we were settled in bed in the penthouse later that night.

At my question, Mila tried to wiggle deeper under the blanket. Since a good chunk of my weight was on her, I didn't know where she thought she was going to go.

"We can start the punishment now," I offered.

"No, nope, that's fine." She was silent again, but it was a different type. A weighty one. After a minute, she inhaled deeply. "When I was little, Veronica had this big shot real estate agent boyfriend. Everyone loved him. Even though it was forever ago, I still remember everyone telling us how lucky we were that he'd come into our lives. That he'd rescued us. They had no clue what a monster he was. He was all about appearances, and everything had to be perfect. But Veronica was a damaged twenty-five-year-old who just wanted attention. And I was a typical five-year-old who made messes. When he..." She took a shaky breath. "When things got bad, I'd hide in the closet. I think that's why I'm claustrophobic and afraid of the dark now. It's just wrapped up in those memories."

"What happened?" I asked.

"I made the mistake of telling my teacher. She reported it, and I had to live with my grandparents for a little while. But Veronica and the guy denied everything, and my nan coached me to say I lied."

I rolled her onto her back and leaned up so I could see her. "Tell me you're fucking joking."

She shook her head. "Nan knew that if they broke up, we'd move back in until Veronica found her next man. To be fair, I don't think she knew how bad it was. She thought he just yelled a lot, and that it was good for Veronica. So I said I got it confused with a movie I wasn't supposed to be watching, the investigation was wrapped up, and he dumped her anyway. And she never forgave me for that."

"What about your father?" I asked.

"Don't know. Veronica tried to pin me on some guy she was seeing by giving me his last name, but he wouldn't sign the birth certificate. And then the paternity test came back negative, so it's one big mystery that I never intend to look into."

"Christ, sunshine. I don't understand how you lived through all that and still turned out so perfect."

She cracked up laughing, but it wasn't a happy sound. It was harsh and bitter. "I'm not perfect. I just made a scene—again. We have to have a night-light because I'm an adult who is afraid of the dark. I'm clingy and needy, and the calmest I've ever felt is when you have me tied up because it's like—"

When she cut off abruptly, I pushed. "Like what?"

"Like I can just *be*," she admitted before rolling onto her side. "I'm still really sorry about earlier."

"No need to apologize. Ever."

"Does that mean there's also no need for a punishment?"

"No."

"It was worth a shot."

I repositioned us and listened as Mila's breathing quickly grew even. I didn't fall asleep as easily.

Holding Mila, I thought about all the secrets I kept. The lies I'd told. The blood on my hands.

I couldn't hide that part of me forever. I just had to hope that when I told Mila, it wasn't already too late.

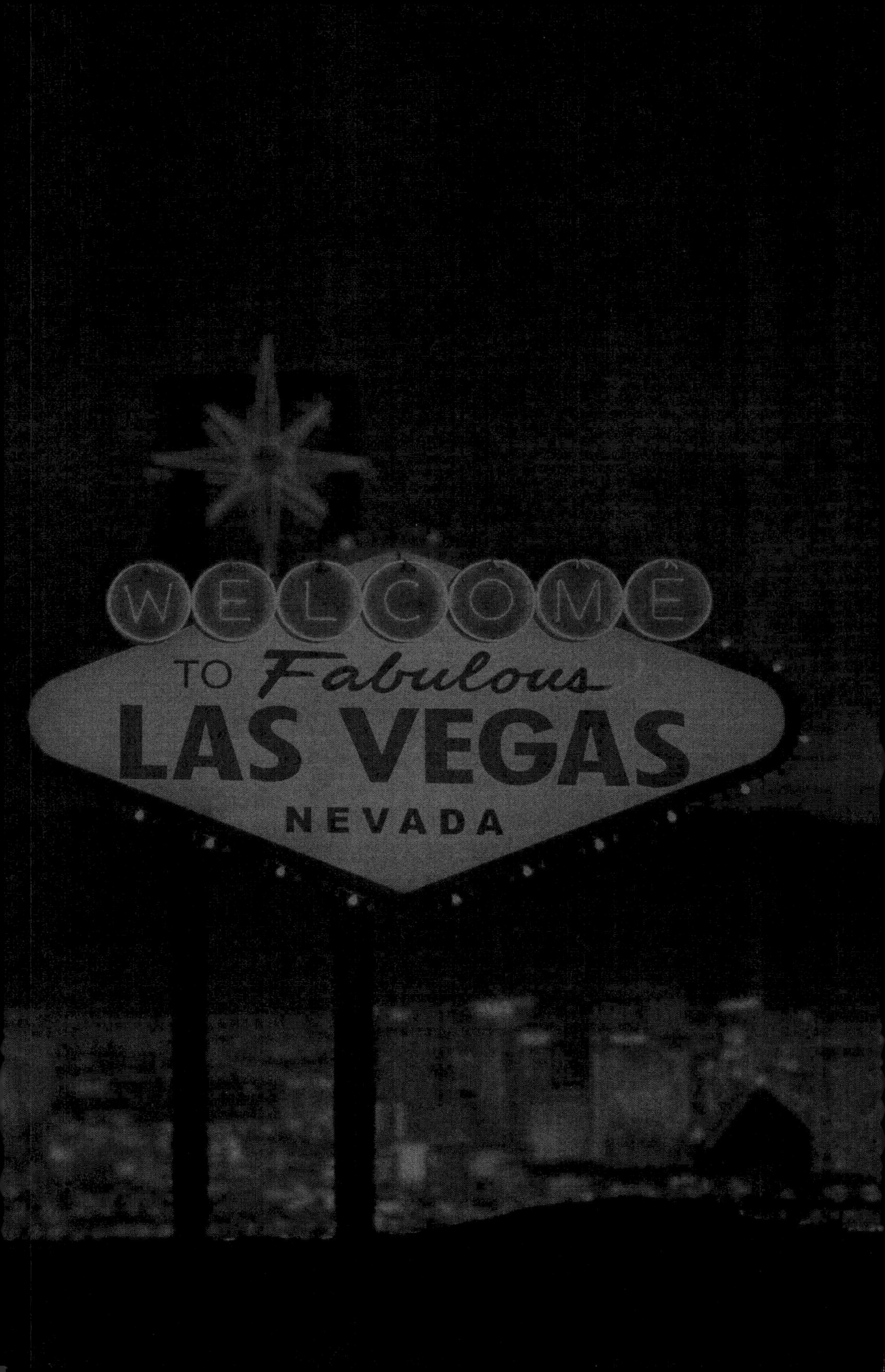
WELCOME
TO Fabulous
LAS VEGAS
NEVADA

CHAPTER 27
ALLOW YOURSELF TO ANTICIPATE THINGS
MILA

WAKING UP THE FOLLOWING MORNING, I opened the door to head out to the living room before Ash's voice stopped me.

"Maximo is here."

Yikes. That was close.

I closed the door again before changing out of the sleep shirt and into leggings and a ripped crop. Since Ash was likely already dressed, I tossed the tee into the hamper.

When I stepped out that time, Ash was coming from the kitchen with a mug of coffee for me. He kissed me—hard and thorough and not at all appropriately in front of an audience—before going back enough to look at my face. "You good?"

Even with the impending punishment lurking over my shoulder—or ass—I whispered, "Yeah, I'm good."

He smiled and handed me the coffee before taking a seat at the table where he had his laptop open.

Maximo sat next to him, but his sharp gaze was on me. His firm tone was almost as commanding as Ash's. "You ever have an issue when he isn't around, talk to me."

I had no idea why, but my gaze shot to Ash. His smile was

immediate as he lifted his chin. When I looked back and nodded at Maximo, he was smiling, too.

Okay then.

I was about to take my coffee into the bedroom when Ash glanced up from the screen and crooked a finger at me. I walked over, and he plucked the mug from my hand and set it on the table before settling me on his lap and handing it back.

All without missing a beat as he talked to Maximo about some bid they'd received. I had no idea what they meant until I glanced at the screen.

"That's awful."

Maximo nodded. "That's what I said."

I looked at the *photo* of a hotel room.

"What's your issue with it?" Ash asked.

I waited to hear what Maximo had to say.

A hand squeezed my thigh. "I'm talking to you."

"Oh. Well, there's a long list. Whoever designed this has clearly never cleaned a room in their lives." I pointed toward the slatted accent wall. "This is cool in small amounts like a headboard, but dust is going to accumulate in that entire wall no matter how thoroughly someone cleans." I pointed at the cluster of futuristic furniture positioned right between the bed and the window. "First of all, it's ugly." I regretted the words as soon as they slipped from my mouth. "That's probably just my opinion, though—"

"No, it's ugly," Maximo agreed. "What else?"

Drawing on my experience as a housekeeper, I pointed out half a dozen other issues between the main room and the bathroom that would annoy guests *and* housekeeping. When I was done, I picked up my coffee and said, "You'd think if they were going to AI a picture, they'd at least make it better."

Ash's body went tight at the same time Maximo asked, "What?"

"It might just be a very bad Photoshop attempt to spruce it up, but I'm almost positive it's AI. Aren't these mockup options for your new hotel?"

He shook his head. "When I told them what I'm looking for, they said they'd done something similar, and I asked for photos. These are supposed to be them."

I pointed out where the shadows didn't match up how they should've.

"Waste of damn time." Ash clicked out of the window and deleted the email.

"If you need an interior designer"—I flung a hand toward all the nothingness—"just have Ash do it."

"If you've got ideas," Ash said, "let me know, and I'll have it done."

I started laughing, but he didn't join me. "I'm serious. You're better at it than those lying bastards. And since my rooms in all four hotels look like this, it's not like I'm an expert."

I didn't say anything, but that didn't mean I wasn't thinking about the possibilities.

Functional possibilities that didn't involve angular chairs that could poke an eye out.

Ash lifted me from his lap and went into the bedroom. He returned less than a second later. "Where's the shirt?"

"The hamper."

His expression was enough to make a phantom burn spread across my ass.

After he disappeared, Maximo stood and gathered his stuff. "Juliet is still sleeping, but text her later."

"I will."

Maybe do that.

His eyes narrowed like he could read my mind, but then he just smirked as he shook his head.

Ash returned a minute later wearing the same dark blue suit and charcoal gray shirt he had been—just with the addition of the undershirt. He pulled me in for another inappropriately intense kiss. "I should be done before dinner." His voice lowered. "And you have a punishment for dessert."

"Isn't there a statute of limitations on those? That all happened last night. Forever ago."

"Never."

"Well, feel free to work extra." I put my cupped hand to my ear. "I think Maximo just said it's mandatory overtime."

He chuckled.

But he did it with hazel eyes blazing in anticipation.

THERE WAS NO RUSH.

It could wait.

I had lots of time.

I...

I was procrastinating because I was a coward.

After Ash and Maximo left, I'd showered before fixing another coffee that I'd drunk out on the balcony with my iPad. Instead of reading like I'd intended, I'd spent a couple of hours looking up different hotel rooms.

I'd always been curious about how a hotel came up with the design they used for rooms. As far as I knew, the bulk of The Roulette's furnishings and decor were a hodgepodge from auctions of failed hotels.

It seemed like bad luck to me.

But for hotels that actually cared, I was curious what went into it. I'd never bothered for the same reason I never window-shopped.

Looking at things I could never have was like sticking my head in a mousetrap I'd set myself—pointless and painful.

When I'd gone back inside, I'd grabbed my phone and...

That was as far as I got.

Staring down at my text thread with Juliet, I wanted to explain—yet again. But there was a limit to how much annoying bullshit someone could take, even from their no-longer-fledgling friend. And despite Maximo's order earlier, I was worried I'd exceeded that quota.

Juliet and I may have had similar-ish backgrounds, but we clearly didn't have the same flaws. Weaknesses.

Issues.

With a sigh, I grabbed the remote and turned on the TV. It was still on the news that Ash had been watching.

I was about to switch the channel to something actually watchable when the man's words caught my attention. Standing outside of a run-down motel that made The Roulette seem like The Bellagio, he pointed to the side. "That poor maid, man. I hope she can sue for emotional distress or hazardous conditions or something because that's just wrong."

"Let's go back to yesterday," a reporter said.

"Well, there's been all those stabbings around, ya know? So when they found the body, that's what we thought it was. That the Vegas serial killer struck here."

The reporter quickly smiled at the camera. "Authorities have already assured the public that those stabbings are unrelated to each other."

He arched a brow. "And cops never lie?"

"About this body," she prompted to keep things on track.

"Oh. So neither of those dudes have been around, but this isn't a summer camp. No one is taking roll call and enforcing curfew. But then the smell started. No AC and all. Management sent that poor maid to check it out instead of going themselves because they're lazy bastards. And that's when she found the guy. He wasn't stabbed, though, so it isn't the serial killer. I overheard them say he's likely been dead for a *week*. Maybe an overdose." He shook his head. "All that time missing, and no one came to check on him. Sad."

"Do you know if the deceased had a history with substance abuse."

"I don't judge which sins people dabble in when they visit Sin City. And dead or not, I'm no rat." He started to walk off frame before sticking his head back on camera. "But yeah, that dude was a tweaker."

The camera panned in on just the reporter as she fought to

stay solemn and professional. "Police are still searching for this man who may have..."

The rest of her words faded to nothing as I stared at the screen. When the picture disappeared, I snatched up the remote, nearly dropping it from my shaking grip. I rewound and paused to stare at the man's photo.

Despite the time that'd passed, my cheeks stung like they were covered in fresh brick burn.

Despite the safety I usually felt thanks to Ash, fear lodged in my throat.

And despite all the showers I'd taken, I could feel his rough hands touching me.

Hurting me.

According to the label under the mug shot, his name was Edward Zale.

According to me, he was the leader. The asshole who attacked me. And I bet that made the dead guy...

When Ash said he'd handled the guys, I hadn't asked follow-ups. I'd just been focused on how good it felt to have someone care enough to make that kind of effort.

'I'll be forced to kill them.'

Ash's words from the night before drifted through my head. I'd assumed the possessive claim was hyperbole. Like when I'd told Juliet that I'd kill for a Diet Coke. I wouldn't actually do it.

But would Ash kill for me?

Had Ash killed for me?

I needed to know.

My thumbs trembled so badly, I had to keep fixing my message.

> Me: Where are you?

Nothing.

> Me: I need to talk to you.

Nothing again.

> Me: I saw the news.

But even that didn't get a response.

I waited for an eternity—or fifteen minutes—before calling.

There was no answer.

He always answered my texts immediately. I'd never had to call him, but that was exactly the point. With the way he worried, he wouldn't ignore me calling out of the blue. He would pick up no matter what he was doing.

Unless he couldn't.

My phone buzzed, and my heart skipped, but it was Juliet not Ash.

> Juliet: I was trying to be patient and not a pushy friend, but... I'm a pushy friend. Boxing isn't for everyone, and I should've thought to warn you. I'm sorry. I grew up surrounded by it, and even then, it can be a lot. If you are feeling self-conscious about running off, remember that I got lost when I thought I could travel the desert alone. And then I tried to leave again because I believed a sweaty, cruel man when he told me that I didn't belong with Maximo.
>
> Juliet: Point is, everyone wants to run sometimes.
>
> Juliet: What matters is whether you have someone who cares enough to chase you.

I skimmed her messages but reread the last two a few times.

> Me: Is Ash, Maximo, or Marco with you?

> Juliet: No.

> Juliet: Why?
>
> Juliet: What's wrong?

Clutching my phone, I rushed to the elevator and went down to the lobby. By the time I stepped off, Elliot was there.

He pointed up. "Cole set it so we get an alert when you or Mrs. Black press the button. Pool?"

I shook my head. "Have you seen Ash?"

"Not recently. What's wrong?"

"I'm not feeling well."

It wasn't a lie. My sour stomach churned like I'd used curdled milk in my coffee.

He went alert, his voice lowering to just above a whisper. "Do you want to leave?"

No, I want Ash to call and tell me what's going on.

Tell me the truth.

I shook my head. "I'll try calling Marco or Cole."

"I've got it," he said, already pulling his phone from his pocket. He put it on speaker.

"Mila with you?" Marco asked by way of greeting.

"Yes, she's not feeling well. Is Ash with you?"

"I'm on my way."

"I can bring her—" he started, but the call disconnected.

Elliot was always kind, but he kept a professional distance from me as he did his job. Even still, there was something Dad-esque about it. Like he was a friend's dad in charge of keeping his chaperone group safe on a field trip.

That vibe was especially strong as he studied me with concern. "Are you sure you're okay?"

"Yeah. I think I just ate something bad. It's causing stomach issues."

He didn't ask anything more.

The elevator I'd stepped out of opened again, and Marco stood inside. He jerked his head.

Taking that to mean I was supposed to join in, I went inside.

"I hope you feel better," Elliot said, still watching me like he thought I'd die at any moment.

It wasn't me I was worried about.

I waited until the doors closed before asking, "Where's Ash?"

"Downstairs."

"In the garage?"

"No."

Confused, I looked at him, but he just stared straight ahead. When it opened again, Marco gestured for me to get out.

And even though the hall looked like something out of a horror film set in an abandoned hospital or prison, I walked out and followed him down a short hall.

We turned the corner just as Ash came out of a room. Before any emotion at seeing him could fully form, my focus dropped to his hands and the blood that coated them. My eyes darted along his body, searching for an injury.

"Not my blood," Ash said, his expression and voice both locked down.

Giving me nothing.

"Maximo or—"

"Not theirs, either."

Like he was simply rinsing spilled marinara sauce from his hands, he went over to the sink and scrubbed them clean.

That's not going to help the blood splattered on his suit.

No wonder he keeps so many backups.

I had to swallow down a hysterical laugh.

The placement of the random sink made me wonder how often of an occurrence it was. While he did that, Marco went into the room and came out a moment later with Cole.

And a man walking between them.

The guy wasn't dead, but his nose was definitely broken. And possibly his fingers or hand, based on the way he cradled it.

As they passed, the guy darted at the last minute and reached for me.

Marco caught him in time and yanked him back. "That was fucking stupid."

"Help!" the guy cried at me. "Help!"

"Wh-what are they going to do with him?" I stuttered when they were out of earshot.

"Log his info with security so he's banned from all Black Resorts properties and then dump him onto the streets."

I released a held breath but couldn't relax. Not yet. Not when there was so much more to talk about. "Who is he?"

"Someone who fucked with the wrong business."

I thought about Ash's irritation earlier, and guilt made my chest go hollow. "The guy who sent the AI pictures?"

"What?" He didn't give me the chance to explain before he shook his head. "Christ, Mila, if I was going to beat every business owner who lied, Vegas would be a ghost town."

"Then what'd that guy do?" I asked.

"Groped a cocktail server. She almost broke his nose herself. I just finished the job. And three of his fingers since that's how many times she told him to back off. It could've been worse."

"How could it be worse than *that*?"

"Did you know there are twenty-seven bones in the human hand?" A cruel smirk curved his mouth, and it was like he was someone else. Not my tender, charming Ash. At least not the version he showed me. "If even the tip of a single one of his fingers would've grazed you, I'd have broken every last one."

Since the guy had it coming for getting handsy with the waitress—and he was still alive—I moved on to what actually mattered. "I saw the news, Ash."

The first show of emotion flashed across his face. Anger mixed with something else I couldn't decipher before both were gone. "We'll talk at home."

"Let's just go upstairs."

"I said *home*."

Ash

Fuck.

I'd known it. In my gut the night before, after Mila finally let me in and shared about her childhood, I'd known I needed to tell her. I'd known there was a chance she'd find out somehow, and the longer I waited, the worse it'd be.

I just thought I had longer than half a damn day.

I wanted to slam my fist against the steering wheel, but I settled for tightening my grip like I could silently choke the shit outta it. Mila was already huddled in the passenger's seat with her arms wrapped protectively around herself. I didn't want to scare her worse.

Not when she'd already called me Ash.

Not Daddy.

Ash.

I'd told her what would happen once I became her Daddy. And when we got home—where it would be harder to run—I would have to remind her.

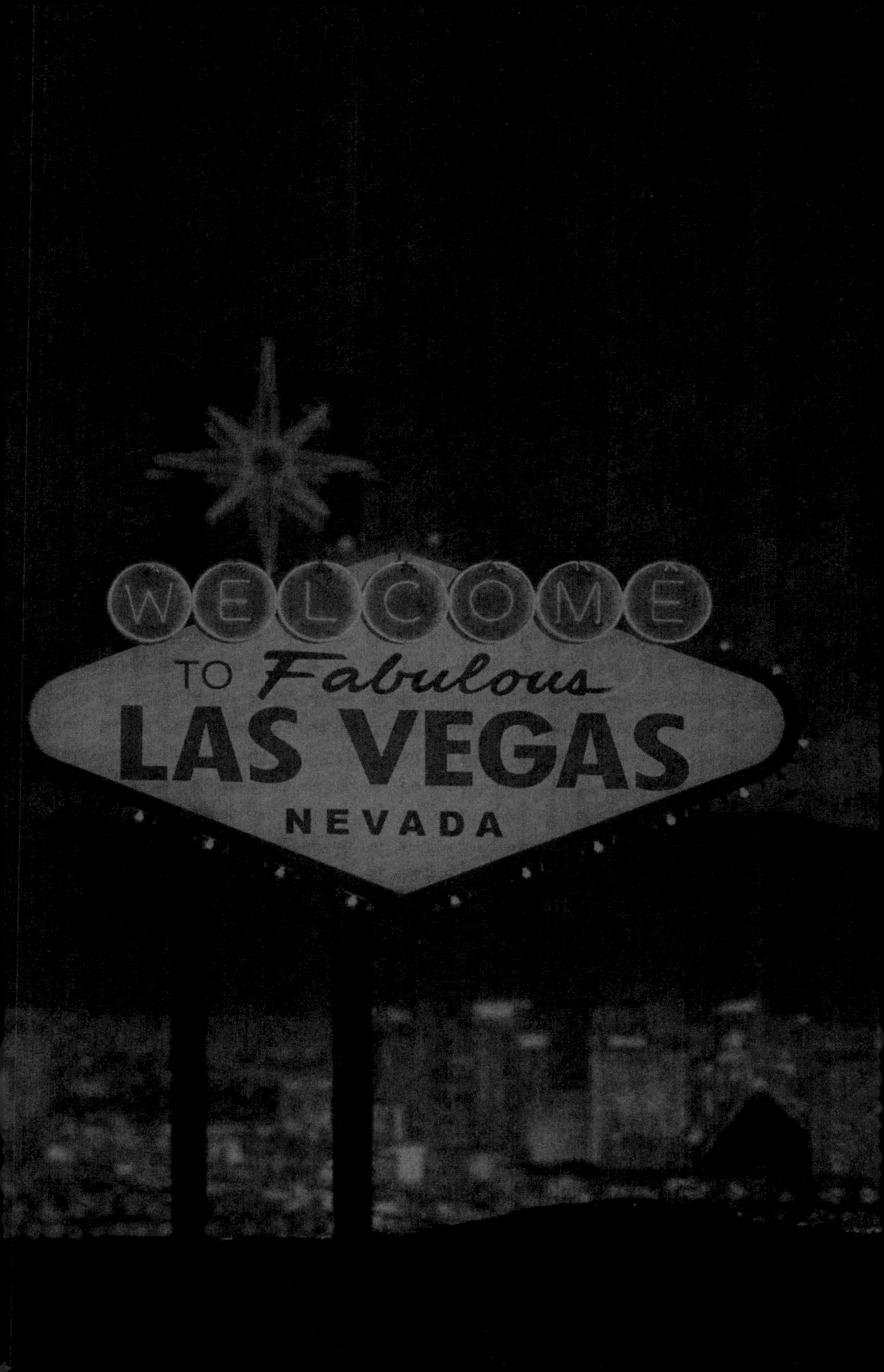
WELCOME
TO Fabulous
LAS VEGAS
NEVADA

CHAPTER 28
ALWAYS REMEMBER WHAT GOES UP...
MILA

Ash said we'd talk at home, and for once, I'd listened. After a long, silent car ride where we both stayed in our own heads, we were home. I stepped through the doorway from his garage into his kitchen.

We were home. And it was as long as I was waiting.

Spinning to face him, I asked, "What happened to the guys who attacked me?"

Ash took his suit jacket off and tossed it aside while he answered my question with a warning. "Think this through, sunshine."

"Think what through?"

He crowded me until our bodies nearly touched. His hazel eyes were shockingly cold as he looked down at me. It sent a shiver through me, and his jaw clenched. "Whether you can live with knowing that answer. If you need some plausible deniability in your head in order to be happy, then drop this now. Because once it's out there, there is no unhearing it. And there is no leaving."

"Ash—"

My words were cut off when he lifted me suddenly and spun

before slamming my ass down on the island. His palms slapped the counter on either side of me. "You do *not* get to call me Ash like that's all I am to you." He pressed in farther, forcing my legs to spread. "I told you what would happen once you became mine. I warned you I could become consumed by you, but that was a lie. I was already consumed. Fucking obsessed. But I still gave you the choice, and you gave me you. Now there's no going back. You don't get to make that decision."

"Then who does?" I asked, lost and confused.

"*Me*. I'm your Daddy because you trust me to take care of you. To do what's best for you." Ash stepped away just long enough to tear my pants down my legs and free his cock. He didn't even bother to step out of them in his rush to be inside me. Holding my legs spread, he filled me in one brutal thrust before freezing. He gripped my chin to crane my neck so I was looking at him. So he was all I could see. "And *I'm* what's best for you. I'll always be what's best for you because I'll live and fucking die to take care of you. And yes, Camila, that includes murder."

My chest tightened until I could barely breathe.

But Ash wasn't done. "Those fuckers hurt the woman I love. They scared her."

"Love?" I breathed, a million thoughts going in a million different directions at a million miles per hour

He kept going like I hadn't spoken. "So I made sure they hurt. That they were scared." He lifted his hands, flipping them back and forth. "And then I came home with their blood added to what already stains my skin and touched you." He wrapped those same hands around my upper thighs. Sliding out, he slammed back in. Even with his hold pinning me in place, I scooted up the island. He pinned me back where he wanted me and then thrust deeper. "Got you off." He plunged in again. "Made you mine." Again.

And again.

And again.

I wanted to give in to it, but I couldn't let myself.

Ash had done so much for me. He let me stay with him.

Supported me. Showed me what it was like to be wanted for once. Made me feel like my neediness wasn't a flaw because it was something he couldn't live without.

True to his promise, he'd taken care of me.

I needed to do the same. "But what about the news?"

His fingers squeezed until they dug in. "Anything I did to them, they had—"

"I don't care about that. What if you get caught?"

He froze again. "What?"

"I watched a segment on the news, and they think it was an overdose. So if they do an autopsy or whatever, and it comes back not drugs, they'll start looking into it more." When I'd seen the news and realized what Ash's version of *deal with them* entailed, panic had seized me. It grew at the possibility of everything imploding around us. "You could get caught."

"You're worried about me?"

I nodded.

The world was filled with bad people. I wasn't going to get in a moral outrage that there were two less of them walking around, trying to assault women in alleys. I didn't have to wonder what kind of person it made me because I already knew it made me a shitty one. I also didn't care about that.

Ash grinned at me like I was adorable.

"I'm serious. What if it traces back to you? Are the police or FBI or whoever going to bang that door down to haul the man I love off to prison?"

Ash's smile fell. His body went so rigid, it might as well have been etched from marble. His hands clenched my thighs tight enough that I could see the veins popping out under the tattooed skin. I wasn't even sure he breathed. "Say it again."

"Prison?"

"Camila…"

It was fast. Illogical. *Insane.*

That didn't make it not true.

I knew without a doubt that I loved Ash.

I wasn't confused, like having never experienced love meant I didn't know how it felt.

I was certain *because* I'd never experienced love. There was no mistaking that untainted beauty for anything else.

"I love you," I said, my words ending in a moan.

I thought I'd seen him desperate.

Wild.

Unhinged.

But I hadn't actually seen Ash lose control. Not until right then, with his mask of civility gone to show me the ruthless monster that hid behind nice suits and charming smiles.

My monster.

My protector.

My Daddy.

His thrusts were vicious as he pounded into me, filling me until I ached and then taking more still. Leaning back on my arms, I wrapped my legs around him to give it all. Little zaps of electricity mixed with fire started shooting through me but didn't have the chance to build. He eased back, and so did my release.

With only the head of his cock pressed into me, his thumb circled my clit. My pussy tightened, greedily trying to get more, but he didn't give it.

He teased me.

Tormented me.

Used my body against me until I wanted to cry and beg.

Ash built my need until I thought I'd die, and then he froze.

"Please," I whimpered.

"Please *who*?"

I didn't hesitate. "Please, Daddy."

He gave me what I needed, but not by fucking me. Gripping my hips, he stayed still and used his hold to move me. Sliding me up and down his length. Making me fuck him.

"Look at how you take me," he growled. When my eyes stayed on his blazing ones, he slowed. "I said *look*."

I stared down my body to where I was obscenely spread

around his width. I could see my wetness coating him, my thighs, and the counter below me. I watched his length disappear as he pressed in, and the visual was enough to make my orgasm hover just out of reach.

He planted deep and stayed there, not letting me move even an inch. I could feel his hand vibrate with restraint as he wrapped his fingers around my neck. "You're not leaving."

It wasn't a question, but I agreed anyway. "Okay."

"You're *never* leaving."

Again, it wasn't a question. It was a deranged order, but I agreed anyway. "Okay."

I tried to rock against him. When that didn't work, I tried begging again. "Please move, Daddy. I'm so close."

"You don't get to come," he shared plainly, like he was telling me a mundane fact.

"What?" But I already knew. My punishment for running the night before. My added one for accidentally calling him Ash.

His fingertips squeezed the side of my throat as he slowly slid his length out of me, ignoring my whimpers and pleading. "On your knees."

Not giving me the chance to obey, he lifted me and set me down on my feet before pushing on the top of my head. I dropped to kneel as I looked up at him. Waiting.

"Christ, how did I get so lucky?" Despite his tender words, his tone was harsh. The way he wrapped my hair around his hand and tugged was even more so. "Open your mouth."

Even though he went down on me often, I hadn't returned the act yet. I had no clue what to do or how to make it good for him.

But I didn't have to worry about that because I wasn't in control.

When I did as he ordered, Ash fisted himself and pressed between my lips. Fed me his cock. I could taste the tangy sweetness of my own arousal mixing with Ash's taste. My mouth burned at how wide I had to open, and I wasn't able to take much before a gag clenched my stomach and throat. He withdrew to just before that point. "Play with your pussy."

I wasn't sure I could do that kind of multitasking, but that didn't mean I wouldn't try. My hand went between my legs, and my fingertip landed on my clit. I moaned around Ash.

"Fuck," he gritted out through clenched teeth as he rocked against me.

I breathed deep through my nose and tried to keep going.

"That's it. That's *my* good girl."

I swallowed around him as my body tensed. Nearly there. On the verge of combustion.

And Ash must've known because he gruffly ordered, "Stop touching your pretty pussy."

But I didn't. *Couldn't.* I was too close.

He yanked my hair harder. "Remember a few days ago?"

I did.

When Ash had wanted to eat me slowly so he could savor the taste, I'd threatened to take matters into my own hands.

And he'd allowed it.

Just not in the way I'd needed.

While he'd watched and lazily stroked his cock, he'd forced me to play with my pussy until my fingers had pruned. But he hadn't let me come. Not until I'd been a whimpering, pathetic mess. Not until I'd been desperate and shaking. Not until I'd promised to never touch what belonged to him without his permission.

It still took all my willpower to force my hand away, and I had to grip the fabric of his slacks that were still pooled around his legs with the effort.

"If I tell you to stay somewhere, that means stay there. Don't know what I would do if something happened to you. It'd fucking kill me." Ash's thrusts sped up but remained shallow. "And never, fucking *ever* call me Ash again. Understood?"

Since my mouth was full, all I could do was nod.

He pushed deeper. "Relax your throat, Camila. Let Daddy in."

I tried to release him and lean back. Not because I wanted to stop. I wanted to *beg*. I needed to come so bad, it hurt.

Trying to pull away from him was the wrong move. His irate gaze narrowed.

"I'm not letting you go." Moving his hold from my hair to my face, he pried my mouth open wider. "I'll never let you go."

He moved me how he wanted me as he used me how he needed. Brutal and unrestrained, he fucked my face until tears blurred my vision before they trailed down my cheeks. That didn't give him pause. He didn't stop or even slow.

Groaning low and rough, he surged deeper. Went faster. Using his hold, he tugged me forward at the same time he thrust, taking me to my limit and pushing past it. My breaths came in whatever small bursts I could get each time he withdrew from my throat.

He pulled free suddenly to fist himself. "Shirt and bra off."

I didn't ask why. I just did it.

I'd seen him touch himself before, but it was always slow. Leisurely. A tease.

That time was different.

Each long stroke was so fast, his hand seemed to blur. It was rough. *Violent.*

With a harsh grunt, he aimed so the first spurt of cum hit my breasts. Gripping my head, he kept it close enough for the rest to splatter across my face.

Marking me as his.

One second, I was on my knees. The next, I was back on the counter. I barely had time to process the change when Ash's thumb began rubbing my clit in tight circles. He used the index finger on his other hand to swipe some of the mess from my face. I thought he was just cleaning it away, but he slid his finger into my pussy.

Pushing his cum inside me.

I was already on the verge of coming apart, but at that, I didn't break.

I *shattered*.

Ash's skilled fingers worked me through one orgasm and straight into the next. When it finally passed, his pressure eased, but his finger still glided in and out.

I tried to close my legs against the sweet torture, but his palm spanked my oversensitive pussy, and my legs shot back open.

Our whole conversation seemed to cycle through my head like my brain was committing each and every moment to memory. His claims of love and obsession, but also the rest. What he was willing to do to protect me.

What he had done.

Like his words were rays of sunlight made just for me, I wanted to bask in them. Let them seep into my soul to warm me from the inside out.

Before I could do that, though...

"We still need to talk," I said.

And I wouldn't be put off—again.

He took his touch away and began redoing his slacks. "I'm not going to get caught."

"But when they do testing—"

"If they bother to—and that's a big *if*—it'll show exactly what they suspect. Drugs. After a week in that dump without the AC on, I doubt they'll look close enough to spot the broken hand. Even if they do, that won't jump out as odd since he's a known shithead."

"What about the other guy?"

"They won't find him."

"Are you sure?"

His expression softened as he shook off his shirt. I tried—and failed—to ignore the wetness on it.

Oops.

"Yeah, sunshine, I'm sure. This isn't something we do on the daily, but we've still done it enough to be good at it."

"*We?*"

"Me, Maximo, Cole, and Marco."

My brows lowered. "They know about the guys?"

"I know you didn't want people to know—"

I waved it away. "No, I mean they know what you did to those guys?"

"They know 'cause they helped me."

I mentally added yet another item to the list of reasons I was dysfunctional. Because at hearing that, my heart melted like I'd just found out they'd gotten together to throw me a surprise party and not a murder.

I set that aside to bask in later, too.

I got momentarily distracted as Ash tugged his tee off, slowly revealing muscles and tattoos like they were works of art.

Because they were.

I forced myself to stay on topic. "If you weren't worried about them overhearing, then why didn't you want to talk until we were home?"

Taking the tee in his hand, he pulled it over my head. I automatically moved to slide my arms in. Once it was on, he kissed me sweetly like he hadn't just roughly used me. And then he smirked. "Because it would be harder for you to run from me here."

That shouldn't have been romantic, yet there we were.

I breathed a sigh of relief. "With how serious Maximo takes security, I thought maybe there were cameras or something in your company vehicle, and that's why you didn't want to talk. I just kept thinking about all the..."

His gaze dropped to my flushed cheeks. "All the filthy things I've said in that SUV?"

Yes.

That.

Ash had given me the reassurances I needed, but it was his turn to demand them. "Why'd you call me Ash?"

"When you didn't answer my texts or call, I was scared you'd already been caught. Then I went down to this mysterious space to find you covered in blood. I was freaked. And when I did it here, it was because I was still freaked and needed to know you weren't about to get taken away from me."

"I fucking dare anyone to try."

"What about the guy today? Won't he just go to the cops?"

He shook his head. "He knows we have footage of him assaulting the server first. And if you think the cops don't know what happens in the back rooms, alleys, or basements of casinos, you're wrong. They know and don't care."

With that settled, I finally let the happiness sink in.

Only it wasn't just warmth. There was also stickiness.

At the way the tee clung to my chest and what was rapidly drying on my face, I asked, "Any chance you're going to let me go upstairs to shower this off?"

"Not a bet I'd make."

I didn't think so.

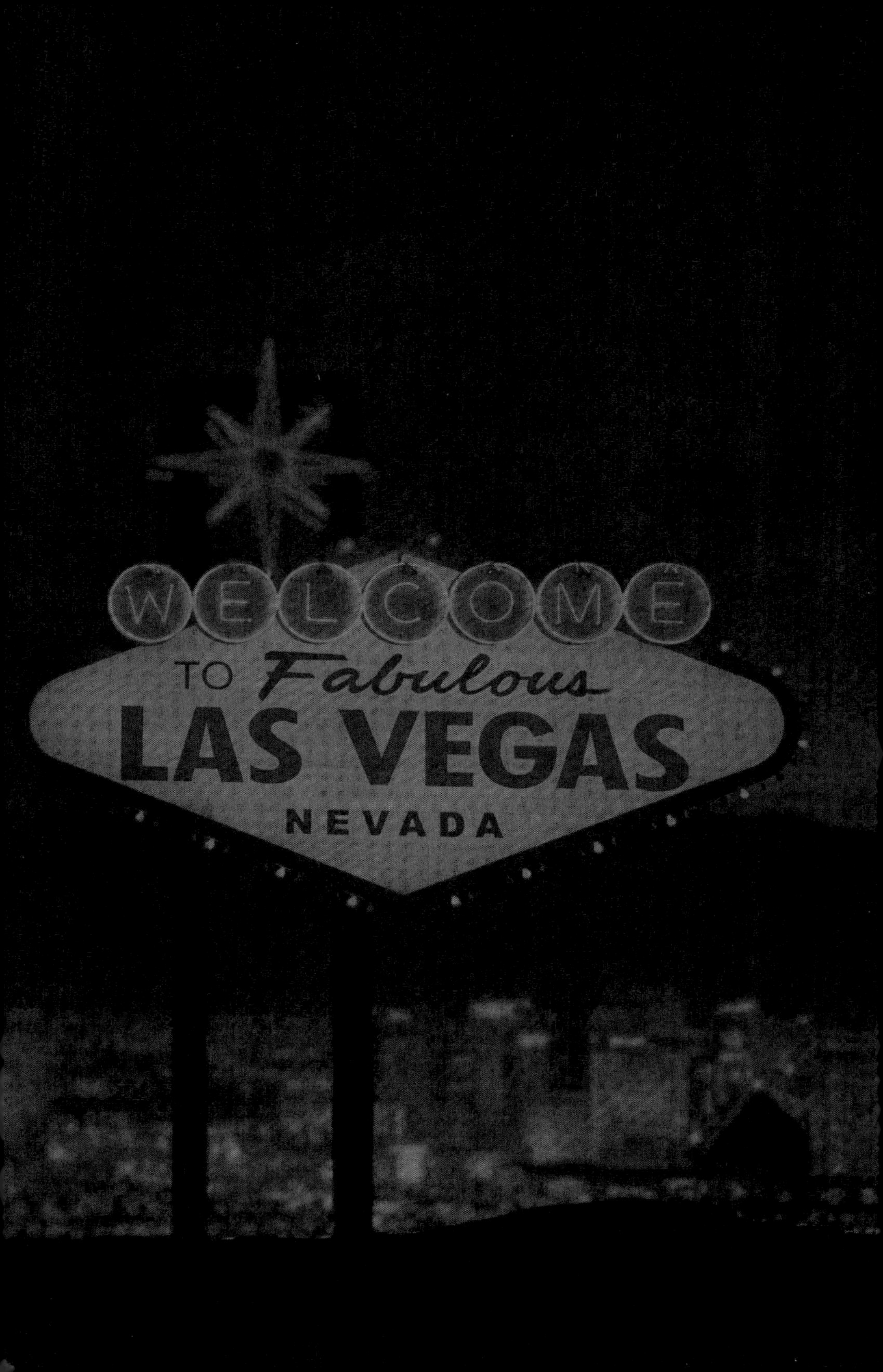
WELCOME
TO Fabulous
LAS VEGAS
NEVADA

CHAPTER 29
...MUST COME DOWN
MILA

My life after Ash came into it was already good. But in the weeks since I'd found out about the other side of him, and the last bit of his restraint disappeared?

It was a dream. Better than anything I could've imagined.

Ash loved me. Actually, *loved* may have been too weak of a word, but it was the best one I had.

Not only was my love life perfect, but I also had friends. Actual friends.

Okay, I had Juliet. But she had to count as like ten friends in one because she was so good.

And beyond all of that, I had big plans for the future. Exciting plans. I'd never really allowed myself to make those before, even in a pipe dream kinda way. In some part of my mind, I'd relegated myself to a lifetime of working at The Roulette or similar places. Imagining anything better had seemed pointless.

Not anymore, though.

With so much good, only one person could mess it up.

And, unfortunately, she was headed right for me.

My eyes scanned the hallway near Moonlight's food court, looking for familiar faces. Other than Elliot, there were none.

After all the years of Veronica trying to hide that she was old enough to have a daughter, something was karmic in the fact I didn't want anyone there to know she was my mother.

For a couple of weeks, she'd texted daily, but when I never responded, she'd given up. I'd assumed she'd moved on. But as she hustled over like the IRS was on her tail, I saw my luck hadn't completely changed.

Elliot clocked her as a threat and stepped to block me before she got near.

"Get out of the way," Veronica said, her voice pitched high with panic.

Elliot never had to act as more than a precautionary sentry.

Until then.

"You need to leave." His hand went to his taser. "Now."

Her pinched face twisted, and I just knew she was building up to a loud fit. Like a tea kettle about to scream.

"It's okay, Elliot," I said, hoping to get whatever drama over with quickly so I could go get my cheeseburger. "She's my mom."

He looked between us disbelievingly, and I could've kissed his cheek for that compliment.

Except for the fact Ash would've undoubtedly sliced the skin right off his face.

"I promise she's not a threat," I tacked on when he still hesitated.

Not one to my physical well-being, at least.

He didn't grab his taser, but he did pull his phone out, likely to check in with Ash.

Since that was fine by me, I turned my focus to my mother. "What's—"

Before I could finish, she gripped my upper arm in the tight way she used to when I did something wrong as a kid.

If she leaves bruises, Elliot's taser will be the least of her worries.

She tried to pull me down the hall, but I dug my heels in and dislodged my arm before she could.

Her frantic gaze darted around, and she kept her voice low. Like she was trying to hide from someone. "I need money."

Oh. Wow. I am shocked. Someone alert Ripley's Believe It or Not *to this groundbreaking revelation.*

"Try your luck at Keno," I said coldly.

"Camila, I'm serious."

When Ash called me by my name, it usually meant he was saying something extra important. Since that almost always meant he was being sexy, bossy, or sexily bossy, I loved hearing it in his gravelly voice.

Hearing it from Veronica was wrong. She may have given me the name, but it wasn't hers to use anymore.

"And I'm just as serious," I said. "I'm not giving you money."

Elliot came closer, but I held a hand out to stop him. The sooner she spewed whatever vitriol she needed, the sooner she'd leave.

In that moment, as I looked at the woman I barely knew, I finally felt ready to sever that connection. I was no longer desperate enough to cling to family just because we shared some blood. I no longer feared I'd be alone. It wasn't a possibility.

I had Ash.

"Fine." Veronica sighed like I'd done something egregious. "Buy me a plane ticket. I don't care where, I just need to get away. Vegas isn't safe for me."

My eyes narrowed. "What did you get into?"

She looked over her shoulder again. "I don't need much. Enough to get by for a while. Maybe a buffer."

Oh my God, she's begging for money and still trying to negotiate for more.

"I don't have any," I said honestly. I'd reordered my debit card and ID. Though I hadn't noticed until it'd come in the mail that Ash had switched my address to his.

It was just as well. He, Cole, and Marco had already cleared my old apartment out.

Even though I had my own card *and* one of Ash's, I never carried them. I never had to.

Just like I never had to stress about money, budgeting, or whether I had enough food to last me the week.

Not that I spent Ash's money—much to his chagrin—but it was reassuring to know it was there if I needed it.

Somehow Veronica seemed to know that because she ordered, "Get it from your man."

"He's not here, so I can't ask," I lied. All I had to do was call, and he'd come. All I had to do was mention it, and he'd give it to me.

I just didn't want to.

"No one said to ask. Take it." Her words spilled out in a distracted ramble as she stayed alert and scanned around us. "He won't even care. You must've gotten something from your mama 'cause he said your man wired over fifty-K like he was paying for a cup of coffee. That's why he wanted me to try to reconnect with you."

I might've been done with her, but at the confirmation that her messages were just another manipulative act, sharp pain sliced through me.

I did something I rarely had to do anymore—suppressed it. "Who are you talking about? What money?"

Veronica's gaze landed on me. "From the... misunderstanding. Your man paid it off. He's not going to care if you give me more. He won't even notice."

"Ash paid..." My jaw dropped. "You owed *fifty* thousand dollars to someone?"

My brain couldn't fathom how that was possible. Hell, a couple of months ago, my brain wouldn't have been able to fathom the life someone could live with fifty thousand dollars. Yet my mother must've blown through it like she always did on her quest for the easy life with more, more, more.

It wasn't a surprise Ash had paid it. If he thought he was protecting me, I wasn't sure there was a limit to what he'd do. That didn't mean I was happy about it. Especially since he hadn't told me himself.

Not giving her the chance to come up with some bullshit lie about how she'd donated the money to kittens and firefighters and kittens who were training to be firefighters, I stepped away.

"I don't care if he wouldn't notice. I don't steal from my man. I'm not like you."

A sharp *thwack* cut through the air as Veronica's palm struck my cheek.

Well, I was wrong...

She is a threat to my physical well-being, too.

I wanted to say it was her pain at the thought of losing me that overwhelmed her to the point of lashing out, but I knew better. It was about the money.

It was *always* about the money.

Veronica's realization that I wasn't going to help her showed she couldn't manipulate me. That meant I no longer served a purpose. She didn't have to watch her temper.

Elliot moved in to grab her, but the behemoth at my back got there first.

Wrapping an arm around my stomach, Ash shifted me behind his big body. His voice was low and calm but so fucking terrifying as he spoke to Veronica. "You're done. I tried to give Mila the chance to come to the decision herself, but that time has run out. And so has yours. You're out of her life."

Desperate to see how she reacted to being put in her place, I peeked around Ash to see Veronica stupidly argue with him. "Who the fuck are you to tell my daughter what to do?"

"I'm her Daddy."

Simple as that.

Her lip curled in disgust. "That's disgusting, you abusive—"

"Shut up," I snapped, dodging from behind Ash. His arm wrapped around me again, but that time it wasn't to protect me. It was to stop me from lunging at the bitch in front of me. When she opened her mouth, I held up a finger—and not the one I wanted to give her. "Don't say another word. I don't want to hear or give a fuck what you think of my relationship. I'm not even going to waste my time and breath bragging about all the ways it's better than anything you could hope to have. I just want you gone. Forever. You're banned from all Black Resorts properties and whatever other ones *my* Daddy has connections at. Now get out. You're dead to me."

Ash's voice stayed low so only Veronica and I could hear. "I don't care if you're walking down the street and coincidentally see Mila. You better turn your ass around and *run*. Because if either of us sees you again, you'll regret it. Understood?"

With hate in her blue eyes that she aimed at both of us, she didn't have the chance to say anything before Ash shuffled us backward. Uniformed guards moved in to grab Veronica's arms.

I'd kind of accepted that making scenes at Moonlight was my thing, but it was nothing compared to the one she created when she was physically removed from the property.

Ash turned his angry eyes to Elliot.

Standing close, he just raised his chin and waited for his reprimand.

But I wasn't done playing the protective hero. Twisting to look at Ash, I explained, "Veronica showed up to ask for money, and I told Elliot I had it handled because I thought I did. I didn't think she'd hit me. Which hurt less than your spanks, so it's not even a big deal." I glanced toward Elliot quickly before returning my focus to Ash. "Anyway, what I'm saying is it's not Elliot's fault."

"He didn't guard you. It's his literal job. Right in the title and everything." His words may have been light and flippant, but the way he glared at Elliot was far from playful.

I put my hands on his chest so he would look down at me. "But I needed to do that. Now I have closure."

Ash jerked his head, and Elliot hightailed it away, leaving the two of us alone.

Well, as alone as we could be in a crowded hall.

His hand cupped my warm cheek gently, and his expression turned so thunderous, I thought he would change his mind and have Veronica hauled back so he could yell at her some more. "Tell me what happened."

I quickly filled him in on the little she'd said that I could remember.

"Did she say what the trouble was?" he asked.

"No, just that Vegas wasn't safe for her." I glared up at him. "You paid fifty thousand dollars for her?"

He shook his head, and I was about to call him out for lying to me again until he said, "I paid fifty thousand dollars for you."

"That's so much... I can't... Why didn't you tell me?"

"Swear to God, I wasn't trying to keep it a secret all this time. I was going to tell you, but then Veronica was quiet, we've been busy, and it slipped my mind."

"You forgot you paid fifty... You know what. Never mind."

His bunched muscles relaxed, and his gaze softened as he studied me. "You okay?"

"Is Maximo going to be mad I banned someone from his resorts?"

"Fuck no. If the cameras picked that up and he sees it, there's a good chance he'll put you in charge of banning people from now on." He lifted my chin and didn't let me joke my way out of anything. "Are you okay?"

"I should've cut her off years ago, but a voice in my head always reminded me she was the only family I had. That if I didn't have her, I didn't have anyone. That's not true anymore. I have you."

"And you always will. I'm not going anywhere."

"Even with a restraining order?" I teased.

"Even then."

"And that's why I'm not even slightly sad." I inhaled deeply, looking at the spot where she'd been. "Drama's done. She's dead to me. Old news. It's time for a cheeseburger."

Who could that be?

I moved through the house toward the source of the loud

banging with my cell in my hand. I wasn't dialing 911 as a precaution.

I called Ash. Except the phone just rang. He didn't answer. A ball of worry took root in my chest.

When I reached the front door, I peeked outside to see two cops.

That's why he didn't answer. He's been hurt.

Or worse.

I was tempted to throw the door open, but I knew better. "What do you want?"

"Police, ma'am. We have some questions for you."

"Let me see your badges."

Two badges were pressed to the glass. They looked legit, but I wasn't an expert. For all I knew, they'd bought them online.

"Business cards, too," I said since it was less likely an impersonator would think to make those.

Two legit-looking business cards were presented, but only one of them was a cop.

I texted Ash, Marco, Cole, *and* Juliet.

> Me: Cops are here.

> Me: Or a cop and an FBI agent.

Disabling the alarm, I cracked the door and looked between the older male cop in a regular uniform and the younger female agent in a suit. "May I help you?"

After identifying themselves with names that didn't register in my panic about why they were there and why Ash hadn't answered my call, the older cop spoke. "Camila Price?"

"That's right."

"What's your relation to Veronica Rogers?"

Since it was the technical truth, I said, "She's my mother."

"When's the last time you saw her?"

"Yesterday afternoon."

Oh my God, if this bitch is trying to lie and press charges, I'm going to hunt her down and kill her myself.

"We're sorry to have to tell you this, but your mother was found dead this morning."

Never mind, someone beat me to it.

The agent tilted her head. "Could you tell us where your boyfriend was last night?"

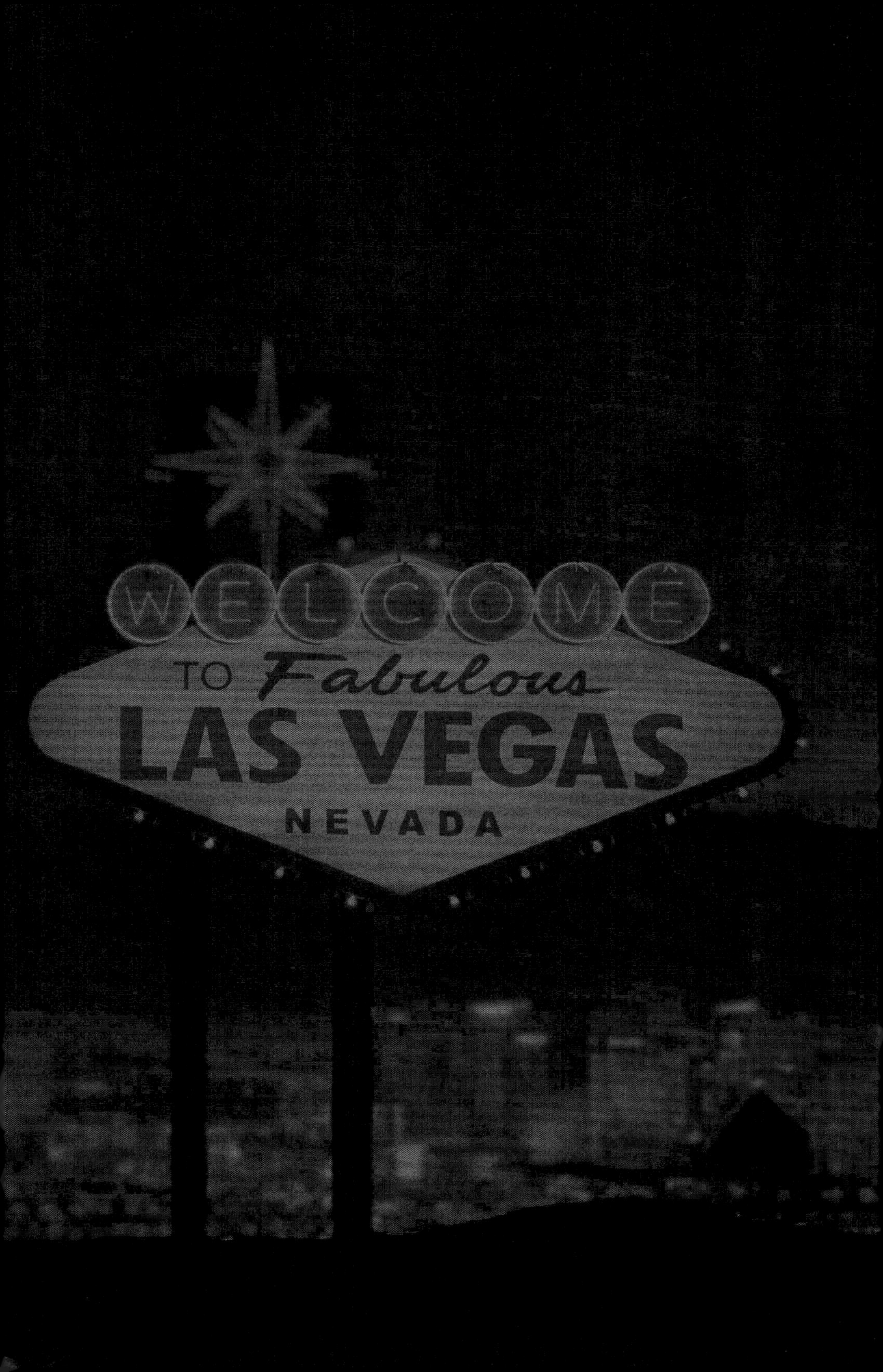
WELCOME
TO Fabulous
LAS VEGAS
NEVADA

CHAPTER 30
YOU DON'T HAVE TO JOIN THE RAT RACE
ASH

"**A**<small>NY IDEA WHAT THIS IS</small> about?" Wes, my lawyer, asked quietly.

"Not a clue." And it was the truth.

"No disgruntled casino guests?"

There were always those, but nothing that any cop worth a damn would pursue.

When Maximo and I had pulled into Moonlight after being at the Black Moon site all day, cops had been waiting for me. They hadn't said why.

Thank Christ Mila stayed home since I was supposed to be in meetings all day. She would've lost her mind and ended up cuffed in the back seat.

My dick twitched.

I was in a police station, not dead.

The door opened, and two suited men entered. One of them looked familiar, but I couldn't place where I'd seen him.

If this is all because he's a disgruntled guest who got tossed from one of the casinos and now he's having a power trip, I'm going to be pissed.

They both sat, but it was the unfamiliar one who spoke. "I'm

Officer Boden, this is Agent Nash. We'd like to ask you some questions, starting with your whereabouts last night."

"Why?" Wes shot back.

"Because we're asking."

Wes answered for me again. "If this is about comparing social calendars, that could've been done without picking my client up at his place of employment. So I'll ask again, *why*?"

"A body was found this morning."

"And? It's Vegas. Bodies are found all the time."

The familiar man leaned back in his chair, his expression stoic. "Do you recall telling Veronica Rogers that her time was up?"

My gut prickled.

"What about that if you see her again, she'll regret it?"

It was nearly imperceptible, but Wes sat up a little straighter. "What is this about?"

"Veronica Rogers was found dead this morning."

Fuck.

Mila. She's going to be a mess.

Wes asked the question before I could. "How'd she die?"

"Stabbed," Officer Boden shared. Wes leaned forward, but the officer just shook his head. "They don't think they're related."

"That's what they always say."

Agent Nash shot me a suspicious look. "Want to explain why you were seen threatening her *twice* yesterday and then she was killed that night?"

"I'm sure I don't have to point it out to you," Wes said, "but part of my client's job is security. He kicks people out of the casino all the time. Including telling them not to return, or they'll get hit with trespassing charges. Something they would surely *regret*. How is this different?"

"Because the victim was his girlfriend's mother."

"Yes, tumultuous family relationships are very sad." Wes gave a slow shake of his head. "That is why my client should be comforting his girlfriend during this difficult time."

"You know," the familiar agent said, "most people in this situation would have verbal diarrhea while they fought to clear their name. There a reason why you're not saying anything?"

Wes fielded that one, too. "Because he pays me a hefty retainer and an insane billable hours rate to do it for him."

"Where were you last night between the hours of seven and ten?" the officer asked.

Wes nudged me.

"Moonlight until almost eight and then home with my girlfriend," I answered.

"Can anyone verify this?"

"Security cameras at the resort, my car GPS, and the security cameras at my house."

Officer Boden scowled, his eyes cutting to the agent next to him.

The agent didn't look fazed by my tripled-up alibi. "But you're a man with money, correct? You come from an esteemed family and have a trust fund, yet you work a demanding job you don't even need. Is telling people they'll be charged with trespassing really that satisfying to you?"

Wes wasn't amused at the waste of time. "Jesus appeared to him on a piece of toast and said it was his calling in life. What does it matter?"

"Because he has the means to pay someone to do his dirty work."

Never. That's my favorite part and the whole reason I deal with the rest of it.

"So coming from money is a crime now?" Wes asked.

"He also has connections."

"Also not a crime."

"It is if he utilized those connections and money to arrange the murder of his girlfriend's estranged mother."

"It's also a crime if he rides a camel on the highway. Or hula hoops on Freemont St. If we're going to sit here listing off all the hypothetical crimes my client could commit, I'm going to need a coffee."

The agent's focus went to me. "Did you spend some time in *your basement* while you were at Moonlight last night?"

That time, my gut didn't prickle.

It tightened with anger because there was no way that was a coincidence.

Must be cheese around because I smell a rat.

Officer Boden looked like he was fighting not to roll his eyes as he shared, "Every casino in this city has a room like that."

"What goes on down there?" the agent pushed.

"Laundry," Wes said.

"What I find myself wondering is, if you're willing to rough up people for cheating or not paying their loans or what have you, then what would you do to the woman who cost you fifty grand?"

That's it. That's where I've seen him before.

The gate guard who was way too chipper.

Clearly, he's good at his undercover act because he's a miserable asshole in real life.

"Which is it? Is he outsourcing the violence with his money and connections or is he a *Rock 'Em Sock 'Em Robot* punching machine? Since there doesn't seem to be any facts or that pesky little thing known as proof attached to any of this, my client and I are leaving." Wes stood and I followed his lead.

Agent Nash kept talking. "It must've made you pretty ticked that you dropped that much money, just for Veronica to run right back to Abraham."

Caught off guard, I couldn't hide my surprise at that.

That dumb bitch got two steps from the end of the maze just to turn back instead.

The agent's *gotcha* smirk dropped at my genuine reaction. "You didn't know."

"I didn't, but I also don't care. I didn't pay the money for her."

He ran a palm down his face. "Start at the beginning."

After getting the okay from Wes, I kept it succinct. "Veronica told my girlfriend she owed someone. To keep Veronica's bullshit away from my girlfriend, I paid it."

"That's a lot of cash to drop because of a woman."

"Then you haven't met a woman like mine."

"Have you been back to Eternal Sun since then?"

"No. That was the end of my interaction with Veronica and that place until Veronica showed up to ask her daughter for money or a plane ticket."

"Why?"

"No idea."

"Did she say anything about Eternal Sun?"

"That Abraham was dangerous."

"Nothing about any upcoming plans?"

"Not a thing."

"*Fuck.*" Agent Nash looked ready to throw the table through the wall. "Nearly a year under for nothing. Think hard. They closed ranks and cut out anyone not in the inner circle. There has to be a reason."

The fact I was sitting there was proof that someone was bad at their job, but I helpfully spelled that out, too. "I went there, paid the money, and left in a hurry because that place fucking creeped me out. I had the displeasure of talking to Veronica a grand total of three times. And they were short conversations. Whoever connected those three dots—"

"Four dots," he cut in. "There's also the Moonlight employee with connections to Eternal Sun."

"Which one?" I asked because that was news to me.

He remained tightlipped.

"Fine. Whoever connected those four dots and thought they had some conspiracy because I'm a guy with money and connections must've had a lot of yarn because they're so spaced out, they're on different corkboards."

"How'd Abraham react when you paid the debt?"

"Like he was happy to be done with Veronica."

The agent shook his head. "He wasn't. He's been obsessed

with her since she dared leave. He didn't give a shit about the money other than it fuels his organization, and he's a power-hungry bastard."

So long as it didn't touch my circle, I didn't give a damn about that, either. "Am I good to go now?"

"Yes," Officer Boden said.

Wes and I were nearly to the door when Agent Nash called, "One last thing."

I turned around.

"If you have such an amazing woman who you're willing to spend such exorbitant amounts of money on... Why was she seen running away from you at your work?"

I whispered to consult with my lawyer. Once I got the okay, I shared, "It's a kink thing."

And then I left to go take care of my woman.

"SHE GOOD?" I asked as soon as I climbed from Wes' car to meet Cole on the sidewalk outside of Moonlight.

"Freaked, but good," Cole said.

After I'd gotten picked up by the cops, Maximo had been on his way to get Mila when she'd texted about her own interaction with a cop and an FBI agent. As much as I'd dreaded breaking the news about Veronica, I still should've been the one to do it. To be there for her.

To take care of her.

I just wasn't sure she'd want me to.

She had to know I hadn't been the one to physically kill her mother since we'd been watching TV together at that time. But like Agent Nash, she could easily assume I had someone do it for me—like Marco, Cole, or even Maximo.

Men who'd already helped kill for her.

"Trust me, man," Cole said, reading my disbelief. "She's just worried about you. I'm pretty sure she's up in Maximo and Juliet's penthouse, baking you a cake with a file in it."

I would feel a lot better once I saw her for myself. But before I could do that, we had to attend to a time-sensitive matter.

Cole and I headed up to Maximo's office to find the three of them already waiting.

When I'd threatened Veronica, the only people who should've been able to hear were Mila and Veronica herself. Since she was dead, that kind of crossed her off the list. My woman would never turn on me, so that left the next closest person.

"I had an interesting afternoon, Elliot."

To his credit, he didn't play dumb. Standing tall like he had the day before, he waited for his punishment.

Only that time, Mila wasn't there to help the FBI rat.

"I need to explain," he said.

"I'm all ears."

"The first day I watched Mila, there was already an FBI agent here watching *you*. They saw her run away from you. When I got off shift, two agents were waiting at my house. They said they were investigating a big case involving kidnapping, false imprisonment, and other awful crimes. They thought Mila was underage, but even once they cleared that up, they believed she was here against her will. Since I'd been guarding her, they asked me to be an informant."

"And you jumped at the chance to do your civic duty?"

"No, I said no. But they kept pushing. They threatened to make my life harder. They said if there was nothing bad happening, then it didn't matter that I was informing. But if there was something bad, and one of you committed a crime, I would be charged, too. I still didn't tell them anything because there was nothing to tell."

"Except about The Basement."

He shoved his hands into his pockets. "Except that. Agent Nash kept pushing me to get incriminating information, and I slipped and mentioned anything bad would probably be down there. He wouldn't let it go."

Not the brightest...

If it was up to me, Elliot would be leaving with a broken nose at a minimum because Mila was going to be so disappointed in his betrayal. But with his FBI BFFs, it wasn't a good idea.

The Basement would be out of order for a while, too.

At least for the major stuff.

My gaze moved to Maximo, and he lifted his chin, giving the okay.

"You're fired, Elliot," I said. "Once it gets out that you're a rat, no one else will hire you. And it will get out because I'm going to spread that message far and wide."

He nodded. "Please tell Mila that I'm sorry."

"Wait." I thought back to what the agent had said. "What do you know about Eternal Sun?"

"Nothing. I don't even know what that is."

I studied him for a moment before giving a single nod.

"Let's go." Marco glared daggers that Elliot pretended not to see.

Once they were gone, I quickly filled Cole and Maximo in on the entire day, including the bad feeling Eternal Sun left in my gut.

"They didn't mention who the employee with the connection is?" Maximo asked.

"No. I assumed it was Elliot."

Cole looked anxious to park his ass in front of his computers. "I'll dig in."

We talked for a few minutes more before I couldn't take it any longer. I needed to get my woman.

Heading up to Maximo's penthouse, I prepared for tears. For hesitancy. For her to be pulled into herself like before.

But the moment I stepped off the elevator, Mila launched herself at me—and not in an attempt to punch my dick again. If I hadn't lifted her, I was pretty sure she would've climbed me like a tree.

Thank fucking hell.

The tightness that'd bunched my shoulders and the acid that'd burned in my gut both instantly lessened the second I had her in my arms.

I cupped the back of her head. "Hey, sunshine."

"Daddy," she breathed, clutching me tight. "Tell me everything."

"When we get to our place."

"You better mean here because there is no way I can make it all the way home."

"Here it is."

With a quick goodbye to Juliet, Mila and I got on the elevator. As soon as we stepped out into the penthouse, she repeated her order. "Tell me everything."

"Camila, baby, you gotta know, I had *nothing* to—"

She waved away my assertion. "I know that."

I was sure as shit glad to hear it, but that didn't mean it wasn't shocking. "You do?"

"You wouldn't physically hurt a woman." A small smile curved her mouth. "Not in that way, and not anyone but me. But that still doesn't explain what happened."

Before I could give her the rundown of the meeting at the station, I had to backtrack to fill her in on Eternal Sun. Like my initial assumption, she'd guessed her mother was indebted to a wannabe mobster or shot caller. A cult leader was a curveball she hadn't seen coming. Even though she hadn't known about her mother's involvement with the organization, she wasn't surprised.

Apparently, Veronica had always been a magnet for an assortment of different fuckery.

When I was done, I gathered Mila closer on my lap and kissed her forehead. "How're you really doing?"

"I feel awful," she admitted. "After everything yesterday…"

"I know. A lot of shit was said and—"

"No, not that. I stand by everything I said. I'm actually really relieved I had the chance to say it all, which makes me feel guilty. And then I feel worse for *not* feeling sad. I'm just left with the same vague sadness someone might feel when they hear a stranger died. But that's it. Does that make me the worst person?"

"No, baby. I think that's normal."

"I still feel guilty."

"What can I do?"

"Would it be awful if we just acted like it's a normal day?"

I squeezed her ass. "Even if that means a punishment?"

She shot me a stern look. "I'm not the one who earned one for lying."

"You're not spanking Daddy."

She laughed. "Nope, your punishment is the infamous lobster story. You owe me that much."

At her sweet laughter, I would've given her the world.

I could give her my shame instead.

Pulling my phone out, I shot off a text to Cole.

He responded instantly, like he'd had the message sitting in his drafts.

Cole: One video

I handed it to Mila. "Press play."

She watched the phone, and I watched her. Her brows were lowered as she squinted at the footage of an empty restaurant. A moment later, she squealed with delight when three dozen lobsters scuttled into the frame. And then she threw her head back and laughed as I drunkenly stumbled onto the screen wearing a tablecloth like a toga.

"I was Poseidon, freeing the sea creatures."

"Of course," she gasped through more laughter. "This is *way* better than the bourbon phone."

For the rest of the night, I gave her what she wanted by treating it like any other day. We watched TV. She rode my face before she rode my dick. And when we went to sleep that night with my body around hers and both of her hands bound together in a prayer tie, I waited.

    For her tears.

    Her anger.

    Her nightmares.

    But they never came.

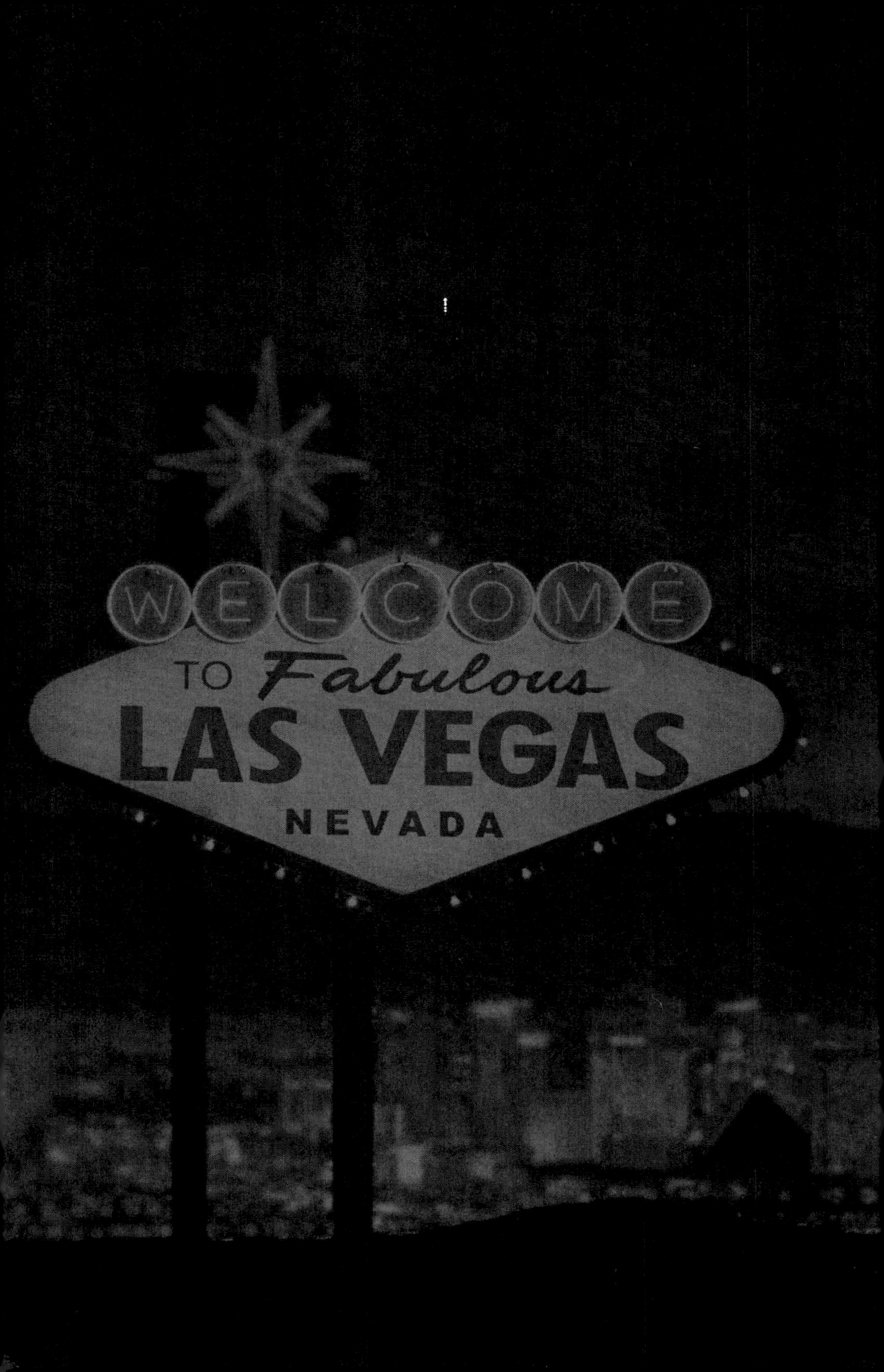
WELCOME
TO Fabulous
LAS VEGAS
NEVADA

CHAPTER 31
YOU'RE ALLOWED TO MOVE ON... TO TACOS
MILA

Contrary to what one of my comfort shows portrayed, the police station was not filled with hijinks and laughter.

It was unfortunate—I could've gone for a little of both.

Ash must've known it. His large hand moved from my lower back to squeeze my hip in a comforting gesture.

It'd been three days since I'd found out my mother was dead. The only thing I struggled with was that I wasn't struggling. I wasn't mourning the way most would grieve and rage at the murder of a parent. I was sad at her death, yes, but that was as far as it went.

I had more guilt over that than I did about my final words to Veronica.

Even though I'd tried to assure him it was unnecessary, Ash had taken some time off work. I knew he was worried that I was still in shock. That it would suddenly hit me, and I would have a meltdown. It wouldn't happen, but that didn't matter. He'd barely left my side.

I was grateful for it right then.

Ash guided me through the station before stopping us in

front of a suited man. He released my hip just long enough to shake the man's hand. When he was done, he looked down at me. "This is my lawyer, Wes."

My panicked gaze shot from the man to Ash. "I thought that agent just wanted to ask me some questions. Why do you need a lawyer?"

"I'm just here as a precaution." Wes held his hand out. "It's nice to finally meet you."

I took it and returned the pleasantry I was too freaked to actually feel. "Nice to meet you, too."

Even though he kept my hand in his, his gaze and words were both aimed at Ash. "I get it now."

"There's no shortage of lawyers," Ash bizarrely bit out with a glare.

Wes didn't look fazed as he released my hand and gave a cocky smirk. "Yeah, but none of them are as good as me. Now, let's get this over with."

We followed Wes as he made his way over to talk to a woman behind a long desk. She made a quick call before escorting us into a small room. After offering coffee that no one accepted, she left, and we each took a seat around the large circular table—with me positioned between Ash and Wes.

It wasn't an interrogation room—at least not the kind they showed on TV—but that didn't matter. The heavy weight of anxiety and past crimes sat in my stomach, making me feel like I was about to barf with every second that ticked by.

Ash plucked me from the hard metal chair and settled me on his lap. "Breathe, Camila."

I inhaled.

The fraction of tension that'd left my body returned tenfold when the door opened, and a man and woman entered. I recognized the woman as the agent who'd come to the house.

I tried to move off Ash's lap, but his arms tightened.

"Thanks for coming in," the man said, his sharp gaze darting between Ash and me as he took the seat across from us. He set a tablet down on the table. His unnerving focus locked on me. "I'm

Agent Nash, and you've already met Agent Grant. First, let me say that we're sorry for your loss."

"Thanks," I said softly, even though I still didn't feel like I'd lost anything.

"I know this must be very difficult for you, but we just have a few questions. What do you know about Eternal Sun?"

"Not much." I gestured to Ash. "Just the little bit that he told me."

"Your mother didn't mention anything about the group or her boyfriend?" Agent Grant asked from her spot near the door.

"We rarely spoke."

The agents shared a look before Agent Nash flipped the tablet over. He swiped at the screen and handed it to me. "Do any of these names or people look familiar? Have you ever seen them around your mother or heard her mention any of them?"

I carefully scanned the names and faces, but nothing jumped out.

For me, at least.

Based on the way Ash's body tightened, his answer was likely different.

I'll talk to him later.

"No, I don't recognize any of them." I set the tablet on the table. "And like I said, my mother and I rarely spoke, so I don't know any of her friends or boyfriends."

Wes tapped the screen. "You finally admitting there's a connection?"

Agent Nash's eyes cut to him, and his tone didn't sound happy. "We think it's worth looking into. To be thorough."

Wes scoffed, but the agent ignored him as he peppered me with more questions. Since I really didn't know anything about Veronica, there wasn't much insight I could share.

He must've come to that same conclusion. His expression was dejected as he handed me a business card. "Thank you for coming in. If you think of anything, no matter how small or insignificant it seems, let me know."

I nodded as we stood.

Like they were hanging out at a bar and *not* a police station, Wes and Ash bickered about hockey as we walked to the exit.

It wasn't until Ash and I were alone in the SUV that I let my questions fly. "Who were the people in those pictures? And why did you recognize them? And what did they mean about a connection?"

He rubbed his palm across his beard as he chose his words. When he spoke them, he watched me closely. "I only recognized a few from the news, but they were recent murder victims."

I remembered the news segment from outside of the crappy motel. "There's actually a serial killer?"

"Don't know for sure, but it's a helluva coincidence if not."

I stared out the windshield, not really seeing anything as my brain tried to wrap around that scary possibility.

Ash hooked a finger under my chin and turned my head so I would look at him. "What do you need?"

After mulling that over for a minute, I started with the most important thing. "I need you to go back to work." He opened his mouth, but I kept going. "The more you hover, waiting for me to breakdown, the guiltier I feel that I'm not more upset." His eyes softened, and his mouth opened again, but I still didn't give him the chance to talk. "It's sad that she's dead. It's even sadder if they're right and all of those deaths are because of a crazy serial killer. But I'm not suppressing some deep heartbreak that is going to burst through at any moment. I just want to move on."

"I'll go back to work in a couple days," he said when I finally let him get a word in.

"Good."

"But you're coming with me."

"Also good."

His voice grew firmer as his hand moved from my jaw to cup the back of my head like he was preventing a retreat. "And you'll have extra security. We can rotate through every damn guard we have on our payroll and hire more until you find ones you're comfortable with."

Learning that Elliot had been reporting back to the FBI—

even just minimally—had hurt. It'd also reinforced my experience that security was always bad.

But I knew it was nonnegotiable. Ash would never back down. And more importantly, there was possibly a serial killer on the loose.

Since I wasn't an idiot, I said, "Also *also* good."

He gave me that small smile that made me want to do anything and everything he demanded.

Only I wasn't done with my own list of demands. "There are two more things I need."

"Anything," he shot back instantly.

"Being in the police station brought back crappy memories and past guilt to mix with my current guilt…"

"You want me to punish you," he surmised without me having to verbalize my need.

"And tie me up," I added.

It was amazing how being in literal knots worked so well to unknot the mess in my head.

His hooded eyes heated. "I can do that. And the other thing?"

"I'm hungry for tacos."

His brows rose in a brief show of surprise before he flashed me a wicked grin. "How about this?" His voice was a low rumble as he tugged my hair to yank me closer. "We'll go home, I'll tie you up and spank your ass, and then I'll keep you tied to me while I feed you the tacos."

I swallowed hard past the surge of lust that stole my breath and turned my brain to goo. "Tied *to* you?"

"Secured to my thigh. You'll be stuck on my lap until I let you go." Another gentle pull of my hair. "And you already know I'm never doing that." Like we were discussing errands or something mundane, he released me and started the engine. "Sound good?"

It was messed up that I found that level of attachment comforting and reassuring.

But it was also true.

And so was my answer. "Sounds perfect."

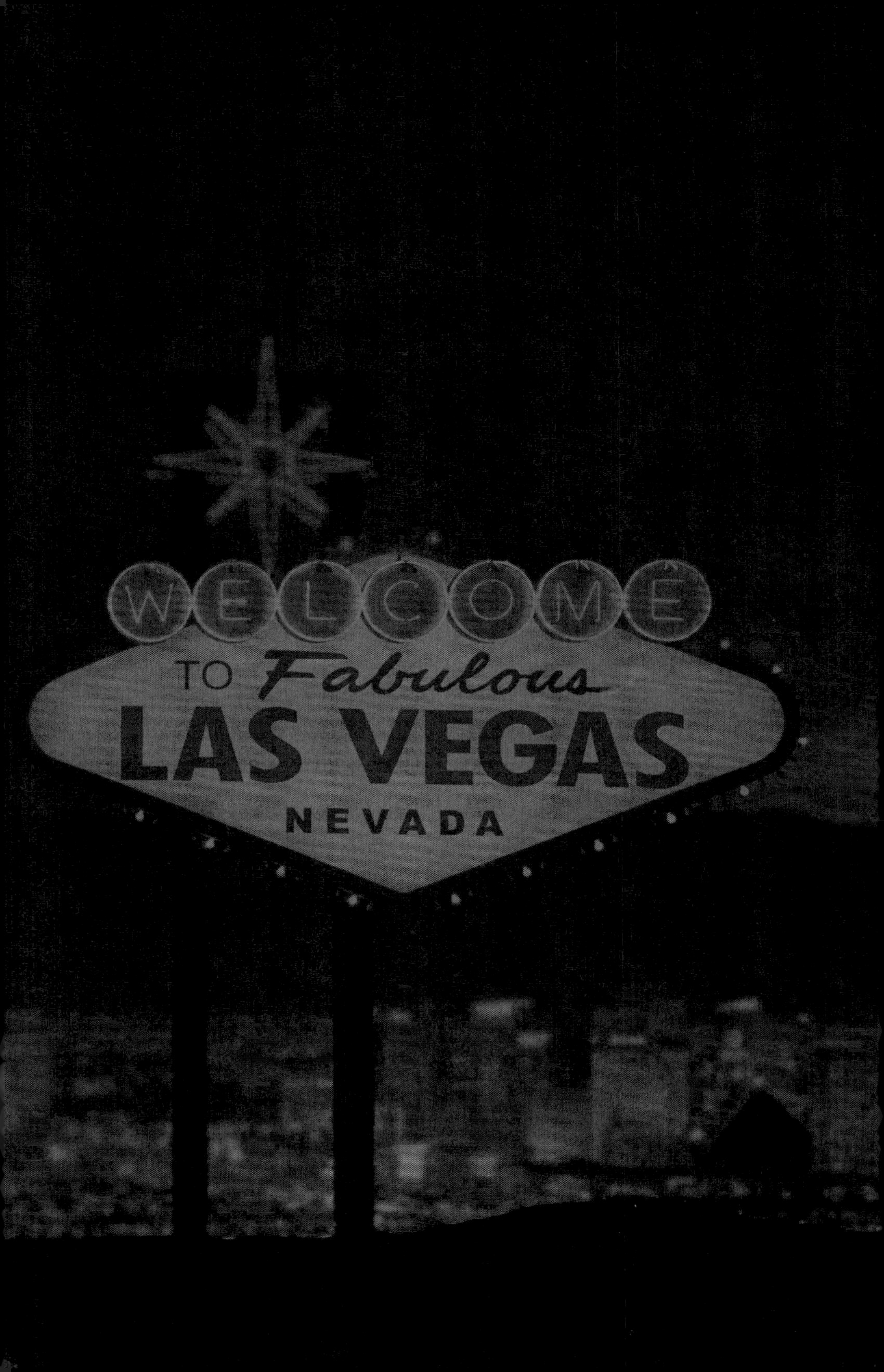
WELCOME
TO Fabulous
LAS VEGAS
NEVADA

CHAPTER 32
DON'T DULL YOUR SHINE
ASH

"**H**ey, sunshine."

Mila quickly put her iPad face down, her pretty blue eyes shooting to me as her cheeks grew pink.

Her embarrassment wasn't from a dirty book—though she and Juliet went through those like lovesick Marco went through tissues.

Marco.

Cole.

Hell, Freddy, too.

Mila's reaction was from the secret she had.

Or *thought* she had since the tracking software Cole had installed meant I could see everything she did on the iPad.

Including her interior design research.

In the two weeks since her mother's death, Mila's casual searches had grown into looking for courses to take. It was like she could finally allow herself to make plans without the fear of Veronica fucking shit up. So long as she left time for me, she could take any classes she wanted. I'd foot the bill so she could get a degree in pig Latin if it made her happy.

Not letting on that I knew what she was up to since I was

waiting for her to tell me herself, I jerked my chin toward the door. "We're going for a drive."

She was up before I finished my sentence. "Should I get changed?"

I never had to worry I came on too strong for Mila. I didn't try to hold back or give her time. I let her see exactly who I was.

And she loved it. Thrived on it. The more obsessive I was, the brighter she shined.

My nickname for her started off tongue-in-cheek at her distrust. But every day, it grew more fitting.

I scanned my giant hoodie that engulfed her. "You got something on under that?" When she lifted it, I saw she wore the tiniest shorts known to man. "Go get Daddy's blue rope."

But again, she was moving before I even finished the order.

When she returned and handed it to me, I ordered, "Tops off."

She lifted the sweatshirt to reveal there was no plural because she didn't wear a shirt or bra. My dick jerked, knowing her bare tits had been rubbing against my hoodie.

Folding the rope so it was doubled up, I wrapped it around her, positioning it above and below those perfect little tits. Her nipples pebbled, and I wanted to pull them into my mouth. But if I did that, we wouldn't be going anywhere.

As I ran the rope up the center of her chest and over her shoulders—creating a harness that framed each tit—I was having trouble remembering why that would be a bad thing.

"Ready?" she prompted when I just stared at my work.

I grabbed her wrist and pressed her palm to my hard-on. "Oh, I'm fucking ready."

With a soft, airy laugh, she grudgingly stepped away and pulled the top back on. "Where are we going?"

"Work errand to check out a property for Maximo."

Sure enough, the fact I didn't want to be away from her for that short trip made her smile up at me.

Or at least that was what I thought it was. Until she fluttered her lashes and asked, "Can we get a drink with the good ice for the ride?"

Since there wasn't a lot I wouldn't give her, I nodded.

And her smile grew.

After we were on the road—and she had her drink with the good ice—she asked, "Why is Maximo interested in other properties when his new build is nowhere close to being done?"

"It's not that kind of property."

"What is it?"

Since I'd stopped holding back, I told her the truth. "Maximo owns a variety of buildings. Some are used for underground boxing matches."

"Juliet told me details about the fight last week." She shuddered. "No, thank you."

If the regular boxing match had scared Mila, the lawless kind held at the warehouses would terrify her. And since I'd rather cut off my left nut than upset her, those nights would be the times I happily left her while I worked.

Well, happily until I had come home to find her sleeping on the couch with *our* show auto-playing on the TV and an empty container of ice cream she'd eaten as her dinner on the table in front of her.

"And a couple of the buildings," I continued, "are for when someone crosses him."

"Got it. Say no more." She might've been accepting of it, but that didn't mean she wanted the specifics.

Which was fine by me since I didn't want those images in her head.

Mia took a sip of her drink before fidgeting with the straw. "So, uh, I've been thinking about something."

"Yeah?"

"After the whole AI-picture thing, I've been looking more into interior design. I think I'd like to take an intro course."

"Go for it."

"It's online, too, so I can do it from wherever we are that day."

We.

Christ, she kills me.

"Go for it," I repeated.

"I just have a lot of ideas for *functional* designs, but if the time isn't right—"

"Camila."

"Yes, Daddy?" she forced out even though I knew she wanted to keep justifying the decision until she eventually talked herself out of it.

"Sign up. You've got my credit card."

Not that you ever use it.

She opened her mouth, and I shot her a warning look.

She closed it without promising me she'd pay me back. Though I knew she wanted to do that, too.

For the rest of the drive, she excitedly shared her plans. She let me in.

Fucking finally.

Pulling next to the only other car in the lot, I parked in front of a building in the middle of nowhere. We climbed out, and Mila scanned the area. "This isn't what I was expecting."

Just wait.

We headed inside where the selling real estate agent was already waiting. He introduced himself, looking curiously between Mila and me. He must've decided that a sale was a sale because he kept his thoughts to himself. "Due to the nature of this property, the seller insists I'm here for every showing. Will your agent also be joining us?"

"No."

He waited for me to elaborate, and when I didn't, he moved on. "I will hang back while you look around. I'm here if you have any questions."

I put a hand to Mila's back and steered her through a set of heavy doors that'd been propped open.

She leaned closer to whisper, "Nature of this property?"

I didn't answer.

I didn't need to.

The first room made it clear.

"Oh my God," she hissed, turning her wild eyes from the room to me. "Is this...? Is it...?"

"A brothel?" I filled in. "Yes."

Each of the four rooms at the front had a different theme and *supplies* left behind that I didn't get close to, much less touch.

"Why even look at this place?" she asked. Her gaze shot back to me. "Maximo doesn't run or uh..."

"Dabble in the oldest profession in the world? No." The side of my mouth curved up as I gestured to the side. "There are hoses and a drainage system in every room."

Mila turned a little green.

We moved to the back half of the building that was one massive space.

She pointed at the wooden trim that lined the painted concrete walls to make it look like a regular bedroom. "That would have to be removed throughout. Otherwise, it'll absorb *liquids.*"

"So what did you folks say you'd be doing with the space?" the real estate agent suddenly asked as he crept behind us. Since I hadn't heard his approach, he'd had to work to keep quiet in the echoing hall.

Should be careful. A nose can easily get broken if you shove it where it doesn't belong.

Very easily.

I opened my mouth to feed him the same bullshit I always used about resort storage since the drop of Maximo's name made people see dollar signs.

But Mila cut in like she was trying to cover for me. "I restore rugs."

"You do what?" he asked.

"Have you not seen the videos online?" She played up the bubbly personality and giggled at him. "You're in for a treat. They're so satisfying. Better than the pimple-popping videos even."

It worked like a motherfucking charm, and she had the nosy bastard eating out of her hand. "What all goes into it?"

I hope she can still bullshit now that she's out of practice.

She could and did so flawlessly. "The hardest part is finding a worthwhile discarded rug. Most end up being cheap ones not worth the cost in soap. Garage sales are good, but estate sales can be goldmines. Once I have something, I work my magic to clean it. It can take a handful of rounds with my big industrial shampooer and squeegee to even see the pattern." She pushed her lip out in the most fuckable pout I'd ever seen. "Our neighbor has started complaining about the noise and the smell, though."

"That won't be a worry here. There's no one else around." He scanned the room. "Privacy was obviously important to the seller." At Mila's random outburst of laughter, he didn't look confused. He looked enamored by her.

I didn't blame him.

Even if it made me want to test the hose system using his blood.

I must not have been hiding it well—mostly since I wasn't trying—because he did a double take at my expression.

"I'll leave you to finish looking around." Without another word, he hauled ass down the hall—his echo sounding loud and clear that time.

I wrapped my arm around Mila's chest from behind to feel the ropes under her clothes. "What was so funny?"

"If my story was true," she whispered, "this place would've gone from polishing wood to cleaning carpets."

I blinked down at the woman who wouldn't even tell me she was hungry before.

Yet there we stood.

In a damn brothel while she made a dirty joke.

I threw my head back to laugh before pressing my still smiling mouth to her head. "Have I told you lately how much I love you?"

"Yes. Daily. But I love hearing it."

For the first time in a while, I held back. If I said what I wanted, I would have to push Maximo to buy the place. Or I'd have to do it myself. Then I would end up fighting a hard-on at the memory every time I was there torturing some poor bastard.

The spirits of the dicks of yesteryear would be proud.

She was close.

But so was I, so I needed her to get there faster.

With Mila on her knees in front of me, I gripped the rope that was still bound around her and pulled harder. She let out a hiss as it tightened around her tits. I used it to rock her back and forth, my eyes glued at where I filled her from behind.

Every view I had of Mila was a view of heaven—my own personal one. But I couldn't deny that watching my dick sink into her was one of my favorites. That, and her smile. And when she laughed. And when she shot me a shy look that was just for me. And...

Like I said, every view of Mila.

The more I stared, the more my control slipped, but she wasn't there yet. She needed a push.

I gave it to her, saying what I'd held in earlier at the property showing.

"We're getting married."

Her body went tight.

Her pussy went tight*er*.

Another thread on my control snapped.

She tried to stop, but I didn't let her. I curved my body over hers and put one hand to the mattress for leverage. My other snaked around her to grab the column of rope between her tits.

"Figure out what kind of wedding you want," I told her. "Don't care if it's a massive party or we elope at a drive-thru chapel. Only requirement I have is that it happens this month."

"It's too fast."

"Got it." I tugged the rope to cut her leeway so she couldn't move as I slid out slowly before gently easing in. Tormenting us both.

"No," she cried, giving a frantic hip wiggle that nearly sent me over the edge. "That wasn't too fast. The wedding. The wedding is too fast."

"You got something specific in mind, I'll make it happen. Not giving you more than a month, though," I said firmly.

She inhaled, but it cut off when I surged forward. "It's too soon for us to get married. We've only been together for like five minutes."

I used my hold on the rope between her tits to move her on me harder.

To make her fuck herself with me as I met her thrust for thrust.

"Already know I'm going to marry you, Camila." I clenched my jaw, grasping at every ounce of willpower I had. "And I already told you, there's no going back. So what's the point of waiting other than wasting time?" Pressure built. "Want you to have my last name."

I slammed in hard enough to take her knees out from under her, but with my hold, she stayed where I put her.

Where I wanted her.

With me.

Always.

Biting her shoulder right near the rope, I lowered my voice to a rough whisper. "Then everyone will know you belong to me. That I'm your Daddy."

Her head dropped as she exploded around me.

Thank.

Fuck.

Her tight pussy milked my cock for every drop of cum and greedily pulsed around me for more.

I'd give it to her.

For the rest of our lives.

When my brain had some blood back in it, I released the rope and gave her my weight until she was flat on her stomach. I kept my cock buried deep and reached into the bedside table to get what I'd stashed there. What I'd fully expected her to find long before then.

Pulling the ring out, I tossed the little box over my shoulder before sliding it onto her finger.

"When did you buy this?" she whispered.

I told her the truth. "Three days after you gave me you. I'd have bought it the very next day, but we spent that weekend together." At the sight of my ring on her finger, my dick twitched. I nipped her shoulder again before brushing my lips over the spot. "You got one month, and then we're getting married."

"You're supposed to ask me," Mila choked out through her tears. I didn't have to see the smile to know they were happy ones.

"No."

"Fine. I accept anyway."

I wrapped her silky hair around my hand and tilted her head back so I could kiss her. "You didn't have a choice, sunshine."

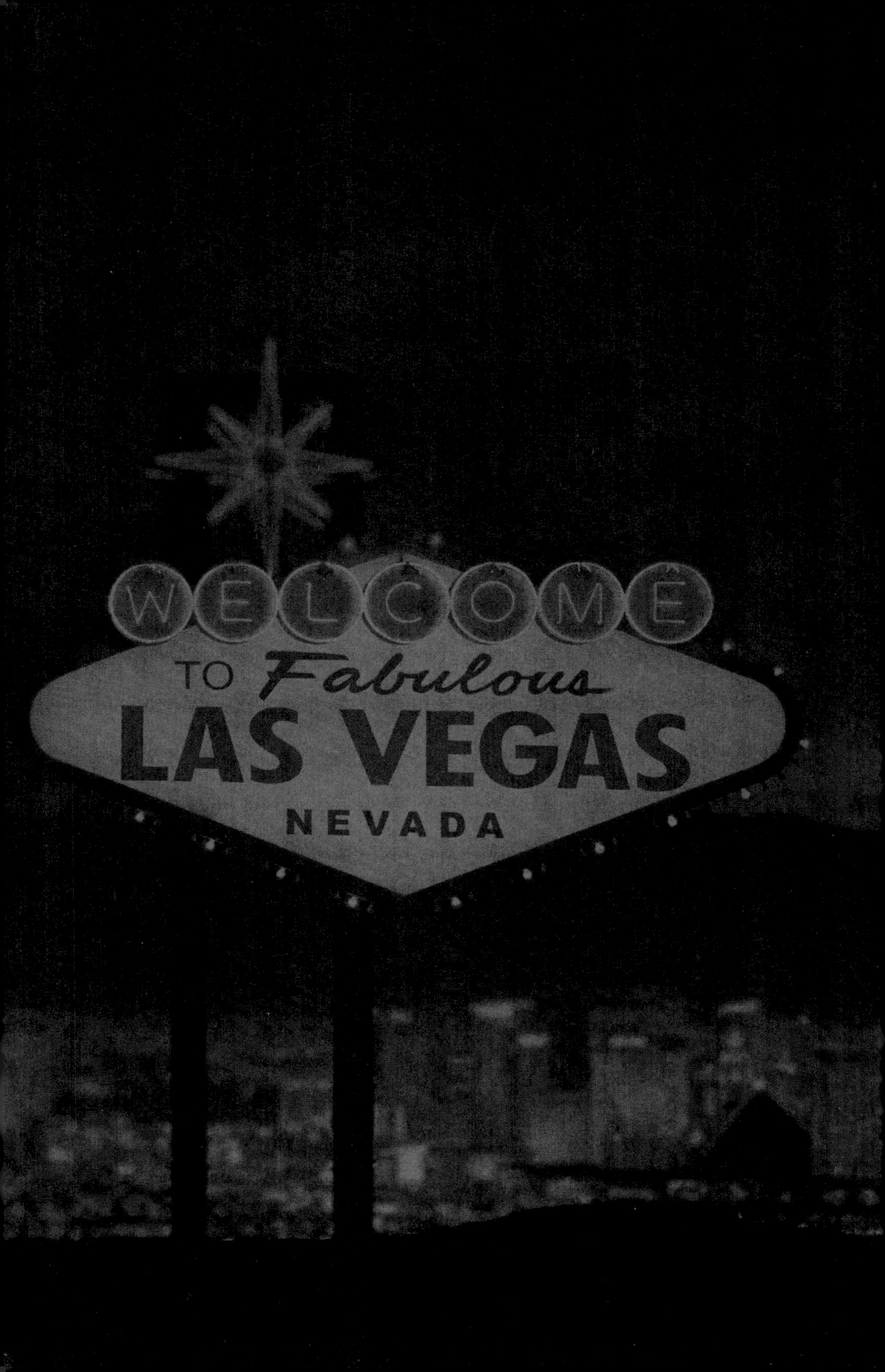
WELCOME
TO Fabulous
LAS VEGAS
NEVADA

EPILOGUE
MILA

THREE WEEKS LATER

"Hurry."

"Who's in charge here?"

"You are, Daddy," I whimpered. He was teasing me. Tormenting me.

Killing me.

It would be a beautiful death.

I made it all of thirty seconds before angling my hip and shifting forward so he would touch me.

"Camila. Do you really want to find out what will happen if you don't listen to me?"

I rapidly shook my head.

"Stand still."

It was easy for him to say. He wasn't the one with white rope being knotted around his naked body.

He wasn't even naked.

That alone was rude. An injustice. Even if he did look so handsome in his charcoal gray suit and black shirt.

After more came out about Veronica's death, Ash had been willing to give me an extension on his wedding deadline.

One more month.

It'd been a considerate offer, but completely unnecessary. I wouldn't have invited Veronica to the wedding had she been alive, so why would I postpone it for her just because of how she died?

It had taken the authorities longer than it should've to admit, but there was no denying that the random stabbings around Vegas were linked. And for the rest of history and Wikipedia, my mother would forever be known as a victim of the serial killer.

More than anything, Veronica had wanted to be famous and adored. In death, she'd managed the first part at least. I didn't need that solace, but it was there, nonetheless.

As messed up as it was to say, I still didn't mourn her death as anything more than a general sadness at the loss of life. Even with the knowledge she'd been a random target of a deranged murderer, she had barely been a blip in my thoughts.

Fitting since I'd never been more than a blip in hers.

I would've been happy to elope, but just because I had no family to attend our wedding didn't mean Ash's couldn't be there—even if I felt like everyone needed to wear name tags. He'd handled getting their flights and rooms booked to ensure that happened *fast*.

His parents weren't what I'd expected. I'd already guessed by the short FaceTime I'd seen and their previous professions that they were traditional. Kind of old-fashioned.

The shock came when I'd found out that they knew about the gray—and sometimes very, *very* dark gray—work Ash did for Maximo.

Even more shocking was that they were okay with it. No. They *approved* of it. Even his father, the former judge.

Witnessing Ash be a *funcle* times eleven was an experience, too. I was unsure I wanted my own children. My family was missing the maternal gene, and I would never put a child through the hostility or the indifference I'd been raised with. But watching him play with the older kids or snuggle the younger ones had made my ovaries perk up.

I got the feeling his thoughts had frequently drifted to the same theoretical stork delivery. On multiple occasions over the weekend, he'd rubbed his thumb across the spot where my birth control implant was buried in my arm.

That would be a conversation for later. Much, *much* later. I had more pressing matters to focus on. Like the torture he was inflicting on me.

I inhaled through clenched teeth when the rope *accidentally* dragged across my clit.

"Done," Ash said before I could attack him—with sex or violence. I was open to either at that point. He stood back to inspect his work.

Length of white rope looped around my thighs and between my legs before it wove up my torso to create a corset. The thin material would be easily hidden under my dress and didn't serve the same purpose as the thicker rope he often used. It was decorative rather than functional.

A reminder that I was his.

A reassurance that he wanted me so badly, he'd tie me down to keep me if he had to.

A secret for just the two of us.

The longer he stared, the darker his expression grew. I could almost see his filthy thoughts, filled with all the depraved things he wanted to do to me.

Biting out a rough curse, he ran his hand across his beard. "Where's your dress?"

"You are *not* allowed to see me in that before the ceremony," I reminded him.

A single eyebrow arched. "Has anyone ever told you that you're bossy?"

No.

Never.

I'd lived my life by flying under the radar. I never fussed or made waves. I never made demands.

But things were different with Ash.

I was different with Ash. Like the me I was always supposed to be.

"I must've learned it from you." I turned to search for the rest of my stuff. "You're teaching me already."

Coming up behind me, he wrapped his arm around my waist and buried his face in my neck. His beard and his groan tickled. I wasn't sure if it was a happy noise at the mention of teaching me anything or an aroused one at the feel of me in his ropes.

I was going with both.

"You keep this up, we're going to be late to our own wedding."

"That's fine," he rumbled, his lips grazing my neck. "What're they gonna do, start without us?"

"Being late means waiting even longer until I'm your wife."

That did it.

He stepped away. "Dress?"

"You can't see it," I repeated.

"Will you be able to get it on yourself?"

"I will not."

"Well I'm damn sure not letting anyone else see you in Daddy's ropes, so I'll ask again. Where's the dress?"

Going into the closet, I shoved a bunch of suits out of the way to reveal where I'd stashed it after my frantic shopping trip with Juliet to a million and ten dress shops.

"You have a lot of suits," I said, telling him something he definitely already knew.

"I need options. They get stained."

Sometimes by my wetness, sometimes by other people's blood.

I was tempted to take my engagement ring off so I didn't snag the fabric, but I'd already learned that was a mistake I didn't care to repeat. Short of an emergency, Ash never wanted it off me.

Fine, I also didn't want it off me. And not just because it was gorgeous—though it very much *was*.

Yellow gold, it had a giant boulder of a diamond that was

surrounded by smaller diamonds to resemble a *very* expensive sun.

Being mindful of the delicate material, I removed my dress from the garment bag and handed it to Ash.

His smile was sweet, but his eyes were loaded with sinful promises as he helped me slip it on.

The long-sleeved, V-neck dress was beige with a shimmery sheer overlay. Once it was on, the beige blended in, giving the illusion that I only wore the see-through layer.

His eyes slowly moved along my body, warming me like a physical touch. "Christ, how did I get so lucky?"

"You were my behemoth in shining armor."

"Your monster in the night-light."

Tears filled my eyes, and I knew I wouldn't get through the day without losing that fight.

I couldn't get over how one awful, horrible, horrendous weekend had somehow turned into so much beauty.

And it was all thanks to him.

"I need you," I whispered.

An inferno broke out in his hazel eyes, and he tightened his fists until his knuckles went white. "After the wedding. And if you keep tempting Daddy, you'll be walking down that aisle with a red, burning ass."

"No, not like that." His eyes narrowed instantly, and I laughed. "I always need your cock and your cum. And I just need you. Period. But at this moment, I specifically need you to help with my shoes." I grabbed the box and handed it to him. I was going to go sit so I could lift my legs, but he didn't give me the chance.

Dropping to his knee, Ash carefully helped me into the intimidatingly high heel before fixing the white bow that tied around my ankle.

"Love the little knots, sunshine."

"I thought you would," I forced out past the ache in my chest at seeing such a big, powerful man kneel to help me put on the delicate shoes. "Thanks."

"Want to know how you can thank me?" he asked, dragging his rough fingertips up my calf as he stood.

I was desperate to know. "How?"

"Get your cute ass outside to the creek and marry me."

I said the only thing there was to say to that.

"Okay, Daddy."

"How're you doing, Mrs. Cooper?"

Standing with Ash's sisters, I was already looking at Violet when she spoke. I saw her own eyes were aimed my way.

But it still didn't register that she was talking to me.

Not until Emily nudged me. "That's *you* now."

Maggie gestured outside of the tent to where their husbands had a competitive game of cornhole going. "None of us are a *Mrs. Cooper* anymore. Well, except Mom."

"But do *not* call her that," Andrea put in.

That was a lesson I'd quickly learned.

While we might've been moving at lightspeed, none of Ash's family seemed fazed in the slightest. There'd been no judgment, apprehension, or even simple curiosity from any of them, but especially not from Lynn Cooper.

From the moment she'd stepped out of the RV, she'd insisted I drop any formalities and had been nothing but warm and *loving*.

It'd kind of freaked me out.

And by kind of, I meant totally.

Belatedly realizing they were still waiting for an answer, I thought about the day.

When Ash and I planned the wedding, I'd told him my one request.

I wanted to get married near the creek that ran through his backyard.

That little piece of undisturbed nature had to be one of the most beautiful and peaceful spots in the entire world. Or at least my world. It was the perfect location for our quick and simple wedding.

Quick?

Yes.

Simple?

Not so much.

I'd had this vague idea that Ash and I would exchange our vows in front of his friends and family, and then everyone would just... do something? Hang out inside. Leave to go visit the more interesting sights.

Maybe order a pizza.

I honestly wasn't sure since neither family gatherings nor weddings were an area of expertise for me. My focus had just been on the whole *getting-married* part.

But like the perfect Daddy he was, Ash had handled everything. The ceremony had taken place at the most picturesque part of the creek, under the sun and blue sky. Closer to the house, a canopy tent had been set up for a reception with food, drinks, music, yard activities, and about a billion twinkle lights.

It'd been casual and intimate and so breathtakingly perfect.

A dream.

Which was why my answer was nothing but the truth. "I'm good." I wasn't a natural hostess, but I could bullshit with the best of them, so that was what I did. "Did everyone get enough to eat? There's lots of cake."

"Speaking of..." Maggie skewered me with a look and lowered her voice. "Do you have any dirt on Freddy?"

The hairs on the back of my neck rose. As did my protective instincts.

Ash just dealt with a rat in his professional life.

He doesn't need one in his own family.

Before I could figure out how to answer, she continued talking. "Or maybe a bribe idea? I'm open to either. I just need him to fork over that cake recipe for my restaurant."

My shoulders loosened. "I don't think you'll have any luck. He's pretty, uh, particular about his methods."

"All good chefs are. But I still want those recipes. I've never had a strawberry cake that tasted so fresh. And the cream cheese frosting—"

"Oh my God," Emily cried, "stop talking about food. I already ate too much. I might pass out on the pool table."

"My, how things change," Violet said. "Instead of sleeping it off from the tequila bar, it's a taco bar taking you down."

"I haven't passed out from tequila in forever."

"It was when we were all here last year."

"Which was forever ago. Exactly what I said."

I did my best to follow along with their easy banter and mild bullying. I could've listened for hours, but their conversation was cut short when there was a loud clatter, and a sharp cry pierced the air.

Maggie, Emily, and Andrea shared a look before hightailing it toward the chaos.

"Not mine yet," Violet said since her only kid was sleeping on her chest. Her hazel eyes scanned me. "Seriously, though, you doing okay? Everyone blowing in at once is like throwing you in the deep end of our insane family pool."

I laughed because she wasn't wrong. "It's been fun."

"Fun. Chaos. Potato, po-tah-to." She smiled. "I'm glad we didn't scare you away. Even if he's annoying, it's nice seeing my brother so happy about something other than work. And I like having you here." Her smile turned mischievous. "And not just because I need someone to hold Charlie while I run to the bathroom. Although..."

Before I even knew what was happening, Violet transferred her baby into my arms.

Her tiny human baby.

Her *vulnerable* baby.

"Just support her neck," she muttered, adjusting my hold before stepping back. "There. Perfect. Be right back."

And then she left.

My panicked gaze lifted from the sleeping baby to search for Ash. When I spotted him, he was already on his way across the tent toward me.

Oh no.

I'm doing something wrong.

But when he reached me, it wasn't to rescue the baby from my incompetence. It was to shoot a dimpled grin down at me.

That alone was enough to make my brain turn to goo, but he wasn't done. His already deep voice was laced with huskiness. "Like seeing you with a baby, sunshine."

"I'm doing okay?" I was terrified I was somehow holding her wrong even though I'd barely moved. Hell, I wasn't sure I'd taken an actual breath.

"You're doing perfect." He wrapped an arm around me and gently shifted me closer, though he made no moves to take Charlotte. "How's your day been, wife?"

Wife.

I'm Ash's wife.

I bit back my smile and shrugged. "Oh. Same ole, same ole. Nothing too interesting."

His hazel eyes narrowed, but it was just for show.

I glanced over toward where he'd been standing with Maximo, Cole, Marco, and Freddy. "I feel bad I don't have any bridesmaids for the three single guys to chat up. This has to be the most boring wedding they've been to."

"Trust me, they're good." Ash's lips curled in a smirk. "They've got their hands full."

I gave him a questioning look, but before he could respond, something flashed.

Lynn held up her phone and took another picture. She let out a happy squeak. "It's like looking into the future. Hopefully, the very near future…"

"Ma," Ash warned, but I just leaned into him and laughed.

It was through a surge of terror, but still. I laughed.

One of the older boys swooped in to distract his grandmother, and Ash gripped my chin to tilt my head. His voice was low so only I could hear. "Let Daddy know if you're getting overwhelmed."

"Don't worry," I said before blinking up at him with fake innocence. "I can't run in these heels."

Despite the blaze of lust that ignited in his hazel eyes, his concern for me was his priority.

I was *always* his priority.

"And I'm good," I reassured before he could worry. "Promise. I like your family."

"They're your family now, too."

My breath caught in my lungs.

I knew how in-laws and all that worked. *Logically*. But the reality hadn't sunk in. Not until right then.

I have sisters.

And brothers.

And nieces and nephews and a father-in-law.

And a mother-in-law who has hugged me more in one weekend than my actual mother did in my entire life combined.

I have a family.

A loving one.

It was yet another thing Ash had given me to make my life a dream.

Ash

NINE-ISH MONTHS LATER

S*omeone's cute little ass is about to be burning hot.*

Mila and I may have been married, but that didn't mean I wasn't still her Daddy. Or that I didn't take that job seriously. My rules hadn't grown lax over time. If anything, I'd gotten stricter.

Because I knew what I had was valuable. Precious. I would live and die to protect her.

Even from herself.

Not much had changed about our daily lives. She still came

to one of the resorts with me more often than not. If Juliet was there, they hung out. If she wasn't, Mila either stayed in the penthouse to work on her online courses, or she hung out with her other best friend.

Miles.

When I'd asked him to walk Mila from the elevator to the arena on the one and only fight night she'd attended, I'd hoped the tiny nudge would be enough to show her that he didn't harbor any judgment or hostility toward her. I hadn't wanted her to continue avoiding him until her insecurities tied her in knots.

That was my job.

I hadn't anticipated that they'd bond over architectural history.

Since she'd known Juliet and Miles would both be there, I'd been surprised when Mila had asked to stay home instead. And after a long-ass day, I'd been counting down the fucking seconds till I got home. I'd expected to find my sunshine tied to the bed where she was supposed to be.

But as I stood in our *empty* bedroom, she was missing.

"Little girl, you better get your ass out here."

Nothing.

"If you come out now, I'll go easy on you."

Not even a creak.

After changing out of my suit and into a pair of basketball shorts, I checked the bathroom. I opened the closet door, but the light was off, so I knew she wasn't in there. I moved through the rest of the house.

Not in the loft.

Not the living room or kitchen.

Not in the guest rooms, the gym, game room, or my office.

Leaning over my desk, I brought up the outdoor security cameras on my monitors, but she wasn't outside, either.

"Where the fuck could she be?" I whispered to myself.

I backtracked up to our room, but nothing looked out of place.

Nothing except my missing wife.

"If you don't come out right now, you won't be *coming* at all," I shouted.

That usually did it, but at the stretching silence, the first hint of apprehension hit my gut.

Is she not here?

With no other choice, I brought out the worst punishment—in her mind, at least.

"Camila Cooper, show yourself right now, or Daddy isn't even going to fuck you. I'll jack off and come on your sweet little pussy instead."

"*Eek.*"

At the quiet noise, I rushed to the door just in time to see Mila round the corner at the end of the hall.

That's why I couldn't find her hiding spot.

Because there wasn't just one.

I took off after my girl, easily catching her as she tried to crawl behind a couch in the loft. In a short, sexy nightie, her bare ass was sticking up.

Wiggling.

Taunting me.

I pulled her back with one hand while I freed myself with the other, filling her in one smooth thrust.

Not just wet.

Soaked.

Always soaked for me.

I ran my palms from her shoulders down her arms to the ropes she'd used to secure her wrists behind her back. "You did so good," I said as I made the few small adjustments she wouldn't have been able to do herself. Gripping the ends, I gave a sharp tug to tighten them so they stayed in place.

My cock surged in and out of her as she rocked against me, fucking herself. I was already close with the frantic way she moved. With the way her pussy choked my cock.

With the mindless desperation we both felt for each other.

But she had a punishment, and I wouldn't be a good Daddy if I didn't follow through.

I squeezed her ass cheek. "You didn't listen—"

Mila launched herself forward. At the sudden movement, I lost my hold on the rope, and she gained a little distance.

But not enough.

Rather than filling her again, I positioned her on her knees before dropping down to eat her pussy from behind. I wrapped an arm around one of her thighs, holding her in place while my finger stroked her clit.

I should've stopped.

I had a punishment to give, and Mila hated orgasm denial worse than any other. Even spankings.

She deserved that for not being in bed. For running from me.

Her sweet taste. The sexy noises that filled the room. And the way she fucked my face like she was greedy for me.

I couldn't force myself to stop.

Her taste exploded on my tongue as she cried out, coming with jerking rocks of her hips.

When she was finished, I carefully rolled her to her back. Her face was flushed with exertion, and her wild hair was spread around her. The way her arms were bound pushed her tits out, and her hard nipples pressed against the sheer fabric of the damn nightie.

Each time I saw her, I thought she couldn't get sexier.

And each time, she proved me wrong.

Fisting my dick, I stroked as I looked down at her.

My own personal wet dream.

My wife.

My sunshine.

Kneeling next to her, I leaned down to kiss her, but she turned away.

"You know the rule," I warned before trying to kiss her again.

She turned her face the other way.

The fuck?

Slowing my strokes, I reached out with my free hand to grip her cheeks and squeeze her mouth open. After I spit her taste in, I kept that hold as my fist began moving faster.

My focus glued to her mouth, I watched as she slowly stuck her tongue out.

Waiting patiently like a good girl.

My good girl.

She startled when the first shot of cum hit her tongue, but she kept it out while more splattered across it and her face.

When I didn't think I had another drop left, I stared—fucking enthralled—as she brought her tongue back into her mouth and swallowed.

I've died.

That's the only explanation.

Collapsing onto my back, I gently gathered her to me before undoing the ropes. I rubbed her wrists and arms even as I fought to catch my breath.

"Happy anniversary, Daddy," Mila whispered, snuggling in like we were on the world's most comfortable bed and not the hard floor.

"At the risk of sounding ungrateful for that gift you just gave me, our anniversary isn't for a while yet."

"I'm not talking about our wedding anniversary." She inhaled softly. "A year ago today, you rescued me from the lobby at Moonlight. You brought me here and made me see what it was like to have someone take care of me. You made me feel wanted. I'd never had either before. You changed my whole life, and I'll always be grateful I trusted a behemoth to keep me safe." She sniffled. "So thank you. For all of it. For everything." Reaching next to me, she snagged the rope and draped it over my chest. "I hope you enjoyed your gift."

That was an understatement.

For whatever Mila thought I'd done for her, it didn't come close to what I got in return. She'd already given me the only thing I would ever want for the rest of my life.

Her.

Mila

TWO YEARS LATER

"I think I have a room idea."

Ash set down his phone and turned his chair to look at where I stood outside of his home office.

He always did that. If I had something to say, he was going to pay attention to it.

Especially when I talked about interior design stuff. He liked to hear what excited me. He liked to see me get excited.

Both excited him.

I was a long, *looooong* way away from doing anything professionally with it. But I enjoyed learning. I felt useful every time Ash or Maximo came to me for my opinion. I'd had fun doing some basic improvements in the penthouses.

And, shockingly, they'd turned out really well.

"What're you thinking?" he asked when I didn't say more.

"You know the second guest room from the loft?"

Leaning back in his chair, he kicked his feet up on the desk and laced his fingers behind his head. He tried to smother a smile, but his dimples gave him away. "I am aware of the rooms in our home, yes."

Our home.

If just those two words can send a butterfly mosh pit through me...

I wonder how he'll feel about my *two words.*

"I think it'd make a good nursery."

It didn't even take him a second to process my words. His feet dropped to the floor as he sat forward. "You're ready to start trying?"

Ash had been ready to try since right after our wedding. Actually, according to him, he'd been ready since we became an *us*. That was why he hadn't bothered to ask if I was on any birth control before he'd come in me. When I'd met his demands with evasiveness, he'd threatened to cut my implant out of me himself until I'd been forced to explain.

Even though seeing him with his nieces, nephews, or Juliet

and Maximo's son always gave me a mega dose of baby fever, it turned out there was a cure for it.

Debilitating self-doubt.

My mother had been a shit mom. Nan had been a shit mom *and* grandmother. I worried that it was hereditary.

That'd changed—okay, the panic had *slightly* decreased—a few months before when I'd had a dream about Ash holding a baby with hazel eyes.

Seeing him holding other people's kids was one thing. But even a dream version of our baby had been enough to make me rethink things.

True to his vows, Ash had given me the world. I was thrilled —and slightly panicked—for the chance to give him what he wanted.

What we both wanted.

"Oh, didn't I tell you?" Tilting my head, I paused briefly for dramatic effect. "I had my implant removed a few months ago."

His mouth dropped open, but I didn't give him the chance to speak.

I pulled the surprise from my back pocket and tossed it at him.

He caught the plastic stick easily, and there was no missing the two *very* dark pink lines.

"I hope you know some ties that can accommodate a pregnant belly," I added.

Ash pushed away from his desk. "Get over here."

"Sorry, gotta run." I took off toward the stairs, even knowing it was pointless.

He was going to catch me.

He would *always* catch me.

"Don't run." His stern voice was laced with fear. "You could *slip*."

Oh man, if Daddy Ash is already protective, Dada Ash is going to bubble wrap this whole house.

For a while, I'd secretly worried that I was more like Veronica than I ever wanted to be. I loved Ash's attention. I basked in his obsession. I found security in his fixation with me. I desperately needed it all *and* him.

And that was exactly how I knew I wasn't my mother. Because I didn't want to be the center of *everyone's* universe.

Just his.

His sunshine.

The End!

Well, the end of the book but not the series. There's still a serial killer on the loose. Not to mention, Eternal Sun's mega creepiness...

If you're excited to read about Marco, Cole, Freddy, and the very lucky woman who's starring in their fantasies and causing a lotion shortage, don't forget to preorder Little Goddess!

CONNECT WITH LAYLA FROST

Please stalk me. I post all the best memes…

www.LaylaFrostWrites.com

Email: contact@laylafrostwrites.com

Join my reader group Layla Frost's Cupcakes!

amazon.com/Layla-Frost/e/B00VJMSYKQ
facebook.com/LaylaFrostWrites
instagram.com/laylafrostauthor
tiktok.com/@laylafrostautho

Also by Layla Frost

BLACK RESORTS

Little Dove

Little Sunshine

Little Goddess

THE HYDE SERIES

Hyde and Seek

Best Kase Scenario

Until Nox: Happily Ever Alpha World

Wild Wicked Obsession

Ring Around the Posey

COURT OF MAYHEM

Until Mayhem

Finding Mayhem

THE DILLON SISTERS

Deathly by Brynne Asher

Damaged by Layla Frost

THE FOUR

Styx

Stoned

Broken

Bones

STANDALONES

With Us

Give In

About the Author

Growing up, Layla Frost used to hide under her blanket with a flashlight to read the Sweet Valley High books she pilfered from her older sister. It wasn't long before she was reading hidden Harlequins during class at school. This snowballed into pulling all-nighters after the promise of "just one more chapter".

Her love of reading, especially the romance genre, took root early and has grown immeasurably until it was time to write her own stories.

When she's not writing, Layla Frost is an insomniac with a deep love of iced coffee, tchotchkes, plants, and her hens. She's also the world's okayest mom, but her kids think she's cool… ish.